FALLEN DESIRE

Sequel to the first book in the series, Fallen Love.

Alex Stargazer

Terran Empire Publishing 1761 Hillside Ct. Placerville, Ca
USA 95667

www.terranempirepublishing.com

ISBN 978-0-9990108-8-4

Visit the author's website at www.alexstargazer.com

To Glenn Guzier and everyone who helped make this book possible! You're all awesome. Glenn and I will let you guys guess what character he will be in my next book.

Fantastic!

Alex Stargazer is becoming one of my favorite authors! His world building is incredible and his storylines are superb. This is a continuation of Mark and Conall's story that started in *Fallen Love*. This series is fantastic and this is a great addition to the story. Cannot wait to read more! —Samantha Cato, Amazon Reviewer

Wow wow wow!

Words are escaping me; this book is everything. The characters and the world building are for lack of better words magical and the suspense and storyline kept me reading well after I should have put the book down. — Vanessa Leighton, Amazon Reviewer

5-Stars!

This conclusion to Mark and Conall's journey was epic in a way I wasn't expecting. I can't believe how much action was packed into this book, and I'm going to have a serious book hangover while I process how everything played out. —Emily Hernandez, Goodreads Reviewer

5-Stars!

Fallen Desire by Alex Stargazer is the second book in the Fallen series. This novel took me on a journey that took my breath away. Magic, action, drama, excitement, and heat Drew me into the story while the beautiful crafted characters kept me spellbound. I highly recommend taking a break, find a comfy reading nook, and dive into this tantalizing and satisfying world. —Kathryn Manzella, Goodreads Reviewer

5-Stars!

Alex Stargazer has stepped up his game with *Fallen Desire*. And I couldn't be happier. The foundation he spent time on in the first book has paid off, for he has started the story's continuation at a sprint. Overall, *Fallen Desire* deserves 5 out of 5 stars. —J.R. Vaineo, Goodreads Reviewer

More Fantastic World Building!

In book one, we got the dystopian world that Conall and Mark have to try to survive in. Here, we get to see an even more amazing world the author takes us to - Hell. Again, Conall and Mark are struggling to defeat the evil ones and be together but they battle separately through much of this story and we get to know them better as the strong individuals they are. That makes it even more rewarding when they come together and get their H.E.A. An author who has quickly become a favorite. —Susie Umphers, Amazon Reviewer

PART ONE: A BEAUTIFUL HELL

Prologue

Mark

The world is not what you think it is. Once, I used to be the same as you: I lived in Ireland, a wealthy European country run by the Party—the authoritarian regime that was (figuratively, not literally, of course) from Hell. But then, most European countries are run by regimes. It's just the way it is. I accepted it as readily as I accepted the deadly mutants that walked the streets; the violent gangs that preyed on the helpless; and the constant, grinding poverty.

You see, I'm a Fallen. The lowest of the low. This was my world, and it sucked, but at least I knew my place within it.

Then came Conall. It wasn't just that he was beautiful and smart and charming, but he was also kind and willing to put himself in harm's way for the sake of me. He rescued me from a pack of devouring scarabs (a particularly unpleasant kind of mutant).

For a while, all was good. I sneaked into his mansion, we made out, and the professionals cleaned up the mess so the Party wouldn't get a whiff.

Things were not to be. The Party discovered me, eventually. But I didn't know the half of it.

They found me, but they didn't do it without help. Somebody else wanted me—someone powerful, more powerful than I could ever imagine. I am not human: there is greatness inside me. But greatness takes many forms. I can choose to do good—or I can join the one who desires me and become like he is.

I can be a demon, or I can be an angel.

Others share this struggle. A witch named Kaylin fights on two fronts: the Party at home and the agents of Lucifer, which come ever closer to Earth. The Barrier—the Great Magic that keeps the demons bound to Hell, once the masterpiece of a long-dead witch—is falling apart. It's only a matter of time before the Devil is set loose, and he will threaten not just Conall, not just my family, but every human on Earth.

I know I must stop him, somehow. But how do you do fight the Devil anyway? And do I even want to? Lucifer may be a monster, but deep down, I know I am drawn to him. He is like the glitter of a knife in the darkness: at once hypnotizingly beautiful and deadly.

Conall once recounted to me the great Latin phrase, made famous by Cato: *Carthago delenda est.* I forgot what exactly it was about (I'm a stupid Fallen boy, remember?), but I got the gist. It means something along the lines of: "Fuck it, let's give 'em Hell!"

Wise words, after all

Chapter One: The Road to Hell

Mark

Would you ever choose Hell over Earth? Would you leave the world you know, the world you hate and love, for a terrible unknown? And would you do it knowing you might have to embrace evil—to become the being you so desperately wish you weren't?

I did all of that, and not because of power; I don't want power. No, I did it for a much more beautiful thing than that: love.

Some would call me stupid. Heck, I would call myself stupid. I would have chosen the alternative—death—if Conall, the man I loved, hadn't begged me to live. My life, I can forfeit; his trust I cannot.

I close my eyes briefly, then try to make sense of what I see. I expected Hell to be a lot of things, but I didn't expect... this. A profound silence blankets the world around us. The sky is deep blue, just shy of pure darkness, and covered in a multitude of stars that shine with a constant, ethereal light. I can see no moon or cloud and suspect I never will. This place has always been like this.

"Where are we?" I ask. Something tells me this isn't our final destination.

"We're on the Road," the female demon replies. They had sent four demons to capture Conall and tempt me into fighting. I destroyed one of them, which left three: the woman who spoke and her two male companions.

I narrow my eyes, shooting a poisonous glare at one of the other male demons. He had been the captain of this little gang.

"What Road? You didn't say anything about a bleedin' road. Also, where is Lucifer? Isn't the Devil interested in his protégé?" Thanks to Conall, I'd picked up some French.

"Lucifer is away. He will meet you when we arrive in Hell. As for the Road, we use it because it is less... painful than the alternative."

"So, the mighty emissaries of darkness do feel pain after all?" As a demon myself, I'd almost forgotten what that was like. Trying to protect my human boyfriend has kept it all in perspective.

"The Barrier, alas. You shall see."

"What's stopping me from leaving?"

The male demon steps forward.

"I would not countenance such a foolish act. Lucifer will punish you for it."

"Diego, stand back and pull yourself together. Threatening him is a poor course of action; it will only undermine our aims."

"Adrianne..."

"I am higher ranked than you. You should know better."

"You were always a cold-hearted bitch."

"Frankly, Diego, one of us, has to be the adult in the room. We've already lost Leila to him."

He snarls. "I know, and he should pay for that."

"Don't be so sentimental—you only had sex with her. Hardly a love born of the stars."

"Unlike our star-spun lover here."

"This dialogue is fun to watch," I point out, "but you still haven't answered my bleedin' question. Why shouldn't I just leave?"

"You made a promise; it is binding."

"I promised I'd follow *Lucifer* into *Hell*. I didn't promise I'd follow you down this road."

She smiles slightly.

"He is cleverer than I thought, Max," she says, referring to the other demon, who'd sat silently through the whole exchange.

"Indeed, Adrianne."

Max, had he been human, would have been imposing: his arms are like tree trunks, and muscles ripple underneath his grey T-shirt. He's quiet, too, and if life as a Fallen had taught me anything, it's that the quiet ones are usually the most dangerous.

Still, I'm not intimidated by him. That demonic sixth of mine tells me that he isn't all that strong—I could take him easily if I wanted to.

"To answer your question, Mark, I don't believe we can stop you from leaving. We can cross the barrier and are, therefore, alas, not strong enough to contain you. I appeal, instead, to your curiosity," Max says.

"I *am* curious," I say honestly. "But that won't be enough."

"And to your cynicism: you know that things in life are never that easy, especially where the Dark Lord himself is concerned. There are many people you care about who we can threaten to ensure your compliance. Conall, for example, or your uncle."

I wince. "You speak the truth, demon."

"You're going to have to stop calling us that, you know. Pretty soon, there will be demons everywhere—and then what will you do?"

"I'll call you 'big demon' and 'annoying demon.'"

Max only snorts at my retort; Adrianne is trying to keep a serious face. Diego is fuming.

"Come on, Mark. Lucifer doesn't like waiting," Adrianne informs me. "We'll explain more as we keep moving."

So, I follow them. I didn't even realise there *was* a road at first, but there it is: silvery, cobbled, and flowing through the landscape like a meandering river. I'm wearing trainers, and the others are wearing boots, but we make no noise as we traverse its length. The silence is absolute.

My breath is a misty cloud in front of me; the air is icy cold, though I feel no need to wear anything warmer than my T-shirt and jeans. Being a demon has its perks.

I have no idea how long we walk; Conall would have said 'an age and a moment,' which is much more poetic than what I can manage.

Then, everything changes. The sky is blotted out by menacing dark clouds, driven by powerful atmospheric winds; the air turns blistering hot, and everything becomes red. The road is visible now: a smooth river of black stone. Beside us, a lake of lava heaves and boils with explosive energy.

"What the...?"

"A common reaction. The road is like this. It alternates between Hell and Earth, passing through the thin cracks in the Barrier."

"So, you can circumvent it?"

"Hardly. The idea is to make the journey easier, but it is still brutal."

I realise that these perfect, aloof beings aren't so cold after all. I'd almost failed to notice it, but Adrianne is right: they all look distinctly uncomfortable, and Diego is even sweating a little.

"I don't feel a thing," I point out.

"That's why you're the Chosen One." Diego snorts.

"You have a connection to both worlds, Mark," Adrianne continues. "Lucifer was right."

We carry on walking. We pass through the lava lake and back into the starlit world. I'm ahead of them now; they're visibly puffing with effort. The road passes next to a grove of trees. I pause to admire it: it's beautiful, the trees' long forms bare and graceful in the light.

"Perfect boy is admiring the scenery," Diego comments.

"Don't be jealous," I retort.

We continue to walk until we reach a gate. What I see fills me with awe. Two massive stone obelisks rise into the boiling red sky, with the entrance suspended between them. Sculpted upon the gate are five words written in Italian.

"Can you understand it?" To my surprise, it's Max who asks.

"Cliché," I mutter.

He only smiles.

The words are *Lasciate ogne speranza, voi chi'intratte*. Conall had taught me enough Dante to recognise the meaning.

'Leave all hope behind, you who enter.'

It turns out the gate isn't decoration—it marks the final entrance into Hell, and it is here that I must cross the Barrier. I simply walk up to it and touch the gate with a finger: it glows a faint blue, then silently glides open.

The others are not so fortunate. Max goes through first; each of his steps seems more painful than the last. After the third step, he's in slow motion; after the sixth, he's crawling. Nine steps, and his back arches in agony.

Now he's through the Barrier. He blinks, smiles then falls unconscious.

"Is he alright?" I ask. Not that I should give a damn about a demon, but as we Fallen would say: he's creamed.

"He will recover," Adrianne says.

Diego goes next. Watching the same process happen to him pleases me, and I have a big smile on my face throughout. Unfortunately, he doesn't lose consciousness—instead, he spits at me from the ground.

"Awww," I exclaim.

Adrianne is the next to go through the Barrier, and it's clearly affecting her more than her comrades. By her sixth step, she falls and begins to crawl. She arches her back by the seventh step and cries out on the ninth. She's unconscious at the gate.

"Well, so much for that," I say.

"Bastard," Diego hisses.

I kick him in the face. His head snaps back with an audible crack.

"You deserve it, demon. You chose to become this." There's anger in my voice now. "Tell me, what did you do? What was your evil act?"

"So, you know about that, eh?"

"A witch kindly informed me."

"I beat a little girl to death." There's no shame in his voice: only a faint pride.

I kick him again, harder this time.

"I don't feel pain, you idiot," he says, laughing.

I stop, realising my mistake. I'm still thinking like a human; I want to beat him up with my fists. But he's not human.

I smile. Electric sparks fly from my hand and arch down towards the prone demon. This time, he screams. I fry him mercilessly, hoping to prolong his pain, but he blacks out.

"Mark!" Adrianne is awake now.

"What?"

"Don't make an enemy of him. You don't want too many of those, not in this place—trust me."

"Why are you giving me advice?"

She shrugs. "I can lie."

"Don't bother."

"Because I can give you valuable advice and turn you into an ally. Power is the dominant force in this world. Politics is the art of obtaining power. And you would make a valuable political pawn."

"Hah. My boyfriend is training to become a politician—you think I don't know this? But Lucifer is omnipotent, or so I'm told. I don't see how you can play power games with a god."

"Lucifer may be omnipotent, true, but there is a sophisticated pecking order below him. Also, the Dark Lord enjoys political intrigue, as you will find out soon enough."

I shake my head. "Is Max awake?"

"I am."

"Grab that idiot, and let's go."

****

Hell is a big place as the road continues. At some point, I stop and sigh in frustration.

"Can't we fly? Walking is slow going."

"We can't," Max explains. He goes on to say, "The lava is thick with creatures who are born of fire, and they are deadly to our kind. We call them firelings."

I raise an eyebrow. "So ya tellin' me that Hell, the kingdom of Lucifer and all his subjects, is filled with creatures that *can kill demons*?"

"Yes."

"You have much to learn," Adrianne mutters.

"So why haven't they burnt this place to the ground?"

"A good question, and one which, perhaps, I cannot answer now. The story is a long one. I do know that there are many roads, bridges, and gates that connect to Hell. Lucifer's magic protects them from the fire and the creatures that spawn from it. If you were to fly above the field that protects a bridge... you would perish."

I never expected the big man to have such knowledge or speak the way he does: quietly, but with excitement, like a scholar or a child.

"You learn something new every day," I comment.

"Wise words," Max agrees.

"Are there any other interestin' details you wish to share with me?" I continue.

"The stones underneath your feet. Remove one and take a look."

The stone must weigh as much as a man, though I lift it easily. On the bottom, inscribed in cursive text, it reads:

For Maria, our daughter, that she be born.

I frown. I walk a few paces and lift another one.

To go through medical school, so I can become a doctor and help people.

Another one.

I love you, Shane. He gave me the power to destroy them: your father, the men who tormented us and hurt us. They deserved to die burning.

I stop and look Max in the eye.

"It can't be true..."

"It is. Every stone here was laid with good intentions. A wish granted by Lucifer. A wish for every person who has walked this road."

I look towards the horizon; the road is long, and the stones are many.

"Come," Adrianne says. "Lucifer awaits."

****

The road finally ends. A large and cavernous space lies in front of us, like the maw of a gigantic animal. It is the entrance to a tunnel.

"As if the entrance wasn't dramatic enough already," I comment.

Adrianne pays no attention to this. "We're about to enter the Outer Circle, where we will start to meet human citizens."

"The outer circle? Really? Are ya going to tell me there's nine of them too?"

"Eight, but nine if you count the Citadel."

"So, Dante only got the maths wrong, then?"

Max interrupts me. "Adrianne, tell him what he needs to know."

"I was going to do just that. There are two kinds of people in Hell: humans and demons like us. Once we enter this place, it would be good to show that the Dark Lord expects you."

"You want me to draw attention to myself? Why?"

"You will see." She lifts a finger, and a symbol is burned into the air: an inverted cross.

"This symbol shows that Lucifer has summoned you."

"Got it."

A few more steps, and we enter the tunnel. Immediately, I realise what they meant: this place is brimming with people. Young and old, men and women; humanity seethes everywhere. I see a haphazard mixture of clothes—jeans mingle with togas, rich colours contrast with dark shades of grey.

What strikes me most are the expressions. Some are the epitome of medieval paintings: broken, melancholy, agonised. I expected that. What I didn't expect to see is the pride, the aloofness, of some of the human inhabitants. It seems some are doomed to suffer, and others benefit from that suffering. Leeches just like the Party.

For a moment—just a flash of doubt—I wonder if the demons are worse than the people.

The people make their way around us, some taking care not to make eye contact, others tipping their hats to us with respect. A few are simply too distracted by their com phones to pay much attention. I guess some things never change.

Still, Adrianne is right: it will take forever to swim through this river of humanity. So, I raise my hand, and an inverted cross burns bright and blue above me.

Instantly, they stop, stand back, and make way.

Adrianne leads ahead, with Max and Diego behind me. We leave the Outer Circle and follow the road until we reach... a bridge. That's the only way I can describe it.

"Holy Hell," I breathe.

"An admirable statement," Max comments. "This is the Cauldron Bridge. It crosses the main area of Hell known as the Cauldron and leads to the Citadel Bridge."

A massive stone bridge, supported by arches, spans the entire length of what looks like a giant volcanic crater. Ordered and arranged at regular intervals are numerous concentric stone circles. Each of those stone circles has layers of buildings and people.

An enormous mountain rises from its centre, and resting upon it is a citadel made of imposing black stone.

"Welcome home," says Adrianne.

Chapter Two: Nostalgia

Conall

A week has passed since he left. A week since the man I loved went to Hell instead of becoming a martyr—all because I couldn't bear to lose him. I had found a Fallen boy, wounded, abandoned, and ready to die; I fell in love with him because he was vulnerable, beautiful, and strong. Yet someone else went in his place: a divine being intent on fighting the Devil himself.

But Mark, despite his newfound demonic power, is still only too mortal. He thought he was invincible, but the being that is Lucifer can slay even the invincible.

Where, though, does this leave me? I may be wealthy and well-connected, but I am human and, thus, vulnerable. Lucifer understood this well, which is why he kidnapped me. I may be free now, yet I know, without the faintest shadow of a doubt, that my freedom is contingent on Mark fulfilling Lucifer's aims. If Mark refuses to obey... I will die. No bodyguard can protect me.

Not that this has stopped Sianna, my mother, from trying. Three men guard me around the clock: one of them, bald and suited, is keeping an eye on me right now. However, I fail to see the point. I am at home in Father's mansion.

I am sitting on a chair in my study. The chair is a deep burgundy leather and lavish in construction and attention to detail. The room around it is equally luxurious: it is dominated by a plush carpet, a tall, elegant ceiling, and a fireplace.

It is not cold enough to light a fire, yet autumn reigns and winter's touch is faint but inclement. The wind races through the trees, occasionally rattling a window frame or howling through some long-abandoned cranny. Leaves fall gently, and the sun shines golden, peaking through the grey clouds.

Some would call the landscape beautiful, in a cool, relaxed sort of way. I find it depressing. Oh, to relive that summer! To touch his golden skin again, to kiss his warm lips, and be cradled by his muscular body.

When the sun burned bright and hot
We burned with it, lovers
Lit by passion.
When the sun grows pale and weak
We forget ourselves and die.

My morose state had, at least, spurned me to write poetry. Father thought it was a waste of time. Mother only smiled in sympathy and ordered more tea for me.

"Sir?"

I turn towards the bodyguard.

"Yes?"

"There's someone here to see you—she claims her name is Diana."

That's a surprise. Diana is human, though capable of practising magic. She is part of an organisation run by a witch named Kaylin. They'd helped us fight Lucifer's minions, though they abandoned us when it came to facing Lucifer himself.

"Let her in; I want to see her."

"She may be a security threat."

"Call my mother on the com phone if you like, though you're wasting your time. Diana could have burned down this mansion—and all of us in it—a long time ago, if she wished."

The man swallows audibly at that.

"Yes, sir."

****

She walks in, her pink dress oddly threadbare in the weather. Though then again, I shouldn't be surprised. Diana can walk through an acid storm; her power over the elements is both impressive and terrifying. Her power manifests itself in other, more subtle ways as well—things I'd subconsciously noticed before but had never put together. To take one example: her eyes. Naturally brown, they alternate into cool grey, mainly when using her power to its fullest.

Today, however, she seems relaxed.

"Hello, Conall."

"Diana." My voice lacks a particular enthusiasm. Diana had been my tutor, and I usually would be pleased to see her, but things have changed, and I cannot forget her actions that day.

"Conall... I know you're upset. But give me a chance. Did you think I'd willingly abandon you to that thing?"

"You did abandon us, though—me and Mark."

"Kaylin teleported me."

"Oh." I hadn't realised she didn't have a choice. Though, this fact doesn't improve my appreciation for Kaylin one bit.

"Come and walk with me."

I follow her out into the garden.

****

The mansion grounds are reasonably generous, at least considering how restricted space is in the Upper Quarter. Guaranteed protection from mutants does not come cheap—and nor is it available to the non-privileged Classes. I had been fortunate to find Mark, wounded as he was, in the Middle Quarter, with a swarm of scarabs not far behind our back.

Our feet make soft crackling sounds on the carpet of leaves—the air is crisp and scented with hints of chestnut and dampness. I cannot deny that the landscape possesses a kind of serenity, yet I know that this is an illusion, an ephemeral hope, flowering one day and dead the next. Mark suffers deep in Hell, and all I'm doing is writing sentimental poetry.

"What do you want, Diana?"

"You're unusually blunt today."

"My patience has been tested too far."

She sighs. "Let me start by apologising. You know I wanted to fight. But... there was very little we could do. You have to understand that: Lucifer is immortal."

"Then why are you apologising?"

"Because we should have been smarter!"

A sudden gust picks up, and my bodyguard—who had been watching a respectful distance away—falls over. It's almost comical, except Diana's eyes are storm-blue, and she seems charged like a thundercloud.

"We always have to act smart. Kaylin taught me that lesson. Magic is what makes us special, but it cannot make up for poor decisions."

I close my eyes, feeling immensely tired.

"I accept your apology. Tell me this instead: what are you going to do about Lucifer?"

"Kaylin has been able to deduce that Michael was right all along— the thing we saw as Lucifer was a projection, albeit a very strong one. His time on Earth would have been limited."

"So, he tricked us?"

"In more ways than one. Lucifer was able to gain complete control over the situation."

"We walked right into his trap." I'd seen that even then. "But what could we have done differently?"

"I've thought the same thing myself, though Kaylin tells me not to ponder. Obsessing about past mistakes is a fool's game; it is wiser to appreciate the circumstances of the present and plan for the future."

"Now you sound just like her. Where's the crazy woman I once knew?"

She smiles at that—just a little, but unmistakably Diana.

"I will always be myself."

"But did I ever really know you? Or did I just know a part of you, perhaps even an imagined part—the doting tutor, the eccentric academic?"

"That part was real, Conall. As real as the more obvious side of me: the woman who likes to burn things."

"Show me your old self, then. Ask me a question."

"About politics?"

"What else?"

Who would have thought that the thing I thought I despised—the Lyceum University, Father's plans for my future political career—would come to haunt me with nostalgia?

"What is a political vacuum?"

"It's when a major controlling figure leaves the scene, usually due to death."

"Can that figure be institutionalised?"

"You mean, can it be represented by a Government or Parliament?"

"Yes."

"Well, historically, that was true... but the Party is no such thing. Parties are associations of like-minded individuals, and they are defined only by their desire for collective power."

"Are we in a political vacuum right now?"

I pause to think. Mark had slain Big Brother—the shadowy figure who had authored much of our suffering before we discovered Lucifer. Big Brother had ruled Ireland with an iron fist.

"We are. I should have seen it before."

"And what happens when there's a vacuum?"

"A power struggle. A faction will try to take control."

The wind blows again, and even the mild autumn temperature seems painfully cold. Diana is giving me a look of approval, intermixed with sadness.

"A storm is coming, Conall. And I'm not talking about the weather this time."

"I guess you and Kaylin are planning something, then?"

"Kaylin is always planning something. I will find you again when the time is right."

"Should I care, though? My boyfriend is a captive of the Devil. The Party can go fuck itself."

She chuckles.

"You *are* very blunt today. But there's something you're missing—something even we haven't figured out yet. The two are connected. Somehow, Lucifer was able to manipulate the Party into doing what he wanted. How did he get that intel?"

"You think the Devil has spies here on Earth?"

"Is there any other explanation?" she asks.

"Maybe he has a scrying glass? Like in the stories?"

"Mirror, mirror on the wall..." Diana smiles. "That's one possibility."

The wind picks up suddenly, and I shiver.

"Are you going to fly out of here?" I ask.

She only grins. "You know me well."

A split second later, she shoots off into the sky. The guard is left completely stunned.

****

I leave my flustered bodyguard to wrestle with his confusion. It amuses me to think he's coming to terms with the supernatural—a process that took me time as well. My mother hinted at what they would be facing, but men like him cannot accept magic until they feel its power.

I return to the mansion and walk up a grand double staircase. The marble is smooth beneath my shoes, the veins of the rock iridescent, blooming in complex shapes, yet I take little notice. Luxury is a given when it comes to my Class. Instead, I make my way down the hall and knock on a tall, mahogany door.

"Come in," Niall, my father, says through the door.

I open the door quietly. Within, I find my father reading an extensive collection of important-looking documents. Despite the dark opulence around him, he seems worn and haggard.

I'd never seen Father look like this, not even when Mark had lifted him two metres in the air with telekinesis. There is a creeping, nervous energy to his movements.

"Father?"

"There you are, Conall! Have a seat. Read through this."

He's never asked me to read official Party documents before. "Father, that's quite unnecessary."

"You need to understand."

"Understand that Big Brother is dead, and the Party is cannibalising itself?"

He freezes. "Of course, you would know... I should have learned not to underestimate you. You are my son and have received the finest political education available to members of your Class."

"That, and Diana told me."

"The witch?"

"No, the woman with the burning hair."

"Ah, yes." He has not fully adapted to the supernatural, either.

"What do you plan on doing?" I continue.

"There is nothing I can do. At best, I can hope to remain in good standing with the new regime."

"And at worst, the Party would have us executed."

"That seems unlikely."

"But it's possible, especially considering what some Party figures are like."

"If only we had Big Brother!" He groans in frustration. "Your boyfriend was a fool to kill the man."

"Big Brother was the reason Mark became Fallen. You don't understand; you can't understand."

"What *everyone* needs to understand is that you cannot enact change by assassinating the leader. That will only lead to instability, struggle, and death."

He says the words with absolute conviction. I can't contradict him—his words are proving themselves correct right in front of our eyes.

"Big Brother is dead," I say instead. "We must move on. Tell me you have a backup plan."

"Your mother has already hatched a plan, though I dislike it immensely."

"What is it?"

"She wants us to... emigrate. To Spain."

"To *Communist* Spain?"

"I told her she was insane, but, well, you know Sianna."

"But she's the most bourgeois woman on the Continent! They'll put her to work in the mines—enemy of the Proletariat and all that."

"She seems to think she can strike a deal."

"Why not France? Germany? Anywhere else in Europe?"

"Extradition."

I close my eyes. "If only I could turn back the clock..."

"You still miss him, don't you?"

"Of course, I do."

"I honestly don't know what to say, son."

"You never approved."

"I don't think it matters."

His honesty startles me. "What?"

"You didn't fall in love with just any man, Conall. You fell in love with a demigod. What can I say to that?"

"Do you think Mark will come back?"

"Ask the witch; I don't know. Such things are beyond mortal men."

"Love is hardly the purlieu of immortals, Father."

"Do you love him, then? Would you follow him to Hell and back?"

"In a heartbeat."

"Then, you have your answer."

Chapter Three: The Dark Citadel

Mark

"Is that what I think it is?" I ask.

"Yes," Adrianne and Max reply at the same time.

The Bridge to the Citadel is enormous, towering over the dark chasm in front of us like a galactic pathway in the deep emptiness of space. There are no arches or supports, unlike the other bridge we crossed: this thing is sheer, steep, and it's on fire.

Yeah. I've seen a few insane architectural designs before—the Party likes them—but none of them were literally on fire.

"Is it safe to walk on?"

"It is: the fire covers and protects the Bridge on the outside," Adrianne explains.

"I guess the effect is purely to support Lucifer's vanity?"

"Lucifer—"

"It serves a practical purpose," Max says, interrupting whatever Adrianne was about to say. She gives him a look.

"Go on."

"The Firelings are most numerous here—the blue fire, which is demonic in nature, prevents them from eroding the Bridge."

"I don't see any of these Fireling creatures," I point out.

"Exactly. That means it works."

"Firelings are extremely dangerous," Adrianne says, taking over. "Although one, on its own, is not much of a threat, a dozen or two have a serious chance of killing more minor demons like us. Lucifer's magic keeps them well away, but if you were to leave the protection of his warded structures..."

"I would die a horrible death—yeah, I get it. Bleedin' hell."

"Do not be so contemptuous," Adrianne warns me.

"It's a common reaction, don't worry," Max says, though I'm not sure if he's trying to calm me down, or her.

"Well?" I continue. "Let's go."

"There's a Gate as well, Mark," Max tells me.

A few short steps, and I see it. It's much smaller than the other gate—the one that opened into Hell. Yet despite that, my sixth sense is telling me that it's the stronger of the two.

"How do we open it?"

Adrianne walks forward, placing her hand on a rock next to the gate. The black granite suddenly glows blue and crimson; the outline of her hand is briefly visible on the rock. The gate opens silently, moving on invisible hinges.

"Only demons can open it," she explains.

We carry on walking. Then I notice more people. No: not people. Demons. Even with their wings hidden, the power they hold is impossible to mistake.

We walk for what feels like miles, almost vertically at some points. It's easy for us, but I wonder how a human being would be able to cope. The Bridge rises and undulates, curving sharply around corners.

Eventually, we pass through an arch. Illuminated by braziers, the black rock shines with a pale, reddish-tinged light. Corridors start to open up, and stained-glass windows rise high into shadowed hollows within the ceiling. Gone is the grey cobblestone floor—instead, its black marble polished to an iridescent shine.

"Welcome to the Citadel," Max tells me.

"Yeah, Max, I get the point."

****

Two massive doors, made from oak, open into what I can only describe as a throne room. Demons mill about, but they stick close to the walls, leaving the centre empty.

Adrianne walks forward and bows. Max sets Diego on the floor, then bows as well, though with less reverence.

I walk forward and ignore them. The throne lies at the very end of the room. It is made from sheer black marble, carved as if by magic, or perhaps by the hand of some ancient giant. Even so, it is nothing compared to the being that rests on top.

I've seen Lucifer before—back on Earth, as a projection. He'd forced me into trading my freedom for my life. But somehow, here, he seems even greater: not merely powerful, but divine. He is reclining on his throne, but when he sees me, he rises. His designer clothing rustles almost imperceptibly.

"And so, we meet again, my dear Mark."

"Did you expect me to bow?" I ask, smiling ironically.

"Oh no, you're far too impressive for that."

"Impressive?"

"Of course. You are no ordinary man, nor an ordinary demon, as I'm sure you've been able to deduce."

"I got the little trick with the gate."

At that, a rumble goes through the crowd. "That's no trick!" one of the demons hisses.

"So, I think," I continue, conversationally, as if it were only him and me in the room, "I can just leave. Fly, teleport, Fade, whatever."

"Is that so?" he asks. The great demon doesn't seem offended or even put off by my show.

"Lord Lucifer, this behaviour is unacceptable," a demon begins. He detaches himself from the shadows of the far wall, moving smoothly, almost as gracefully as Lucifer himself.

"Acheron, oh, Acheron. Did I make you a demon merely so I could teach you obedience? Are you an *Arch* Demon, no less, because you have no will of your own?"

"I see," the demon named Acheron continues.

"Stand down," Lucifer orders. The other demon backs away silently.

"Some palace you have here," I continue. I don't know what I'm thinking, but something burns through me: defiance. I never did like authority, especially when that authority abuses its power.

"Do you like it? I think it quite grand."

"Yeah. The burning bridge is a nice touch—though I think the first Gate was nicer. A bit of Dante."

Lucifer only chuckles.

"But still," I say. "Big palaces are to impress stupid people. You're no King; your ego is regal, maybe, but that's about it."

"Kill him, Lord! Smite the fool boy down to the pits!"

"You're free to do it yourself," I say to the demon in the crowd.

He flies at me, wings outstretched, fire alight in his hands. My power rises automatically to meet him: my wings unfurl, my body glows electrically, and strength floods my body.

His fireball just glances off me. He slams into me, but I don't move an inch. I grab him by the neck and send him flying into one of the stained-glass windows.

The demon does not go through it, as I hoped. Instead, red and blue runes burst into life on the glass as the man crumples to the floor.

Lucifer claps. "Oh, how dramatic! How strong you are, Mark.

"Zi-Xuan, pull yourself together. I'm surprised you ever made it through the ceremony—you're determined, yes, but not always intelligent in your pursuits."

"Yes, Lord Lucifer."

"That's just the way he is—obedient and adoring of power," Lucifer explains to me casually. "The latter is an excellent quality in a demon; the former, less so, alas."

"What do you want?" I ask him simply.

"Walk with me, Mark."

He gestures widely, and the other demons part, making way for us. The Dark Lord strides smoothly ahead; I follow, drawn by an inescapable compulsion.

Damn it, but I never expected Lucifer to be so... intriguing.

****

"What was the point of all that circus there?" I ask, following his stride, the corridor vast and silent around us.

"Drama. A point that needed to be made."

"Is that how you keep them in line? With... spectacular shows of drama?"

He smiles this time. It's a strange expression on him: I can imagine the Devil smirking, contemptuous, or amused, but this is a genuine joy.

"Political power rests on an image, as well as true power."

"So even a god needs to project his power? To show who's boss?"

"Yes. Demons are not so dissimilar to humans, you understand. We are all monsters underneath. We all admire the strong—the difference is that humans only follow the strong out of fear and awe, whereas demons follow me for more intelligent reasons."

"A calculation, to get more power for themselves."

"Precisely."

"You think I'll follow you, then? You're wrong. I don't care about power."

"Oh, everyone cares about power—one way or another. But that is a question for another time. I wish to return to your original postulation: leaving Hell, my domain.

"You see, what you describe is not so easy to accomplish. As I'm sure you already know, fading to Earth is impossible. Flying is also impossible unless you want to be consumed by Firelings, which leaves walking. There are many Gates, and they only open when I allow it."

I close my eyes, trying to remember Earth: uncle's house, Conall's bedroom. The memories come thick and fast... but I can't focus on them. It's like there's a filter, blurring everything just slightly.

"I admire you for trying," he says, still smiling.

"Why...?"

"The Barrier is not the only wall between Hell and Earth. You can pass through it easily—as you saw—and you logically concluded that you should also be able to Fade. But these worlds are... how shall I put it?" I notice the accent again. Latin, probably.

"Out of sync?" I suggest.

"Yes, very much so. Fading is a rather precise form of magic."

"So, how were you able to be there on Earth?" I ask. "Your power..."

"I was not a projection, but I was a Spectre—a much greater kind of Sending."

"Let me guess, though. You couldn't maintain it for too long."

He pauses. "No."

"You tricked me."

"I did. But that is the way of things: we all desire power, and deception is a time-honoured way to acquire it."

"But deception also means I can't trust you. Whatever your plans are for me—they'll fail."

"You are correct: trust can be as valuable as deceit. There is more than one way to earn trust, however."

"Oh?"

Before I know it, he's in front of me, eyes dark and captivating.

"Stare long enough into the abyss, and the abyss will stare into you..." I whisper.

"Nietzsche. Very appropriate and pleasing."

I close my eyes, turning away. "No. You're too..."

"Captivating. Irresistible. Perhaps even... attractive."

There's no way for me to miss that. The jaw, the perfect form of his arms and legs...

A touch on my shoulder gliding over my arm. I shiver.

"You are beautiful, Mark. You may be the most beautiful man I have ever seen, and I have seen many."

"Is the Devil trying to seduce me?" I can't muster up the sarcasm, even though I try.

"Oh, yes, he is. In sex, Mark, I will always be plain with you."

The effort is too much for me. I open my eyes, and Lucifer turns my jaw in his hands, his fingers smooth and perfect. Those eyes of his—so vast, so divine, yet so human—leave me utterly helpless. He leans in, and his lips brush mine.

Then he's gone.

****

I find myself startled, blinking with confusion, the hall empty around me. Well, maybe not empty: a woman is walking up to me. I can tell she's human. She looks young, in her twenties perhaps. There's something... odd about her. I can't put my finger on what.

"Sir Mark?"

"That's me—without the sir if you please."

"Yes, Sir."

"Whatever. What do you want? Do you know where that bastard went?"

"Bastard?" Her accent is received pronunciation, like the Queen's; it laces the word with contempt.

"Lucifer. He almost kissed me; then he Faded away."

"Well, the Dark Lord is known for playing such games of fancy."

"So, he was just messing with me?"

"I would not go quite so far as to say that—I understand he's quite besotted with you, at least insofar as is possible for him. But he likes to toy with his subjects."

"He's going to get punched in the face next time."

"You can try, but you won't succeed."

I raise an eyebrow. "Really? How do you know?"

"I've seen him fight in the annual Games. But regardless, that's not why I'm here; I am to escort you to your rooms."

"Oh? Am I a guest, then?"

"No, you're a permanent resident. I should perhaps say 'suite,' as it is a more accurate descriptor."

"Lead on then. What's your name?"

"Suzanne."

"A nice, simple name."

"It's in your native language, that is why."

"True. How many nationalities are there in Hell?"

"Many, some long-extinct. A lot of the original demons were Roman citizens or subjects."

"I got that from the Latin. But original demons? What does that mean?" I realise that she probably knows a lot about this place, and, being human, she would be a less dangerous informant than another demon.

"I should not say... Lucifer will tell you when he thinks the time is right."

"Oh, come on... just for me?" I smile at her. I've never done this before, so I have no idea if it will work. I guess she is pretty enough. Her pale skin frames her long, dark hair, and her eyes, I observe, are crystalline blue.

She turns away slightly, blushing faintly. "The original demons were among the first to join Lucifer, before the Barrier."

"When was this?"

"Around the year 30."

I frown. "Should that be familiar to me?"

"No. It wasn't to me, either. The Church is dead on Earth—a fact that pleases Lucifer greatly. I never learned any of the Christian myths here."

I've only ever heard about religion in books, and the books I read didn't make it sound too cool.

"So you're telling me that's when Jesus was born?"

"When he died, rather. It is complicated, and to be honest; I'm not sure I'm qualified to inform you. Perhaps Shahar will be willing to teach you."

"Shahar?"

"Hell's chief scholar. You'll find him if you ask for him. Now, as to your room..."

We arrive at an ornately carved door. Suzanne opens it for me, and I walk in, then stop.

"Flippin' Hell!"

She chooses not to comment.

A massive chandelier hangs from the ceiling; the floor is black marble, and each candle shines either red or blue, casting a kaleidoscope of colours on the dark surface. Three windows tower into the cavernous ceiling.

I walk towards the bed—a solid, four-poster unit that wouldn't look out of place in a medieval castle—and jump right in.

"I guess you'll be comfortable?"

"Sure."

"There are clothes in the dresser," she says as she motions to the other furniture in the room. "There's a bell by the door; ring it, and the bell boy will come."

"What about locking the door?"

"There's a... stone pad next to it. Place your hand on it, and the door will lock."

"Like the gate?"

"I don't know—only demons can work magic."

"But you've never seen them do it? Surely you must have."

"True. I understand that demonic magic works through Will."

"Like, wish it hard enough, and it will happen?"

She laughs. "No, more like... if you want something bad enough, and if you're willing to do anything to get it, then the doors will open for you." There's a passion in her voice now. She's suddenly very animated.

"Are we speaking literally or metaphorically now?" I ask her quietly.

"Both," she says coyly. "Is that all?"

"Yes, you can go."

She bows elegantly, then leaves. I shake my head, bewildered. Religion, ancient history, and my very own piece of Hell... it's going to be a long ride.

Chapter Four: Awakening Rebellion

Kaylin

I lead a clandestine organisation dedicated to fighting the Party; my life is definitely not meant for leisure. Despite my status as an Upperclass-woman, rebellion has forced me away from luxury: I've dedicated most of my wealth to purchasing equipment and paying salaries to my men.

It would therefore surprise many (and I include myself in this) to discover that on this day, right now, I am not engaged in plotting, killing, or reconnaissance. The autumn day is chilly but pleasant; the seaside breeze gives Cork a cheery atmosphere, like the seaside resorts depicted in postcards.

Even the people seem more at ease than usual, though I know that chaos lies just behind the surface. Big Brother's death caused a shock-wave in the Party hierarchy. My visions had revealed some of the complex machinations going on within—and frankly, I would not want to be a Party member right now. I'm sure there are quite a few officials marked for removal.

But murder seems so far away right now. I find a terrace and order an ice-cream. It's been so long since I've eaten the cold, sugary desert; the experience is almost novel. I contemplate closing my eyes but resist, just barely. Years of instinct won't let me lower my guard that easily.

Diana? How are you?

Since when do you ask me that? she responds telepathically. She has gotten better at the magic; it's easy for both of us now.

I realise that it is a question one should ask of friends, at least once in a while.

I'm fine; I'm working on improving my skills as you told me to. I flew last week.

Really?

Conall had a hell of a shock.

Be careful—

I know., I know

Have you taken note of more Party activity?

Nothing major. You haven't had any more visions, by the look of it.

No. It seems odd—

I don't finish the thought. The world around me blurs and flickers into oblivion: I see something else instead, as if through a haze. A Gardá base. Then, in shadow, I see men and women wearing a symbol—a gold star on a red background. I see the men loading weapons.

In a flash, the vision ends.

Diana, I've had a vision. Someone is planning to raid a Gardá station.

What? Who?

I'm not sure yet. Stay put: I will deal with this myself.

Are you sure?

Though I know she can't see it, I smile. *You're not the only one who's been practising her magic.*

I neatly finish my ice cream, pay the bill, then rise. I quietly make my way under an alcove. I burn the rune into my skin; instantly, I feel it grow, mould over me, and act.

I return to the crowded street, passing unnoticed through the throng of people. Shadow isn't the only one who can go invisible.

****

I deduce enough from my vision to head towards the Gardá compound's rear and wait patiently. Soon enough, I see two men wearing ragged clothes. One has a plasma cannon on his shoulders; the other is also armed but is acting as his spotter.

The right man raises a hand, and a pulse of plasma flies out. It smashes through the force field and takes out a tower.

The men scramble to make a getaway. I shake my head: they will be dead in moments from return fire. Quickly, I draw a rune in the air. The shield activates a second before a machine gun starts firing. The bullets fall harmlessly against it.

The men have now changed positions. Another plasma pulse destroys a second tower, and from another side of the compound, a similar pulse takes out the third tower. They have disabled a good part of the compound's protections—but there are still many armed men there, and the force field is intact.

But this seems to be part of the plan: the two men retreat, and I watch them reach a getaway car and drive off. Gardá troops pour through the gates. I easily manoeuvre around them, curious to see whether the attack was indeed a diversion.

My assumption is correct: another group of men, wearing Gardá uniforms but still distinct to my senses as rebels, waltz through. In the chaos, they pass unchallenged.

I shake my head again. The audacity of their plan! It almost works. The two men would probably have died, but still.

Knowing that the mission will become more dangerous still, I burn another rune into my skin. A shielding rune, like the one I cast previously, though it acts only on me. My mind burns with the effort; this process requires me to keep both spells working simultaneously, and the magic takes its toll on my skin, too, which itches and aches.

All magic has a cost. The trick is to use it wisely.

The rebels find their way to the headquarters. They draw weapons and open fire. Several important-looking Gardá members fall dead, though one of the rebels takes a laser flash to the head; he dies instantly. A bullet hits another on the shoulder. Several shots and laser flashes bounce off me.

The Gardá are now dead. The men move quickly: they set up explosives (using some of the Gardá's stock against them) and hack one of the computers.

I have to run to follow them out, though they slow to a stride once they are outside. We pass through the gate, take off down a road, and hit the beach. Moments later, an explosion tears through the compound.

****

"Mac, you're wounded."

"Never mind me, Eoin is dead," the man named Mac replies.

A moment of silence passes. I can understand the feeling well: the burden of command is hard to bear and makes the tragedy more painful.

"I'm sorry, Mac."

"I get it, Ness. I don't blame you. Those Gardá bastards... we should've killed more of 'em."

"The order from high command was clear: we go in and plant the bomb. We couldn't have done it anyway—they outnumbered us."

Another of the group leans forward and helps Mac onto the floor. "Let Andrew take care of you; he knows what he's doing," Ness continues.

I somehow doubt that. I pause, thinking of what to do next. These men and their organisation could prove valuable assets, but they are clearly too inexperienced; someone else is leading them. I need to know who the "high command" is.

It's too soon to reveal myself just yet. So I bide my time, waiting for an opportunity: a younger man, I notice, is a little away from the group, who by now has moved to the inside of a cave.

A minute later, the opportunity presents itself.

"I need to take a leak."

****

The young man leaves the cave, and I follow. I drop the shield spell; I won't need it, and the power is more useful in other areas. I sneak behind him, then place my hand on his neck.

He drops, paralysed.

I lean down, letting the invisibility spell fade as well. The young man's eyes widen, but he cannot speak; the spell holds him tightly.

Alex Stargazer

"Promise me not to scream."

He tries to move, vainly. "Or to run. It will only make your life more difficult."

He stops—I'm pleased to note the intelligence. I reach into the spell, changing it subtly.

He sucks in a breath. "Who the bleedin' hell are you?"

"I am no friend of the Party if that's what you're wondering."

"Why should I believe you?"

"Your friends with the plasma cannon would have met an unfortunate end were it not for my intervention."

"*What* are you?"

"I am a witch—or something close to it, in any case. Now, listen: I don't have time to explain, and I need information."

"Do whatever dark magic you want to me; I'm not spilling."

"It would be to aid the people you fight for, not to betray them. Besides, I can always take the information directly from your mind—it would be a much more uncomfortable alternative for you."

He thinks. "Okay, what do you want to know?"

"Where is your high command?"

"Somewhere in Donegal, I don't know more than that."

"What is your name?"

"Will."

"No, I meant the people you work for."

"The Red Army."

I laugh. "Impossible."

"So you know about the past?"

"Of course. I take it you are communists, then?"

"We are."

"And you wish to overthrow the Party."

"We do."

"Well, we have one thing in common then."

"Who do *you* work for?"

"I'm the one asking questions here, Will."

"Yeah, I get it."

"How would I go about making contact with you?"

"Send a message to one of our pickup locations: 18 Armagh Street, Cork."

"Excellent." I notice an iron pendant hidden on his neck, forged in the shape of a hammer and sickle. I grab it.

"Hey!"

"You'll get it back later, along with your memories."

Before he can protest, I quickly draw a bit of blood, cast the spell, and blanket this memory from his mind. I don't erase it; that would make it impossible to return. I create a fake memory in its place, then move back.

He sleeps, knocked out by the spell. I touch the hammer and sickle—it's iron, rough and cold in my hand.

It's time to return to base: my men will need to hear of this. Before I leave, I spare a thought for poor Will. He doesn't look older than eighteen. He didn't need to be summarily interrogated by a mad witch like me.

Still, sometimes these things are necessary. The Party is not dead yet—and we're going to need all the help we can get if we are really to follow through with the dream.

A new government. A better future for this country and Europe.

Chapter Five: The Scholar and his Cat

Mark

I rest for a bit, overwhelmed at everything that Hell has to throw at me. It doesn't last long, though; I don't need to sleep, and I'm too restless, too anxious. I've no idea how long it's been since I left Earth—or since I saw Conall.

I wince at the memory. The way he'd looked at me as I went through that portal... I'd never realised how deeply someone could love you. And I'm not some sentimental pussy to say that loosely, either. I'd promised him I'd come back, but can I fulfil that promise?

For a moment, I feel crushed. It's not just the memories—the feel of his skin against mine, that confident smile, his sarcasm, and poetry. This place is like a vice, pressing me in with its blank stone walls, relentless heat, and constant darkness. Dante had been right after all.

I get up from my bed. It's not like me to sit here and complain about my life: I need to go out, actually *do* something. I remember what Suzanne had said about a guy named Shahar—the scholar. I'd not survived being Fallen without learning a few essential things, and one of them is this: information matters. Without it, I'm blind, and it's only a matter of time before someone tries to stab me in the back.

Before I leave, I pause to look through the wardrobe. If I'm Lucifer's favourite, maybe I should wear something other than a days-old T-shirt. (I can thank Conall for teaching me about fashion.) Still, there's no way I'm wearing any of *this*: the wardrobe is full of Italian suits and expensive leather shoes.

I ring the bell, sit on the bed again, and wait. A minute later, a boy rushes in. Okay, he's not a boy: he's not much younger than I am, maybe seventeen. Still, he has the boyish good looks down to a T. He has loose blond hair and bright blue eyes; he's tall and thin and a bit shy.

"Sir Mark?" He has a strange accent I've not heard. Maybe... Dutch?

"That's me. Don't bother with the sir."

He bites his lip; he's so cute I want to laugh.

"Yes, S—"

"Look, I need something to wear."

"The wardrobe—"

"I'm not prancing around in designer suits. Find me something a bit more... casual."

He nods. "Sure. A moment please."

A minute later, he comes back with a pair of grey jeans, a grey shirt, and a denim jacket.

"There's underwear as well," he adds. He carefully places the clothes on the bed next to me.

I throw off my jeans and T-shirt, then my boxers. He turns away red-faced.

"Put these clothes in the wash for me, will ya?"

"Demons don't usually... wear the same thing twice. At least, not unless it's special."

"Well, whatever." He still can't look at me.

"You're attracted to me, aren't you? Damn it." Lucifer probably engineered this himself: it would be just like him.

"I—I'm not..." But he can't turn his eyes away from me now.

"Did Lucifer set you up to this?"

"The Lord Lucifer did ask me to serve you, yes."

"That manky bastard!"

"Sir—"

"I know I shouldn't call him names; I've been told already. Look, kid. What's your name?"

"Steijn." Definitely Dutch, then.

"Why are you in Hell?"

"I was born here."

"That sucks. Well, let me tell you one thing: you're young, and you don't realise when you're being manipulated, especially when it comes to sex. Lucifer and his cronies thrive on sexual manipulation—don't give in, and don't let them know you're affected."

He gulps. "Ja. Oké, I understand. It's just..."

"Believe me; I already know how hot I am. My boyfriend knows too."

"I've heard rumours. Is it true he's still on Earth?"

"Word gets around fast, eh?"

"In Hell, words are power."

"Well, how about you tell me some of these rumours then?"

"I can do that."

I hear the catch in his voice. "For a price?"

His eyes roam my body; he licks his lips. "For a price."

I move like a viper; he doesn't have a chance to react. I push him up against a wall and hold him there. His breathing stops.

"You don't know much about demons, do you?"

"I... no. I've lived with my parents, helped them with their work." There's fear in his voice now.

"I could have lied and pretended I'd give you what you want. Hell, I want you too. But that's the thing with demons—they never give you what you want, not if they know what that is. If I were like them, I would have raped you repeatedly until I got bored with you and snapped your neck.

"Do you understand?"

He nods; he's crying now. I soften a little, letting him relax.

"How about this: if you tell me what you hear about me, I'll do my best to protect you. How does that sound?"

He nods again, still crying. Feeling guilty with myself (though he needed to learn this lesson), I wipe away his tears.

"Don't cry."

"I know."

"I'll get changed. Try not to molest me," I joke.

He laughs, just a bit. "Got you."

I throw on the denim, then head out the door. I have someone more important I need to meet.

****

I walk through the Citadel, my footsteps quick and confident, though I've no idea where to find Shahar. A few demons give me curious glances; I ignore them. They can stare at Lucifer's chosen one as much as they like.

He finds me. As I turn a corner, I come face-to-face with a man—if you could call him that. He is incredibly ancient. His hair is entirely white, his skin mottled and grey. I tower over him; he is stooped and frail.

He can't be a demon: Lucifer must be millennia old, and *he* looks like he's in the prime of his life. But neither, I sense, is Shahar entirely normal; there's a power attached to him, and a demonic rune glows on his forehead.

"Shahar?" I ask cautiously.

"You must be Mark! *Shalom*, pleased to meet you."

The old man raises a hand, and I shake it carefully, trying not to break any of his bones. The man's handshake is surprisingly firm. I can't sense anything more to him—he seems otherwise human.

"Not to be impolite, but do you mind if I ask how old ya are?"

"Oh, that's a common enough question. I'm just turning 2600 years old, actually. I'm as old as the Dark Lord himself." He winks.

I stare at him, unable to come up with a response.

"You are young, aren't you? Eighteen?"

"That's right. You speak English very well, by the way; Lucifer is not as fluent."

"Oh, languages are one of my passions—I manage to speak about eleven fluently and have an understanding of more. But come; I have much to discuss with you."

"Really?"

"Lucifer asked me to fill you in on some important facts, and according to my sources, you've already heard of me."

"That's right—a woman told me about you."

"That would be Suzanne, no?" He chuckles. "Come, we can converse more freely in my tower."

"You live in a tower?"

"Yes. Lucifer claims one of two; the other is mine."

The little man runs forward, and I walk swiftly to stay ahead. For a human, especially one nearly three thousand years old, he sure is quick. We pass through several corridors and reach a narrow flight of stairs. Up he goes, and I follow right behind. About a minute later, he pauses for breath.

"So, you really are human?" I ask.

"Quite so. I refuse to go through the ceremony, and Lucifer accepts that; he values me more for my knowledge than for any potential use as a demon."

"But..."

"How am I so old, you wonder? Well, I can thank Lucifer for that. The rune you see on my forehead, along with a sister rune above my heart, are responsible for keeping me alive. And also mostly immortal, aside from that."

"People have tried to kill ya?"

"It pays to be cautious. And humans can die in many ways, be it a disease or an unfortunate fall down a flight of stairs. That was quite unpleasant, let me tell you."

He regains his breath, then carries on. A few moments later, we arrive inside a room. Or, well, "room" is a word I use loosely: it's a vast, circular space and resembles an alchemist's hideout more than it does a place meant for human habitation. Maps, charts, and alphabets adorn every wall. Books are everywhere, on shelves and strewn across tables.

I also spot a com phone and a computer, both in advanced stages of disassembly. Shahar is no stranger to technology.

"Impressive," I say.

"You think so? Excellent. My occasional guests usually mock me for my disorder and lack of taste in luxury."

"Demonic guests?"

"Especially."

He walks up to a shelf and grabs several books. Worried he might fall over, I'm instantly at his side and take several of the thick tomes in my arms. He blinks in surprise.

"You never do that."

"What? Help you carry books? Sorry to point this out, Shahar, but I'm a bit stronger than you."

"No, I meant that you demons never offer to help me."

"What? Why?" But I think I already know.

"A mere human, even blessed as he is by Lucifer's magic, is beneath them."

"Why not become a demon yourself if Lucifer lets you choose?"

"Would you *choose* to become what you are?"

"I... no." I can't believe he's asking me this question.

"Well, there you go. Also, it is not as simple as it was for you—the ceremony is complex and... risky. But you will learn about that in more detail later. For now, the basics." He thumps the books on the table.

"You want me to read all that?"

"I would not demand such a thing from you, Mark. Besides, you wouldn't read it anyway." His eyes twinkle, and he chuckles. "No, I will merely use these books to illustrate some concepts. To begin with: Hell and its geography."

He flips one of the books to a page showing a map. I wonder at the intricate detailing—it's all handmade.

"The inhabited portion of Hell is known as the Cauldron. It is essentially a series of concentrically arranged platforms and buildings—some of which rest on naturally formed rocks—which are all interconnected via bridges and gates."

"Yeah, I got that. There's an uninhabited part of Hell too?"

"Yes, a remote cave system. No one goes there—not unless they wish to be eaten by firelings or worse."

"I've been told a lot about these firelings, but I've never actually seen one. What are they?"

"Good question. Firelings were among the original residents of Hell before Lucifer was exiled here."

"What do they look like?"

"Like little sprites. They are very bright to look at and radiate heat."

"And they can kill us?"

"Indeed, their fire is magical in nature."

"Right."

"Let's go back to the original topic for a bit. The Citadel—the place we are in now—is Lucifer's palace and also holds many rooms for demons, though most demons don't live here normally."

"How many demons are there?"

"Eight hundred and ninety-four."

"That's very precise."

He smiles. "Everyone knows. As for how many humans there are, the figure would be around two and a half million."

"That's... a fair amount."

"Yes. They are allowed to live on the various platforms arranged around the Citadel."

"With other demons?"

"The higher ranked demons effectively act as liege lords for humans."

"How feudal," I point out.

"Things are different here," he offers by way of explanation. "But back to the topic, you were asking about." He opens another book and shows me... a mural, I think. It depicts a proud, black-winged figure—Lucifer—leading a group of wearied demons. Small, flame-like creatures dance around them.

"What does this show?" I ask.

"Lucifer, as you can guess, and the Originals."

"Those are the first demons that followed him into Hell, right?"

"Yes, indeed. The first days were agony; very few thought we would prevail. Yet Lucifer did just that—he built all that you see today and banished the firelings and their master to the caves."

"All of it himself? The bridges, the gates...?"

"All of the magically warded structures. Naturally, various build-ings have been added, by human hands in particular; but the bridges, gates, and Citadel required Great Magic to create."

I'm still struggling to come to terms with all this. I felt Lucifer's power used against me—I *know* he's strong. But to carve all of those structures out of sheer stone? And toward them as well?

"What's Great Magic?" I ask, instead.

"That is... a somewhat complex topic, to put it mildly."

I already know what it is—Michael, my father, had explained it to me briefly. It needs three things: activation, foresight, and sacrifice. I close my eyes, holding back the memory. Damn it, but I wanted him to be my dad: I didn't want him to flee as soon as Lucifer looked at him side-ways.

Before he can explain further, we hear a loud, insolent *meow*.

A cat strolls in with its tail raised high; its body graceful and lean.

"Naem! My beauty!"

The feline glares at the Scholar.

"No luck finding mice?" Shahar asks her sarcastically.

"Meow."

I watch the older man as he withdraws a piece of cured meat from a cupboard and deposits the prize over to Naem. The little furball quickly devours the food, then curls up on a chair.

"Cats," I say.

"Oh, but I am quite besotted with her."

"Why do you call her Naem?"

"It means 'graceful and beautiful' in my native Hebrew."

"Ah. How old is she?"

"About as old as me; I've had her for such a long time..."

"What? That cat is two and a half thousand years old?"

"Alas, no. I call all of my beloveds Naem, though technically, she is Naem 201. They all have different personalities, but I've loved them through the Ages."

"That's..." Mind-boggling, I want to say.

"Sentimental of me? Lucifer certainly thinks so. Whenever Naem gets old, I ask him to make her immortal, as he did me."

"And what does Lucifer say to that?"

"He just laughs."

"Right."

A bell rings nearby. It has a deep, resonating timbre that reminds me of a bronze bell. Shahar sighs and makes himself comfortable next to his cat.

"Alas, I would teach you more, but it will have to be later. That bell is very distinct: it is a Summoning Bell for the Games."

"What?"

"Summoning Bells are when Lucifer calls his demons over to the throne room. The Games are an annual activity—a tournament, I should say. Lucifer is very fond of it, though of course I never watch."

"Why not?" I have a feeling I'm not going to like the answer.

"The purpose of the Games is to pit demons against each other to determine who is stronger. The Games are usually held a week later than this, but it seems Lucifer has moved the date forward."

"Because he wants me to participate?"

"You guess correctly. Doubtless, you will be a guest of honour and will be permitted to observe the combat, but fight you will, I am sure of it."

Something within me relishes that possibility. The power burns inside me, and my wings quiver.

Shahar looks troubled. "You're a lot like them, you know."

"How can you say that?"

"Your eyes." He detaches himself from Naem (the cat growls in discontent) and brings a mirror to me. The polished obsidian is an excellent reflector: I can see that my eyes are black, absorbing the light like a void.

I close my eyes, forcing my power back. It is like a chained beast: contained but always ready to spring at a moment's notice.

"I'm impressed. It's unusual for a young demon to have that level of control over their magic."

"What can I say? I had to learn on the job."

"That you did. I understand you were attacked by agents of the Irish government?"

"That's putting it mildly. The Party had me imprisoned, and when they couldn't come up with enough evidence to prove I killed Fintan, they kidnapped my boyfriend and me."

"They couldn't have had you tried and sentenced? Why bother with kidnapping?"

"Conall hired the family lawyer to defend me. It would have been in breach of the rule of law."

"Ah yes. I have studied this "rule of law"—a fascinating concept, but a short-lived one, on the whole. Humanity had it for maybe a couple of centuries. The Romans did not bother with such ideas, and nor does Lucifer."

"Well, ya see, the Party still has to pretend to follow the rule of law. De facto, Fallen, like me, don't have its protection because we can't afford expensive lawyers—or even read very well in some cases. The rule of law is there to protect the rich and the aristocracy—Upperclassmen and Owners, mainly—from the Party's whims. It's a kind of implicit power-sharing agreement."

"Interesting. So they kidnapped you covertly?"

"Yup. They tried to threaten my boyfriend to ensure my compliance, but I was having none of it."

"I can imagine. You have great power, Mark: use it wisely."

"I'll take your advice."

"Now, I really mustn't keep you away from the Games; Lucifer wants to see you there. Although this conversation was certainly intriguing— I read a great deal about Earth, of course, and I have access to social media... but hearing first-hand accounts is more enlightening."

"Glad to be of service."

I leave the scholar, his cat, and the tower. If Lucifer wants a fight, he's going to get it. (I still want to punch him for trying to kiss me. Guess this could be the right opportunity.)

Chapter Six: Assassins

Conall

Radio silence. That's the only way I can describe these past few weeks—nearly a month since Mark left for Hell. Kaylin has given me a few hints about a new political entity on the scene, but nothing more than that. Of course, Mark has not returned, and neither have any of Lucifer's minions come knocking.

I try, vainly, to make conversation with my mother's hired bodyguard.

"So, what's your name, soldier?" I ask, a little sarcastically.

"I don't think that's in your interest to know, Sir."

"That's rather impolite of you, don't you think?"

"Maybe, but it's my professional code."

Before I can ask him anything more, he raises a hand. He's listening carefully to the com phone in his ear. He shakes his head; I frown.

"What are they saying?"

I'd learned that mother's bodyguards had taken control of the mansion's defences; the existing guards my father employed are under their command.

"Nothing. That's the problem."

"Maybe something is wrong with their com phones? Or there's a storm nearby?" Though I can see perfectly well that the sky is clear.

"Stay down. Do not move from this room."

He un-shoulders his laser rifle—he is noticeably well-armed and not hiding that fact. I hide under the table (the time for bravery is not now). He inches up against the wall, then peeks out from the open door. A split second later, he fires.

The laser flash is silent and visible only as a brief flash of light. The choked sound from the other end is distinctly human, though.

"What do we do?" I ask, afraid now.

"We're under a planned attack; I don't know what's going on with my colleagues, but we can assume they are dead. The assailants probably don't know your position, so let's not make it easier for them—we need to move."

"Are they after me?"

"We were hired to protect you for a reason."

"You were there when Diana came. Believe me, if I'm the target, the assailants won't be human."

He seems very uncomfortable with my pronouncement but accepts it rationally. "Your father, then."

"Will you protect him?"

"My priority is you; if I can protect your father, I will try my best." He doesn't sound too hopeful, though.

He beckons me forward, and I follow behind him. I spot the smouldering remains of a body; he pauses to investigate. I can see that the man is armoured, though not enough to stop a full laser rifle hit (it's a ballistic vest meant for bullets). My bodyguard curses under his breath.

"Party agents?" I guess.

"Almost certainly."

"And armoured?"

"My sidearm will be useless."

"How much energy do you have in your laser battery?"

"Enough."

We walk forward, but a moment later, he tackles me. The wall above my head explodes in flame.

"I thought—"

"Be quiet and keep your head down."

More laser flashes tear through the room. A moment later, another series of laser flashes—but from somewhere else. Human screams ring out.

"So my men are still alive," he comments. He raises his rifle, and then... he falls. I crawl over and see that a bullet has hit him in the chest.

His armour stopped it, though. The reason he's unconscious is that he hit his head on the wall—he's bleeding from his scalp.

"Damn it." Seeing no other option, I grab his rifle, then crawl to the other corner of the room.

Seconds pass. The battle—firefight, whatever you want to call it—continues erratically. A brief silence. Then, a man walks into the room.

He's wearing black armour, and I don't recognise him. I pull the trigger twice; he dies. I don't have time to ponder the swiftness of his death or the ease with which I could take a life. Nor can I afford to contemplate my impending doom. I need... I don't know what I need to do. Should I get out of the mansion? But what if someone is watching the exits?

Besides, trying to leave this room would expose me. The Party bastards have already proven happy to shoot at me, unarmed as I was, so I can't count on them to obey the rules of war. The Party has never followed the rules anyway, especially when dealing with internal threats.

I can only hope that the guards prevail, though I know that's unlikely—there's no way the Party would send an inferior force against us. The other alternative is Kaylin. I don't know if she foresaw this attack in a vision or knows it's going on right now; I can but hope.

Then I hear it, a sound that's hard to mistake—it's too mechanical, yet resembles human footsteps. Androids.

We have one android guard, but there's more than one out there. There is a storm of gunfire. Then quiet.

"They're dead now, cap'n?"

"The guards are dead, and their android is out of commission."

"So, where's the target?"

"I don't know, but I suspect he's hiding somewhere, maybe in a panic room."

"We should have brought the androids sooner; we've lost three men, and we'll need them to get in a safe room too."

"Perhaps, but it would have cost us the element of surprise."

I don't know if the target is my father or me. I can try running and hope my father will survive long enough in the safe room... The thought tapers off. I know it's unlikely. I don't want my father to die, even if he's sometimes a bastard. Nor do I want to run like some coward—but then, what choice do I have?

I start as a hand grabs my shoulder, and a voice whispers in my ear. "Conall, man, stay still and don't make a sound."

"Shadow?"

I recognise his voice even when it belongs to an invisible hand.

"That's me."

"Diana—"

"I'm right here," she says, her voice unnervingly close.

"Be quiet," Shadow continues. "We'll distract them, then take them out."

I nod my understanding.

Two seconds pass, then a window shatters. Androids and men both turn around. Then fire bursts from Diana; robot and human alike perish in a flash.

The duo turns visible now. Shadow has a pleased smirk on his face; Diana is smiling widely. They don't see a badly wounded Party soldier grab hold of his gun and raise it towards them...

But I do. I fire without thinking, adrenalin sharpening my reflexes into lightning. The hand drops. Diana turns around, shocked, while Shadow gives me an appreciative look.

"Good work, Conall."

I throw away the laser rifle, faintly disgusted.

****

Diana takes a tour of the mansion, eventually collecting Father from his safe room. (I didn't even know there was one.) Shadow calls my mother, and she finds us among the desolation.

"Oh my," she exclaims. "Conall, are you quite alright?"

"I killed two men."

"They deserved it, darling. Party agents, I presume?"

"Yes."

"We need to get out of here."

"Will we be safer in your place?" I ask doubtfully. "We're wanted now."

"I know that, which is precisely why we're going further afield."

"To Spain? Are you—"

"Mad, dear? Choose your words carefully. You've seen what they're capable of, now that we're in their sights. Your boyfriend, I must remind you, is not here to save you."

"Thanks, Mother."

"It is necessary, sometimes, to point out the truth."

"But I protected him," Shadow points out. "I'm sure—"

"The witch has other priorities," my mother interrupts.

"You're wrong," Diana tells her. "Kaylin considers Conall important; he is Lucifer's leverage over Mark."

"True, but I know she is busy fomenting rebellion with the local Communists."

Both Shadow and Diana are shocked. "How... ?"

"The Spanish government supports them; I was able to deduce the facts from my Spanish contact. I know, therefore, that you are allocating your resources towards that goal. You cannot protect my son."

"Do you honestly think we'll be safer there, then?" I ask.

"It's better than being in the middle of a civil war; have your lessons not taught you that much?" I wince. My mother knows how to win an argument.

I turn to my father, but he just shakes his head. "She's right, son."

I sigh, closing my eyes. Assassinations, civil war, and demons. What did I do to deserve this?

"When are we leaving?" I ask her.

"Soon, though not right now. I will bring you all to my underwater compound, which should be more difficult to assault."

"What of the valuables?" Trust my father to think about money.

"That will be taken care of as well, Niall. Now, follow me."

"Wait! What about our guards?" Trust me to think about human welfare.

"Most of them are dead; your bodyguard is the only one alive," Shadow informs me.

"I should fire that man," Sianna mutters.

"He was brave in the fight," I defend him. "He had the focus of a hawk."

"Very well, we'll ask him if he wants to continue being your bodyguard."

"What about Minnie?" I ask. "I hope she survived the attack."

"Your dog probably ran off," Father chastises me.

"Minnie!" I cry. Naturally, my father is wrong: a distant yelp, the scrape of claws on marble, and our dog is suddenly here—well, in my arms. She's barking at the unfamiliar faces, including Diana.

"Let him take the dog," my mother says with a trace of amusement. Diana smiles indulgently. Still, she remains serious.

"Do you want us to come with you?" she asks me.

"I—"

"I can protect my son just fine, thank you very much."

"Mother, listen to your logic. Diana and Shadow are powerful—they just took out three androids and a score of armed men. You should make use of them while you still can."

She ponders my words, her eyes cold and blue. Even in the destruction surrounding us, she is the epitome of regal: her posture is tall, her white suit immaculate.

"Very well, you may join us."

And so I find myself inside my mother's limousine, Shadow and Diana by my side. Minnie stays in my arms, though she eventually goes to sit next to Diana. Huskies are curious and friendly by nature.

"Your mum—"

I finish Shadow's sentence for him. "My mother is quite a piece of work."

"That's one way of puttin' it." He's smiling.

The limousine rolls away silently. We know our immediate waypoint, but what's our final destination?

Chapter Seven: Let the Games Begin!

Mark

Following Shahar's instructions, I find myself among a multitude of demons congregating in the throne room. The throne itself is empty, its master fashionably late. The hairs on the back of my neck stand up; the large number of demons here makes me defensive, the power inside me boiling nervously. It's strange: Lucifer is an immensely powerful demon, the worst of them all, and yet he doesn't make me uncomfortable. Not like they do.

A part of me—some very naïve corner of my mind that I didn't know still existed—wants to think that he's better than they are. That somehow, a being as beautiful as he cannot harbour such ugly, monstrous evil. But I know that's a lie. The other demons reflect their creator; they are only inferior, but their nature is the same.

My philosophising is finally interrupted when he shows up, Fading to somewhere high up in the roof and gracefully floating down to his throne. His wings are outstretched and glorious in their size, the individual feathers velvet and dark. The effect is magnificent—he's showing off. Even so, I can't help but admire his grace.

"Welcome!" he calls out, his voice reverberating massively. Magic, probably.

The demons shift excitedly, though they're silent as mice.

"I have called you here, my valiant demonic subjects, to invite you to the annual Games."

"Aren't you a bit early?" I call out sarcastically. Several demons give me looks—either of fear, disgust, or quiet admiration.

"Indeed, I have called the tournament a week early, on account of the *special occasion.*" He smiles knowingly; the other demons chuckle.

"What are the rules?" I continue.

"I will show you, my dear Mark. Follow me."

The Great Demon glides—not walks, that would have been too proletarian of him, to borrow Conall's language—and we all follow. His wings are partially folded; I don't think he needs them to glide. A few doors and corridors later, we're outside.

Suddenly, he takes off, flying high into the air with unbelievable speed.

I shake loose my wings and follow after him. The entire procession of demons takes to the air; we are a vast horde of dark-winged beings, equally beautiful and terrifying. I whoop, unable to contain the exhilaration. It doesn't last long—soon, he's landing next to a lake, and what I realise is an amphitheatre.

We all land around him, though none of us land on the water, which I realise is boiling.

"Normally, we fight on the Boiling Lake," he says, "but this is a special occasion and calls for a little more variety." He raises his hand; a burst of power emanates from him, like a shockwave.

The lake freezes instantly.

He smiles and flourishes. He creates several ravines, depressions, and boulders out of the flat expanse of ice. The end result is like something out of Hell.

With the show over, the demons make their way to the front row of the amphitheatre. I suspect they know their rankings from last year—it must be important to them.

Lucifer walks away from the lake, and several runes on the rocky ground activate. I feel the shimmering field burst into existence, magic flickering across its ethereal blue surface like lightning. It's not so different from a force field on Earth, I guess.

Lucifer floats upwards towards a regal-looking seat higher in the amphitheatre. He waves at me; I fly up next to him, still giddy with the sensation.

****

"Enjoying the show?" he asks with a twinkle in his eye.

"Sure." I swing for his jaw. All of my power is behind the strike.

Nothing happens. I realise the Great Demon is holding my hand; I hadn't even seen him move. He caresses my fingers, opening them up. Before I can complain, he pulls me forward, next to him. There's only one seat, but it's large enough to hold the both of us, with his arm annoyingly comfortable on my shoulder.

"Damn you," I say through gritted teeth. "You're fast."

"Oh, you'll see. But I admire your enthusiasm, nonetheless." He chuckles darkly. "If you want to hit me, there will be an excellent opportunity tonight."

I don't miss the innuendo: I go red, my cock involuntarily hardening a bit. Lucifer chuckles more deeply.

"You promised me you would tell me the rules," I say, trying to put myself on a more even footing with him. His legs are pressing against mine, and he even smells good, dammit—like tobacco and musk, the kind of masculinity that makes you want to lick his skin to see how it tastes.

"There are two rules: To win, you have to throw your opponents against the barrier. You can use magic, but you are not allowed to attempt to destroy another demon wilfully."

"Really? I thought you would appreciate a little bloodshed."

"I do, but there are other ways to accomplish that. We have human gladiator fights, naturally. Demons, however, are too valuable to waste."

"What are the human gladiators fighting for?"

"Various things, but mainly money, status, or a shot at becoming a demon."

"And the demons themselves?"

"Pride."

"Pride goeth before the fall," I point out. "I learned that much from the books I read on religion."

"A Bible quote. I wouldn't pay any attention to it: Christianity, in the eternal words of Nietzsche, is a slavish religion."

I know only a little Nietzsche and damn as near nothing about Christianity, so I pick a different topic. "Have you ever been surprised or impressed by a demon on the arena?"

"Yes, many times; it is why I enjoy the tournament so much. Cunning, strength, and will; that is what I admire most."

"More than raw power?"

"Will *is* power."

Before he continues, I notice that the amphitheatre is no longer empty—humans have started showing up. Many of them, even. I spot Suzanne and Steijn among them. Suzanne gives me a wave; Steijn catches my eye briefly.

"Why do people watch?" I continue questioning him.

"A variety of reasons. Humans are easily awed; some watch it out of fear, and a few are here only for the festivities." A human servant walks up to us.

"Lord Lucifer, how may I serve you? I have—"

"*Vin, s'îl vout plait,* Pierre."

The servant pours him a large glass.

"*Et pour le monsieur?*"

"Wine as well, please," I say, not trusting my French.

I also receive a glass, which I drink curiously. Lucifer watches me with amusement.

"To think that you are not used to alcohol! You must drink more. *Pierre! Un Autre!*"

"*La carte de cognac,*" Lucifer continues.

Lucifer selects a vintage from the menu, and Pierre serves it to me. I can taste the alcohol on my lips and feel a vague burning sensation in my throat, but nothing more. Instead, I notice the aromas: the caramel sweetness, the dark flavours.

Lucifer drinks his glass with pleasure, then claps his hands. A hush falls over the amphitheatre.

"Now, for the games!"

He doesn't need to say more: two demons enter the arena, gliding over the ice, albeit clumsily compared to Lucifer.

"We start with the weakest first," he adds for my benefit. "How is the cognac?"

"Nice."

"And the wine?"

"Also nice."

"Drink up. Would you like Pierre to bring you cider next, or something else? Rum? Tequila?"

"I have no plans to get drunk."

He pauses; I realise I've made a mistake. "Wait, *can* I get drunk?"

"An interesting question. Only if you want to."

"Do you ever get drunk?"

"Occasionally."

"How much did you drink?" I'm not interested in alcohol, really, but he makes me curious.

"I don't keep track, but enough to kill a human, perhaps more than one human. I was told I went through roughly a few bottles of wine, a bottle of cognac, as well as whisky, cider, and numerous cocktails."

"In a day?"

"Three; I was continuously drunk and did not sleep."

"If only..." I don't finish the sentence. *If only Conall could have seen the debauchery!*

"If only...?," he prompts.

"You had sex too." I cover myself quickly, but I haven't fooled him— I can tell.

"Naturally, I did. I went through four women and two men."

Those dark eyes of his watch me intently, like a snake. His hand moves down underneath my trousers, lightly touching the tip of my arse.

"Keep doing that, and I will punch you again; I don't care if you are the devil."

He withdraws his hand, chuckling. "You can try the arena then."

I notice that there's only one demon in the arena now—the victor. "I missed the fight. Was it any good?"

"His opponent was weak."

A new challenger steps up. She walks smoothly, confidently, the ice being no impediment. They face each other for a brief moment; then, he attacks. He flies high, then dives, barrelling towards her with tremendous speed. She sidesteps, avoiding him, and smashes the back of his head. He crumples forward, hitting the barrier.

He's on his feet again in a moment, but he's lost. Dejected, he walks away.

"Victory through deceit," I comment.

"Indeed. The victor is weaker than him but more devious. I like her style."

Another challenger comes forward, this time, another woman. She's tall and has blonde hair down to her hips.

"Vilde, a Norwegian," he says.

The blonde woman jumps at the other demon but Fades just before they collide. Instantly, the dark-haired woman twists around, lightning forking from her hands. Vilde, however, has Faded at a side-on angle next to her; she throws the other woman across the arena. She hits the ward.

"Deceit countered with ingenuity," Lucifer exclaims with pleasure.

"I'm going to fight her," I say, feeling annoyed.

"I would suggest waiting for the strong demons, but if you need to blow off some steam, as they say..." He smiles broadly. "Be my guest."

I shoulder my way through her challenger—a tall, blond male demon, maybe another Viking—and step into the arena. She regards me with a lot of curiosity, though she doesn't show fear. I loosen my shoulders and crack my knuckles.

She doesn't attack me physically; instead, she throws a fireball at me. I dodge it easily.

"That's illegal!"

"She can't kill you anyway, Mark. I'll let it pass." It's Lucifer's voice, but no one else seems to hear it.

Vilde smiles, then launches a lightning attack—likely to stun. I Fade next to her, ignore the lightning, grab her, and throw her across the arena. She crumples against the barrier.

It seems too easy.

My next challenger approaches more cautiously, his broad frame taut, his piercing blue eyes following my every move. In an instant, he Fades and punches me in the face. His fist glances off. He raises his other hand; it's alive with blue fire. Before he can burn me, I strike him, twisting my body to avoid his attack while I do it.

I don't need to bother; my strike throws him across the vast expanse of ice, almost to the barrier. He regains his feet, but I follow up with some magic of my own: I blast him hard, immobilising him against the barrier. He's howling with pain, unable to escape.

"You've proved your point," Lucifer's voice echoes out. I let go of my magic, bow with a flourish, and take up my seat next to Lucifer again.

****

Lucifer soon calls for a break. The demons mutter among themselves restlessly while the humans drink, cheer, and relieve themselves. In a way, it's bizarre—I've heard of stuff like this, seen it in sports stadiums, but this is no sport we're playing at. It makes me wonder if the humans of Hell idolise their divine masters; it's not a pleasant thought.

I leave Lucifer and make my way down to the demons. I recognise Diego giving me a baleful look—he had been defeated earlier—though Max seems amused. A few demons stand apart from the rest. I feel raw power emanating from them: they're strong and different from the others. Archdemons, I guess.

I turn and find myself face-to-face with one of the Archdemons. There's no mistaking it—the sheer power that emanates from his body is like lightning off a violent sea. But there's more to it than that. The other Archdemons are beautiful in the way polished diamonds and fine suits are beautiful; they are dark, sensuous, and perfect.

He smiles, revealing pointed teeth. His hair is a wild mess of electric blue, fiery red, and an impossible shade of green.

"Who the bleedin' hell are you?" I ask.

"That's no way to greet someone, now is it?" Even so, his smile does not falter. "Call me Tim."

"Is that an American accent I hear?" I've never actually heard one in real life before; it's a cultural artefact from a bygone era, something I learned from watching old movies and songs.

"Yup. I'm a native Oregonian, but there's a bit of Cali in there too."

"What?"

He waves my question away. "You wouldn't understand—my country is gone. Lost to time and nuclear war."

"You're the only American I've met so far."

"There aren't a great many of us left, even in Hell. Lucifer always considered us a crude, ignorant, and violent nation; he was surprised when I became the youngest human ever to Ascend."

"How old were you?"

"I was twenty."

"Why do it so early if you're not sure you would survive the ritual? I thought becoming a demon reversed most of the ageing your body experienced up to that point—otherwise, you wouldn't all be so hot."

He waggles his eyebrows suggestively. "Really?"

"You know what I mean."

He only chuckles. "In answer to your question: I didn't have that much longer to live. The doctor gave me ten years."

"Huh?"

"Things were different back then. It was the year 1990, and I had just been diagnosed with HIV; I was 18. So really, it was either Ascend or die horribly from AIDS. And immortality is *rocks*."

"Couldn't Lucifer have used a spell, like the one on Shahar?"

"He considered that, but there was one important difference between Shahar and me: he was healthy, and I was not. It might not have worked. Besides, I preferred to perish seeking immortality than let some stupid monkey disease kill me."

"Okay, I get it. You're a tough, sexy demon and want to impress me. Or are you jealous that I might take away your crown?"

"Not at all. I was impressed by how you fought the lesser demons; there is immense potential in you. If you Ascend properly, no one except Lucifer could stand against you."

"I don't want to Ascend."

"Let me convince you." He winks. "Just watch."

I realise everyone is sitting down and getting ready for the next match—the Archdemon fights. Intrigued, I glide over to Lucifer.

"I see you met Tim." There is amusement in his voice.

"Cool guy. He's different from the other demons, though."

"Was it the hair that gave him away? Or the tank top?"

"I didn't notice what he was wearing—but his teeth were sharp. Like a shark."

"It's an affectation; we demons are capable of some limited shape-shifting, but it's a difficult skill to learn. Tim is probably better at it than me."

"What? No way."

"Just you watch."

****

The previous fights had been nothing compared to this.

Tim is in the arena facing another demon: Dacia, a slight, beautiful woman. She shares Lucifer's grace, but she carries herself differently— Lucifer is like a god, whereas she seems alien and inhuman. The effect is uncanny. Tim, on the other hand, is prancing on the arena. His wings are outstretched, and they take my breath away. They aren't black, like angel wings; instead, they're silvery and translucent, like a dragonfly. Each new angle reveals a different hue—from blue to green and everything in between.

The audience holds their breath; the icy lake glistens red in the light. The two beings circle one another, and power crackles in the air between them, hidden but potent, ready to spring at a moment's notice.

Dacia attacks first. I expected a fireball, but I didn't expect to see *dozens* of them, their trajectories overlapping in a deadly cone of flame.

None of them find their mark. Tim seems to effortlessly evade the attacks, flitting from one place to another with impossible speed. I'm not even sure if he's Fading or if he's just *that* fast. The crowd is cheering.

Dacia looks very irritated. She Fades, heading straight for him, blue fire coiled around her wings. Tim is expecting this, clearly: at the last minute, he sidesteps, and Dacia flies straight past him. Before she can correct her mistake, blue energy coils from Tim's wrist—it reaches out, twists around Dacia, and slams her into the magic wall.

But Tim's not done yet; I can see the smirk on his face. He twists his wrist again and pulls Dacia—still struggling and cursing—back like a yoyo. He slams her into the barrier one more time; the crowd erupts into laughter.

"Enough. You've proven your point, Timothy; there is no need to add humiliation to injury."

"I am just as magnanimous in victory as I am in defeat." He releases Dacia, then saunters off the arena.

"Wow. Tim sure can work the crowd," I comment.

"The humans love him, although the demons think he's a bit insufferable. He scorns them—he takes his lovers from among the humans."

"Interesting."

Lucifer claps his hands; it is time for round two. Another Archdemon enters the fight. Julius is his name—I know because part of the crowd is chanting his name. The rest of the rabble is cheering: "Tim! Tim! Tim!"

The mechanics of this fight seem to unfold differently. Dacia was like a bull in a China shop; Julius is much calmer. With his perfectly coiffed hair and tailored clothes, Julius is the picture of ancient Roman aristocracy. His countenance is smooth, quiet, and collected, though there is just a hint of amusement in his dark brown eyes.

Tim attacks first. Glowing candy canes and gift boxes magically materialise above the frozen lake, then accelerate towards Julius. He doesn't bother with evasion; he draws his magic outwards and forms a shield. Tim's attacks smash against the magic and explode into multicoloured glitter. Julius's shield flares as it absorbs the attack. Even the glitter triggers the protection ward—it must be dangerous.

"Spoilsport," Tim cries out.

"Why don't you come and get me, *mentula*?" Julius is smirking so much that I think Lucifer might have been wrong—there's something between these two. The crowd picks up on it too, and they laugh uproariously.

Tim leaps at Julius, breaks his shield and tries to wrestle him. The demons stand locked together in a strangely macabre imitation of an embrace. Their power swirls around them, waxing and waning in tendrils of fire (and pink).

Still, I know he's made a mistake. Tim is faster, but Julius is stronger. Tim staggers back; Julius follows up with a bolt of dark fire. Everything moves in slow motion: I see Tim's eyes widen; the bolt is milliseconds away from killing him.

The bolt stops inches from his chest. Looking sideways, I see Lucifer smiling.

"A smart attack, Julius, and no doubt it would have succeeded in turning Timothy to dust were it not for my intervention." I gulp: I have no idea how he can keep Julius' magic frozen like this.

"Timothy, you fought well."

The bolt finally shatters, and I jump. It makes no sound, but it makes my nerves tingle.

Tim bows at Lucifer and then at Julius, though he does so half-mockingly. "I'll get you next time."

Lucifer smiles at me; he seems pleased, like a cat that stole the cream.

"Impressed?" he asks.

"I'm not going to lie—that was a good fight. How did you stop Julius's attack?"

"My will was stronger than his."

I doubt he'll tell me more than that. It disturbs me: Lucifer isn't just more potent than the Archdemons—he's in a different *league*.

"Would you like to pit yourself against Julius?" he asks smoothly.

I freeze. "You think I can beat him?"

"Perhaps. I would certainly appreciate seeing it."

I stare at the Archdemon below, my fist balled up and power radiating through my body.

"I'll do it."

****

As I fly down and walk into the arena, a hush descends among the crowd and the other combatants. They've seen what I can do, and now I relish the chance to show them more. Frankly, I'm not sure why I accepted Lucifer's offer to fight Julius: the Archdemon is no paperweight.

Then again, if I can beat him, I can beat anyone. Maybe even Lucifer, with luck.

He looks at me; his eyes are ethereally blue, his hair luscious and black. A small part of me complains that he shouldn't be as beautiful as me—it seems almost too much to gift to someone already so strong. I understand demons are naturally more attractive than humans, and stronger demons can only be more beautiful still.

His attack is blindingly quick.

Three fireballs hurl at me from different directions while he flies like an arrow. Instead of Fading, though, I roll on the ice. To my pleasure and surprise, he misses, skidding ever so slightly on the slippery surface.

I follow up with a counterattack, aiming a fist at his handsome jaw while burning him with fire.

He Fades, and I hit thin air.

Knowing that another attack is imminent, I Fade too. I'd counted on Julius being at the other side of the arena, and I'm right: I've Faded to his right, close to the edge. I attack him with three shadow bolts; it takes all of my concentration to maintain them.

I've tried three different trajectories, but none of them hit. I realise the Archdemon Faded twice.

There's no way I can beat him at this game: I have to get close. But I also need to surprise him—he'll Fade away otherwise. So I pull my power close to me; the air next to me hums and flickers. I lift slightly off from the ground, send a fireball his way, and charge.

As expected, he dodges the fireball and Fades next to me. I barely have time to roll before his palm passes inches above me, glowing bright blue. I pull my wings forward, knowing he'll succeed in hitting me and bulldoze into his abdomen.

I send him flying. A fireball grazes my wings, stinging slightly. Even in mid-air, he twists, rights himself, and throws three fireballs my way. I dodge two and catch another on my wings—it burns, but the damage isn't going to be permanent.

He Fades, and I twist, but it's too late. His attack catches me, and I go flying.

I force myself to stop mid-air, but this time he hits me with magic. His power drives me into the barrier.

As I lie winded, applause rings through the arena.

"Well done, Julius. And well done, Mark."

"But—"

You lost gracefully, putting up a good fight against a strong demon. You also used your environment to your advantage, unlike Julius, who was arrogant.

I realise he's speaking to me in my head. Telepathy was one ability I didn't know I had.

Getting off the ground, I glide gently towards Lucifer; he's smiling at me.

"I'll beat him next time," I promise.

"With more skill in Fading and controlling your power, maybe you will," he says.

I grab another glass of cognac, willing myself to get drunk. Soon, I'm feeling the hot buzz of alcohol, and for a time, I allow myself to drift.

****

Lucifer calls for another intermezzo, and I find myself wandering the arena. Demons and humans alike are buzzing about a fight—not just *a* duel, but *the* duel. I pay them no attention.

A regal-looking woman steps in front of me, rudely blocking the way.

"Who the bleedin' hell are you?" I ask.

"My name is Domiziana, and I expect more politeness from you."

I raise an eyebrow. Domiziana is a woman of medium height, with olive skin, brown curls, and green eyes. She is wearing a dress as black as a moonless night.

"You must be Lucifer's favourite plaything!" I exclaim with cheery falseness. "That explains why you're such a bitch."

"It looks to me like you're his favourite plaything."

"Jealous?"

"No. I am merely warning you. Those who fall from Lucifer's grace tend not to survive long."

"Is that a threat? A human is telling a demon to watch their back?"

"You have no idea. But you'll find out soon enough."

She turns around and leaves. I can only scratch my head. Domiziana is either playing a game I don't understand—and I'm in real danger—or she's the dumbest woman I've ever met. I guess I'll have to find out.

****

A growing quiet tells me something is happening; Lucifer is standing in the arena.

"And so we come, at last, to the greatest event of all. The three remaining Archdemons—Julius, Acheron, and Renesmé—have succeeded in besting their fellow Archdemons, leaving me, the one and only, to face them in the arena."

I start. I didn't realise I'd get to see Lucifer himself fight; he seems too aloof, too grand, for such a feat. Yet, it seems he relishes the opportunity.

"Who are you going to fight first?" I ask him.

He laughs; the sound is full of mellow confidence. "Oh, Mark. I'll fight the three of them at once."

"Oh."

The Great Demon places himself right in the centre of the arena. It's a position I would not have picked had I to fight three Archdemons simultaneously: I would have found a corner and forced them to meet me one by one.

But then, they would have found a way in Fading. I realise that my instincts—which had served me so well in fights against humans— aren't quite right when battling demons. I need to learn their weaknesses.

For precisely three seconds, the four figures stay statue still. The arena holds its breath.

A circle of fire builds around Lucifer; I realise the three demons are co-operating. It flickers and crackles as if the air itself has turned to fire. It forms a sphere around Lucifer, then seems to collapses in on itself.

Except that it doesn't collapse, not really; instead, it stays still, and through the flames, I see Lucifer smiling. The fire suddenly expands outward with incredible speed. His opponents try to protect themselves, but the attack takes them by surprise.

Lucifer cashes in on the opportunity and Fades. The Great Demon smashes the Archdemon named Renesmé into the Barrier.

The other two demons attack with a hail of fireballs. Lucifer's fireballs rise to meet them, and the flames extinguish one another.

Julius and Acheron don't stop, though: they Fade in and attack up close. I watch, amazed, as Lucifer dodges. He's subject to a flurry of blows, but not one finds its mark. He avoids the strikes so smoothly I barely see him move.

Then he lashes out, catching both demons and sending them sprawling into the Barrier.

Lucifer bows with an ornate flourish, then leaves the arena. The crowd erupts into a cacophony of cheers, and I stand motionless, in awe of his skill.

Chapter Eight: Salvation

Mark

The Games are over, and for a time, I wander through Hell. There is no daylight to mark out the progress of time, nor stars in the dark sky. There are only the boiling lava and the various magical lanterns illuminating the houses. I walk through the streets. Away from the amphitheatre, the humans are more fearful, and they shy away from me. Some even bow.

It annoys me. No man should have to bow to another; there's something unnatural about power. Still, what can I do? Lucifer's rule is not something I can challenge.

I look for a bench or some other relaxing spot, but without any luck. In the end, I end up gliding and perching on the roof of a house. From here, I have a bird's eye view of the Cauldron. Many buildings are obviously old, some medieval, and some plausibly resemble Classical architecture. Though a few structures are different: they resemble huge greenhouses, and they shine with brilliant light, like beacons of hope in this dark forgotten world. It's silly, of course. The greenhouses are just lit up in order to grow plants.

I'm just not sure how they do it. Where do demons get the soil from? (There is nothing but rock here.) And do they feed animals?

Trying to get a better look, I take off and land on a roof that's closer to the greenhouse. I have to admit that flying gives me an incredible feeling of freedom—even if I'm trapped in this place, effectively to protect Conall.

I shudder. Through all the chaos, I'd almost forgotten about the boy I'd loved. No dreams had been there to haunt me—because I hadn't slept. Being a demon is a curse, not a blessing, despite the extraordinary abilities it gives me.

I close my eyes, trying to banish the visage before me from sight: the great lake of fire, the dark stone buildings, the shifting shadows. Instead, I think of Conall's hazelnut eyes, his soft skin, the memories we'd shared. I think of Uncle and the secrets he'd kept from me. I think of my father... who abandoned me.

I laugh bitterly. Truly, Lucifer is not someone you can fight. But if he'd stayed...

A sudden *whoosh* startles me from my thoughts. I open my eyes to see Lucifer next to me on the roof.

"Enjoying the view?" he asks.

"It's a bit... gloomy. Except for the greenhouses."

"Those are hydroponic farms. But I quite agree: Hell is not the most idyllic place. Perhaps you'll find it more interesting once you see it from my tower."

"Is that an invitation?"

"Correct."

"Can we fly there?"

"Follow me to the Citadel first."

We drop from the roof, and he begins moving. His speed is immense; we're like wraiths gliding through the street, moving in a way impossible for mortals. Soon we're at the gate. Then, we fly.

We spin in circles, swoop down, and then up again. I'm laughing, and Lucifer is laughing too, almost as giddy with joy as I am. Hell stretches out below us. The concentric arrangement becomes evident; the Citadel lies right at the heart of the edifice. Fire and stone are around us, and above, there is only infinite darkness.

Suddenly, he grabs me and flies me through a window.

The room in which we land is opulent and large, though not as massive as the throne room. The floor is black marble and crisscrossed by multihued veins. A colossal chandelier occupies most of the ceiling, though the mood is predominantly of shadows. Lucifer casually takes off his shirt, then arches his back, hanging in mid-air.

"Gravity not cool anymore?"

"I find I prefer the soft comfort of the air."

"You're such a show-off."

He chuckles. "That I am. Follow me."

He twists around and floats over to an archway. There, lit by candles, lies a small pool. The water is completely still, and reflections dance across its surface, a perfectly formed mirror.

"A pool?" I ask.

He smiles, standing up next to me. Lucifer is breathtaking with his clothes on, but without his shirt, he is unmistakably divine. No man could hope to match a body like this: he has broad, strong shoulders that taper into muscular abs; he has long, powerful forearms and legs to die for. His bronzed skin reminds me of art depicting Apollo. There is no hint of blemish to disturb its smooth perfection.

Noticing my eye, he smiles more deeply and runs his hands across his chest, pausing below his jeans.

"Aren't you going to take those off?" I ask casually. "Or will you be getting your fancy designer jeans wet?"

"Don't you want to do that, Mark?"

"I'm taken."

The room turns freezing, like the most brutal Arctic winter, before returning to its normal temperature. His expression doesn't change, but I can feel his anger. No, not anger—something different, something more like... jealousy.

"I see I need to work harder for you. Few resist me."

"I'm not just anyone, now am I?"

"Indeed, you are not."

It doesn't stop him from jumping into the pool; wet clothes be damned. I roll my eyes, strip down to my underwear, and jump in. The water is pleasantly warm; it's just right for bathing. I spread out in my wings in a narrow arc and propel myself through the water, almost but not quite flying.

"You have our instincts," he comments.

"I know how to swim."

"That's not what I meant." He, too, glides towards me, no less graceful in the water than he is in the sky. Our wings become entwined, and before I know it, he is resting his head on my chest.

"You are powerful like us; you understand our tactics, but more than that, you do not think like a mortal."

"I'm a demon by accident," I insist. "I did not commit my evil act."

"Not when you killed Finn? Or that guard?"

How does he know, I wonder?

"You orchestrated it all, didn't you?"

"I did. I wanted to push you to see if you would respond accordingly."

It's my turn to be angry: the air grows frigid as the Antarctic, and the water seethes and boils.

"You got what you wanted then, didn't you?"

"Yes, but not in the way you think, Mark."

"Well, fuck you!"

I throw him off me like a rock. He disappears. A moment later, he's beside me—hand on my shoulder, eye to eye.

"I can answer all your questions, Mark."

I don't have time to reply because just then, Domiziana enters the room.

"Lucifer?"

"Amata, dear, not now."

"You call me your beloved, yet I see you are still with him. Why do you insult me so?"

Lucifer regards her calmly, with a mixture of desire, amusement, and—just barely, in the depths of his eyes—pity.

He says nothing more, and instantly we Fade.

****

We Fade back into the bedroom. My arms are around Lucifer's chest; his smell is strong, musky, and utterly intoxicating. I look him in the eye.

"She's jealous of me," I say.

"She is."

"You're not interested in her, are you?"

"Domiziana is beautiful, but no, I am not interested in her. Not in the way she imagines, at least." He laughs, and it is a soft, beautiful laugh. The kind that makes me shiver.

Domiziana enters the room; a scowl fixed on her face.

"You'll regret the day you met him," Domiziana warns him. "Mark will betray you; he will tear your black heart from your immortal body."

"I've made my intentions clear, Amata. Spare me your soothsaying, will you?"

I hear her footsteps as she walks away.

Lucifer hasn't turned away from me, though. His eyes are obsidian black, fathomless, a black hole in the centre of the universe.

He leans in gently. At that moment, I should be absorbed by him. He is the most beautiful man ever to live; he is powerful, cultured, seductive. Yet instead, I remember the face of the boy I love. Conall, in his skin-tight jeans with his cocky smile, charming and yet never malicious, always honest. More than anything, I remember the day the Gardá came for me; how we laughed and larked about in the sunshine. Darkness came for me then—yet I defeated it.

The kiss is sweet but oddly unsatisfying; he tastes of burnt caramel and tobacco. Then he tightens his body around me, and before we know it, we're on the bed.

"Before we do anything," I say, holding his jaw, "I want some answers."

"Ask me anything, *amator*."

"Latin? I prefer the Greek *eromenos*."

"Ah, but that would imply a pederastic relationship: you, the beloved, and me, the lover. I prefer to think of us as equals."

"Equals? You and me?"

"In you, I see someone very much like me."

The observation strikes me in ways I can't comprehend. "Who are you, Lucifer?"

"I am nightmare and desire; I am feared by the weak and worshipped by the strong. I am Will and Power."

"Okay, a different question. Why are you the master of Hell? Why is there a Barrier?"

"One question at a time, Mark. You can ask more as we progress."

He takes off my shirt, kissing me on the neck. I lie still, trying to enjoy the sensation. If I have to convince him that I'm really into this—because I need him to tell me everything, every secret—then I can't think of Conall.

"I am not," he says, breathing in my ear, "in fact the Lord of Hell. I am a prisoner."

Before I know it, we're in the air, flying high. Lucifer holds me tight, wings wrapped around my body.

"Look into the sky."

For an average human, it would be too dark, too distant. But my eyes see it: faint and yet unmistakable. The Milky Way.

"Is that...?"

"Earth. The only small part of it visible from this dark pit."

"And the Barrier?" I ask.

"The work of a witch and a traitor."

"A traitorous demon?"

"Unfortunately."

"Do you know the names of the witch and the demon?"

"Everyone knows their names. The demon was called Jesus. And the witch was known as Mary Magdalene."

I try to make sense of what he's telling me.

"Christianity...?"

"Got it all wrong. Humans forgot the truth and fabricated stories in their place. But they got this much right: the fool Jesus sacrificed his life to fuel the binding spell placed upon me."

"So this place, Hell, is—"

"Too many questions."

He glides back down and places me on the bed. For a time, he kisses me, and I kiss him back. Or at least, I pretend to.

After some minutes, he twists me around and starts massaging my back.

"Questions?"

"This place—Hell, I mean—wasn't empty when you were banished to it?"

"Hardly. It was infested by firelings, not to mention the dragon. The old witch thought it might be the end of me."

"A dragon?"

"Yes. Big. Red. Don't ask me its name—you don't want to know."

"Is it safe?"

"I tricked him into a cave and bound him to it for all of eternity."

"That's incredible."

"That's another question." He kisses me hard and pushes my head down towards his abs. He slides off his jeans.

I resist. "Lucifer, I—"

"Did she spoil the mood? Women."

Then I'm sucking his dick. Would it be fair to say that he forced me? Yet, despite everything—kidnapping me, threatening Conall—my body responds. I do not love Lucifer, but he is any man's dream. I know I will need to suffer much tougher challenges than this.

Can we communicate telepathically? I project my thoughts to him.

Of course.

Tell me, how do you plan on breaking the Barrier?

Oh, how I've waited for you to ask that. The Barrier has become weak—

Why?

Because the spell relies on humanity, specifically, on his faith, and the Barrier will hold so long as man rejects power. But many more humans have gone over to the dark side and become demons.

Which is why there are mutants on Earth, I realise.

Yes—that's a side-effect from the witch's meddling.

So when will you break the Barrier?

It's not enough to turn ordinary demons. To undo the Great Magic that cast it... well, it requires something special.

Special?

You, Mark.

I break off, shaking my head. He wants too much from me, and I'm not just talking about sex. I realise the full extent of my meaning to him. I'm not some tool in his arsenal—my ability to circumvent the barrier is just a bonus. No, I'm so much more than that: I'm his salvation. His greatest equal.

He senses my withdrawal. "Mark? Come here. Maybe I spoke too soon—you know so little."

But I'm already Fading away.

****

I've Faded to my room, where I crash on the bed, weary. A startled yelp tells me I'm not alone: Steijn is in the room with me. Naturally, I'm still naked, thanks to Lucifer; the boy looks at me like I'm candy.

"Don't even think about it."

He turns away and stutters a response. "Y-yes, Sir Mark. Mark, I mean."

"It's Lucifer, dammit. I just Faded away from him."

"Right now? The Dark Lord...?"

"We were together. No, I didn't want to have sex with the devil, but he was persuasive. Also, I got some important information out of him."

"Such as?"

"Tell me what you've found out, first."

"You have enemies."

"I already guessed that. Who?"

"Several people, including some higher-ranking demons. The Lady Domiziana, for one, is jealous and is said to despise you."

"Let me guess: Lucifer's favourite plaything?"

"I suppose that's an accurate description."

"What's she going to do? Besides skewer me with her sharp wit, I mean. She's only human."

"Don't underestimate her. She has demon friends too."

"Any I should be scared of?"

"Diego hates you, but you already knew that, I think. There is the question of the Archdemon, Acheron."

"What about him?"

"He dislikes you and has questioned Lucifer as to your real importance."

"Would he turn against me?"

"Maybe, given the right push."

"Anything else?"

"Not yet; I still need to meet up with my source."

"Your source?"

"I'm not saying anything until you tell me more."

I pause, deciding what to tell him. (I at least take the opportunity to put on my jeans.) In the end, I don't think it's best to say to him too much—it's dangerous knowledge.

"I'll let you know this much: Lucifer needs me bad."

"To break the Barrier?"

"You know about that...?"

"I figured it out."

Maybe Steijn isn't as dumb as I assumed. He's young, a little naive, and thinks with his lad too much, but he has a good head for logic.

Then I hear it: a hollow thud in one of the wardrobes. In a flash, I open the door.

Instantly, I am face-to-face with the most fantastical creature I've ever seen. It's red, small—almost child-like—and has little horns on its head. He glares at me with an indignant expression.

Not knowing what else to do, I try and grab him. To my amazement, he evades my demonic speed and jumps straight for the door. I Fade, blocking his way. He leaps, pushes against a wall, and shoots towards the ceiling. Realising I can't catch him any other way, I focus on my magic and pin him with my telekinesis mid-air.

"Fuck you! Fuck you! You demon! You whoreson! Your mother—"

"Was human, and I didn't become a demon by choice. Now shut your potty mouth."

Somewhat surprisingly, the creature goes silent.

"Steijn, what the hell is this?"

"That's Javalook. He's an imp."

"An imp? They're real?"

"And you're a demon," the creature points out. "Why the surprise?"

"Fair enough," I respond.

"Javalook is helping to spy for me," Steijn continues. "That's one of his specialities."

The creature draws himself up, showing pride, though my magic keeps him dangling awkwardly in the air.

"Put me down, you idiot!"

"Promise you won't run away?"

"I promise. I owe a favour to your star-crossed bell boy there."

"Hey!" Steijn complains.

"I agree. Steijn, stop staring at my bum."

He blushes. Turning my full attention back to the imp, I gently lower him to the floor, then release my magic. He puffs contemptuously, then hops on the bed.

"Do you have more to tell us, Javalook?" I ask him.

"Little to add to what Steijn has already told you. But I do have a suggestion if your mightiness is willing to listen."

"Go on."

"I have heard a little about you, Mark. I've heard more than a little, actually; eavesdropping is my speciality."

"Keep talking."

"You are powerful but still clueless. You know very little about the history of Hell and what kind of character our master is."

"Lucifer."

"Yes. You didn't even know we existed."

"But what are you, exactly? How are imps different from demons?"

"Shahar will explain everything to you. I can start by telling you that Lucifer created us from firelings."

"What?"

"A long time ago, not long after he imprisoned the dragon. He intended us to fight off the firelings—which we're pretty good at doing—and to be his loyal subjects."

"So why are you helping me, then? Would Lucifer approve of it?"

The imp, who before had seemed a comical figure, smiles a very chilling smile.

"I love my master; we all do, for he is kind to us when no one else is. I even delude myself into thinking that Lucifer loves us too."

"He doesn't?"

"He is very fond of us—which is rare for him—but he is incapable of love."

Something about all of this seems a bit suspicious to me.

"And you're telling me you're different? Imps, beings wrought by Lucifer's hand?"

"We don't desire violence, Mark. We are tricksters; we love a good practical joke. A bit like you Irishmen, if you don't mind me saying so. Evil, though—that's something we're not."

"I don't believe you," I say. "I need proof."

The little imp sighs. "He's not stupid, Steijn. I'll give him that."

"No, he's fierce," Steijn agrees playfully.

Javalook stares me in the eye. "Come with me; I have something to show you."

"What is it?"

"It's... hard to explain. You have to see it for yourself. The location is public if that's what you're wondering."

Life as a Fallen had taught me too paranoid, so I'm always on the lookout for a trap. But his offer seems genuine. "Very well, lead the way."

****

The imp leads us to one of the main areas of the Citadel; the entrance is marked "Gallery." There are people everywhere: some well-dressed, others bedraggled; there are young children mixing with old men and women; a few are hawking wares. I observe popcorn, candy, and various trinkets among the offerings. Most of the items are priced in sestertii; the more expensive items cost one or two denarii, which I understand is a modest amount of money.

"So this is some sort of exhibition?" I ask Javalook.

"If you could call this by such a polite name."

"How much is the entrance fee?" I ask. "I haven't got any money on me."

"Lucifer subsidises the museum," Steijn informs me. "Entrance is free."

We make our way past the entrance and into a large hall. At first, the exhibitions are banal, the kind of thing you might expect to see in a museum: there are bronze statues of Greek men and women, along with more resplendent marble statues of demons. Some of them are truly captivating—the artist really captured the arrogant poise of the demon and the snarl of cruel contempt.

"Are these magic items?" I ask, noticing a handful of crystals. They glow in various iridescent shades of blue, green, and violet.

"Lucifer took a handful of crystals from Earth into Hell," Javalook explains. "They are, indeed, magical."

"What are they used for?"

"Aiding spells, storing power, all sorts of things," Javalook says.

We follow the imp as he leads us away from the central exhibition to a room marked "Enemies of Lucifer." I feel a cold shudder pass through me.

It takes me a couple of seconds to realise what I'm actually looking at. At first, I assume it's just another statue. Yet the proportions are too lifelike; the grimace of pain seems too real. The man was perhaps thirty years old when he was turned to stone.

"Who was this man?" I ask quietly.

"This was a human who displeased Lucifer. He attempted to escape Hell, breaking his promise to remain here all his mortal life," the imp explains casually.

We keep going. There are numerous petrified humans, along with quite a few ice sculptures. Which, of course, aren't really ice sculptures at all. The next room shows three winged beings, and each turned into different elements: stone, ice, and wood. The last figure is the most intriguing—I've never seen a demon turned into a tree before.

"Is it... alive?" I ask.

"That particular demon was named Maferath, and Lucifer was particularly proud of his creation. He turned Maferath into a living tree, yes, though little remains of Maferath's consciousness. Some say they hear whispers in this room. I don't know if it's just their overactive imagination at work or if the old demon really speaks."

The imp bounds away, leading us to the final room.

I jump, thinking the first imp is alive. But the little creature seems a bit too solid, and far too still, to still be alive.

"This is a special kind of petrification," Javalook explains. "It is specific to imps."

"It looks very lifelike," I say in an awed whisper.

The next imp is blue-skinned and strangely beautiful, in a macabre sort of way. Ice has crystalised on his eyelashes, and icicles dangle from the edge of his little tail.

"What did she do?" I ask, referring to the frozen imp.

"She aided a human child," Javalook says sadly. "A child who was born in Hell but dreamed of seeing Earth."

"How many?" I ask.

"These are not the only imps Lucifer has executed," Javalook tells me. "They are simply the ones he chose to make an example of, in quite a spectacular fashion."

"Pour encourager les autres?" I ask.

"Exactly."

The last imp Javalook shows us is the most disturbing of all. He is a ghastly caricature, his face twisted with madness; the creature is stooped and warped-looking. Tumour-like growths spurt from his face, body, and tail.

"What... what happened?" I almost don't dare to ask.

"This is Wazoo," Javalook says, averting his eyes.

"Even I've heard of him," Steijn says. "Wazoo was one of the kindest imps ever to have lived; he was well-known among the human community for his healing abilities."

"Imps can wield healing magic?"

"Not many of them can, actually, but Wazoo was a natural. He was one of the most respected people in Hell; Lucifer adored him."

"So what went wrong?"

"Wazoo could not stand Lucifer's cruelty," Javalook says. There are tears in his eyes.

"I'm guessing he did something to piss off the Devil? It must have been bad."

"Wazoo was not content with trying to repair the pieces after Lucifer broke someone," Javalook explains. "He came to think of Lucifer as a monster, a being devoid of compassion. In the end, Wazoo wanted Lucifer to die. So he tried to contact the dragon."

"I'm guessing he wasn't successful?"

"He foolishly revealed his plans to a human friend," Javalook says. "It is unclear whether the human betrayed him or if they were simply overheard."

"Why would his friend betray him?"

"The human was trying to become a demon. This might have been his Great Act, though the human did not survive the transformation."

"What punishment did Lucifer mete out to Wazoo? Why does he look like he does?"

"Lucifer tortured him by causing him to develop an aggressive form of cancer; Wazoo tried to heal the cancer, but the effort only prolonged his agony. We imps eventually convinced Lucifer to kill Wazoo out of mercy, but by then, the damage was already done. Wazoo was a shadow of his former self."

"Lucifer is a monster," I say darkly.

"You have to know what you are up against; what we are up against," Javalook informs me.

"Can anyone hear us right now?" I ask.

"I cast a spell to prevent eavesdropping, either with magic or the banal kind. We do actually know what we're doing."

"Smart thinking. So Wazoo is what turned the imps against Lucifer?"

"Yes. We cherished him deeply. We have been biding our time for more than a century; you are a blessing for us."

"Thank you for showing me this—it can't have been easy."

"No. It wasn't."

We leave the museum and its grizzly trophies behind. Neither of us says a word.

****

We return to my room, and my mind wanders back to the problem at hand.

"So what's the plan, Javalook?"

"You are powerful, Mark, and you are not dumb. Still, you are ignorant about Hell: it is a place with many hidden secrets and many traps for the unwary. We will do our best to spy for you, but you must arm yourself with knowledge."

"Are you talking about Shahar?"

"Yes. The old scholar has a great deal to teach you."

"What if he finds out we're plotting against Lucifer?"

"I wouldn't worry about it. Shahar was once a close friend of Lucifer, but that was a long time ago—times have changed."

"Right. You spy for me, and I learn magical juju from an old scholar. Sounds grand."

Javalook grins. "You have the right idea. Now I must be off. Farewell, Mark and Steijn."

"Farewell, Javalook."

The little imp bounds out of the room, finding an unseen hole in the ceiling.

"Some informant you have," I comment. "He can disappear through cracks in a wall, hide in the ceiling, and I bet he can hear the hairs growing on your head."

"He can do all of those things. Lucifer's imps are good enough to rival MI6 or the Stasi. They don't need to threaten anyone to be effective."

"You've heard about MI6?" Everyone knows the English spy agency is one of the best in the world.

"We do have books in Hell. And our own Internet, too."

"So how did you meet Javalook? Why does he owe you a favour?"

"You wouldn't believe it."

"Try me."

"I played wingman to Javalook when he was trying to woo a lady imp."

"You're right; I don't believe you."

The boy chuckles. "Whatever."

"So what can imps do? I understand some of them have the power to heal?"

"Some of them, yeah. None of them can teleport as you do, though."

"Good to know. Anything else?"

"They might not be able to teleport, but they're swift, as you can see. Imps also have control over ice and fire, to kill both demon and fire-ling alike."

"Really?"

"Yup. One imp wouldn't stand a chance, but multiple imps could kill a demon. I don't know if that has ever actually happened, though."

"Thanks for the information, Steijn. You've been great."

"Do I deserve a hug?"

"Yes, but behave yourself," I warn him.

We hug, and I ruffle his hair for added effect. He is sweet; I realise I'm starting to like him. Maybe he's the younger brother I never had.

Chapter Nine: Returning Memories

Kaylin

Memories are precious things; they define who we are. Without memories, we are nothing. And to take away a memory—even one as small as I did—is not something to be done too lightly.

After delivering the message, along with the hammer and sickle, I stole from Will, Diana, my men, and I have come to Cork.

Unable to explain how he lost it, the boy and his superiors should be willing to meet me at the agreed location—a bar right in the city centre.

My party and I are sitting at a table we've booked for the evening. I have several men posted around the building and in the bar-room itself—Shadow leads them, with whom I've managed to form a telepathic connection. Grumman has an ordinary electronic link with the other men.

"What are you thinking, Diana?"

"We could do with some allies. Blanketing the boy's memory was an interesting move."

"And you, Grumman?"

"I agree with Diana—we can't fight what remains of the Party and kill demons on our own. These guerrillas can help us with the former if not the latter."

"Can we trust them, though?"

He smiles coolly. "We can trust them so long as we have a common goal. After that, who knows? If this revolution of theirs succeeds, well, we know our history. Don't antagonise them—and make sure you always have something to bargain with."

He says no more because just then, four men and a woman enter the bar. To their credit, my men keep their eyes away from them (that would have given them away).

"Just five?" I whisper.

"They'll have a backup," Grumman tells me.

"Good evening," I say to them, holding out my hand. A large, ageing, and thickset man shakes hands with hearty warmth. Grumman and Diana do the same with the others.

They sit down. I observe the group with interest: the man I just shook hands with is probably the leader. The woman is the oldest—I'd say she's at least sixty. The other three men are younger, although the youngest is about thirty. I pay special attention to him: there's something in his brown eyes and intelligent expression that attracts me.

"Who are you?" the leader asks me. "I'm Andrew."

"And I'm Kaylin, but that's not really what you wanted to know."

"Go on. Cut to the chase."

"I know who you are and what your plans are. You're revolutionaries."

"And you, we're to think, are a revolutionary as well?"

"Who do you think helped kill Big Brother?"

His eyes widen. "You did?"

"Indeed. But as you can see, it wasn't nearly enough. We killed the head of the snake, but the body is still writhing in its death throes. We need to deliver the fatal blow while the Party remains weak."

"Naturally, I agree. I don't quite trust you, however. Where did you get the hammer and sickle?"

"From one of your men—Will. You must have figured it out."

"We suspected."

"Bring him in then; I would like to see him."

"He's—"

"I know he's here."

Andrew pauses, thinking. He exchanges a meaningful glance with the others. He speaks through a hidden radio; then, some moments later, Will walks through the door.

He's just as young as I remember. He looks at me strangely, recognising something.

"Will, I'm Kaylin. I believe I have something that belongs to you."

He sits down in front of me.

"Lady, I think I know you."

I smile. "No wonder. Give me your hand, palm up."

He complies but wears a puzzled expression on his face while he does so. I touch him and briefly enter his mind. As I thought, the blood bond is still strong.

I locate the memory; then, I uncover it, removing the fake one.

He yelps like a startled cat. "You!"

Everyone reaches for hidden weapons; I raise a hand.

"Yes, it's me. Tell your comrades what you know."

"She's a witch!" he whispers. "She had me with a spell."

"Calm down, boy," Andrew starts. "You look like you've seen a ghost."

"Or a witch," the brown-eyed, younger man interrupts, smiling. "I'm Leo, by the way," he says to me.

"Pleased to meet you."

"Leo, explain," Andrew commands.

"Andrew... you know I'm a little bit special. The supernatural exists. Kaylin, here, is the real deal."

His pronouncement shocks his comrades, though I sensed something in him the moment we met.

"Right. That explains a few things," Andrew mutters.

Will seems too shaken to say anything more.

"Gentlemen," I interrupt. "We have precious little time. I revealed myself to you in this manner as I was there when you attacked the Gardá base; I aided your men."

"Thank you," Leo says.

"Your help is appreciated," Andrew concurs. "So, this is what you want? Co-operation?"

"Yes. Such an arrangement would be mutually beneficial, perhaps even necessary."

"We'll need more time to decide if we can fully trust you," Andrew warns me.

"You have time, but not forever. There have already been multiple assassinations among the ranks of the Party and one attempted murder," I say, thinking of Conall's father. "We will meet again soon. I take it our men have exchanged means of communication?"

"We have," Grumman says.

Andrew nods. "Very well. We have another mission planned—we'll let you in on the details and see how you can help."

I nod. "Until then, Andrew."

"Until then."

Before they walk away, I send a telepathic message to Leo, hoping he can hear it.

Leo? I want to talk with you.

Kaylin? You can use telepathy?

Yes. Can you?

Barely, I... I still don't know or understand very much.

Meet me tonight if you can.

Yes. Where?

I live not far from here. I'll send one of my men, Shadow, to accompany you. He, too, has a gift.

Are there others like me? Are you not the only one?

There are others like you, though... I've yet to meet other witches. I seem to be unique.

I want to know more; I'll come.

Pleased with myself, I tell Diana the news.

"Good. We could do with knowing another Familiar."

"Do you know what he's capable of?"

"I have no idea, but I'm sure you'll find out. I'm sure you'll know everything about Leo."

"How so?"

"Come on, Kaylin; it's obvious. I haven't seen you in love with someone for years. I mean, *really* in love, not just now-we're-friends-it's-complicated."

I blink, realising she's right.

"Do you think... ?"

"Don't act like a teenager. Yes, he likes you too. Now let's get out of here—it's risky, meeting like this."

"I know, but we had to meet face to face."

"And Will deserved his memories. I agree, Kaylin. Grumman, let's move it."

We leave the bar, my thoughts ablaze.

****

That night, he comes to me.

I wait for him at my home. I could have picked a different location—someplace more anonymous and better for my safety. But I detest that kind of secrecy. Somehow, I trust Leo; I wouldn't want to treat him like a threat.

I open the door. Leo is wearing jeans, a long-sleeved shirt (with fashionable cuffs), and a bomber jacket. A little too bourgeois for a communist, maybe, but appropriate given the circumstances. I'm wearing my usual black clothing (I am, after all, supposed to be a witch).

"Good evening, Kaylin," he says.

"Come in, Leo."

I bring him to my living room, where I serve him warm tea—he accepts graciously—and cake. I considered cookies, or maybe gingerbread men, but deemed them to cliché.

"So, can we get straight to the point?"

"I like a man who speaks plainly."

"I have a lot of abilities. I can use telekinesis. I have some control over fire, too." He opens his hand and produces a small fireball.

"Interesting. I've never met a Familiar with so many Abilities, except for Diana, but she's different."

"How?"

"She can't use telekinesis, but she has control over the elements and can fly. Can you also fly?"

"No, not really. I can jump telekinetically, but that's it."

He telekinetically lifts a book from a nearby shelf and brings it towards me; I focus and oppose the motion. Simple telekinesis is easy enough, even without a spell.

He's strong, though, and I flounder. I quickly draw a rune in the air, then refocus. The book flies off into a wall.

"Sorry about the book," he says.

"Don't worry; it wasn't valuable. You're pretty strong—I wonder how I ever missed you."

"You were stronger than me, though."

"Not without a spell."

"How is it that you have so many others like me under your command?" he asks instead.

"I'm a seer; I find them in my visions."

"I had no idea."

"I don't either. The early days are always the hardest. But I learned, and then I found the book."

"The book?"

"It's called the Black Book; it's a spellbook. It was a priceless artefact I stole from the Chinese authorities, in the mountains of Tibet."

"Bloody hell."

I laugh. "I guess that's a good way of putting it."

"So this book—does it say anything about us?"

"No, which is what puzzles me. I have my suspicions, though."

"What suspicions?"

I sigh. As much as I like Leo—maybe even *because* I like him—I can't let him in on this. It's too dangerous for him to know about Lucifer.

"Leo... I want to be upfront with you, but there are some things I just cannot reveal yet. Ask me anything else, but not this. I can only reveal that we have an enemy—a powerful enemy, well beyond the Party and supernatural. I don't want to implicate you in this. You can't under-stand how dangerous it is."

"Okay... I believe you. What about the Party? How did you kill Big Brother?"

"Let's just say I had some help, which I can't count on again."

"What's your beef with the Party, then? Surely you don't fight them just because you can?"

"That would be good enough reason. But no: you're right. The Party tried to hurt my friend, Diana."

"So it's protecting your friends then? Or revenge?"

"I killed the bastard who tried to hurt her. After that... it became something more. I interacted with people of the lower Classes; I fought alongside them, learned their struggles and hopes. I began to dream of something better."

"I know. I'm a Technical myself, but my powers made me feel like an outcast. Andrew found me and gave me a purpose. Maybe that's what we all need—purpose."

"But tell me," I say, "what is this purpose? Do we see eye to eye?"

"What do you want, Kaylin, besides the Party gone?"

"I want a government that's better than the fascistic kleptocrats in charge of the world right now."

"Including the Chinese?" he questions.

"Including them."

"We want to set up a government too. Something fairer. But it's not easy... sometimes I wonder how we'll ever do it. Or if, after drinking from the fountain of power, we too will become corrupted."

I smile knowingly. "A fate with which I am all too familiar. But strug-gle, we must—if we don't, who can? Truly, I'm amazed by how far you've come. Even with my magic, I've had some close calls."

"Aye, we too."

"And to think of how this horrible situation all came about. Two great powers were annihilating each other, driven to war by the pride of their presidents, by propaganda, hysteria, and hatred."

"And to think," he fills in for me, "that we, Europe, took over in the aftermath. That we succumbed to fascism and jingoism in the face of uncertainty; that we rediscovered our old colonial roots, and built an Empire just like the Chinese."

We mull over the words in silence.

Then, weary with the gravity of the conversation, I ask, "Wine?"

"Yes, please."

We continue to discuss everything—our lives, futures, and the fate of the world—as we drink. Soon we've finished the bottle.

Throughout the evening, I'd noticed the warmth of his body, his dark matted hair, and his eyes, so gleaming with passion. I abandon discretion and kiss him. He kisses me back.

"Kaylin?"

"Yes?"

"I want you to know that... I like you very much."

I smile with amusement. "You're telling me this after I kissed you?"

"Well, I thought the words could add to it."

I laugh, just a little. "Leo?"

"Yes?"

"I like you too."

Then I kiss him again, and we speak no more.

Chapter Ten: Destination Unknown

Conall

I stand upright, staring hard at Kaylin. I'd requested to see her, and she'd brought me to her base in the heart of the city. An invisibility spell kept me hidden on account of the danger involved.

"What do you want, Conall?"

I've never seen her like this, but then I don't know her all that well, do I? I've always thought of her as calm, contemplative, and smart. Yet the woman who stands before is *driven*, almost possessed.

"Do you know what's happening to my boyfriend?"

She looks taken aback by the question.

"I can't see into Hell, or at least, not consciously; I've tried, believe me."

"And have you no other sources of information?"

"Information into another dimension? How?"

"Honestly, I do not care *how*. I only care that you find out what Lucifer is planning and how we fit into it."

"I—"

"I know you're planning a revolution, Kaylin. There's no need for excuses. I'm telling you that the revolution isn't as important as you think it is: if Lucifer escapes from Hell, it won't make the slightest difference if you rule Ireland, or the Party does. Lucifer will control the entire *world*.

"And unlike the Party, he cannot be killed. The world will endure his torment until the end of time."

I can see I've got her. She deflates, palpably, as if she were five again, and I've just popped her balloon.

"You are right. I have allowed myself to become distracted, to... hope."

"You think I'm a typical Upperclassman, blind or indifferent to what the Party does?" It must seem like that, I realise. I don't care for communism, but I saw what the Party did to Mark. He deserved better. All of the Fallen do.

"Do you care about any of it or just your boyfriend?" There's a faint note of anger in her voice now.

"I would be lying if I said I didn't care about Mark most of all." I shrug. "But then, you'd be lying if you said you didn't care about Diana more than anything."

She looks at me more carefully now, as if seeing me for the first time. Her eyes shift colours, switching from their iridescent blue to bright green, amber topaz, and back again.

"Are you doing that just to unnerve me?"

"What?"

"The eyes."

I can see she's confused. "Your eyes are changing colour."

She asks one of her men for a mirror and studies her reflection carefully. Her surprise is apparent.

"A witch thing," I suggest.

"Yes, but what does it represent?" She shakes her head. "You're right, Conall. I must discover what Lucifer is plotting by any means possible. Are you ready to leave?"

"My mother is adding the final touches for our relocation to Spain."

"I will need to protect you, even there. There will be men watching you; I will cast spells to see you. You understand this?"

"I'm always going to be in danger, so long as I continue to love Mark. I accept that."

"Then goodbye. I hope you survive this, Conall."

"I'll hold you to your word, Kaylin."

I exit the compound. Kaylin's spell will keep me invisible until I leave the city—although I have to avoid bumping into people, which is easier said than done on the busier thoroughfares. I dodge the crowd and take a side street. The base is in the Middle Quarter, which makes sense: it avoids being in the heavily guarded and monitored Upper Quarter while not being as dangerous as the Fallen or Lower Quarter.

The sun is bright, though lower in the sky than before. A breeze blows, still pleasant in the temperate autumn. If only my thoughts were as pleasant.

I know there's a Q-car waiting for me just outside the boundaries of the city. It will take me to Mother's house by the sea, where another Q-car will fly us to Spain. I recalled a strange co-incidence from reading the map: the location is very close to Jake's house.

Even thinking about it brings back sharp, bitter memories. When the Party had imprisoned Mark under false charges, despair had struck me; and in my desperation, I'd sought Jake for company. He'd abused that trust.

I have no intention of seeing him again.

****

I manage to escape the city and arrive at the meeting point I established with Mother. The invisibility spell has faded away by now, so the pilot should be able to see me. There's just one problem: the air is thick with black smoke. I can barely see in front of me.

"Hello?" I cry.

"In here," a voice calls out. I turn and see the glowing blue Q-car: the door is open, and a woman is at the steering wheel.

"I need to get you away from the smoke."

"Why? What's happening?"

"A mansion has been set on fire—I've heard reports on the intercom that it's another Party raid."

The realisation slowly dawns on me. I tell the driver the address, and she checks it on the Q-car's display.

"Yes, that's it."

"Can you drive us there? A... friend is in danger."

She looks at me more carefully, and I notice her eyes are bright green and glint with apparent intelligence. I also see some concern on her face, though not fear.

"I can get you there and help you, but they might not be alive."

"I accept the risk. Please." I step into the Q-car. She nods, and the vehicle begins pushing forward. Wondering what I'm getting myself into, I lie back in the seat and contemplate my next move. I've already saved one boy from probable death—and look where it got me. Why must I try to rescue another?

I don't have long to ponder my choices because soon, the Q-car is slowing down. The woman hands me something—it looks like a portable cannon of some sort.

"This is an ultrasonic cannon; I'll need you to use it to break down doors and obstacles."

"What are you going to do?"

"First aid. Kaylin made all of us learn the basics."

Then we're off, running towards the enormous burning building. The gate is closed; there's no time to be polite now, and I aim the cannon, charge it, and fire. The entrance explodes outward, straight off its hinges.

"Dial down the power! The shrapnel might hurt your friend or me."

"Understood!"

I follow her, thumbing the dial next to the trigger. Glowing LEDs on the weapon indicate power level—I bring it down from ten to five. As we reach the door, I fire again. For the space of about a second, the huge door groans then collapses.

As we enter the building, the smoke is blinding. The woman puts a mask on me, motioning at me to keep it on. I blink in disorientation: the mansion is huge. How will we ever find him?

Fortunately, Jake is still alive, and screaming too. "Help!"

We find him coughing on the floor, dragging himself towards the door. My driver helps him up, and we half-carry, half-drag him outside. The fresh air is a relief; I rip off the mask.

"Who are you? Conall?"

"Shut up and get in the Q-car," I snap. I might have saved him, but that doesn't mean I've forgiven him.

****

I sit still, watching the ocean. The sun is dropping below the horizon. Jake had suffered minor wounds, which Kaylin's men have successfully treated. Now he's arguing with my mother—or rather, begging since nobody argues with my mother.

"You weren't honest with my son, so why should I assume you will be honest with me?"

I ignore Sianna's question and Jake's reply. There are more critical things on my mind.

"Mother, find me a Q-car pilot—I need to see someone."

For once, she does not bother asking questions, instead gesturing to one of the two Q-cars she had procured for us. I settle myself inside; the man at the controls gives me a firm nod.

"Where to, sir?"

I give him the address, and soon we're in the air. As a precaution, I know he has activated the Q-car's stealth mechanisms, rendering us invisible. The journey is short; the distance is not great. We land next to the house. I thank the pilot, then knock on the door of the house. It is just as I remember: an elegant white house with a well-tended garden.

Mark's uncle opens the door.

"Hello, Conall. Do you wish to speak to me?"

"Yes. May I come in?"

He chuckles, though there is bitterness in it. "I don't have much choice, anyway. Come on in."

We sit on the sofas, and I can't help but remember everything: the day Mark and I first kissed, the delight and apprehension. I even remember the day I first met his uncle—I behaved so arrogantly, and yet the older man had been completely unimpressed.

"I'm not sure if you are aware, but my father and I were attacked a few days ago. Our mansion was destroyed—"

"Why were you attacked?"

I bite back a stinging retort; he's the kind of man who gets to the point. "Father has fallen afoul of the new Party regime."

"So, Mark really did kill Big Brother?"

"Yes."

"I almost wondered if it was a lie, some new propaganda invented by the Ministry of Information."

"No. The Party is close to collapse."

"Which is why they attacked you?"

"Yes. We are leaving—for Spain."

He whistles. "That takes some guts; I'll give you that. So why have you come to me then?"

"You may be in danger too, and I don't want Mark to lose what family he has left. If you come with us, you'll be safe."

"I think I'll manage. More importantly, I don't have people to take care of patients who depend on me." He says the words with stoic determination. He might look grey and worn, but there is steel in his voice.

"It is your choice, but I ask you not to be a hero." With a pause, I add, "The time for that will come later."

"What do you mean?"

"Ask Kaylin. I am sure she will find a good use for a doctor in a rebellion."

"Mark mentioned something about that witch, but a rebellion?"

"Mark put in motion what Kaylin had planned for a long time. And it's about damn time, too."

I sense new respect from him. "You're going to support this rebellion?"

"With all my power, yes. Good luck to you."

"Good luck to you too, Conall."

We shake hands, and I return to the Q-car.

****

We will leave Ireland in a matter of days. Mother is putting her finishing touches on the plans—we will need two Q-cars, she tells me, and we will leave under cover of darkness. We will land on a secret airfield near Santander.

I wonder if I will miss Ireland. Perhaps it is better for me if I do not.

Chapter Eleven: Let Sleeping Giants Rest

Mark

"So, how did it all begin?" I ask Shahar as I make myself comfortable in an armchair. The leather is dark tan, soft, and luxurious. I've been trying to read some of what Shahar's assigned to me—everything from treatises on demonic magic to technology and medicine—but none of it interests me as much as this.

"Be a bit more specific. I've been teaching you that to reach the right answer; you first have to ask the right question. That's why the great philosophers studied mathematics and formal logic."

"Did you know any of the great philosophers like Socrates, Aristotle, or Plato?"

"They were a few centuries before my time, those three, and I've been living in Hell for nearly two and a half thousand years. I'm afraid I must disappoint you."

I pout, and he shoots me a wry grin.

"But back to the subject. Did you mean Hell or Lucifer?"

"All of it, I guess. When were the first demons created?"

"Lucifer was the first demon; he was born in 60 BCE, but he became a demon in 30 BCE."

"And all the other demons?"

"He created two hundred and twenty-one, about a quarter of the present population, in the years between 30BCE and 1CE. They are now called the Originals. The other demons have been created over the last two and a half thousand years."

"And... how are demons created, exactly? My case is pretty exceptional, I understand."

"It's divided into roughly three stages. The first stage is choosing to enter Hell and to be bound to it all your mortal life. Lucifer follows these humans carefully; he selects a pool of candidates to whom he offers the opportunity. The second stage involves carrying out several acts of power—"

"Wait a minute. Are you sure you mean 'acts of power' and not 'acts of evil'? That's what everyone told me."

He smiles, but it is a cynical smile, and it oozes contempt.

"That's a lie."

"What? But Michael, my dad—and Kaylin too—"

"Are both quite wrong. It takes acts of power to begin the transformation, and the majority of such acts are indeed evil—but an act of power can also be a good one. Morality makes no difference in magic. It is a force of nature; it is no more concerned with good and evil than the tide or the stars."

"But what exactly is an act of power?"

"That's a question even I can't answer—I know it theoretically, and the demons have an inkling of the practice... but true knowledge belongs to Lucifer, and only to him."

"Can you tell me what you know?"

"I believe that an act of power is something that makes you stronger; it is something that changes who you are."

I lie back, thinking. Shahar's knowledge is terrifying. To believe that all of those demons—those rapists, child-murderers, and fanatics— could have been angels? Had my father misunderstood his nature? And what about me? I revelled in killing my enemies, in destroying the Party. I am powerful; that much is obvious, but am I dark or am I light?

"Everyone believes the lie," Shahar continues, noticing my discomfort, "because of Lucifer and because of appearances. We are conditioned to believe that good men wear white and carry lanterns of truth." With an amused chuckle, he adds, "Ideally, the men should have beards."

I laugh. "And no one expects a creature with black wings and a six-pack to have a good heart."

Sicut in Terra et in Infernum. That means in Hell, as on Earth (Shahar has been teaching me Latin). The Party holds the sceptre, the trust placed in authority—and behind closed doors, they kill, threaten, and destroy families. We Fallen are just assumed to be liars or criminals.

"Okay, what's the third stage?" I ask. "You've mentioned two so far."

"The third stage—which you skipped—is drinking from the Infernal Cup."

"Is that... metaphorical?" It's a new word I learned from Conall.

"No, it's quite real; I've seen it. It is a black chalice inlaid with rubies."

"What do the candidates drink from the Infernal Cup?"

Shahar shrugs. "It is usually water. Blood if Lucifer is feeling dramatic. Either way, it makes no difference."

"But I became a demon without drinking from it?"

"You were born with the power, latent though it was. Other demons need to drink."

"And Lucifer can't make any demons without it?" If so, it would be an excellent opportunity for me to steal it—and hopefully destroy it.

Shahar senses my intentions; he quirks his mouth in another ironic grimace. "Some have proposed the Cup is a powerful artefact that Lucifer merely stumbled on all those years ago. They are wrong; I was there. Others think the Cup might just be a bauble—another of Lucifer's theatrical props. This, too, is wrong. No: the Cup is a tool. It allows Lucifer to create other demons, but he can forge another one if he needs it."

"It sounds like you were there when he was making the demons."

The old scholar closes his eyes as if remembering. "I thought nothing would stop him. He could slaughter whole armies on his own, but that wasn't enough; he had to make others like him. It made him stronger, true, but he did it because he didn't want to be alone."

I shiver despite the warmth. "That's... terrifying, but also sad."

"How about we change the subject? You wanted to know more about Hell."

"Yeah, Lucifer mentioned something about a dragon."

He chuckles, this time with genuine glee. "He always mentions that—he's proud of it."

"So there was, like, an actual bleedin' dragon living in Hell?"

"He had many names: Niðhöggr, to the Vikings; the Irish knew him as Lig-na-Baste, and in English, we prefer to call him the Sleeping Giant."

"Is he really asleep, though?"

He shrugs. "I have no way of knowing. Given that Lucifer bound him to a cave system that lies below us, it is quite likely he got bored and went into hibernation. On the other hand, the old dragon certainly bears a grudge."

"Why did Lucifer trap him in a cave, anyway?"

"The dragon did not appreciate the demons' presence here; he thought they were abominations. He tried to destroy Lucifer and his subjects. Indeed, he almost succeeded—even Lucifer could not defeat him in open confrontation."

"So he used trickery instead."

"Precisely."

My mind is a whirlwind of ideas. This information is something I only dared to hope for—a being capable of defeating Lucifer, a being *stronger* than he is!

A demon Fades into the room, interrupting us. I whirl, but it's only Max.

I raise an eyebrow. "It's usually polite to knock."

They both laugh. "I know Maximilian well," Shahar explains mirthfully.

"We have been friends for a long time," Max confirms.

"So, what do you want with me, Max?"

"I want to show you around Hell and explain the bridges."

"I'm down for that."

"You two have fun," Shahar orders. "Although, we will still discuss propositional logic in our next session. I expect you to have at least mastered truth-tables for implications."

"Yes, Professor," I reply sarcastically.

"The thing to remember is that implications are always true unless the antecedent is true—" Max starts.

"And the consequent is false. Yeah, I get it."

Shahar looks at Max, smiling. "He is stubborn."

"Yes, he is," Max agrees. "Come on, Mark."

"Do we have to walk down the stairs?" I ask.

"No, we're flying." He spreads his wings wide. He unlatches a door (with telekinesis, nothing as profane as manual work) and takes off. I follow him a moment later.

****

We fly, circling the tower; at first, he glides gently but then accelerates at a hurried pace. I explode through the air, catapulting myself in front of him.

"Who is the fastest?" I taunt.

I'm not even going to try, he says telepathically. *But I have to warn you that the wards only extend to the towers, Citadel, and other populated areas.*

I swerve, heading for the gate. I'm not dumb enough to ignore Max's advice. He follows behind me, landing a few moments later.

"So, what's the deal with the gates?" I ask him.

"They mark off warded areas from the dangerous parts of Hell. They also act to control everyone in Hell."

"The humans, I get, but the demons? Can't we open the gates with magic?"

"Did you think it would be that easy? We can only do it because Lucifer allows us to; he controls the magic of the gates."

"Right... and it's either the gates or the lava."

"Don't forget the firelings."

"What about the dragon?"

"Ah... how interesting that you should ask. It is the dragon who is master of the firelings."

"That would explain why they're so aggressive," I muse.

"Exactly. But let me move on and explain how the gates operate. You need to place your hand on this pad here—" He demonstrates, and I follow his instructions. The stone pad feels surprisingly cold against my hand and very smooth.

"The *intent* is important," he explains. "You have to want the gate to open."

I concentrate, willing the gate to open. Moving on silent hinges, it responds.

"Good. Now—"

"You two! Listen!" A voice suddenly interrupts him from the shadows. An imp jumps out, though it's not Javalook—this imp is smaller and looks female.

"Who are you?" I ask.

"I'm Piripira, known to my friends as Pip. Stop gawking at me. I'm here to warn you that we've overheard a demon named Diego talking with Acheron—they're planning to kill you!"

"What? We need to tell Lucifer right away—" Max protests.

"We're on it."

"Then we should Fade!" I grab Max by the hand, picturing ourselves in the throne room of the Citadel. But nothing happens. I can feel something opposing me: it's like a bubble of magic, pressing hard against my power.

"Did you think it would be so easy?" The voice belongs to Acheron, who appears before us. The Archdemon is not alone: Diego is with him, along with Zi-Xuan, and two other demons I don't recognise. Five against two. I'm confident we can beat the four weaker demons, but I know how strong Acheron is.

I look around for the imp, but she's disappeared, which I guess is the smart thing to do.

"You take care of the others; I will handle Acheron—"

"No," Max says. "We fight them together, or we go down."

I nod, and then we attack. One thing I've learned as a Fallen: initiative counts in a fight, and offence is sometimes the best defence, especially if you find yourself outnumbered.

We attack Zi-Xuan first, assuming he is the weakest. We're right: the demon goes down in an inferno of blue fire, screaming curses at us before he burns to ash. Then we're fighting hand-to-hand, overwhelmed in the melee. Max and I are back-to-back; at this moment, I trust him with my life. If I don't, I die.

Max is right, I realise. Without being able to Fade, the other demons would be able to overwhelm us individually. Max throws off a demon, and I slam my fist into Diego's pretty, ugly face; he falls, then comes back for more. I burn him instead, and that gets me a satisfying yelp.

Then fire surrounds us. *Acheron*, I realise. "Max?"

"I'll lend you my power," he tells me. "You are stronger than me; you stand a chance."

I feel a rush of power. Max sags against me, eyes rolling in their sockets. With grim determination, I push my power outwards, holding back Acheron's fire.

The three demons slam into me. For a moment, we hang in the balance: I feel their power, ready to rip into me and destroy me. But I am stronger than they are. I snarl and send them flying.

"What's your feckin' problem anyway?" I growl.

"You're an arrogant shit, and Lucifer is a fool," Acheron explains. "It wouldn't be the first time he fell for a pretty boy, but it will be the last. The one Judas was enough."

The Archdemon's power lashes at me like a whip. It takes all of our combined power to resist; there is no way I can retaliate. His power crushes me, pushing me to my knees; the rock underneath me cracks. I fight him with everything I have. Through the corner of my eye, I spot something impossible—an imp is jumping between buildings, and Shahar is following him.

Then all Hell is unleashed.

****

It is like a massive floodgate is opening. The magic washes over me, making my nerves tingle. Acheron's magic suddenly ceases. I realise why: the demons are under attack. Creatures of fire pour through an opening in the wards, moving through the air like will-o-the-wisps. They seem— and I know how bizarre this sounds—to be grinning. And they like throwing fireballs.

Two of the demons fall in the firestorm. Diego and Acheron defend themselves with their demonic fire, and I see a score of firelings writhe in the conflagration. Then, incredibly, imps join the fray. They jump and hide, weaving their way through the buildings, throwing blue bolts of ice at the firelings.

I can't help but smile. The imps are grinning and laughing, clearly enjoying themselves.

I feel his presence suddenly: Lucifer is here. The Great Demon does not look amused.

"Shahar, close the wards, will you, dear?" A moment later, I feel it like a colossal door locking with steely finality. Lucifer takes out a few stray firelings, but it's clear he's letting the imps do most of the work. Or have most of the fun, depending on how you look at it.

Acheron tries to flee, but Lucifer immobilises him with a look. I've seen malice before—Hell, I've killed my fair share of enemies—but this is something else. This is pure and savage. This is a darkness that can swallow you whole.

Acheron screams in agony, crumpling to the floor. Raising his hands, Lucifer casts a spell: I feel it like a savage wind, a coldness so profound it can extinguish even the memory of warmth. Magic surrounds the Arch Demon, and he freezes instantly. Through the ice, I can see he's screaming.

Moments later, the imps finish off the stragglers. All that remains is silence. Max is crumpled on the floor, unconscious but alive. Diego seems to have been grazed by a few fireballs but is otherwise still standing. (He isn't dumb enough to flee; Lucifer would kill him instantly, enraged as he is. Better to wait and hope for some leniency.)

To my surprise, Lucifer places a hand on my shoulder, his voice soft and soothing.

"It's okay, Mark. Maximilian was brave to protect you as he did, and though it will take him time to recover, he will survive."

I nod mutely.

"I'll take you two to Shahar's. I shall deal with Acheron and Diego later."

I'm surprised he doesn't want me to come with him. I don't have time to ask because moments later, his power envelops us like a warm wave. We are back in Shahar's tower.

****

We are on a bed; the room around us seems strangely similar to an infirmary. It probably is. I seem to be in a part of the tower I haven't seen— it's a small room, something hidden away, with a narrow window gazing outside. Several lamps keep the room well lit. I can feel their warm glow. They remind me of the LEDs in my uncle's house, though this is magic, not technology.

I wince, remembering Earth and Uncle and Conall.

I decide to think about something more productive. The story about the dragon had given me a glimpse of an idea, inchoate though it is. I need some more information to hatch a plan. Meanwhile, I lift Max— his big muscular frame is still no match for my strength—and make him comfortable on the bed. It feels strange to be doing this, given that Max is a demon and the last person I'd expect to be helping.

Then again, why not? He put himself in danger to protect me. Mine is not a story about a damsel in distress. That's a myth for children and dumb straight guys; the damsel in distress is often faking it to trap the unsuspecting hero. In real life, the people you should trust and protect are those who earn it.

A distant echo tells me someone is coming up the stairs. Soon, I hear Shahar huffing and puffing. He opens the door, peeking in.

"Mark?"

"Yeah? What is it?"

"Lucifer wants to know if you would like to punish Diego."

"And Acheron?"

"Lucifer will punish him personally."

"Right. What about Max?"

"Max is immortal; if something doesn't kill him, then he will recover. It was quite clever of him to lend you his power and brave too."

"He's like this because he lost his power giving it to me?"

"It's depleted, yes, but it will return to him in a few days."

The old man sits on a chair in front of me.

"Go on, ask; I can tell you're curious."

"How did you turn off the wards? You're not a demon. And I don't think you're a witch either."

He smiles, just faintly. "I am neither of those things, but Lucifer's magic has rubbed off, so to speak. You have to understand that it does not take great power to turn the wards on and off; it takes great power to create them, yes, but what I did was more like turning off a switch."

"Right, that makes sense. But does every demon know how to do this? My attackers were caught totally off-guard."

"They didn't expect me of all people to intervene—they always underestimate me. But you are correct: it takes specialist knowledge to operate the wards."

I mull over his words, thinking them through. I'll figure out the implications of what this could mean later. For now, I have a more immediate decision to make.

"I'll go and take care of Diego," I say.

"Be careful, Mark. Vengeance is a powerful force; it can punish the wicked, or it can be cruel and ruthless."

"I haven't decided if I'm going to kill him yet," I point out.

"I suggest you give him a quick death; that is what I would do. But only you can decide."

"Thanks for everything, Shahar. You saved my arse out there."

"Good luck."

I concentrate, then Fade. It's time to meet Lucifer.

****

I've teleported to the throne room, where I'm guessing Lucifer will be waiting. I'm right: Lucifer is sitting upright in the throne room (not lounging), and his expression is thunderous. His countenance mellows a little when he sees me.

"Good to see you, Mark."

I nod in return. I can see Acheron encased in a block of ice in front of Lucifer.

Diego is bowing to Lucifer next to the block of ice; he looks genuinely afraid. We're not alone in the throne room—there are several other demons here, along with Domiziana, who is stone-faced. Something tells me she might be involved in all this.

"I am pleased to see my loyal demonic subjects here," Lucifer begins. "Alas, these two have proven themselves disloyal: they attempted to kill Mark and his friend Max, along with three others who are now dead, and whose names I've already forgotten."

The audience gasps.

"Archdemon Acheron and Diego Rosales, you are to be punished for attempted murder and treason. We already know that you are guilty, but you may plead for mercy." Lucifer grins at the mention of the word "mercy."

"Will Acheron be allowed to speak?" Domiziana asks.

"He will soon, darling," Lucifer replies. "For now, we wish to hear what Diego has to say. I am allowing Mark to decide his punishment."

The audience shuffles nervously; they did not expect this. Diego clears his throat and starts to speak.

"What I did was wrong," he begins, addressing himself to Lucifer. "I allowed my dislike of Mark to cloud my judgement, and I deserve whatever punishment you see fit to give me. But Mark is not fit to judge me; only you can judge us, Master."

Lucifer rolls his eyes. "Oh Diego, you're such a fool. Don't try appealing to my vanity. It's not me you should be apologising to; you attacked Mark, not me. The only reason I'm letting you live is that I never seriously thought you could kill Mark. If you had, you would have kept us all trapped here for, oh, I don't know, *millennia*. At least a few centuries if I'm optimistic.

"You wronged Mark, and you will answer to him."

Diego shudders, steeling himself. "Then kill me," he begs.

I walk up to him, grabbing him by the jaw. He squirms, trying not to look me in the eye.

"Look at me," I say, and my voice sounds alien to my ears. There is power in it, a power that the demon cannot disobey. The words echo inside the throne room, and the other demons twitch nervously.

I've never looked at Diego very carefully, but I'm not surprised to see he has brown eyes and dark hair; his beard is soft and thick against my fingers. He looks at me with hate but also jealousy and fear. A lot of fear.

"You believe I am just a kid, yet you're jealous of me because Lucifer treats me like an equal," I whisper. "You fear me, yet you don't understand why. I am greater than you, Diego. There is nothing you can do—you must accept this fact as surely as the wounded gazelle accepts that the lion will eat it."

I remember how Lucifer looked at Acheron. There was rage, yes, but something more too: there was malice forged into strength. I tap into the part of me that is vicious and strong, and I drive the darkness into his heart, twisting it like a knife. He screams, dropping to the floor. The demons watch in stunned silence.

I stop.

"I could have killed you easily," I say. "But I don't have to."

The demons are whispering to each other in frightened voices, some more loudly than others. Lucifer regards me with appreciation and something akin to respect. Diego, after recovering from the pain, bows to both Lucifer and me before dragging himself out of the throne room.

"The Dark Stare? On another demon?" I hear the demons whispering. "Only Lucifer can do that..."

Lucifer claps, stilling the voices. "Thank you, Mark. Take a seat beside me. It is time to judge Acheron's actions." With a casual gesture, Lucifer unfreezes Acheron. The ice block cracks then crumbles into a million crystalline shards. The Archdemon gasps, then blinks, taking in his surroundings.

"Don't bother trying to Fade," Lucifer warns him.

Acheron bows his head. "Yes, Master."

"Now, you must speak and defend yourself. Why did you attempt to kill Mark and his friend Max?"

"I did not intend to kill Max deliberately; he was—"

"Collateral damage," Lucifer supplies.

"Yes. I attempted to kill Mark because I considered him a threat to you and demonkind."

"Why?"

"Sire... We all knew the way you looked at him. He is gorgeous; that much is obvious to anyone with a pair of eyes. But so was Judas."

The audience stills; Lucifer's expression darkens.

"Do not mention that traitor by name. I know what he did, but Mark is not like him—not like him at all. Do you think I am a fool? You tried to kill Mark; your actions would have condemned us to many more centuries of imprisonment in Hell."

"I have proposed some alternatives—"

"Which don't have an icicle's chance in Hell of actually working." Lucifer waves at the molten ice next to Acheron; I have to admit he makes the point very spectacularly.

"Perhaps I made a mistake," Acheron admits. "Would you be willing to forgive me?"

"If it had been only a mistake. Had you discussed your concerns with me, we might have reached an agreement." Lucifer shrugs. "But you did not. You took matters into your own hands, contravening my express authority. You tried to murder a valuable demon—and a man I have come to care for." His tone gets colder. "You will suffer for it."

Lucifer's power swells like a raging tornado. The ground tremors; the lights flicker. An icy chill sweeps through the room. Am I witnessing the death of an Arch Demon?

"NO! PLEASE!" We all turn to look at Domiziana. She's frantic, eyes wild. "I MADE HIM DO IT!"

"At last," Lucifer says. To my shock, I realise that Lucifer *knew* about Domiziana's involvement. He was trying to get her to admit it. But this doesn't make Lucifer any happier: the frost storm rages on, and ice forms on the windows.

"Please, I would die to protect him!" Domiziana continues.

Acheron looks shocked. "Domiziana, no—he'll punish me—but you, he will kill—"

A ball of blue fire extends from Lucifer's hand and shoots towards Acheron. I watch the events unfold in slow motion. Acheron stands still, waiting for Lucifer's wrath to fall on him. Domiziana is running, and then...

The fireball collides with her, incinerating her instantly. Acheron screams, rage overtaking him, and heads straight for Lucifer. By the look on his face, he has nothing left to live for; he knows attacking Lucifer is tantamount to suicide, but he does it anyway.

Acheron never reaches Lucifer. A circle of runes lights up on the floor around Lucifer; for one brief moment, Acheron is held in place. Then it happens. I feel it like an explosion, but that's too trivial a description for it, too crude: this magic is unbelievably powerful and *subtle*. This is magic on a whole different level.

The magic reaches out and plucks Acheron from the room in the same way a toddler might grab hold of a toy before throwing it out of the pram. The Archdemon is gone.

Chapter Twelve: Ambush

Conall

"Sir, Ma'am, we are twenty minutes away from entering Spanish airspace," our pilot informs us through the intercom. My dad and I are in the first Q-car, along with Minnie and my bodyguard. Sianna, Jake, and two other bodyguards are in the second Q-car.

The sky is dark outside, and an infinity of stars glimmer in the clear night air. Wispy clouds shift below us; we are flying high and fast. I preoccupy myself with examining the various switches, dials, and screens dotted around the flying craft. The pilot holds something resembling a steering wheel, which controls pitch and roll; he has two pedals that he uses to determine the yaw of the Q-car and execute a turn. The aircraft has to both roll *and* yaw to turn.

I know the layout is the same you'll find in more traditional jet planes. Of course, the Q-car doesn't work in anything like the way a jet does: it uses powerful magnetic fields to control gravity and airflow. Still, some of the principles remain the same. (Besides, a pilot only has so many arms and legs.)

"I'm surprised we've made it out," I say. "I didn't expect it to be so easy."

"Careful what you wish for, son because it could come back to bite you. We're not in safe airspace yet," Father admonishes.

As if on cue, a massive shockwave smashes into the Q-car. The seatbelt saves me from injury, but only just. I realise the pilot has just been knocked unconscious.

"We're under attack!" I shout at the intercom.

"Affirmative," the other pilot replies. "John? Can you hear me?"

"He's unconscious," I supply.

The other pilot swears. I watch our attackers through the screens: the Party has sent three Q-cars to intercept us.

"If this keeps up—" Another explosion blasts the Q-car. We're no longer flying level; the aircraft is tilting sideways and towards the ground.

"Conall, grab the steering column!" Father tells me. "If you don't fly it, we'll all go down."

"But—"

"Do it!"

I turn towards my bodyguard as well, looking for confirmation. He nods grimly.

The Q-car's controls are accessible to either of the pilots, and since John is unconscious, he doesn't leave me much choice. The Q-car's nose is drooping, and several alarms blare on the cockpit screen. I focus on the heads-up display, which has the essential instruments: speed, altitude, and a virtual horizon. I pull back on the steering stalk, and slowly, the Q-car's nose rights itself.

I grab the lever next to my arm, forcing the Q-car to maximum power; I hope that maybe we can get away from them and leave the other Q-car to fight. The aircraft shudders and vibrates—another alarm pops up on the HUD.

I realise that if I keep it on full power, the Q-car will tear itself apart.

So I try a different tactic: I bring the power down, lower the nose, and angle the aircraft to the right. As I hoped, our attackers fly above us. But Mother's Q-car is all alone now.

We are targeted by missiles and lasers. Our Q-car uses decoys to fool the missile and retaliates; the onboard AI struggles to target our attackers. Without a proper gunner or at least someone picking targets, the AI does its best, but I fear it may not be enough. One of the attacking aircraft is damaged, but Mother's Q-car is damaged too.

"Shoot them!" Dad orders. "You have to help her!"

"I have no idea how to fire this thing!"

I fumble at the controls, trying to figure out what to do. One of our attackers has broken off from the main group and is now turning towards us. We're losing altitude fast.

The realisation sinks in: there's no way we can survive this. Our Q-car is damaged almost to the point of no return—a single well-placed shot will doom us if it doesn't kill us outright. Maybe I can shoot down one of our assailants, but there are three of them.

Then, I remember that I still have the medallion that Kaylin gave Mark and me. It doesn't work in Hell, and Kaylin is so far away... but it's all I have. I grab the medallion, feeling the cold obsidian against my fingers. I focus on a message: HELP. The medallion does something strange—I don't physically feel it, but it's like a beacon in my mind.

I turn back to the cockpit, finding a red button and what looks like a targeting system. Splitting my time between targeting and flying proves complicated, but I manage to program the targeting computer quickly and mash the red button. A laser flash shatters the darkness of the night, hitting the enemy's Q-car head-on. A blue light blinking on my HUD explains that the Q-car absorbed the blast with its shields.

Knowing the laser will have to cool down, I look for the plasma cannon. If I could get one more hit...

The enemy Q-car explodes in a pillar of blue flame. Shocked, I swerve our aircraft to avoid the oncoming debris. I half notice a black figure swoop away from the fire. What did I just see?

"What was that?" I ask.

"Whatever it was, it saved us," Father points out.

"I saw a pair of black wings," my bodyguard says simply.

I lift the nose, trying to get us to rejoin my mother's Q-car, but our vehicle is too short of power—and too unstable—to contemplate that. We can only watch the drama unfold above us. A fireball tears through the second enemy Q-car; it goes down in a smouldering pile. The third Q-car finally realises the new threat and fires a plasma cannon. The plasma burst collides with something—a figure with black wings.

To the shock of my father and bodyguard, though unsurprisingly to me, the demon remains unharmed. He vanishes, then re-appears a split second later. The Q-car tries madly to avoid him, but they're on a direct collision course; it's a one-way trip to Hell.

The winged figure scythes through the Q-car, cutting it neatly in half. I can almost imagine the men inside screaming before they perish.

Still, the danger isn't over yet. We must be a hundred miles away from Santander; there is nothing but the deep, dark sea below us. The Q-car is still controllable, but it doesn't have much power left. I bring us lower, relying on the denser air to maintain level flight. Our velocity is two hundred and fifty miles an hour.

We fly for nearly half an hour, and they are the most terrifying thirty minutes of my life. The Q-car shudders, sometimes swinging to one side, forcing me to manhandle it into submission with the controls.

Then, finally, we see lights on the horizon. I breathe a faint sigh of relief.

"Sir, is John awake?" the pilot in the other Q-car asks.

My bodyguard takes his pulse, then touches the man's head. His fingers are slick with blood. He looks worried.

"Negative," I reply. "John is seriously injured."

"Shit."

I now realise the problem. "I'm going to have to land the Q-car, aren't I?"

"Your power generator is damaged, and so are your control electronics."

"Will I be able to land it?"

"Hopefully. I don't think even a trained Q-car pilot would find it easy."

"Thanks for the confidence boost," I mutter sarcastically.

Then I hear my mother's voice on the intercom. "Darling, be brave. Listen to my pilot when he tells you something, and stay on guard."

"Yes, Mother."

"The location of the airfield is in your flight computer's memory," the pilot continues. "But if you can't land on it, any field will do."

I thumb through the flight computer menus using a touchpad. I find the GPS coordinates, then set the computer to guide me there; it works like a satnav, but it's not good enough to land the Q-car for me, especially damaged as it is.

The airfield is a couple of miles away. I ease on the throttle levers, reducing our speed to a hundred miles an hour.

"This thing doesn't stall, does it?" I ask.

"No, it shouldn't. But the control electronics are damaged. It may be safer to land it like a plane as opposed to a vertical landing."

"I get it."

I see that our altitude has dropped by a few thousand meters, and we are now just a couple of hundred meters above ground level. I reduce the speed to as low as I dare—about seventy miles an hour—and search for the landing gear.

"Here," the bodyguard helpfully points out.

I flip the lever, being careful of the increased drag. The GPS tells me the airfield is just a mile away; I only need to maintain the Q-car's bearing while descending.

"Does this thing have lights?" I ask.

"Trust your instruments, not your eyes," the pilot orders.

"I need to see where I'm landing!" I cry.

My father hits a switch, and light blazes forth from the Q-car. I give him a look.

He shrugs. "I've been driven around in these things long enough."

The ground is coming up fast. Just then, the control stalk starts to shake. The Q-car tilts and yaws dangerously; I force it back. We hit the ground just in front of the tarmac (there are no lights), bounce, then skid. I engage the brakes, and eventually, we come to a silent halt.

I breathe out.

The other Q-car lands next to us, descending vertically. We exit our vehicles and begin to regroup. The other pilot rushes towards John, who I realise must be his friend.

"Well done, darling," Sianna says.

"Thank you, mum." I haven't called her mum in years.

"But where is Michael?" she asks.

"Michael? It could have been another demon—" I start.

"I am here."

A black-winged figure emerges from the shadows. The Q-car lights seem not to affect him: darkness clings to his body like a second skin. It's a power I saw Mark use when he rescued me from the Party; it's a kind of Glamour.

My bodyguard raises his pistol, but he's shaking violently.

"I really wouldn't try to shoot me, human," the demon remarks wryly. "You cannot kill me, and it may end badly for you."

I motion towards my bodyguard, and, visibly relieved, he holsters the pistol.

"How did you know where to save us?" I ask.

"I felt a pulse of magic coming from you; it was obviously a distress signal."

I thumb my medallion, wondering at the smooth volcanic rock. "I didn't think it might work. Kaylin gave it to me—I didn't realise you could feel it as well."

He chuckles. "Kaylin must be an inexperienced witch if her talisman works like that. Every magical being in the vicinity would have felt it."

"I'm just glad you saved my life," Sianna comments. "How can I repay you?"

"Well, I believe the debt of the table has been settled."

"The—what?"

"I broke your table, remember?"

Sianna just laughs. Then she bounds towards Michael and embraces him. The old demon awkwardly pats her back.

I clear my throat. "I have another question."

"Go on."

"How did the Party know? They might have figured we'd leave the country, but why not attack us while we were still in the country? And how did they know which way we were going?"

"Is that one question or several?"

"My son has a point, Michael," Sianna corrects. "If the Party had known our plans, they would have caught us in Irish airspace, or sooner. Catching us in the ocean was desperation mixed with luck."

Just then, Jake comes out from the other Q-car.

"What on Earth *was* that?" he asks.

We all turn towards Michael, wondering how to explain the situation, but the demon is gone. Well, maybe not gone: he may simply be invisible.

"Jake, dear, we have a seriously wounded man who needs medical attention," Sianna begins sweetly. "Perhaps we should leave this for later."

"I saw something—a bird? —but it looked like a man—"

"He's not responding," the pilot cries out. "He's breathing, but he could be in a coma! Can we call an ambulance here?"

That distracts Jake from whatever he was about to ask, and we all turn to Sianna, expecting her to answer.

"Just a moment," she says, thumbing a number on her com-phone. She lets it ring three times before hanging up.

"A code," she explains. "The airfield is rather remote, and it may take them some time to get here."

"Michael," I whisper, knowing he can hear me. "Can you help our wounded pilot?"

No. I start when I realise he's talking to me in my mind. Mark had never done that with me.

"But you're—"

A demon, a being of darkness. At most, I can teleport the pilot somewhere, but I do not know healing magic. Also, your friend Jake is here.

"He's not my friend," I mutter. "And how do you know his name, anyway?"

Sianna just mentioned it. May I reveal myself to him? I can put him to sleep if necessary. It's a simple enough spell.

I think over his words. As tempting as it would be to make Jake shut up, I will have to eventually tell him the truth. He's in this with me, whether he likes it or not.

I think it's best if you let him know about you.

"Good evening," Michael says. Jake jumps about a foot in the air, slips on the wet runway, and lands on his arse. We all have a good laugh at his expense. Michael offers him a hand, and Jake takes it gratefully.

"Who... who are you?"

"My name is Michael. I rescued you from that unfortunate run-in with the Party fighter aircraft."

"You blew up those Q-cars? Wow. That's incredible. What *are* you?" Jake seems enthralled by him. I've learned that people typically react in three different ways when they learn about demons: with fear, blasé nonchalance (maybe that's only my mother), or total awe.

"I am a demon."

Jake blinks, then smiles. It's a very wide-eyed, stupid smile, and not very like Jake at all.

"We need to deal with the pilot," I interrupt. "Michael, can you Fade him to Kaylin's?"

"You think the witch might be able to help him?"

"Witch? What—"

"Jake, shut up," I order. "Yes," I say, talking to Michael. "I know she has doctors in her team if nothing else."

"So do the Spanish," Sianna points out. "They should be here any minute now."

"Pilot, what's your name?" I ask.

The man hasn't even noticed Michael in our midst; he is trying to get John to wake up. I realise how much he must care for him.

"Stephen, sir."

"Stephen, we have the means of taking John back to Ireland right now. Or you can wait for the Spanish emergency services. It's your decision."

He doesn't even stop to question how we can do this. "Take him to Kaylin. Your mother told me about her," he says, seeing my surprise.

Michael moves towards John. Before he reaches him, Sianna intervenes.

"Hang on a minute! Conall, we have yet to determine how the Party found us."

"I thought you said it was dumb luck?"

"Maybe, but I'm considering an alternative hypothesis. What if someone tipped off our attackers just after we left?"

"But who? I didn't tell anyone, except..." I pause. I *did* tell Mark's uncle, and he would never have told the Party. Not unless the Party made him talk.

"Mark's uncle could be in danger!"

"You told his uncle we were leaving Ireland?"

"Yes."

"And you think the Party might have interrogated him?"

"Precisely."

"We can contact Kaylin," Sianna suggests. "She should be able to get him out."

I shake my head. "No. I put him in danger; it's my responsibility. Besides, Mark would never forgive me if something happened to him."

"Surely you're not suggesting you want to go back to Ireland?" Father asks. "We risked so much to get us out of there."

"I am suggesting exactly that. Michael, can you... ?"

"I can Fade both of you, no problem."

"Son, don't do this."

"It's no use, " Sianna tells him. "I know when he's made up his mind."

Michael has slung John over his shoulders; it looks completely effortless. It's as if John weighs no more than a toddler.

Michael offers me his hand. I stare into his glittering dark eyes.

"You're getting yourself in deeper," he says quietly. "A war is coming, and you're joining an army."

"Didn't you do the same thing all those years ago when you joined Lucifer?"

The demon smiles grimly. "I did."

I grab his hand, and we Fade away. The experience is unlike anything I've ever felt before: it's as if time and space are warping around us. The effect is unsettling. My vision goes dark, then explodes into light. Instead of the chilly breeze blowing in Spain, I now feel the warmth of an indoor place.

I blink a few times, re-orienting myself. We're in a room with a handful of Kaylin's men, who are all staring at us.

"We need to see Kaylin," I state.

"Conall? I'm Grumman, Kaylin's head of operations," a man says. He has steel blue eyes and greying stubble. I shake his hand firmly.

"I am Michael."

"I know who you are. I'll get Kaylin on the com phone right away—you have a lot of explaining to do."

"Can you wait just a minute?" I say. "We have a man who needs medical assistance." I point to John.

Grumman nods solemnly. "We have a doctor right here in the base. I'll get her on the job. It's good to see you, Conall."

"I wish it were in better circumstances. I have a feeling the Party has apprehended Mark's uncle."

"But we put cameras and men around his house—"

"And the hospital?"

Grumman swears. "Kaylin will need to help you with this. No one can locate a missing person better than a seer can."

"Thank you, Grumman."

I can feel the adrenaline of the past few hours catching up with me. I'm woozy with exhaustion; my hands are starting to shake. I look for a bed in a quiet room and collapse. A dreamless, wearied sleep overtakes me.

Chapter Thirteen: A Witch Needs Her Magic

Kaylin

"Kaylin, we need your help," Grumman barks into the com phone.

I rub the sleep from my bleary eyes; the sun is a pale-yellow light on the horizon. I turn towards the com phone on my nightstand, stabbing at the hologram button. Grumman's stern face is projected above my bedroom in 3D.

"What is it?" I ask.

"It's about Mark's uncle," he begins, then quickly explains the situation.

I have to run to catch the 6 am maglev train, which travels at five hundred kilometres per hour and reaches Dublin in just thirty minutes. I find two people waiting for me at the base: Conall and Michael.

I pause; I did not expect to see the demon again. The immortal is just as I remember him—dark, composed, and serious.

"Grumman told me about Mark's uncle," I say to Conall. "He mentioned you too, demon."

Michael raises his hands. "I wronged you when Lucifer attacked; I admit that. I made a hasty decision, acting in error."

"You were a coward with a poor sense of judgement. Lucifer couldn't maintain the Projection for long."

"I realise that now. Don't for one moment assume I feel no guilt. Mark is in Hell, trapped with that monster—"

"We have bigger problems on Earth right now," Conall says with a hint of anger. "Eoin could be in serious danger as we speak."

"What about the wounded man—John?" I ask, suddenly remembering the man Grumman had mentioned. Just then, Elizabeth walks into the room.

"We have the doctors looking at him," she tells me. I smile at her: Liz has, among her many talents, excellent driving skills. She'd driven a remote car into a Party base, destroying all of their fighter craft in the process. I recall the memory with fondness.

"Is he conscious?"

"No. They think he might be in a coma."

I sigh, rubbing my forehead and eyelids. *Prioritise, Kaylin.*

"Okay, Conall, I'm going to need a moment to try and locate Mark's uncle. Besides his name, can you give me any distinguishing features? What kind of person is he? It's not easy for me to locate a random person, especially if they're not someone huge like Big Brother was."

"Let me think... Eoin has blue eyes and dark hair, tending towards grey. He is a doctor, but he also had a stricter side." He smiles wistfully. "He didn't like it much when I started dating Mark."

"That will have to do. Liz, Conall, Michael—give me a moment."

They clear out of the room, and I close my eyes. It's not easy being calm; the process of Seeing requires absolute concentration. It necessitates that I forget the immediate world—my early-morning exhaustion, the pressure to save Mark's uncle from captivity and death—and focus on what *is* and what *can be.*

I blink hard. The pressure, combined with exhaustion, is almost too much. I try it again. This time, smooth calmness envelops me. The world seems to melt away; the visions come to me.

A fortress of bare concrete and murdered innocents. The march of many men; the hard grating noise of android footsteps. The harsh bark of orders.

I focus: it needs to be more specific. *A room, a torn and bleeding man with haunted blue eyes. A flash of a name: The Belfast Barracks.*

I breathe deeply, and the vision recedes. Then I curse loudly. Ever since this country had re-unified, the largest military installation hasn't been in Dublin—but in Belfast. The city serves as a local capital of sorts. As for the Belfast Barracks, it's one of the most infamous and heavily guarded in the country.

"Grumman!"

He comes running. "Yes, Mistress?"

"I need to know everything you know about the Belfast Barracks, and I need it now."

He pales slightly. "Tell me he's not there?"

"He is."

Grumman breathes out slowly. "We need to plan."

****

"Call the damn Communists," Grumman orders my men. "We need their help with this."

"Do you really think the Communists will agree to help us with this?" I ask. "It's a difficult and risky mission."

"You mean it's suicide?" Grumman asks flatly.

"I didn't say that—"

"I have Andrew, the Communist leader, on the com phone," Liz interrupts.

"Put him through the main speakers," I order.

"Hello? Kaylin?"

"Yes, it's me. Andrew... We would like to ask for your help. A friend of ours, Eoin, is being kept hostage in the Belfast Barracks. He doesn't have much time."

"Are you sure? The Belfast Barracks is a god-damn fortress. We need time to plan—"

"If we don't rescue him by tonight, he will die."

"How do you—right. I shouldn't ask how you know." He sighs. "Look, Kaylin, I can't just send my men to attack the base head-on. It's a suicide mission."

"I told you so," Grumman mutters.

"What about... a diversion?" I suggest.

There is a pause on the other end. "I could do something like that. Belfast isn't too far from our base in Letterkenny; I'm sure we can manage something."

"Excellent. We'll stay in touch."

The com line goes dead. I turn towards the people assembled in the room.

"We should get everything ready. We'll need Diana and Shadow as well, plus all the men we can muster, and..." I pause to think. "Michael, you should also come with us."

The demon shoots me a dark look.

"Do you want me to be your shock-and-awe? I go in, kill everyone, and your team bundles him away to safety?"

Now that he mentioned it, I was thinking something very much along those lines. He notices my expression and continues.

"There are consequences to revealing the supernatural. The whole world might find out. So far, you've operated under secrecy and anonymity; if the world discovers magic, how long do you think that will last?"

"If you don't help us, demon, this could end very badly for Eoin. Your son would never forgive you," Grumman says coldly.

I raise a hand, silencing him. "Michael, you are right, but so is Grumman. I will need another moment to See."

Michael shrugs. "As you wish."

I leave the room, returning to my meditation room, the one place in this city that calms me most. I close my eyes; this time, the visions come quickly. *I see blackened fields of death—a murder of crows is circling above.*

Bright light. I see a lovely park and smell the breeze on my hair; Eoin is smiling brightly. Darkness. I see a man with eyes like coal and an expression of calculating contempt. Burning meteors fall from the sky; the Party lies broken.

I blink, confused. I return to the main room.

"Well?" Grumman asks.

"It's all just a mess—there are too many possibilities." I sigh. "If my visions won't help, I will have to trust my good sense. Michael, I want you to come with us, but you should only reveal yourself if the situation turns dire." I address the rest of my team, "This will be a stealth mission, aided by distraction."

Each member of the team nods.

"What about me?" Conall asks.

I sigh. "Bringing you along would put you in needless danger—"

"I promise I'll stay back and avoid doing anything stupid."

The boy gives me a hard stare: there is determination there, and love, and something else, something new. I realise that Conall isn't a boy anymore; he is a man. And that look? It is ruthless.

"No stupid things, OK?"

He smiles darkly.

****

We stand back, examining the grim fortress before us. I recall a line from a poem, now almost forgotten: *Two vast and trunkless legs of stone / Stand in the desert...* I smile coldly. This black concrete monolith adorns the desolate landscape like a plague. The surrounding area is a desert; only it is hewn from concrete and sulphuric smog rather than desiccated earth.

At least the Q-car has an air filtration system. Liz, the driver, is next to me. Seated behind me is Diana, who is grumpy because my men shook her awake (and Diana loves her beauty sleep). Shadow is sitting next to her. His normally cocksure expression melts in the face of this fortress. It's one thing to be told that the Belfast Barracks is a kill box and quite another to see it for yourself.

"We're going to storm that building? It's a bleedin' deathtrap." He stares pointedly at the array of androids, machine gun nests, and gun-toting soldiers.

"We will sneak into it, not storm it. Michael is also here as a last resort." He'd flown with us, easily keeping pace with the Q-cars.

"Can't we wait it out?"

"No."

"What about a spell to disable their electronics?" Diana suggests.

"The whole place is proofed against EMPs. And I only know one spell that can do it."

"Let me guess," Liz interrupts. "It was the spell you used last time when everything went wrong?"

"That's... exactly the point. I don't have enough control over it."

"Why did you bring Conall?" Diana asks.

I give her a sideways glance. "He wasn't going to just stay behind. That's Mark's uncle in there."

The com phone suddenly crackles to life. "Kaylin? This is Andrew. We put some bombs in a nearby warehouse, but we would like to go over the details of your plan again. How much time is there left?"

I rub my forehead, trying to relax. Diana turns off the com phone and silences the others. It takes a long minute—I gradually slow my breath, emptying the thoughts from my mind. A scene slowly comes into view. *Eoin is bleeding; he is bound, and two of his ribs are broken. A cruel man twirls a sharp knife in his hand, and there is murder in his eyes.*

"So, how do you want to die? There's the easy way, and then there's the hard way."

I gasp, blink, and return to the world. There is a look of sharp concern among my friends.

"He doesn't have any more time." I turn the com phone back on. "Andrew, blow it up."

"Roger that."

"Wait!" Conall shouts. He's running at us from the other Q-car.

"What the hell are you doing here?" I ask him.

"If this goes pear-shaped, you need to communicate with Michael. Technology might not work."

"I can use telepathy—"

"You need something more immediate. Here," he says, handing out his medallion. "Take my medallion and use it to signal Michael."

"That's pretty smart," I say, impressed at his ingenuity.

"Now go!" he exclaims.

We don't have to wait long. A series of bombs go off—Andrew's diversion. We are lucky it's a Saturday, and the warehouse should be empty. The diversion goes as planned: several men, vehicles, and androids leave the compound. It is time for us to do our bit.

"Remember what I said about the shields," I tell Shadow and Diana. I concentrate, drawing the spell on my skin and theirs. I've never placed a shield spell on three people before, and the effort is extraordinary. The magic pushes against me; I am literally shaking.

"Kaylin? Are you okay?" Diana asks.

"I'll manage. Shadow, hide us."

He nods, holds our hands, and we leave the Q-car invisible. We still have to get through a force field, but I'd thought about that. I use a spell to cut a hole through the forcefield; we hurry through, and I close the gap before any of their sensors can pick up on it.

You all know where in the compound we need to be, I telepathise.

But we don't know the exact layout of the building; it's top-secret, Diana responds.

She is correct. It takes us several minutes to locate the holding cells, and we have to dodge several men and androids in the process. When we arrive, we find the holding cell blocked by a steel door.

His torturer is in there, I say. *And we have to blow this door open without anyone else noticing.*

Do you have a spell? Diana asks.

Yes, but I will need to turn off the shield spell.

I pull my consciousness back, and the magic surrounding us fades. I quickly draw a symbol on the door; its name is Shatter. The rune burns itself into the steel, glowing blue, then vanishes. Seconds later, hairline cracks appear on the door, and after a moment, it merely collapses into metal rubble.

"Where are you? I know you're here." The cruel man inhales deeply, and his eyes roam towards us. Instantly, I realise what my vision did not convey: this man is a Familiar, like us. He has power, but I do not know what exactly he is capable of.

I file this piece of information into a drawer somewhere in the back of my mind. I draw a spell, focus my mind, and attack with telekinesis. The torturer's neck snaps audibly.

Eoin? Can you walk? We need to get you out of here.

Eoin looks around wildly, then slowly nods. Smart man.

I will cut through these manacles with magic. He watches in confusion as the Shatter spell turns the steel manacles into junk metal.

His eyes widen in terror. It's the only warning we get.

The man I just killed—or at least, I thought he was dead— smiles wickedly. "There you are."

The Familiar lifts Shadow in the air, strangling him with one hand.

I attack with blind instinct, ramming my telekinetic power into him. It's not as effective as when cast with a spell, but sheer, raw will-power is enough to send the guy flying, separating him from Shadow. He snarls and lunges towards me.

A ball of violet fire catches him an instant before he reaches me. With a shrill cry, he explodes into flame, then turns to dust.

"What the hell *was* that?" Diana demands.

"He was some sort of Familiar. If you hadn't reacted, he might have killed me, Shadow, and Eoin."

"Well, if it burns, I can kill it."

"He healed from a broken neck; I didn't expect that," I admit. "We never met a Familiar like him."

"Maybe he just healed very quickly?"

"Ladies? We're runnin' out of time here," Shadow wheezes still bruised from nearly being strangled to death. "Get Eoin, cast the shield spell, and I'll conceal you. If we don't get out of here—"

A host of men run at us. I cast the shield spell, push my mind out-wards, and place the shield on the door opening, the way I might lace a curtain. Gunfire and laser pulses collide with the shield.

"We're trapped!" Shadow says. "Kaylin, is there another way out?"

"If I could use Shatter on a wall and hold the shield..."

"Can you do that?"

"I think so—"

The events unfold in slow motion. An android turns the corner, powers up its main plasma cannon, and bombards the shield spell. It smashes into a million pieces; the impact sends me flying. Diana turns around, fire bursting from her hands, but it's too late, we're going to die...

He appears before us like a dark god, Fading into the room, his wings outstretched. Bullets, plasma, and laser pulses fire into him without harming him. And when he retaliates, I realise that there is truly nothing else on Earth that compares to a demon's power. Michael destroys the android and expertly sends its pieces flying towards the enemies.

Michael's aim is true: the men are speared straight through the heart, but he is far from over. Blue fire uncoils from his wings and explodes through the building. It incinerates everything in its path. Men perish screaming, and androids melt into plastic candles.

The fire is ravenous; there is no end to its hunger. Metal is instantly liquefied; concrete catches fire and blackens. In less than a minute, the compound is destroyed.

The demon turns towards us; his eyes are black abysses, and for the briefest moment, I am afraid. Then he visibly regains control of himself.

"Get Eoin out of here," he croaks. "He needs medical attention now."

I nod. I turn on my com phone, which I had Glamoured to avoid detection from electronic sensors: "Men, I need the medical Q-car here now!"

****

Dawn light filters in through the windows, tingeing the white blankets with fuchsia hues. The early morning is chilly, though the room is warm.

It smells faintly of disinfectant, cleanliness, and healing. A machine beeps quietly in the background.

It is Sunday morning, and Eoin lies on the bed, asleep but alive. He sustained several injuries, but none were life-threatening—the strange Familiar was torturing him and wanted him alive until the end.

I step away from the room, smiling faintly, though there is sadness in me too. In the next room—an equally warm, quiet, and pleasant space—John lies unconscious, deep in a coma. None of my medical personnel had been able to treat him; they say there is brain damage. I had tried a spell instead. I had been able to enter his mind to see his memories, but I have no idea how actually to fix him.

I leave the room and head over to the main chamber; Conall, Diana, and Michael are waiting for me. Shadow is also waiting on the sidelines (he never likes being the centre of attention). My men vacate the room as soon as we are together.

"We need to determine what happened," I start. "To figure out the aftermath."

"Are there more Familiars like the guy we just killed?" Diana asks.

"I don't think so," I say.

"But how can we be sure? You can't possibly know about all of them, Kaylin, even with your visions. What if the Party has more men like him locked away somewhere?"

"I'm not even certain if the Party knew what he was; hell, I don't think even *he* knew what he was capable of."

"It's not surprising," Michael says, interrupting our conversation. "With the Barrier weakened, more of Lucifer's magic is leaching out and tainting humans into Familiars."

"Kaylin?" Diana asks. "Is it true?"

Michael has dropped a bombshell on us. "Are you saying what I think you're saying? That Familiars are created by demonic contagion?"

"That is exactly what I am saying."

"It makes sense," I whisper.

"Okay, but assuming this is true," Diana begins sceptically, "what makes us so different from the demons?"

"You still have free will," Michael points out. "Demonic magic is powerful and dark, but it does not rob you of the ability to choose what is right."

"That guy was a bastard," Shadow agrees.

"By the way, Michael, how did you manage to Fade in front of us?" I ask, remembering what he did.

"It was a special type of Fading magic. It is bound to a person rather than a specific place."

"So, you can find anyone in the world like this?"

"Almost—it's not nearly that simple. I do have to have some idea of the place, even if not to the extent that a normal Fade spell requires."

"Guys?" Conall interrupts. "Are we not forgetting something important here?"

We all turn to look at him.

"Such as?" I ask.

"Do you really think the Party isn't going to find out about this? You waltzed into their base and destroyed it."

"I was careful to burn everything—communications, cameras, human beings..." Michael starts.

"Even if you destroyed all the cameras, there would have been a live feed; it would have been backed up on a remote server."

I realise Conall may be right.

"Software Man!" I shout.

It takes my men a few moments to locate him, but he soon comes running through the door.

"Yes, Kaylin?"

"Could the Party know about us? Has any of the footage survived?"

"Well, if a live feed were being transmitted through to another base, then, potentially—"

A vision interrupts whatever he says next. I feel myself sagging; the world starts to spin. *A man with dark eyes is pacing around a table. Several important-looking men and women sit at the table watching him. A computer displays a video. The man says something, but his speech is indistinct—I can make out the words "angel" and "monster."*

"He knew there might be supernatural beings," I whisper. "And now he's discovered us. He can't explain it—yet."

"Who is he, Kaylin?" Diana asks.

"I'm not sure—"

"It has to be the Party leader," Conall says. "Who else?"

I nod in agreement. "Yes."

"Just grand," Shadow says.

"This isn't good, Kaylin," Diana agrees. "Our fight just got tougher."

****

Days pass; I visit Eoin and John whenever I can. John remains comatose. Eoin, thankfully, is awake, though his mending ribs hurt like hell.

"Kaylin," he says, smiling. The morning sunshine reflects off his blue eyes, and for a moment, he seems happy.

"Hello, Eoin. It's good to see you well."

"Are you saying that because Mark would have your head if I weren't OK?"

"True, but I am motivated by the desire to protect the innocent. I wouldn't be risking my life otherwise."

"I'm sorry I revealed that Conall and his family were leaving Ireland—I put them in danger, and the man in the other room is in a coma because of me."

"No, Eoin. He's in a coma because the Party tried to kill him. If anyone is to blame here, it's me for not guarding you better and for not being able to heal injuries. I have a book full of spells, but it's all binding spells and teleports and glamour. Smoke and mirrors."

"Is there any magic that can heal and not destroy? None of you can mend people."

"No, I can't. But I think there's a way to change that; I believe there is more magic out there."

"Do you believe, or do you know?"

I smile. "I haven't told anyone about this yet—you're the first person to see this."

"What is it?"

"Two days after we raided the fortress, I got a book."

"Like, through the letterbox?"

"No, it simply appeared next to my spell-book."

I withdraw a small, white book from my pocket; it is cloth-bound but plain. I open it to the first page; the paper makes a soft rasping sound against my fingers. Eoin is staring at it with a mixture of confusion, fear, and wonder.

"There's a spell on the first page; I can show you." I touch his cheek lightly, focusing and drawing a rune with my finger. I put my willpower into it; I channel my desire to protect him, to make him better, the way I want to protect everyone from the Party.

A warm glow emanates from my hand, though it lasts but a moment.

"That's... I feel better already. The pain in my ribs—it's not gone, but it's a million times more bearable."

"This is a simple pain spell."

"So, what else can you do?"

"Nothing. The other pages are indecipherable to me—except for one thing. A message."

"Show me."

I turn the page, revealing what I saw the day I opened it.

IF YOU WANT MORE, MEET ME NEAR MOUNT EVEREST.

Chapter Fourteen: Three Words of Power

Mark

"So, what exactly happened?"

"Why do you even want to know, Steijn?"

The young man shrugs and sets to work tidying up my wardrobe with new clothes. I told him not to bother—I can damn well do it myself—but he insisted.

"I told you so."

"That Diego and Acheron were planning to move against me? Yes, you did. I believed Lucifer would take care of them if they tried anything. And he did take care of them, but I almost got killed."

"What did he do to Acheron? I hear he didn't kill the Archdemon, which figures, seeing how few of them there are."

"He wrought a spell, an act of Great Magic. I couldn't believe it; I've never felt anything like it."

"You realise that for Lucifer, Great Magic is as easy as clapping his hands?"

"But you need—"

"Activation, Foresight, and Sacrifice. I know, Shahar told me. I also know that Lucifer is a brilliant strategist and a master of deceit."

"How—what—" Steijn has left me speechless. I'd thought he was just a naïve teenager. It amazes me that he knows so much.

"Why the surprise? I've learned. Anyway, I asked you what he did to the Archdemon."

"I think he trapped him, maybe in a prison of ice. He likes freezing things."

"I saw it when he froze the boiling lake—it's theatrical and awe-inspiring, which fits him perfectly."

"Mark?" I spin around. Max is in my room, eyeing Steijn curiously. After days asleep on the infirmary bed—giving up his power to bolster mine had not been easy for him—he's finally awake.

"Max! You're awake. This is Steijn, by the way—he's my..."

"Butler," Steijn adds.

Max only smiles. "You're not letting him be your butler, are you?"

"No."

"But he very much wants to do his job. Steijn, I think you simply enjoy Mark's company too much."

He looks away, flushing.

"Max, are you OK?"

"I am fully recovered. Fear not, for I am still an immortal being."

"Do you know if Lucifer will want to see me now that you're awake?"

"He will, soon, but not now. Go on. I'm sure you want Steijn to teach you some of the ropes."

I turn and meet Steijn's gaze. "Can I meet your family?" I ask.

"You may. It is a long walk—"

"I'll fly you out of the Citadel. I can do that much."

He gulps audibly. "I've never flown before—"

"The first time I flew was when my boyfriend, Conall, took me in his ornithopter. I was a bit scared as well, but you'll soon get to love the feeling. Come on."

He makes a squeak, which sounds like "okay." I offer him my hand, and he takes it.

****

I am flying, and Steijn is in my arms. The sensation has me whooping with joy, but it freezes Steijn with terror. Yet, after a tense few moments, Steijn relaxes, and soon he's shouting *WEEE!*

The moment does not last long, for soon, we arrive at the gate and are forced to walk. Steijn takes me through various streets and alleys, moving with the quiet confidence of a long-time city dweller. I do not show my wings, and I don't stare or project hostility; but even so, people shrink away from me. A few questionable people—criminals, the same in Hell as back in Dublin—look away and hide in the shadows.

"Steijn, does everyone know I'm a demon?"

"No, not everyone. But you're fucking terrifying. You realise that, don't you?"

"But how? I'm not carrying weapons; I'm not making myself obvious; I don't stare—"

"You're clearly *not human*. No one is as beautiful as you are; you're the stuff of Greek sculpture. And you're clearly not *afraid* of anything—because no one can hurt you."

I open my mouth, then close it. There is nothing I can say to that. I realise that I am no longer the boy who met an Upperclassman and fell dangerously in love; I'm not a Fallen anymore. I'm not vulnerable, afraid, or a social outcast. *Maybe*, some small part of me thinks *Lucifer wasn't so wrong about me after all.*

"This is my home," Steijn declares. He stops in front of a terraced building: it has sash windows, a steep slate-tiled roof, and a facade of red stone, blackened by centuries of Hellfire.

"This is... Victorian. This stuff only exists in museums in my country—I hear there are a few left in Scotland and England."

"It's more than six centuries old," Steijn tells me. "The demons have used magic to re-enforce it."

"Why bother?"

"Nostalgia? I don't know." He knocks on the door, and a woman opens it. She has long blonde hair and bright blue eyes. She is perhaps forty or fifty years old.

"Steijn! Hoe gaat met je? En is dit... jouw vriend?"

"His name is Mark, and he is my friend, mum."

"Oh, how silly of me!" she says. "I should have spoken English with you straight away. Where do you live? I've not seen you before."

"I'm new here," I say ironically.

Steijn rolls his eyes. "Mark, if you don't tell her, I will. She has to know."

"Know what?"

"He's a demon."

Steijn's mother jumps back as if electrocuted. "You're friends with a demon? But... how...?" Then, remembering her manners, she curtsies towards me.

"He's not like the others."

"And you don't have to bow to me," I say, annoyed.

"Your name is Mark?" she asks instead. "Is it true you fought off an Archdemon?"

"He tried to kill me, but he failed. I had help, though."

"Please, do come in. My name is Femke."

"Femke." I taste the word on my lips, making sure to pronounce it correctly. Uncle had taught me some foreign languages when he had the time, but I've never had the chance to travel outside of Ireland. Hell has been a learning experience—I can say that much, at least.

"Would you like something to drink? Orange juice?"

"Do you have tea?"

"Tea? I have mint tea."

"But do you have just normal tea?"

"Normal tea?"

Once more, Steijn rolls his eyes. "Moeder, Mark bent iers."

"Ik heb geen zwarte—I don't have black tea," she says, correcting herself.

"Then, mint will be fine, thank you."

We sit around a small coffee table, me with tea, Steijn with a glass of orange juice ("sinaasappel sap"), and Femke with a glass of wine. I let my eyes roam, taking in the house. A faint tingling on my arms alerts me to a draft, which is precisely what I'd expect from an old house. The air is hot—but then, we are on top of a lava lake in Hell. The overall atmosphere is one of darkness; there is one magical lamp on the table, and that's it.

"Do you own this house?" I ask.

"No, we rented it from the local demon lord, who was Acheron. We now pay rent directly to Lucifer."

"So, all the other archdemons are landlords?"

"Yes, and they pay a share to Lucifer."

"Feudalism? Just like the old days."

"It's not easy, but we manage," she says. "It helps that Steijn works for you."

"What happened to your husband?"

"I divorced him. He was too fond of the drink."

I nod. "I know what it's like not to have a father. Or a mother."

"What happened?" Steijn asks.

"My mother died giving birth to me, and my dad fled Lucifer's minions."

There is a moment of silence while they process what I've told them. At that moment, as if he had been listening, Lucifer sends me a mental message. *Mark, where are you? I have to talk to you.*

"Shite!" They stare at me. "Lucifer wants to talk to me. Steijn, hold on, and I'll teleport you to my room. I have to go and meet Lucifer afterward."

Steijn gives me a knowing look, grabs my hand, and says goodbye to his mum. I Fade us back to the Citadel.

"Do you have any idea what he wants?" he asks me.

"I've no clue. Maybe he wants to lecture me?"

"Be careful, Mark."

"I will."

Lucifer, where are you?

I am at the Tower opposite Shahar's. There's no rush; I will always wait for you.

That isn't very reassuring, but I say goodbye to Steijn and make my way to the other tower. I find him immediately.

The chamber is vast and lavish. I realise the architecture here is different: the rest of the Citadel has smooth, dark granite and stained-glass windows—a homage to Gothic architecture. This room is more like the Art Deco of the 1930s and the Revival Deco of the 23rd century. (Conall had taught me art history, but I never believed it ever would be useful.)

Lucifer is lounging on a fine leather armchair; he has a cigar in his mouth and a bottle of cognac next to him.

"Want a smoke?" he asks as I make my towards him, taking the other armchair in front.

"Uncle told me never to smoke."

"Because it would give you cancer?" He smiles. "Humans are so foolish. They throw away their brief, precious lives by smoking or going to war for despots."

I shrug. "Fine. I'm immortal anyway; I might as well make the best of it."

The cigar smoke is not like... I thought it would be. Some of my drug dealer roommates liked to smoke. I smile—it's a memory that seems like it belongs to another lifetime. Tobacco smoke had been utterly intolerable to me. But free from disease and fragile lungs, I can now savour the full flavour of it: an intoxicating blend of caramel and sharp-edged bitterness.

"So, what did you want to talk to me about?"

"How did I deal with Acheron?"

"You froze him into a demon-flavored lollipop?"

He laughs. "Besides that."

"It was public," I say.

"Yes."

"And it showed how powerful you were—you dominated him."

"Exactly."

"Did I do a good job with Diego?" I ask, suddenly curious.

"You did exactly what I would have done."

"You would have let him live instead of making him suffer for eternity?"

"He was a bit player; he joined a more powerful demon because of personal dislike. It was a foolish mistake, and he paid for it—but not for eternity. Moreover, I think he respects you now. Demons respect power if nothing else."

"Right. But I want to know more: how did you cast the Great Magic? Why did Domiziana and Acheron want to kill me?"

He stretches and purrs; it is a very feline gesture. He motions towards the bottle of cognac. "I think we should discuss this over some good cognac—this is a LaFayette. It's perfect for that cigar you're so fond of."

With a start, I realise I had not stopped smoking; I'd been enjoying it.

"I'm not going to let myself get drunk," I warn him. "I know you."

He only grins. He pours us both a glass, and I take a sip. The drink is like burnt cinnamon: it tastes earthy and smoky and burns wonderfully down the throat.

"Do you like it?"

"I do, yeah. I still don't think it beats a nice cup of tea, though."

"You Irish amuse me—though then again, I ought to admit my love of cognac is a recently acquired taste."

"Really? How recent?"

"I've only been drinking it for about five hundred years. For millennia, I thought wine was the best drink on Earth, and nothing could sway me."

I blink in confusion. "Five hundred years? And why wine?"

"I've lived two and a half millennia, Mark. I was a Roman citizen back when that was—how would you say? —still a thing. I've seen empires rise, and I have seen them fall."

"So, this is a lecture, I'm guessing?"

"I would never pontificate to you. If you like, this can be fun." He expertly unbuttons his shirt and lies back in the armchair, enjoying the way I stare at him. Bastard.

"It's still no."

"Very well. In regards to your question: I performed an act of Great Magic using Foresight, Activation, and Sacrifice."

"Domiziana was the sacrifice."

"Yes, and Acheron provided the activation when he jumped into the circle. The foresight, now, that was the tricky bit."

"You *knew* Domiziana and Acheron were plotting to kill me?"

"I suspected it and made plans accordingly. If I had accused them, they would have reacted appropriately, and my plan would have failed. Also, their crimes needed to be made public and punished rather dramatically. We Romans always understood the value of a public execution." He smiles wistfully.

"But why? Why did they hate me?"

"Domiziana was a jealous bitch; I saw potential in her, but this was a fatal character flaw. She proved herself untrustworthy when she tried to kill you behind my back."

"You slept with her—"

"I fucked her. There's no need to use a euphemism."

"You did it so that you could tell how she would behave when jealous?"

"Yes. And as for Acheron, he... mistrusted you."

"He said something about Judas. Wasn't that the guy—"

"Who betrayed Jesus? That's a myth. Actually, he was in cahoots with Jesus; they both conspired to betray me. But Christianity had to come up with another scapegoat, who was conveniently Jewish."

"But you loved him?"

"I only deluded myself into thinking that I loved him. He was beautiful, and he took cock so well—"

"I don't need all the details."

"Alright. I'll tell you this much: Judas was nothing like you. He never said what he really thought. I found it amusing at first—a game I was always destined to win."

"But, he tricked you."

"He did; it's part of the reason why I'm trapped here."

"How come?"

"It's... complicated. Mark, have you ever tried sharing a memory?"

"What? We can do that?"

"If another demon consents, yes. I'm very good at this kind of magic, as I am at all magic." It's a cocky boast, but Steijn was right: Lucifer can do Great Magic just by clapping his hands. There's no point in contradicting him.

"I'm curious," I admit.

He places his hand on my chest. "Most demons need to touch the head, but I can do it by touching the chest. It feels much nicer, doesn't it?" I gulp, trying to ignore the innuendo.

"You have to be open to it," he tells me. I nod, closing my eyes.

****

The feelings are incredible. I can feel everything Lucifer feels: the raw lust, the tenderness, the affection. I can feel the way he touches Judas; his skin is like silk.

Lucifer is staring Judas in the eye. The boy—he looks like a boy, though the hardness in his muscles tells me he's a man—has eyes the colour of walnut. He is stunningly beautiful. He possesses a combination of delicacy and masculinity that is rare to behold: a tall neck, a square jaw, and just a hint of stubble.

"Tell me your secrets," Lucifer breathes.

"I have no secrets."

"You have many; it's why you so enrapture me." Lucifer kisses Judas, and I feel it through him. Judas has lips that are soft and full; his tongue is strong. Judas kisses just as hard as Lucifer.

"Take this tunic off me, and I'll tell you."

"You're not wearing a loincloth underneath it?"

"Fuck, no."

Lucifer gradually removes the tunic, kissing his nipples and abs. Judas has bronze skin and lean, tight muscles.

"Anything you want to say before I fuck you so hard you can't breathe?" Lucifer asks.

"Yeah. Go to Hell."

The spell is nothing like I've ever felt. What Lucifer did with Acheron pales in comparison to this: this is epochal, the most extraordinary spell ever wrought by a mortal hand. The magic rips Lucifer away from Judas. Reality itself seems to tear and fracture.

Even as Lucifer flies into the abyss, he sees that Judas is smiling. And his rage is endless. He curls his fist mutters a word, and Judas falls dead. The memory ends with a picture of his glassy eyes, staring emptily into nothingness.

I snap back to the present. I'm breathing hard, and my heart is doing a hundred miles an hour. (I don't need my heart to stay alive, but that doesn't mean it's not there.) Sweat has pooled on my forehead, and my dick is hard too. I take a moment to calm down.

"Now, you know."

"The lying, twisted fucker—" I stop and turn to Lucifer. His eyes are downcast with anger and shame. I've never seen him ashamed before.

"What he did—I was a lovestruck idiot—dumb and naive—"

I hug him. I don't know why I do it: he looks so wounded, so sad. Lucifer is a monster, but even monsters deserve a hug from time to time. He slowly returns the hug, and I sense that for the first time, I've truly surprised him.

"I'm sorry for what he did to you."

"You... are?" Almost instinctively, he touches me, grabbing my bum and trying to kiss me.

"Don't push your luck. I haven't given you carte blanche to bang me."

He laughs. "No, indeed, you have not. May I still hug you?"

"Yes."

We embrace for a long moment before we break it off.

"Goodbye, Lucifer."

"Thank you, Mark."

"And do me a bleedin' favour, will you? The tenants who paid to Acheron?"

"Yes? What of them?"

"Don't charge them rent."

I turn and walk out of the room.

****

I wander the corridors for some time, feeling lost and alone. Lucifer has given me a lot to think about, but what I feel is more than that. Partly, it's worry: I had been careless, and that carelessness had nearly killed me. Partly, it's futility—there is no way I can recreate the Great Magic that trapped Lucifer here. This seems like an impossible fight: a war that has raged for millennia, the stuff of myth, the legends that created human history.

But more than anything, I miss Conall. I can't keep doing this. It's hard enough turning down to Lucifer's sexual advances, but to live in eternal darkness, never seeing so much as a glimmer of Conall's eyes? That's too much to bear.

I eventually find Shahar in the other tower.

"Mark! Good to see you. I hear Max has fully recovered."

"I'm not here to talk about Max."

He senses my disquiet. "Have a seat."

He points to a rickety wooden chair, where his cat, Naem, is lounging. I walk towards the chair, waiting patiently for her feline majesty to give up the seat. Naem stares at me with one eye open, and the message is clear: *Fuck off, human.*

I sigh, grab the cat in my arms, and seat her on my lap. Her claws dig into me, indicating her displeasure, but I know I can win her over. I rub her behind the ears to appease her.

"What is it you would like to discuss?"

"Lucifer tells me I can't Fade to Earth; the road is the only way."

"That's correct. If somebody removed the Barrier, you would be able to fly away through the opening above the citadel." I file that piece of information away.

"But Lucifer could project to Earth?"

"Indeed, he could."

"Can I do it?"

"I think you could manage a simple projection. A material Sending would require a lot more power and some pretty sophisticated spell work."

"Could you at least tell me how to make a simple projection?"

He examines me critically. I continue rubbing Naem, and she starts to purr.

"Is this about Conall?"

"What do you think?"

He sighs. "Lucifer wouldn't approve of this."

"Will that stop you?"

He smiles, though it is a sad smile. "No, it won't. Very well. I will teach you some of the basics of spellcraft."

"You mean you're not going to do the spell for me?"

"I could, but teach a man to fish—"

"And he'll be independent forever. I get it. I just had no idea I could do *magic* magic, like with spells and stuff."

"Of course you can; you're a demon. Now listen carefully." He removes a book from the shelves, showing me a series of symbols. "This rune is Menis; it means rage. This rune is Inlusio, which means a cruel illusion. And this is Virtus, which is strength and courage."

"I can understand Inlusio and Virtus, but Menis? Why rage?"

"Rage is what powers a spell, especially the stronger ones. We can modify it to see what works best, but let's start with the basic formula first."

"Inlusio and Virtus are Latin, but Menis is Greek—"

"Yes, Lucifer named the runes after various languages, but especially his native Latin. There are a few in Hebrew as well. Menis is from the Iliad, of course."

"Right. And all I have to do is draw these runes?"

"And name them correctly, and you have to *will* the spell. That's the most important element—the spellcraft is to aid you, to give structure to the magic, but it is your will that powers it."

"Lucifer is always going on about will."

"Maybe you've learned the lesson then."

"Okay, let's do this."

Shahar shows me a clear area on the floor and provides chalk. He instructs me to draw the three runes in a triangle.

"Inclusio, you are but a cruel illusion; Virtus, you are courage; and Menis, you are rage, loss, sorrow," I say, pointing at each of them in turn.

"Now, it's up to you."

I nod, drop down on my knees, close my eyes, and focus. *Come on, Conall. I want to see you again. I want it more than anything else in the world, and I don't care if I have to break into another dimension to do it.*

The runes glow a dark red, and then everything goes black.

Chapter Fifteen: A Cruel Reunion

Conall

Like a phantom, he appears, though he is not born of darkness but of shining light. I am in a guest bedroom inside the Dublin base; the early morning sunlight blazes through the window, and where it meets the outlines of his form, it gilds him in warm, silvery hues. His hair is molten gold, and his eyes shine like jewels.

"Mark?" I ask.

"It's me, Conall."

"Are you real?"

He smiles bitterly. "In a manner of speaking, yeah."

I lose control of myself and leap, embracing him. I pass right through him, and the sensation is a strange one: a tingling, a resistance as if moving through sound. I turn around and face him.

"I'm only here as a projection. Shahar tells me I'm not ready for a material Sending yet."

"Shahar? Who's that?"

"He's a... mentor; I guess you could say. He has lived for over two millennia."

"He's a demon?"

"No, he's actually human."

"Right. Well... Damn it, Mark! I want to kiss you and hold you."

He raises his hand, and his fingers open wide. I touch him with the tips of my fingers, and for a moment—a beautiful, memorable, and terrible moment—it's as if he's there. The distance between us is like a vast ocean, a great mountain, the very fabric of another universe.

"So close, but so far away..." His voice is husky, his breathing ragged.

"Lost in another world," I say. "So, this is all we can do? You can't do magic?"

He strains, and his eyes narrow in concentration. I feel only a hint of it, like a breath of air on my hips.

"If that's your version of a blowjob, this is going to suck."

He laughs. "Yeah, I'm sorry."

I sigh. "We need to talk to Kaylin. She's going to want to know about this, maybe try a spell on you."

"That witch—"

"Saved your uncle."

He blinks. "What? What happened?"

"He was kidnapped and tortured by the Party, but we got him out, and he's healing up in the infirmary. He should still be here; you can ask him yourself."

He nods. I walk out the door, navigating the corridors, and he moves behind me, silent as a ghost, but somehow a tangible presence.

"You haven't lost your taste in fashion—you're still wearing those tight black jeans," he comments.

"Just like old times, eh? Remember when I first showed you the mansion, and you kept staring at my ass?"

"I was not staring at your ass—I was admiring the marble floor, the motifs on the ceiling, and your jeans."

"You were admiring my ass. You never gave two bleeding fucks about the motifs or the marble floor."

"Yes, you win, Conall. You have a great ass, and I'm not ashamed to admire it. I'm glad you came to my house and made me fall in love with you because I would never have had the guts to do it myself."

We arrive in the infirmary, and the conversation ends abruptly (though I've not forgotten what he's said). Eoin is sitting on the bed, packing his bags. He leaps into the air when he sees Mark.

"Mark? What the hell?"

"I'm only a projection, Uncle."

"You're not really here?"

"No. Are you OK? I heard the Party—"

"The Party bastards nearly killed me, but I lived, curse them. Kaylin helped fix me up. But are you OK?"

"I nearly got killed, but I survived; Lucifer punished those who tried to hurt me."

Eoin looks confused. "What—?"

"I am also very interested to know." We all turn to see Kaylin at the door. "Hello, Mark. You didn't tell us you were coming."

"I'm here as a—"

"Projection, I know. I've been consulting the Black Book."

"Pity it didn't help you when we needed it."

"I regret that too."

"Hey! You two!" I interrupt. "Mark won't be here forever, and I think we have more important things to discuss."

"You are right," Kaylin admits. "Mark, who attacked you in Hell?"

"An Archdemon named Acheron and some other minor demons. One of my friends, Max, gave up his power to bolster mine."

"Max is a demon?"

"Yes."

Kaylin nods, filing that piece of information away to a mental drawer marked "Important."

"You said Lucifer punished them?"

"Lucifer used Great Magic to freeze Acheron into an ice cube; he's going to be an ice statue for a long time, as I understand. I punished the other demons."

"He used Great Magic just for that?"

"He didn't want to kill Acheron, and Great Magic was the only permanent solution."

"I understand—or at least I think I do. And you punished the other demons personally?"

"I discovered I could hurt other demons purely with a malicious gaze."

"Michael told me the Dark Stare did not work against demons."

"He's wrong about that—both me and Lucifer can use it."

"Only you two? No one else?"

Mark pauses, thinking. "No, only us two."

We all look at him more carefully. "You're badass," I tell him.

"Thanks, Conall."

"Tell me more about Lucifer," Kaylin orders. "What is he like? What motivates him?"

"He's motivated by power and anger. A witch imprisoned him in Hell by sacrificing a demon named Jesus."

"Michael told me about the Barrier, and the Book says it was a powerful spell. But *Jesus*? The actual prophet?"

"That's the one. He was the demon sacrificed to power the Great Magic."

"Is there anything else I should know?"

"Lucifer is smart, cunning, and brilliant. He predicts how people will act, and he has a plan for everything."

"I figured as much."

"Also... I hate saying this, but Lucifer is in love with me. If you think he's motivated by nothing except power and rage, you've got him all wrong—he's not like the Party autocrats. He's sexual and emotional."

Kaylin nods. "Thank you for this, Mark. Now give me a moment to cast a spell on you; I want to get a feel for your magical signature. It might help me track you in Hell, possibly even create a portal like the one that was used to capture you."

"If you say so," Mark agrees.

Kaylin traces a series of symbols in the air, which Mark and I follow closely. A faint blue light glows on Mark's forehead before fading away. Kaylin examines him critically. "This may be the best I can do, given you are here only as an illusion."

"Don't you feel any pressure to leave?" I ask him. "Demons usually can't maintain this magic for too long."

"The Barrier does not affect me, so no. I can stay here as long as I want."

"Then come with me," I order. Kaylin looks like she's about to protest, then thinks better of it. Eoin simply nods.

As soon as we're a reasonable distance away, I ask him, "Did Lucifer try to fuck you?"

"He sure bleedin' tried."

"It can't be easy fending him off all the time." I'm not stupid enough to be jealous: Mark is in an unenviable position.

"It isn't, but when I think of you, it helps. You have no idea how much it means for me to see you again."

"For me too. I was afraid I lost you down there. What is Hell like, anyway?"

"It's built on top of a concentric rock formation which lies above a lake of lava."

"Wow. Dante got it right, then?"

"I'm starting to believe one of Lucifer's demons actually did manage to sneak him into Hell—the descriptions are just so accurate. It makes sense too."

"Lucifer would want humans to fear Hell."

"Because people who are afraid are easy to manipulate."

We look into each other's eyes and smile. "When did you get so wise, Mark?"

"You taught me the basics!"

"Yes, but Lucifer made you master politics. Anyway, what else is there to see in Hell for the lost tourist?"

"Old houses and Gothic architecture. Oh, and an arena built on a frozen lake."

"A frozen lake?"

"It was boiling to start with, but Lucifer froze it."

"Right. So Hell really does freeze over?"

He chuckles. "If its master wants it to freeze over."

"And what are the people like?"

"The people are like here—lots of them are poor and struggling to pay rent. The bastards in charge are much the same."

"Except in Hell, they're immortal, and there's no hope of revolution."

"You telling me there's a revolution here? Besides Kaylin's petty vandalism and sabotage?"

"We have a Communist movement."

"What? Feck me. With an actual army and stuff?"

"They're getting there—I'm sure the Spanish government will offer them a little sneaky help, thanks to my mother."

"Your mother is in Spain?"

"My family is. Somebody attacked us at the mansion; the Party is out for blood."

"They just don't stop, do they? And what are you still doing here?"

"Playing hero like an idiot."

"Welcome to the club. Losers' Club."

"Thanks."

We laugh. Then Mark grows serious again.

"I have to go back—Lucifer might find out if I'm missing for too long, and I always need to keep my guard up."

"Good luck, Mark. I love you."

His ethereal fingers brush against my cheek, and I shiver. The sensation is one of warmth and sweet summer days. Remarkably, he even smells nice: I taste the salty ocean, the fragrance of blooming flowers, and underneath that, a hint of sweat.

"Go," I croak. "I want to fuck you, and I can't, and it hurts."

"I'll come back to you, and then you can do whatever you want to me. I promise."

Then he fades away.

Chapter Sixteen: Mount Everest

Kaylin

Before making any major decisions, I always plan. Mark's temporary arrival had delayed me, but not for long. I have to leave for Mount Everest; it is the only way to discover the truth of the two Books. It may even be the only way for me to increase my power and fight my enemies.

That doesn't mean convincing my men will be easy, though. They stand waiting, Diana and Grumman observing me.

"I've called you here," I begin, "to explain a decision that will seem paradoxical, even mad."

They all groan.

"I will be travelling to Mount Everest, starting soon."

"How long is this exotic pleasure cruise going to last?" one of my men calls out.

I smile patiently. "Potentially a good while, especially since it isn't a pleasure cruise."

I withdraw the White Book from my jacket pocket. They all stare at it, many with confused expressions; only Diana and Shadow seem to recognise what it could be.

"Is that another spellbook?" Diana asks.

"It is. It appeared on my desk with no other explanation than go to Everest. It is a book of healing magic, though I can only access a small part of it."

"How do we know it's real?" Grumman asks.

"I've used one of the spells successfully."

"It could still be a trap," he points out.

"That is true, but it's too good an opportunity to miss. Moreover, I fear we cannot defeat either Lucifer or the Party without better magic — especially healing magic. Many of our men might end up like poor John otherwise."

Many people grimace at the mention of John.

"I'm not convinced yet," Grumman says. "We need you here, especially now that the Party has figured out the supernatural. We're also not sure how trustworthy our allies are. I fear what might happen to us without your leadership."

"I will do my best to communicate, Grumman," I say, sighing. "But you are at least partly correct: I have to appoint an interim leader in my absence."

They shuffle at the mention of "interim leader."

"Who do you have in mind?" Diana asks.

"As much as I trust you and love you, Diana, I think Grumman is best-placed to handle this."

"I don't like it, Kaylin. You're weakening this organisation at just the wrong time."

"Do you refuse then?"

He just sighs a weary, exhausted sound. "I will do my best to fill your role."

"Excellent."

"Wait!" Diana interrupts. "When do you leave? Don't you need a security detail?"

"I will leave tomorrow morning. I have a feeling that I need to do this alone, and a security detail would be unwise."

"You could be walking into certain death," Diana says stonily.

"If this person is a witch or some other supernatural creature, I doubt a security detail would be able to protect me—I would only be putting you all in danger."

"I should come with you!"

"You're better off helping Grumman."

The air suddenly grows violent, swirling like a hurricane. Diana is on *fire*. She is like a god; she swells with enough power to light up the stars. My men dive for cover.

The spell is only a whispered word and a hastily-drawn gesture, yet it rips from me like a corded whip. It ensnares Diana, thickens, hardens, and traps her. It extinguishes her power like a small, beautiful flame.

"I can handle myself, Diana. You need to trust me." I release the spell and reach out, helping her back to her feet.

"You're stronger than I thought," she admits. "That was awesome!"

"But let's not do it again, shall we?"

My men murmur in agreement, and Diana pouts. "Have it your way then."

"I know you think this is unwise, but it is for the best."

"That's what you always say before something goes horribly wrong."

"I promise to watch my back, okay? You take care of the others. Grumman isn't very good at understanding magic."

"I'll be your right-hand woman if that's what you want me to be."

Diana and I shake hands to seal the deal.

I order my men to prepare a Q-car for tomorrow morning. I pack my bags—I take warm clothes with me, a large wad of cash, and a pistol, just to be safe. But before I leave, I have one more thing to do.

****

"Good evening, Conall. Hello, Eoin."

They turn towards me; it's clear both are surprised to see me. I more or less ignored them since yesterday, and they've made themselves temporarily at home in the base. That cannot continue any longer.

"I'm leaving for Mount Everest tomorrow morning," I state.

"What? The actual mountain in Nepal?" Conall asks. Eoin only smiles at the question.

"Yes. While I am gone, I want you to return to your family in Spain. You are not safe here."

"I helped save your life with the medallion, remember?"

"You did, and I am grateful. Even so, it's dangerous for you to remain, and there is little you can do to help us right now."

"I can still do more here than I would be doing on some beach in Spain."

"You're cleverer than that, Conall. Do you think we can win this war alone? Not kill the Party, but actually govern this country? The Spanish government can provide invaluable help, and you—along with your mother—can negotiate."

He considers my words carefully, stroking his chin with a finger. "Okay, you win."

I offer my hand, and he shakes it. "You did well. I respect you."

"Thank you."

"Now, I best get to sleep. I have a long day ahead of me."

"Kaylin?" I turn around—I had almost forgotten about Eoin. "Can I go with him?"

"Not so tough anymore?" Conall mutters.

"You certainly can. What changed your mind?"

"I realised Conall was right—there is a time for being a hero, but it isn't now. Not with the Party out to kill me."

"A wise choice," I state.

****

The morning is bright and distinctly chilly. It is the last day of September, and autumn will eventually fade to winter. Grumman, Diana, and a handful of my men await me next to the Q-car. I have prepared as well as I possibly can.

A breeze lifts Diana's hair, and she smiles. There is a trace of sadness in the expression.

"Watch out for yourself," she tells me.

"I will."

"Don't stay long," Grumman warns me. "I'm not you."

"Thanks for the compliment," I say sarcastically.

He does not smile.

I haul my bag into the Q-car, close the door, and instruct the pilot. I've said enough goodbyes. Ireland soon fades to a patchwork of green fields, dark forests, and then the ocean's flat blue expanse. Even travelling at Mach 1.5, it will take more than four hours to reach Mount Everest. I have a long trip ahead of me.

I review my notes on a com phone, idly scribbling down thoughts with my finger. Mount Everest is famous, but it's remote, inhospitable, and wild. Aside from the apparent threats—freezing to death, altitude sickness, and the identity of the mysterious entity I am meeting—the most unpredictable element is the Chinese. The European League of Nations is still technically at war with China, though a ceasefire is in place. The Europeans control the Near Middle East: Turkey, Iran, Saudi Arabia, and Turkmenistan. Things get tricky in India, as the country is split in two. Nepal belongs to China.

I know a Glamour spell to change my appearance, but not being able to speak Mandarin, I doubt I would ever pass for a Chinese citizen. So I ordered my men to forge a diplomatic passport; that would buy me some time to escape in case I get caught. The hard part will be getting the Q-car into Chinese airspace.

Eventually, the ocean melts away, and mountains rise from the horizon. At first, they seem distant and small, though that is an illusion. The Q-car slows down to subsonic speeds and engages all of its stealth features. Gradually, the horizon resolves into a vast chain of mountains.

I am left speechless. I see one of the world's great wonders: these rocky peaks reach out and touch the sky, like the Tower of Babel reaching for heaven. Sunlight glitters brilliantly against the snow, and clouds swirl around precipices.

"We're approaching Chinese airspace, Mistress," Elizabeth, the Q-car pilot, informs me.

"This is the most dangerous part of the flight, isn't it?"

"That's right. If we trip something, the Chinese air defence systems could—" An alarm cuts her off. "Shit. Someone just fired a SAM at us."

"Chinese defence networks are getting more sophisticated. Can you evade it?"

"I can try, but it's fast. If I shoot it, the heat signature of the plasma cannon will make us an even bigger target."

I nod. "Do your best. I'll try a spell."

The Q-car angles sharply to the left, dives, then lifts. I close my eyes, concentrating carefully. I could try destroying the missile telekinetically, but casting a Glamour would be much easier. The spell is similar to what I use to conceal the base back in Dublin; it is harder to apply it to an object in motion, but not impossible.

Runes appear in my mind's eye, and I draw each of them in quick succession. The Q-car's alarms are blaring; the G-forces make my eyeballs pop. But I'm determined, and with a heave of effort, I cast the final rune in the spell.

The magic is like a balloon, expanding from my body into a sphere before becoming more like a fabric. I drape it over the Q-car like I would a bedspread or tablecloth. The edges of the Q-car appear to shimmer and darken.

The alarms go silent in an instant.

Elizabeth breathes a sigh of relief, wiping the sweat from her hair. The Q-car returns to its standard flight path.

"That was pretty close," she says.

"It's harder to do magic when you're going 500 miles an hour upside-down," I point out.

"But you did it anyway. Thanks."

"No worries."

The Q-car starts to descend and lands at the base of a giant mountain. I exit the Q-car, marvelling at the pleasant temperature and beautiful sunshine: it is the first day of October, and it is perfect.

"Think you'll manage on your own, Mistress?"

"I'll be fine. You can fly back to base."

"You know, this has to be one of the dumber decisions you've made—I think it ties with misusing that spell and taking down a bunch of communications."

"You'll have to trust me, Liz."

"Go on then."

I salute her, and she smiles briefly before turning the Q-car around and flying away. I'm on my own now. The trouble is, I don't know where to start: the note I received in the White Book wasn't exactly super-specific. Everest is a colossal mountain set in a vast wilderness. How do I find the mysterious person? At Base Camp? At the peak? In a cave?

There's one way to find out: a spell in the Black Book allows me to find hidden things, uncover glamour, and locate missing persons. All I need is a fragment that belonged to the missing person—and the note I found is just enough. I don't waste any time. I draw six runes in the air, forming a circle; this will act as a sort of radar dish for the spell. I draw a more massive rune in the centre and focus.

This spell is different from all the others I've used before in the way it *feels*. My awareness seems to extend outside of my body and then split. I can hear the chirping of a small black Bulbul and the echoing cries of a Himalayan Golden Eagle; I see small rodents burrowing in the forests; I can taste the sweet water of glacial streams and the cold Autumn air as it flits across the landscape.

A raven caws, and I blink; the spell shatters instantly. There's something strange about it: the raven is staring at me, and there is intelligence in that gaze. I feel like it is watching me, or indeed, judging me. Whatever the bird wants, it has my full attention.

I refocus the spell, aiming the magic in the direction of the raven. The corvid takes off as if sensing my intentions.

Then I feel something else—something hidden, powerful, and deadly. I retreat, but it's already too late. The magic leaps out like a hungry beast circling its prey. It is a trap, and I fell straight into it.

I try to whisper a protection spell, but the words refuse to come out of my mouth. I try to draw a rune, but the spell paralyses my hands. *Shit.*

I bite down my rising panic: if the magic wanted me dead, I would be a corpse right now. I need to break free—I just can't figure out how.

Chapter Seventeen: Birthday Boy

Mark

"That was great!" I say. "Can you teach me how to do a true Sending? So I can be there for real?"

"You did the spell very well, but I'm afraid that a Sending of that kind is rather less trivial to do than a projection," Shahar explains.

"Why?"

"You need the stars to align."

"What? Really?"

"I am not joking. There are only a few rare instances within a year when it is possible, and usually, the window is less than an hour long."

My enthusiasm deflates. Shahar smiles warmly.

"Come, Mark. It is your birthday today. *Yom huledet sameach.*"

"Thank you, but it sucks without Conall."

"I can teach you some other spells," Shahar offers. "You are a natural."

"I quite agree." We both jump when Lucifer Fades into the room. "*Felix sit natalis dies!* We Romans usually celebrate birthdays on the first of the month, so you are lucky."

"Thanks," I say.

"And I can teach you spells better than Shahar ever will. With all due respect, friend."

"No offence taken."

"Will you teach me how to fight?"

Lucifer smiles widely. "Most certainly."

****

Lucifer Fades me to a place at the bottom of the Citadel's perch—a garden. I've never seen it before, sadly, for it is beautiful, and that's rare in this forsaken place. I see roses, which are dark crimson, like spilled blood. There are stranger colours on display, too—from iridescent violet to indigo blue. A small stream gurgles gently; it overlooks a clearing in the middle.

"We're going to learn to fight... here?"

"No, not here. I will teach you duelling magic soon enough, but here, I want to show you that demonic magic is capable of far more than slaughter and destruction. Nor do you need to use demonic runes, though it helps."

"I've always been able to use my powers without any formal spells," I say, "but I always assumed that the greatest feats of magic—"

"Runes do not represent the strongest magic, only the most sophisticated. Let me show you."

Lucifer walks up to the clearing and traces several runes on the paving stones. They form a complex, overlapping circle. The Great Demon offers me his hand, and I take it, curious to find out where this is going.

"I need you to think of a tree—the most beautiful tree you can imagine."

"Right."

"My magic will blend with yours, and we will create this together."

I nod, closing my eyes. I think of all the trees I've seen on Earth: I remember their grace, their majesty, the warm green earth, and the pale blue sky that gives them life. The magic is like a song, a duet, and it threads between us, weaving a strange and wonderful tune.

The magic coalesces into a dark mass, then gradually takes shape. A tree rises from the inky depths, but this is a tree-like no other. The tree's trunk looks as if someone has carved it from marble, but this is a living thing, a stone that breathes fire and air. Its branches glisten gold and proud. And its leaves are smooth, dark obsidian; they glitter like polished darkness, their edges sharp and wicked.

"This is... amazing."

"Do you like it? For all of its beauty, it is not like the trees on Earth."

"You can't make a living tree?"

"I can, but what would be the point? It would not survive long in Hell."

"So what about those greenhouses?"

"With the aid of modern technology, sure, a lot of things can be made to grow. It isn't the same, though, is it?"

"True."

Then I begin to wonder about how things may have grown here without the benefit of greenhouses or LEDs.

"But how did you manage in the days before technology? Magic?"

"We did indeed use magic in the early days, but today, technology does it easier and cheaper. We only keep the magic lights because they do the job well, and it's not worth the cost to electrify."

"How much *would* it cost?"

"Hundreds of millions of denarii. It would be quite a hit to my finances—especially since I am the lender of last resort. Humans joke that I'm the Central Bank of Lucifer. It's not like Hell has a big international banking system, in case you haven't noticed."

At that moment, I realise something incredibly crucial about Lucifer: he may be tragic, and he may dream of greatness, but he is a pragmatist down to the bone.

We are interrupted when Suzanne enters the garden, watering pot in hand. She is busy feeding the roses I spotted when I entered through the gate. There's something... strange about her. The cut of her clothes, the graceful way in which she moves—it's at odds with the domestic chore.

"Who is Suzanne, really?" I ask him.

"Why do you want to know? She is a servant I assigned to you."

"But was she born in Hell? Or did she cross over from Earth?"

He grins. "That is an excellent question."

"You're not going to answer me, are you?"

"You'll figure it out on your own. Enough about Suzanne. I take it you want to duel me?"

"Yes."

He offers me his hand. "Then follow me."

****

He Fades us to a room. The word room seems too anodyne a description, though: this could be a ballroom or a king's hall. It is enormous; it must be the largest room in the citadel. The ceiling stretches high above us, and the farthest corners are shrouded in darkness. Elegant stained glass windows cast a pale, reddish hue, though it hardly seems to pierce the darkness. The floor here is not marble—it is a hardwood parquet.

"No more marble?" I comment.

"It's rather impractical, I'm afraid. I have to have the parquet repaired regularly, despite the warding spells I cast."

"So this is—what? A dojo?"

"Something like that. I used to call it the pankration chamber, but the word dojo is much simpler."

"A what now?"

"Pankration is a Greek sport that involves boxing and wrestling; I quite admire it."

"So, we'll be wrestling?" I fancy myself a decent wrestler.

"No. As I'm sure you've realised, wrestling is not an effective technique against demons who can Fade—and are impervious to physical damage anyway."

"Then, we'll learn magic?"

"Magic and weapons."

The Great Demon raises his right arm high into the air, and a sword suddenly appears in his hand. I've never seen swords in real life, only in photographs. But this is something else: its blade is black as night and s seems to shimmer depending on the angle. The cross-guard is golden and ornate but not entirely decorative...

"Is that really a sword? Or is it magic?"

"In a manner of speaking. It's a manifestation of my power, and it can harm immortal beings like demons."

"Can I make one?"

"You can. Listen carefully now."

He draws several runes on my hand and makes me memorise each one. "This is *sideros*, and it means iron. It is the most important rune in the spell, for it gives the sword its strength and power. You must have Will to use this rune."

He shows me another rune: "*Adamas* is steel; it is unconquerable. Finally, *aes*, which is bronze: golden and poetic, for a blade must have poetry as well as strength."

"Aes?" I try to pronounce the word, hoping I get it right. "Is it Greek or Latin?"

"Latin. The cross-guard on my sword is gilded, but it is made from bronze, not pure gold."

"Right."

I trace each of the runes he has drawn on my hand, whispering their name, understanding their meaning. As the magic forms inside, I struggle with understanding the complexity. I reach the final word, *sideros*, and strain. The other runes require grace and imagination, but this needs raw power. I might as well move a mountain or tame a sea, as power this spell.

So I do something a little different: I draw my strength from anger, hot passion, and fury. A different word appears in my mind: *Pyr*, which I realise means fire. The words coalesce into something like a sentence, and the spell explodes into flame.

I don't shy away from it—it doesn't hurt me. Instead, the fire creates an object, which slowly gains the proportions of a sword. The cross-guard is golden, like Lucifer's sword, but the blade is silver, like ice. The memory of its creation seems to linger, though, as the blade shimmers with golden fire.

Lucifer raises an eyebrow. "Interesting. I did not expect that."

"So, how do we fight?"

"Let me start by teaching you the basics of the thrust, cut, and parry." He moves over to me, placing his hands next to mine. I shiver faintly.

"You parry with the forte of the blade, near to the hilt. Doing so gives you more leverage to deflect a thrust or a cut."

"Show me."

With a flourish, he withdraws his blade and aims a thrust towards me. I catch it with the back of the blade, turning it away smoothly.

"Good," he says with warm approval. "Fencing relies on your ability to control distance and estimate range. We can Fade, which is devastating in a sword fight." In an instant, he Fades next to me, sword flashing. I barely have time to parry the attack.

"Now it's your turn," he says.

Grinning, I teleport, launching an overhead cut. I expect Lucifer to block it, and once he does, I circle the blade, aiming for the lower part of his body. The sword passes through thin air.

"Impressive," he says. "You've already figured out the basics of the bind without any instruction from me."

"I still didn't hit you."

"You were too slow, and that is still a fairly simple attack. Nonetheless, it is on the right lines. Again."

I lie still, for just a moment, before rushing in. I Fade halfway through the attack, aim another upward cut, then grab Lucifer by the arm as he parries. I smash the pommel into his face, which feels oddly satisfying.

"Very impressive."

"I got you that time."

Before I can say anything more, he attacks. I don't even see what he does—the sword simply flies from my hand. Then he's on top of me.

"You have more work to do before you can fight at full speed," he murmurs against my ear. I gulp, trying not to show how uncomfortable he makes me feel.

"I'm a novice."

"Hmm, yes. You did very well with the spell."

"The spell?"

"That little Projection to Earth."

"How did you know?"

"Did you think you could conceal it from me? I live and breathe magic, Mark. I can hear a spell cast from the other side of the Citadel; I can smell the magic on your hair and skin. To me, illusion magic tastes like pine needles and sunshine."

"The Party attacked my uncle," I blurt out. "The Party you turned against me," I added bitterly.

"The Party was a means to an end, nothing more. They have outlived their usefulness. I do not plan to let it continue once I am free of this place—I will rule Ireland the same way I will rule the world."

"And the world will run red with blood."

"Not so; I can be quite reasonable. It will require force to crush both China's imperial ambitions and the European League of Nations—we both know that. I do not think you would mourn the passage of either."

"No, but—"

"Master, master!" We both turn to examine the new arrival. The imp looks familiar to me (was her name Pip?). Lucifer extracts himself from me, offering me a hand; I take it, and he lifts me quickly.

"What is it, Pip?" Lucifer asks.

"It is a secret," the imp explains. Lucifer just smiles.

"Very well, hop on to my shoulder."

The imp jumps, makes herself comfortable, and whispers something in his ear. Lucifer leans in melodramatically. I want to laugh: the scene is absolutely comical.

A few seconds later, the imp bounds away, and Lucifer straightens himself.

"What was that about?"

"Some gossip. Not particularly important. The imps make a show of secrecy for everything they tell me—from banal rumours to the most priceless intelligence."

"Why?"

"So that no one guesses when they're telling me something important."

"That makes sense," I realise.

"Happy Birthday, Mark."

I blink at the change of subject. "Lessons are over, then?"

"For now," he says.

****

As I walk the corridors of the Citadel, I bump into an acquaintance: Archdemon Tim.

"Hello Mark," he says, offering a handshake while puffing on a cigar. (Though I can tell it's weed, not tobacco. I can recognise the smell thanks to my old life alongside dealers.)

"Why are you smoking cannabis?" I ask while giving him a handshake.

"To get high."

"Can demons get high?"

"You did with it the alcohol, didn't you?"

"Yeah, but that was different."

"Fair enough. Indeed, herb doesn't affect me the same way it does a human; I suffer no memory loss or psychosis. But old habits die hard, especially when you're half a millennia-old."

"What do you want to talk to me about? Get to the point."

"It was you who started the conversation, darlin'. Now that you ask, I would like to show you my art collection. Do you admire art?"

"I never got the chance on Earth."

"Then you will learn in Hell. Come with me," he orders, fluttering down a side corridor. I realise that he's actually levitating and leaving behind glitter.

"I've never seen a demon like you," I say.

"Nor have I ever met a demon who is so much like Lucifer in his abilities," he points out.

"Yes, but all demons are somewhat like Lucifer—except you."

"With freedom, books, flowers, and the moon, who could not be happy?" he asks.

"That doesn't answer my question. You're also plagiarising Oscar Wilde."

"Oh, so you *do* know something about art?"

"Enough to recognise a famous quote."

"Quotation is a serviceable substitute to wit."

"You keep telling yourself that."

He only laughs. After a few moments, we arrive in what must be his private living quarters. I stop: there's a birthday cake on the table, emblazoned with the numbers "19". The candles burn pink.

"You made me a birthday present? No way! Thanks."

"Well, it would be more accurate to say I ordered the cook to do it. I just put the finishing touches," he says proudly.

"Like the pink flame on the candles?"

"Precisely."

"How come you're the only demon to know what a birthday cake is?"

He shrugs. "It's something the older demons never experienced, so they don't have the cultural context to do it right. Take a bite."

I cut myself a piece, and then another. "Mmm. The cream is lovely, and it has so many fruits. How did you know it was my birthday?"

"Lucifer mentioned it in passing."

"So, how close are you to him? He seems to know the Archdemons very well—"

"Oh, but he remembers me even better. I'm not someone you forget."

"I get that. Tell me more about yourself."

"Is this going to be an interview?"

"I'm just curious," I say between mouthfuls.

He grins. "Where should I start?"

"From the beginning," I say, munching on another mouthful of cake.

"Aristotle once said that a good story has a beginning, a middle, and an end. I don't know where my story finishes, but I do know where it began. I was 14, and it was the summer of 1986."

"Ah, you're like one of those old American movies the Party used for propaganda."

"I was too naughty to be in a propaganda movie. My parents barely paid any attention to me, and I was drinkin', getting' high, and fucking."

"So that's how you got HIV?"

"Guilty as charged."

"They really didn't have treatments then? We have a vaccine for it now."

"Honey, they didn't even know what it *was*. It took years until we got real therapy. I was sunning myself in Hell by the time they got to a vaccine."

"I see your point, although I must point out that there is no sun in Hell."

"Don't be so pedantic."

"But what made you want to be a *demon*? How did Lucifer recruit you?"

"Oh, you know how the Devil does his business. You hear voices in your dreams, and then you start to hear them awake, too."

I knew exactly what he meant. "And then?"

"Then a bunch of bullies show up, and the voice in your head tells you to kill them. So you grab a baseball bat, and you kill them all."

"That's definitely familiar. I'm guessing a demon shows up after that?"

"Right you are. A handsome man with dark eyes suddenly appears and makes you a deal. You can try to become a demon, but you have to go to Hell forever. I said yes, he opened a portal, and after that, it's history."

"Cool," I say, finishing the cake. It is delicious.

He pouts like a wounded cat. "Can I show you my art collection now?"

"Go on."

I follow him into another room, and I'm amazed by the amount of *light*. The other places in Hell always seem shrouded in darkness; the light is simply a pale, reddish tinge, no more than a shadow of proper illumination. But the light is here bright, neither reddish nor blue, but a perfect simulacrum of sunlight.

The walls are a light grey, and I see either a painting or a photograph everywhere I look. Two pictures stick out at me: one shows a baby seal, or at least, I think it's a seal since I've never seen one in real life. The animal is simply adorable. Another shows a road leading towards a mountain; the peak is rocky and snow-covered, and golden sunshine illuminates the landscape.

"I love the photographs. Where were they taken?"

"The seal you're admiring was photographed in Denmark, and the landscape is from the Cairngorms in Scotland."

"You took them...?"

"No, it was photographers who took their work with them when they entered Hell. I bought the photographs from them. There's more." He walks over to the far side of the room, where a vast painting hangs over a wall.

I realise it's a depiction of Hell. An enormous black mountain juts out high into a sky filled with stars; below, a cauldron of lava seethes with firelings.

"I'm guessing this was painted in Hell?"

"Absolutely. I've seen the medieval depictions of Hell, but they don't really do it justice. We demons don't waste our time with pitchforks."

"Nor do we have horns."

He smiles. To my amazement, two horns start protruding from his forehead, then curl around towards each other.

"How...?"

"I can teach you how to shape-shift, but I've only met a handful of demons who could do it. Even Lucifer struggles with it."

"He mentioned that. Honestly? I would love to try. If I fail, then at least I gave it a shot."

"I like your attitude."

"So what spells or runes do I need to know?"

"I do it without any formal runes. There are some which help, but good shape-shifters don't use them."

"Give me something to start with."

"*Circe* is the rune you want." He draws it on the wall, where it appears briefly before fading away. "She was a sorceress and an expert in transformation magic. You can use the spell to change someone else, but I don't recommend trying that until you've mastered it on yourself."

"So, do I draw the rune on myself?"

"On your chest or forehead is best. You have to Will the transformation you want."

"What's easiest to do? Wings? Horns?"

"The wings are the hardest; the teeth are the easiest."

I nod. "OK, let's do this."

I draw the rune on my forehead, name it *Circe*, and imagine the magic coalescing around my teeth. The rune tingles and magic pours into my body like fire, but this is unlike any I've used before. All the magic I know acts in some way externally, usually with destructive intent. This magic works inside me, and its purpose is to shape and create. It is much more challenging.

I realise that this kind of magic is too fluid to control using spells. It can do anything, which also means it can do nothing at all. I have to imagine something particular, and yet at the same time, I have to be open to whatever the magic wants.

I carefully focus my intent. The magic follows my lead, working inside my body in ways I don't understand.

I smile, and he smiles back.

"Awesome."

"Do you like them?"

"Oh yeah. I went through a vampire phase too."

The fangs in my mouth are long and sharp and force me to speak carefully.

"What about reversing the change?"

"That's easier—you sort of have to just to let go."

I close my eyes, imagining myself before the transformation. The magic pulses in response then begins to recede. I explore my teeth with my tongue, finding normal human incisors.

"You did well!" he says with excitement.

"Can I make myself sparkle like you do?"

"You'll need a bit more practice."

I take that as a positive sign. "It was nice meeting you, Tim. Thanks for the birthday cake."

"You're welcome," he says with a wink.

I Fade myself out of the room. I enjoyed my birthday today, but I'm not blind to the fact that I'm still a prisoner here and that I need to be stronger to win. I've learned that I can shapeshift and create magical swords; I have two more weapons to fit into my arsenal.

Chapter Eighteen: Crystal Cave

Kaylin

I have to think quickly and get myself out of the trap. I cannot speak or move, which leaves me no other choice: I have to use my mind to cast the counter-spell. But first, I have to understand how this magic works. I extend my mind outwards, feeling, probing, understanding. The spell is like a snake, smooth and slippery and primed to strike, but it can be charmed.

Runes appear in my mind's eye, and I form them carefully, composing a kind of sentence. Anything too aggressive will cause the spell to bite me, with potentially fatal consequences. I extend the magic outwards, blending it with the spell that binds me. I slip out of the binding like an eel.

I breathe a sigh of relief; I am free.

"That was well done," a voice comments. I spin towards the speaker's direction.

She gradually becomes visible: a woman, an ancient woman, and one like no other I have ever seen. She could be centuries old. Her physiognomy suggests an Indian origin; her skin is dark and wrinkled. She's wearing a sari decorated in bright colours.

"Who are you?"

"My name is Roshika. I already know who you are, Kaylin."

"You're the one who sent me the White Book?"

"And the Black Book, too. Did you think it a coincidence that you found it here?"

"No. So you've been following me for how long? Years?"

"Ever since I sensed your power growing."

"Are you... like me?" I've never met another witch. Diana's powers have always been very different from mine, and even Leo is not like me. Meeting another witch feels terrific, but at the same time, frightening.

As if sensing my thoughts, she smiles. I notice she still has most of her teeth, but not all.

"Yes, I am a witch, like you. You have a lot to learn."

"Why did you cast that binding spell? Was it to catch intruders? Or to verify my identity?"

"It was a test, and you passed it."

"I'm embarrassed I didn't see it beforehand."

"I went through a lot of effort to conceal it; I did not expect you to sense it. I wanted to know if you could think on your feet, even when you are completely trapped. You showed quick thinking and a strong under-standing of the magic."

"Thanks."

"Now follow me! There is much you have to learn."

"Will you teach me spells from the White Book?"

"Yes. In time, you will progress to the Red Book as well."

"What's that?"

"You will learn when the time is right. For now, I want you to con-centrate on the Glamour."

I reach out, trying to see past the web of magic that surrounds this place. I sense the edges of something murky, and with a whispered word and gesture, I part the veil away. Above us, the entrance to a cave lies open.

"Good. Follow me."

We walk a disused path, climbing over the more difficult sections. The cave is only a small fraction of the way up, but I am exhausted by the time we reach it.

"Is there no—" I pause, breathing hard, "—no way to land a Q-car in the cave?"

"A Q-car could get in. A plane wouldn't."

"How come you aren't tired?"

"I've been doing this trek a long time; I have lived centuries."

"Wait; what? How old are you?"

"I was born in the year 2000, which makes me just over five hundred years old."

I can barely believe it. "But you're not an immortal—surely we don't live that long?"

"I have been using White Magic to repair the damage caused to my body by ageing. I am one of the oldest witches to have ever lived, but I was the last witch remaining until you. You are the first witch born in centuries."

"So you've lived this long to do what exactly? Keep the flame burning? Pass the baton?"

"Yes and yes."

"Way to put pressure on me."

She only smiles. "You can handle it; I wouldn't have chosen you otherwise. Now pay attention to what you are about to see."

We enter the cave, and for a moment, I am speechless. I wasn't sure what to expect. An ice cave? A dark, neolithic cave with hand-painted murals? But no. The inside of the cavern contains giant, gleaming crystals. Some are ruby red; others emerald green; and many in colours too fantastic for the eye to believe—violent purple, icy blue, and one crystal that is black as a demon's conscience. It is the largest of the crystals and grows right in the middle.

"What is this place?" I breathe.

"These are the crystal caverns. My home."

"If you don't mind me pointing out the obvious—what are all the big crystals for?"

"The big crystals," she says, arching her brow, "are to contain, amplify, and tap into magic. Use your sense to explore them."

I don't think she's referring to my sense of smell. I reach out with my mind, probing into the crystals, finding a vast current of magic—a river, or a raging waterfall, especially around the black crystal.

"So much magic..."

"Precisely. The magic we normally use—the magic demons use—is based upon our power. We witches will always be at a disadvantage compared to immortals; their bodies are capable of much greater feats of magic. But there are some things we can do to turn the tables. Magic exists in nature, and we can tap it—with the right tools."

"So, I can't just use the power of a storm as Diana can?"

"Diana is not like you. Her power is demonic in origin."

Michael told me as much, but I guess I still had my doubts.

"So it's true?"

"It is. You must have figured it out once you met more Familiars."

"Yes, but they're not like demons—"

"No buts. A similar process creates all your Familiars—demonic magic escapes through the weakened Barrier and contaminates the beings here on Earth. Some humans develop mutations that allow them to use demonic magic; that makes them more attractive to the magic, which naturally coalesces around them."

"But Diana and Shadow aren't evil."

"No. It is intent that makes people good or bad; magic just is."

I breathe a small sigh of relief. "So that man we met in the Barracks—"

"He was just a bad apple. Michael is an example of a demon with a conscience. What he did will never be erased. But it is always possible to choose better."

I nod solemnly. "Will you teach me how to use these crystals?"

"Yes. In addition to the magic of the Books, it will give you a fighting chance."

A loud CAW suddenly interrupts our conversation; Roshika rolls her eyes. "Marten again," she explains.

"Who is Marten?"

"He is my pet raven. You saw him a couple of minutes ago, though he did not introduce himself to you. Marten, come meet Kaylin."

As if understanding the command, a raven flies down from the roof of the cave, settling on her shoulder. The corvid eyes me with interest.

"Marten, meet Kaylin."

"Is the bird sentient?"

"Sentient? Definitely. Can he talk to you? Well, almost."

The creature ruffles its feathers, almost as if offended.

"Sorry," I say meekly. Marten perks up, and then I feel it—a telepathic presence, a hint of personality. There are no words, but I grasp a sense of... approval? Amusement?

"We can talk to animals telepathically?"

"If you can call it talking. You are communicating with Marten telepathically. Make no mistake about that—but although he can understand human language, he cannot formulate a reply into words."

"Do all ravens have this capability?"

"It varies. Marten is a particularly intelligent example of the corvid family."

The raven seems pleased at the compliment.

"Come with me; there's more."

****

We walk to a room above the cave, which is pleasantly illuminated by large windows. The walls are stone, but this is masonry, not a natural formation. The room is sparse: there is a chair, a table, and not much else.

"This is a room I use for practice and meditation. I want you to learn more magic from the White Book."

"But what am I supposed to heal?"

"I will show you in a moment. Give me the Book." She takes the book, draws a rune, mumbles a spell, and produces a knife. She makes a small incision on her finger, dribbling the blood on the cover. The Book seems to glow for a moment, then the aura subsides.

"You may access all of the spells now. I will bring you Cassandra, who has not been eating for a while."

I don't even bother to ask what Cassandra is (this woman clearly loves her animals). Instead, I begin familiarising myself with the spells in the book. I've only just scratched the surface; this book is enormous, and there is a spell for nearly every kind of illness: various cancers, auto-immune diseases, infections—even acne.

Roshika returns with a snake wrapped around her arms.

"Meet Cassandra, my female ball python." The snake seems almost sleepy. Its skin has a beautiful pattern of orange stripes on a black background.

"How long has she not been eating?"

"About a month. I tried feeding her live prey—she particularly savours New York sewer rats—but to no avail."

"New York sewer rats? I thought New York was a burnt-out husk?"

"Teleportation magic works wonders. How do you think I sent you the Book?"

"But why New York sewer rats? What on Earth gave you the idea?"

"I lived there for a while when the city still stood. I always thought the rats were particularly well-grown and plump."

"Right. Let me get to work."

She transfers the snake over to me, who coils around my arm. I pet the animal, more in confusion than anything, as I have no idea how to handle reptiles. I look up a spell for metabolic illnesses like diabetes.

I reach out with my mind, mumbling the words of the spell and drawing runes on the snake's head. My consciousness expands to encompass the reptile's body. Theoretically, I know how medicine is supposed to work—it's all about enzymes and receptors, and chemistry. But the magic is nothing like that. Instead, it's more about *sensations* and *ideas*. The snake feels cold, discouraged, and too tired to live.

"How old is this snake?"

"Cassandra is 52 years old, which is quite old, even for a python."

"She's older than me, dammit. Are you sure you want me to perform this spell?"

"There is no harm if you do, and no harm if you don't."

I refocus my attention on the spell. Patterns dance in my mind's eye, and with them, I feel *warmth* and *life* and desire. The magic tingles against my fingers; the snake seems to grow warm, then gradually cool again. Cassandra seems to brighten up and starts exploring me with her tongue. I gently pry the snake away from my neck.

"I guess that did the trick?"

"Yes, well done. The spell you used is moderately advanced magic, though not too difficult."

"Do you have any other pets?"

"Newt is my spider—"

"Do you have any mammals?"

"You can try and make friends with Daimon, my cat. He does not like strangers, so you'll have your work cut out."

"Just great."

"Cheer up, Kaylin. You're only just getting started with magic; there are many feats magic can accomplish that technology can still only dream of."

"Like what? Bringing back the dead? Healing brain injuries? Giant fireballs?"

"Healing brain injuries is advanced, difficult magic, but it is possible; I once healed a woman in a catatonic state. Fireballs are rather trivial. As for bringing back the dead, do not attempt it! I have healed people whose hearts stopped beating—cardiac death—but go further, and you need necromancy."

"What's wrong with necromancy?"

"It is a horrible cruelty to bring back any living creature as an animated corpse. Moreover, necromantic magic is inherently unstable, with many devastating unintended consequences. Just don't even think about it."

I mull her words in silence. Outside, the sun has dropped below the mountains, casting an iridescent twilight across the landscape. The snow, bright silver in the shadows, is glazed in fuchsia, where the light peeks through. I wonder how a human being can survive to be alone all these years—decades, centuries perhaps? —and remain sane. A landscape like this surely helps, but I suspect Roshika is mad as a bat. I smile. The crazy old lady may be mad, but she is mighty and wise.

I stretch and leave the room. I've made a mental list of what I need to do; it isn't really in order.

1. Learn powerful magic juju.

2. Save the world.

3. Find that damn cat.

Chapter Nineteen: Diplomacy

Conall

Kaylin's men fly me and Mark's uncle to Spain. I am told that Eoin has volunteered to work for a hospital in Madrid; he brought his life savings with him in cash.

Mother, on the other hand, has procured for herself a villa just outside of Madrid. I've no idea how she did it, but nothing surprises me when it comes to mother. We left Ireland in the morning; it is now noon.

The aircraft lands on a strip of bare earth. In many ways, the villa is just what I expected—built in the Roman style, with terracotta roof shingles, white plaster, and four walls surrounding a courtyard. Yet in the distance, I see mountains covered in thick forest, and I even spot a dusting of snow on the taller peaks. Mother mentioned the villa was near to the Manzanares mountains, just south of Cercedilla.

This place feels rustic but hides a hint of wildness.

"Welcome home, darling," my mother says, smiling in her white dress. "Bienvenido."

"Buenos días to you too, Mother. How are you? Did everyone make it here in one piece?"

"Your father has found the move most difficult. Your *acquaintance* Jake has adapted quite well, on the other hand—he has befriended the resident cat and even your husky, Minnie."

"How diplomatic of you to call him that, Mother."

"Diplomacy is essential. Besides, any other word would have sounded rude. What would you prefer? Whore? Player? Fuckboy?"

"I never actually had sex with him."

"But he was dishonest about his intentions and tried to take advantage of you in a moment of grief. Do not forget that."

I brush past her, making my way into the central courtyard. "Your bedroom is to the left," she tells me.

I open a sliding door and examine my new home away from home. The room's terracotta tiled floor is warm and welcoming; the walls are white, and a skylight bathes the room in light. The ceiling, I notice, is made from dark wood.

A cat is sleeping on the bed. I stroke the feline on the head, and he responds with a low purr but does not otherwise acknowledge me. Looks like I'm sharing the bed. For a moment, I lie back, trying to figure out how I ended up here and what life holds in store for me next. I had it all planned out—I would graduate from the Lyceum and get a cushy, well-paid job in the Party ranks. Instead, my boyfriend is in Hell, and I'm a political asylum seeker in what is (officially, at least) a communist country.

I hear barking and laughing; I recognise it as belonging to Jake and Minnie. I find them playing in the courtyard. Jake is throwing a Frisbee, which Minnie loyally catches and returns. He's wearing medium-length shorts and a long-sleeved shirt, open at the chest. I've never seen him wear white before—only black and variations thereof.

For a moment, I simply watch him. Is he a changed man? Does sadness lurk beneath that visage of carefree happiness? Does fear touch his soul whenever he is alone? Or am I simply a fool taken in by his dark-haired beauty?

I catch the Frisbee in mid-air; Minnie looks at it expectantly. I throw it hard.

"Hello, Jake."

"Hola!"

"Don't bother with the happy greetings. I'm not really in the mood."

"Ah, so this is one of those talks."

"How is Spain treating you? Is life pleasant for the political refugee? Have you debauched yourself yet?"

"Your mother makes life much easier, for which I am grateful. I've been eyeing some of the maids—who are so very cute—and I've already made out with Fernando. Spaniards aren't shy, let me tell you."

"Glad to hear it," I say sarcastically.

"But that's not really what this is about, is it? I'm sorry about your boyfriend, by the way."

In a blink of an eye, I tackle him, slamming him down against the ground. He is too surprised to resist.

"Is that insincerity I sense in your words, Jake? Should I have left you to burn in that sordid mansion?"

"I—No. Conall, you probably saved my life. The Party wants me dead. And I recognise that my actions were unethical, base, foolish. I really do want you to get your boyfriend back; I want you to be happy."

"Really?"

"You've been unhappy for a long time; I think you deserve better."

I relax, letting him catch his breath. We look at each other in the eye.

"What did you do to piss of the Party, anyway?"

"Nothing in particular, really. Let's just say my family doesn't support the new Prime Minister, or Taoiseach as you Irish call him."

"So it was politically motivated murder?"

"Maybe murder, maybe a warning. I am not welcome in Ireland anymore."

"But why come with us to Spain? Don't you have family in England?"

"Ah, it's not so simple, you see. My parents are already on the political shitlist as it is—things have been harder; business deals haven't panned out. The English government has always had a complicated relationship with the Irish Party, so Ireland was a reasonably safe haven until now. But the new taoiseach has the support of the English government."

"So you could be walking from the frying pan into the fire."

"Precisely. Moreover, it would cause a diplomatic incident. My parents basically told me to grab whatever I could and fuck off. They've tolerated my bad grades and behaviour until now because they could afford it, but no longer."

"Your parents disowned you because you would be putting them in danger otherwise?"

"They haven't disowned me—they've smuggled me some bonds—but my financial situation has deteriorated considerably."

"You've never had to live with nothing but the clothes on your back. Normal people don't have bonds—they have to sell their labour to capitalists to make a living. It sucks."

"You sound like a communist."

"And you sound like a spoilt brat."

"Touché."

We do not speak for a moment; the silence stretches on. I go through Jake's words carefully, trying to understand his situation and the importance of what he is telling me.

"So the new taoiseach—Big Brother—"

"I understand the new leader doesn't like that particular epithet. He wants to change it."

"So, the new guy running the party is supported by the English government?"

"Yes. The Brits have wanted an ally in the Irish, particularly since the Scots have their own priorities, limiting English power within the European League of Nations. The death of Big Brother seemed like the perfect way to change the régime."

"That probably explains why this new guy has been able to consolidate his power so quickly—he has outside help."

"Is it true your boyfriend killed Big Brother? Your mother told me, but, well, I couldn't quite believe it."

"He did. If Lucifer gets out, he could conquer the whole world, and no one would be there to stop him."

"Nukes and plasma cannons won't?"

"You saw what Michael did to those Q-cars, and Mark is even stronger than his dad."

Jake whistles.

"Thanks for telling me all this," I begin. "I want to discuss this new development with Mother. It might help negotiations with the Spanish government."

"Officially, the ELN forbids Member States from interfering in each other's constitutions. That's why the Spanish are reluctant to intervene—but if you can prove the English government has been meddling in Irish affairs, it would delegitimise the new taoiseach and make the Spanish more likely to act. It might also make the other states more sympathetic to the Spanish if word got out."

"Ah, Jake. You're really not dumb, even if you have terrible grades."

"Thank you for the compliment," he says mirthfully. I slap him across the shoulder blades playfully.

"Have you met the cat?" I ask.

"El Presidente? How could I not?"

"Is that his name?"

"In English, I call him President Meow."

"But why?" I ask him.

He only chuckles. "You'll find out soon enough."

****

I meet Mother as the sun is setting. She has foregone her white dress— which was uncharacteristically casual—for a blue suit. She's clearly meeting someone.

"Meeting with the Spanish government?" I ask.

"Yes."

"Can I come with? I want to share some information about who is backing the new taoiseach—incorporate it into our strategy."

"I already know, dear. But you should come with me. You will learn a great deal. Have you been practising your Spanish?"

"I've been doing my best."

"It will have to do."

A Q-car flies in and lands in front of the villa—I realise it must belong to the government. I settle on the bench next to my mother; the pilot is the only other person inside. In an instant, the Q-car is away, though our airspeed is pretty low: Madrid lies just a handful of kilometres away.

The city gradually fades into view. Dublin is not a small city, at more than one and a half million residents, but Madrid's population is more than quadruple. It's a true metropolis to rival Berlin, Paris, or London. The Q-car lowers its altitude, treating us to an aerial tour of the city: we see the Plaza Mayor, alongside medieval and Renaissance architecture; but equally, the city is built to modern fashions. Many buildings have garden roofs and solar panels (apparently, Spain is less polluted than Ireland).

The Q-car approaches a large complex, which at first glance, resembles a beautifully laid-out garden. A body of water, perfectly flat and painted crimson by the setting sun, surrounds a building with marble columns. Numerous visitors enjoy lush grass.

Nothing in my country compares to this. It was possible to visit Big Brother's tower in the Upper Quarter, but only for higher Classes, and the taoiseach was rarely actually there. But here we are to meet the government in a *public building*—not an underground bunker! It's hard for me to comprehend.

We are not greeted by a security team but rather by a man wearing a fashionable white suit. His eyes are warm and brown, and he sports a well-groomed beard.

He's also wearing a cap with a red star, which I have never seen anyone wear before.

"Buenos días señora Sianna. Mi nombre es Javier. ¿Quien es el señorito?"

"Me llamo Conall, y Sianna es mi Madre," I say helpfully.

"Será un placer atenderle," he says, shaking my hand.

"Does anyone here speak English?" I ask my mother.

"They have translators. Mariano speaks English fluently."

"The Spanish prime minister?"

"Yes, as do some of his cabinet members and officials. I expect the conversation will be held in English and translated to Spanish for a handful of other politicians."

"So, they really have democracy in this country?" I whisper, eyeing our escort. He is a safe distance in front.

"Not officially. Sort of. It's more than what we have in Ireland—we haven't had even a sham election in ten years. They have honest elections here, but it's mainly for mayors, regional government, the autonomous community of Catalunya, and so on. The Communist Party still controls the national government. The system seems to work for them."

"Aside from Mariano, do you know who else we're meeting?"

"General Francisco is his right-hand man. He's a clever one—watch out for him."

We proceed to a room where several men and a few women sit next to a round table. It's not a long table like in a boardroom—it's round like in Camelot. A sturdy man with a long mane of blond hair is carefully examining us.

"Hello, and good day, Mariano."

"It is nice to see you again, Sianna. And who is this?"

"I'm Conall."

"My son," Sianna explains quickly. "I believe he understands the entity we are dealing with very well. May we sit down?"

"Yes, of course."

We take two empty chairs next to Mariano. I've never been this close to a head of state before, and I didn't think I ever would be—only the most senior Party figures ever met with Big Brother. Things are different here.

"The situation is rapidly evolving," Sianna explains. A woman with tightly cropped hair is standing in the corner of the room, translating. Mother pauses after each sentence to give her time. (It's a courtesy I've never seen her show to anyone.)

"The old Party leader, known colloquially as Big Brother—" this elicits an amused chuckle from them—"is dead, and the new leader, following several assassinations, has succeeded in gaining power."

"We already know the Party kills unofficially," Mariano interrupts.

"And we've known for a long time," another man adds. This must be General Francisco, the brilliant strategist Mother just told me about. He doesn't look older than thirty-five.

"Yes, but did you know he has support from the English government?"

There is a noticeable silence in the room.

"I thought not."

"When did you learn of this?" Mariano asks.

"Recently."

"Why are the English supporting this new Taoiseach? Do they know about the rebels? I thought they stayed out of Irish affairs."

"Not from what I've heard. The English government is notoriously anti-communist—"

"An understatement," General Francisco interrupts. "We consider the English our worst enemy."

"But in this case, I suspect they don't know; they support this taoiseach because he shares their priorities within the European League of Nations. The English want another ally—they are isolated."

"That's a state of affairs we worked hard to achieve. We exploited the French contempt and the German antipathy so that the English wouldn't be able to spread their ideology, which we see as directly hostile to our interests," Francisco says.

"In which case, you surely see the wisdom of supporting Ireland's incipient communist movement?"

"I didn't say that. Your suggestion carries considerable risks. It would damage our relations with the other European states if word ever got out. Moreover, it's not the first time we've supported our "comrades" abroad, only for them to turn into monsters once they got hold of power.

Remember Romania? It took us years of diplomacy and hard work to topple the brutal regime we helped to power."

What about Kaylin? I whisper to my mother. She nods.

"I understand your concerns, and in truth, I wondered the same thing. But another entity can obtain power in Ireland."

"Who?" Mariano asks. "And why didn't you mention it before?"

"It's... complicated. I didn't think you would believe me. But Conall can explain—he knows them better."

I clear my throat nervously; they are all looking at me. "A woman named Kaylin runs a well-funded, well-organised clandestine organisation. They want to topple the Party, and they're working alongside the Communists to do it."

"Interesting," Mariano comments. "Do you think they can beat the Party and run the country?"

"They are very technocratic. But they are also very effective—they killed Big Brother."

"Really? We heard rumours, but we didn't know what to believe. Stories about men with wings and top-secret EMP weapons. Do you actually know what happened?" Francisco asks sceptically.

"I do; I was directly involved."

The silence is so perfect. You could hear a pin drop.

"What? How? You never mentioned this, Sianna," Mariano says.

"I wasn't going to tell you everything I knew, was I?" Mother responds coolly.

"I can't tell you how exactly they accomplished the feat," I say. "I'm also not sure if this group can do it again. The new Taoiseach has caught on. He will be better protected this time."

General Francisco is scrutinizing me carefully, I notice.

"We will need time to adapt our strategy. You've thrown us a bombshell," he says.

"I agree," Mariano adds. "We will speak again. Thank you for the audience, Sianna and Conall."

We leave the room and exit the building. The evening air is fresh on my skin.

"So do they believe me? Will they help defeat the Party?" I ask.

"They believe you. Francisco, of course, is suspicious. He is always suspicious, and since you didn't mention Mark and Michael, that gives him a reason to pay extra attention. Something is clearly missing from your account—but they'll never figure out what. Who has faith in the supernatural? Certainly not these men, who are proud of their rationality and lack of superstition."

"Was I... okay?"

Mother smiles. "You were good. I'm proud of you."

Well, that's not something I get to hear every day.

"So what do you think motivates the Spanish government?" Mother asks.

"They don't seem too keen on regime change, fighting oppression, or helping their comrades fight for the cause."

"You're right," Sianna agrees, a twinkle in her eye.

"So I'm guessing this is really about the English. They don't want the English government to have an extra ally as this upsets the balance of power."

"Precisely. Perhaps those lessons did you some good after all."

"Nothing in the Lyceum prepared me for real negotiations," I complain. "That was pretty intense."

"Negotiating is a skill you develop with practice, dear. It's not something you learn in a classroom. Given enough time, I am sure you will become a skilled negotiator."

"If I live," I mutter darkly.

Chapter Twenty: A Deadly Plot

Mark

I used to think that Hell was an ugly place, devoid of life, beauty, and light. Now I realise that Hell is beautiful in its own right: it is a place of darkness, but here, the light shines brightest; it is sharp as obsidian, precious as gold. But a cage, even a gilded one, is still a cage.

Can I get out? Is it even possible? I pose the question to Steijn, who asks Javalook.

"No," the imp explains simply. "It would be difficult for an imp; it is impossible for a demon or a human. Lucifer can shut the gates whenever he wants, and he knows who is using them. An imp might brave the Cauldron and evade the firelings—which is not something you can attempt."

"Can't I fly through the opening—"

"Lucifer would stop you instantly. Do you really think something that obvious would ever work?"

I pace around my bedroom like an enraged bull.

"Well fuck it, I have no idea what to do."

"Might I make a suggestion?" Javalook asks.

"Go on; I'm out of ideas."

"Why not destroy the Infernal Cup? It would send a clear message to Lucifer, and it would hamper some of his designs."

"Shahar told me it's just a tool—"

"But an important tool."

"This isn't a permanent solution."

"There are no permanent solutions; you can only resist."

"Wait. What about the dragon?"

Steijn and Javalook share a glance. "You don't want to meet the dragon," Steijn says.

"The dragon kills demons on sight," Javalook explains. "Also, how do you plan on getting to meet him? It's the same problem: gates, wards, and firelings."

"Doesn't he live in a cave? Can't we, I dunno, tunnel?"

"He does live in a cave, but you need to cross the Cauldron to reach it. You'd need to tunnel through several kilometres of rock otherwise."

"Can't you get a message across? I want to talk to the dragon if I can't meet him."

"I doubt the dragon would be pleased to see us. He would probably just eat us," Javalook says.

"Technology can't do it? Magic?"

"The dragon doesn't own a com phone," Stein points out.

"Nor do I know any magical means," Javalook adds.

I sigh, deflated. "Fine. Then we destroy this stupid Cup."

"Got it. Talk to Shahar; he will explain what you need to do. I'll meet with my friends," Javalook begins.

"You sure this won't leak to Lucifer?"

"We imps know how to keep a secret. We don't tell Lucifer everything—and he doesn't suspect a thing. Trust us." With that, the little creature vanishes from the room.

****

I find Shahar in his study, as usual. He's reading a complicated-looking tome on the arcane arts; his cat, Naem, is nowhere to be seen.

"I need your help."

"What for?" he asks without missing a beat.

"I want to destroy the Infernal Cup." No point beating around the bush.

He stills. "I see. What you want will not be easy, nor will it solve all your problems. Indeed, it might cause a lot of new problems. Are you prepared for that?"

"Yes," I reply without hesitation.

"I will not be able to convince you otherwise, so I shall help you against my better judgement. To begin with, you will need a distraction."

"I figured as much, but why?"

"The Infernal Cup is held in the Arsenal, a room containing Lucifer's most powerful spells and artefacts. It is, naturally, glamoured, and warded."

"Can you teach me how to break the wards?"

"Break them? Normally I'd say a simple demon can't do that, but given your strength, you might succeed. The problem is simple—Lucifer would instantly know."

"So, do you have like... a key?"

"No, only Lucifer can operate the wards like that. However, I can teach you a spell that's more like a safecracker, to use your analogy."

"And this spell will take time?"

"Precisely. Thus, I will also teach you how to create a kind of magical bomb, which will serve as a distraction."

"It won't hurt anyone, will it?"

"No, it's more like the magical equivalent of an EMP than an explosive. It will burn some lamps, that's all."

"That still leaves the million-euro question: how do I destroy the Cup?"

"The million *denarius* question, you mean?" he asks, smiling.

I never really paid too much attention to the currency they used in Hell: if I needed anything, I asked for it, and I got it.

"But yes. Destroying the Cup is probably the easiest part of this whole equation—I will teach you some suitable destruction spells."

"Can't I just hit it? Fry it with a fireball? Throw it in the Cauldron?"

"It's a powerful demonic artefact; you can't destroy it *that* easily. You will need a formal spell, albeit not a very complex one."

"Okay, so I need to start studying."

"I am glad you understand. I want you to practice for at least two days to make sure you get it right. I will erect a spell around the tower to block stray magical energy—otherwise, Lucifer will know what magic you're using. As it is, I recommend avoiding him during this period."

"He can smell the magic on me."

"Is that how he put it?"

"Yeah. He said it tasted like pine needles and sunshine."

Shahar chuckles. "Lucifer is poetic like that."

"I'll talk to Steijn and the demons; you set up the spell. See you later."

****

We are five in total: there's me, Steijn, Javalook, Pip, and one other imp who, apparently, is named Beelzebub. I thought it was a joke, but no. There aren't any demons at our co-conspirator meeting: I briefly considered letting Max in on the plan but immediately rejected the idea. I can't trust a demon with this, not even brave Max.

"So, what's the plan? Why have you brought me here?" Beelzebub asks.

"We're going to destroy the Infernal Cup."

"Well, that's sure to piss off Lucifer, and it will put a dent in some of his plans. But how do you plan on accomplishing this?"

"I'm going to make some kind of magical bombs, plant them all over Hell, and detonate them at the agreed time. Then I storm the Arsenal and destroy the cup. You guys act as my lookouts."

"You're going to plant the magical fireworks? You know you're a celebrity, right? Everyone has their eye on you," Beezelbub points out.

I have to admit I didn't think of that.

"I agree," Pip says. "You should get someone else to do it for you."

"Will you do it for me?"

"We can manage," Javalook agrees.

"I want to help too," Steijn interrupts.

"I don't want you to put yourself in danger—"

"I'm putting myself in danger as it is."

"I agree with Steijn," Beezelbub interrupts. "Besides, a human can be of some use. Hell is designed for big humans with long arms, not for little imps like us."

"Javalook? Pip? What do you think?"

"It's not the worst idea I've heard," Pip comments.

"If Steijn wants to help, let him help. I won't stand in the way," Javalook agrees. "Let's go over the rest of your plan. How do you plan on storming the Citadel?"

"Shahar will teach me a bunch of spells for disarming the wards, going past the glamour, and destroying the Cup."

"Have you scouted the area? Are you sure no one will be there?"

"No."

"More work for us," Pip comments. "Let's get busy, boys. See you later, Mark."

I nod in acknowledgement, and the three imps bound away.

****

Steijn is stalking back and forth across my room.

"You don't have to do this, you know," I tell him.

"You're treating me like a child."

"You're seventeen."

"And you're not my brother."

"No, but I love you like one."

He stops. "You do? *Echt?*"

"Yeah, *zeker.*"

"And you even paid attention when I tried to teach you Dutch."

"I'm still hopeless at it."

He comes towards me. "No, you aren't. Damn, I—"

"Please don't make this a declaration of love. Before you ask," I interrupt him, "I think of you more like a hot younger brother I would bang.

But I'm still very much in love with Conall. Maybe, if we survive all this, you'll get to see Earth—and meet my boyfriend."

"I would very much like that. Do you think he would be open to a threesome?"

I pause, thinking. "Conall is pretty adventurous in the bedroom. I think he would."

He wraps his arms around me, kissing me on the cheek.

"That's enough love talk," I say huskily. "Get ready. You still have to live through this shit."

"And if I don't, I die remembering you."

"Don't say that."

"I'm not afraid of death. But you're right: we need to get this show on the road. I'll see you again in two days, right?"

"Yes, once I've perfected my spellcraft to Shahar's satisfaction."

"*Veel succes.* See you then."

****

"Inlusio is the rune you want against glamour, combined with *veritas*, which means—"

"Truth. Yeah, I get it."

"My, you have been practising," Shahar comments. "I will create a glamour, and you will try the spell against it."

The old scholar draws three runes in a triangle in the middle of the room. A larger triangle forms three points at the edges of the room; that's the spell he's using to conceal magic, which works a lot like a glamour does, from what I understand.

I focus on the smaller triangle. A house appears above it. Not, not just a house: a villa, surrounded by trees, mountains, and a stream. The stream burbles gently, and I can even feel the wind and smell the faint tang of ocean salt.

"This is amazing, Shahar."

"It is nothing that Lucifer cannot recreate. Pay attention."

I form the two runes in my mind's eye, naming them: *Inlusio, you are a cruel illusion, and veritas, you are truth, honesty, substance.*

My consciousness seems to expand and stretch. I feel the glamour like a cape, a rippling being of magic. I snuff it out like a candle. Instantly, the villa disappears.

"Good. Only two spells left to learn. Let's move onto the bomb spell: you need to know the words aphanizo, phronesis, and *fulmen.*"

"Aphanizo, phronesis, and fulmen?" I say, trying to pronounce the Greek words.

"Yes. It means destruction, prudence, and lightning, though the Greek is difficult to translate. You must inscribe the runes on these stones," he says, gesturing to a bunch of rounded, flat stones.

"Okay. How are we going to test the spell?"

"I will create a ward in the centre; you must place the stone there."

I nod. The scholar draws another series of runes, and I concentrate, burning the spell's names on a stone. He motions at me when he's ready.

I place the stone, then activate the spell. There is a kind of fizzing and flashing, but nothing spectacular.

"It didn't work," he says. "Try again. Remember the intent behind each rune. You are trying to cause *controlled destruction* using lightning."

I nod and try again, this time paying more attention to each rune. When I place the stone in the triangle this time, it explodes in a flash of blue lightning. The ward glows, containing the magical energy.

"That will do. Now for the final spell: I recommend using *apoleia,* though the Hebrew *Abad* will also do the job."

"Apoleia? But *abad* sounds catchier."

He smiles. "As you wish. I'll ward this stone; you must destroy it."

He draws a series of runes on one of the flat stones and holds it out to me.

"You sure this won't fry you too?"

"You can control it; I am confident in you."

I am pleased by his trust in me. Concentrating on the stone, I whisper the word: *Abad*, willing it to destroy, to annihilate.

The stone seems to just... implode. It's as if it never existed.

"Wow. I expected fire, sparks, or for you to shatter the stone. But you are on another level."

"Thanks," I say, beaming with pride.

"Don't get cocky. I want you to practice."

"I promise."

"And good luck."

Chapter Twenty-One: Operation Rolling Thunder

Kaylin

"Pay attention," she orders. "You must mend the wing correctly. Otherwise, the bird will suffer further injury."

The bird is small and colourful. I believe it's a blue-fronted redstart, though I don't know much about birds. Roshika wanted me to fix her broken wing.

"This is like, the ninth animal you've asked me to heal? I'm tired of being a wildlife hospital. I want to heal people. There's a man, John—"

"Who is in a coma, I know. But I will not allow you to attempt complex healing until you've mastered more basic healing magic, even if it means helping ten animals or a hundred. His condition is stable; he will survive a few more months."

"But we might not *have* that long. I place my men in peril by staying here with you. At least teach me some more offensive magic."

Her wizened, wrinkled face curls up into a frown. "I do not like introducing a witch as inexperienced as you to the Red Book... but the circumstances are exceptional, and you've proven yourself highly able. Very well. Finish with the bird and follow me."

I refocus on the spell, taking care to make sure the bones align correctly. Roshika is right, of course: an improperly healed wing can put stress on the joint, break ligaments and connective tissue, and put the bird in great pain.

After a few minutes, I finish up. The bird chirps happily, and I feel her consciousness: a small, energetic mind, always focused on food. She wants to get back to her mate, which makes me smile. I wave as she flies away.

I find Roshika in a small, dark room, which is adjacent to the cave. She is thumbing through a large volume that sits on a pedestal. As I get closer, I see that it has a red cover; it very much resembles blood. It wouldn't surprise me if it *were* blood.

"No, it's not blood," she says.

"Did you read my mind?"

"Nope. There was no need."

"So you *can* read minds?"

"In a manner of speaking. I can pick up on emotions, stray thoughts, that sort of thing. To rifle through someone's thoughts, I need a blood link and a spell."

"Can demons do it?"

"No, it's not possible. Mind control is likewise challenging and impractical; Lucifer has never bothered."

"Good to know."

"This is the Red Book, and it contains the most dangerous spells available to witches."

"Speaking of demons," I ask, my curiosity piqued, "can they do what we do? Does Lucifer know about the books?"

"Most demons lack the skill and training to accomplish what a good witch can do. Lucifer, naturally, knows all about the books. He even created some of the spells in here."

"Wait; *what*?"

"Oh, come on, did it never cross your mind? How do you think the first demon came about?"

"I have no idea." I had never even paused to consider it.

"He was a witch, Kaylin."

"There are no male witches—" I protest.

"Of course there are. You're working with outdated terminology and insufficient data. It's true: most witches are female. But Lucifer was not only a witch; he was the very best."

The world seems to spin around me. All this time and I never asked myself this question? But then, I had too many other mysteries to ponder. The more I uncover about magic, the more I realise how little I know.

"How did he become a demon?" I ask.

She quirks her mouth in a grim imitation of a smile. "Even after all these years, I don't know the full story. I've been able to piece together a few pieces, but not the whole puzzle."

"Can you tell me what you know?"

"I will, but not now. You need to focus on your magic first; this is too distracting."

I nod, understanding. "OK. Back to the Red Book then. What kind of spells are in there, specifically?"

"There is a fireball spell on the first page." She shrugs. "Even simple fireballs do the job sometimes. Then there are the stronger spells, the darker ones. Blood runes. Death spells."

"Is there such a thing as *avada kedavra*?"

She raises an eyebrow all the eye up to her forehead. "I had no idea people still read that in the 26th century."

"I found some old books," I explain sheepishly.

"You're correct, but there is an important caveat. A death spell kills mortals instantly; it cannot kill immortals. The protection charm is easy, but you must always be on your guard. When you face a demon, you should have it active at all times."

"Anything else I should be worried about?"

"You too can cast death spells. But you must always use the protection charm, because otherwise—"

"The spell would kill me too?"

"Precisely."

"And the blood magic? What about that?"

"I hope you never have to use it... but I will teach you the spells, knowing you might need to. Blood magic is essentially using the power of others to bolster your own."

"That doesn't sound so bad."

"And it isn't, necessarily. It can give you the edge to prevail over a much stronger demon. But it can easily turn you into a bloodthirsty murderer; the temptation of all that living power is a huge one. Even if you don't intend to kill, it is tricky magic, and humans die more often than you think."

"What about using demons?"

"Doesn't work. Demons are not really *alive* in a way that allows you to use blood magic on them; they are divine, immortal beings, and they're not made from the same stuff as we mortals."

"What about other Familiars?"

"They would be excellent candidates. They're alive but much stronger than a normal human."

"Animals?"

"Too weak to fuss over. Maybe if you slaughtered a whole herd of cattle."

"I get it; it's impractical. Will you teach me the blood magic?"

"Defence from death spells comes first. We'll warm up with some fireballs. Come to the cave."

****

I join her in the crystal cave. She leads me to an area separated from the main cavern by several glowing red crystals. At the centre of this small antechamber lies a circled transcribed with runes.

"Why circles, by the way?"

"They are quite useful for a lot of spells," Roshika explains. "They have no gaps, and they represent infinity. But triangles also work quite well. Heck, I even use the odd pentagram."

"So, you want me to shoot fireballs at the circle?"

"That's pretty much it. The spell will dissipate the fire magic. Are you ready?"

"Yes."

She shows me the shape of the rune, and I draw it in the air, concentrating. I imagine Fire in all its forms: the warm hearth that gives us life in cold winter; the rebirth of forest fires; and the ultimate expression of the element, pure, unbridled destruction.

I feel powerful and alive. No spell has ever made me feel quite like this. Flames materialise in my hands, and with a shove of will, I send a fireball at the circle. It explodes in a shimmer of light.

"Good. That was not going to be difficult. The next spell is not difficult either, but I want you to practise on an animal first."

"Let me guess: another snake?"

"No, a raven friend of Marten. You have to want to protect the animal for the spell to work." She whistles, and, right on cue, two ravens fly into the cavern. I recognise Marten, and with him is another raven. The animal flies down into the circle—I can tell she's feeling nervous. My telepathy has never been so acute.

"The name of the spell I will use is *Nekros*, which means death," Roshika explains. "The protection spell is named *Sanctum*. The spell works differently for individual users—I imagine the cool scales of a powerful snake protecting me, but I expect something else will work for you."

"Let me try."

The word *Sanctum* does not bring to mind any kind of building but rather a meadow, a place in the sunshine where wildflowers grow. A gentle breeze brushes my forehead; the air is thick with pollen and alive with the sound of bees. I'm not sure if I'm imagining it or not.

Roshika whispers the word, *Nekros*, and I smell the magic like the putrid smell of freshly decaying corpses; I feel it like a cold wind on my shoulder, insistent and inescapable. But I imagine that warm meadow, and I trust it to protect the raven.

"You can open your eyes now," Roshika tells me. "You did it right."

"I didn't feel your magic attacking mine," I say.

"No, but Marten's friend is alive, which is proof enough. Anyway, the death spell does not work like that—it isn't like a sledgehammer against your door; it's more like a virus you need to detect. There's no need for raw power."

"How *does* the death spell work? Why is it named in Greek?"

"The spell is more like a... shortcut. It cuts short a living being's life. Against one person, it is a terrifying weapon. Against many people? Not so much."

"Why?"

"The skill and power required to use it increases exponentially when used against many."

"Good to know."

"As for why it is named in Greek," she continues, "that is just a convention; there are variants in Latin and Hebrew as well. Lucifer invented the spell, and he initially named it *Nex*."

The very name makes me shiver. "Why doesn't that surprise me?"

"Remember, it is intent that makes a spell. We name spells, or draw them, to create a functional language."

"When will you teach me how to use the spell?"

"Soon. Be patient. Now, back to healing."

I sigh. How did I know she was going to say that?

****

Diana

It arrived under cover of darkness, at the stroke of midnight, in a shipping container. The container is labelled 'Agricultural produce'—olives, wine, and chorizo, mainly. Hah! The Party had no idea that a ship loaded with deadly weapons got smuggled right under their noses—and to a bunch of ragtag communists, no less. The Spanish, to their credit, planned it meticulously, with a bit of help from Grumman and me.

But Kaylin always warned me: be careful what you wish for. The Communists aren't interested in waiting, planning, conducting espionage—any of that shit. They want to declare war. And they want to start it with a bang.

So we find ourselves meeting at their Letterkenny base. It's a not-particularly-well-concealed concrete building in an industrial park, and it's teeming with fighters.

"They're not trying to be discreet," I say.

"No. The Party has a minimal presence here, and from what Andrew tells me, they've either bribed or assassinated most of the local figures already," Grumman replies.

"So, they already rule this part of the country?"

"Unofficially, perhaps. I have a feeling it won't last."

"The unofficial bit you mean?"

"Exactly."

Several armed men escort us to a bunker. We pass through multiple sensors and X-ray machines, mainly perfunctory, as they can see we're armed. Well, I'm not armed, but then, I *am* a weapon.

"Hello, Grumman and Diana," Andrew, their leader, introduces us. I recognise most of the faces in the room from our first meeting. I catch Leo's eye, hoping to see a friendly face, but he seems anxious.

"Hello, Andrew. I received your communiqué earlier today. We must discuss your plan for *Operation Rolling Thunder*."

"What is there to discuss?" one of the men asks. "We bomb the Party base in Derry. We cripple a decent part of their equipment and put the Party bastards on the defensive."

"The base is next to a populated town. Civilian casualties are likely," Grumman continues.

"We won't shoot civilians," Andrew says defensively. "The bombs—"

"Will kill civilians, perhaps many civilians, despite your best efforts," Grumman interrupts.

"Sometimes, you have to break a few eggs to make an omelette."

Grumman and the Communists have a long argument, which I tune out. It's clear there will be no agreement. I manage to corner Leo alone while they're shouting.

"Leo? You don't look happy. Talk."

"I'm worried this plan is going to go horribly wrong. I'm afraid we'll kill a bunch of innocent people, and that will turn people against us."

"Oh, I agree."

"But where's Kaylin? She might have convinced them. No one is as intimidating as she is."

"Really?"

"She's a tough woman who knows her stuff."

"Kaylin is... away. But she will be back."

"You're not allowed to tell me?"

"I'm allowed to tell you. But there are ears in this building if you get my drift."

"Okay, I understand. But get your boss to come back, will you? We need her."

"Do you mean my people or yours?"

"Both of us are going to be in a considerable amount of trouble without her."

Sometime later, we leave the building, the matter undecided.

"So, do we help them?" I ask.

"We have no choice."

"Don't we? It seems they have enough resources to execute this mission."

"But if we don't help them, they'll cock it up even more. At least this way, we might contain some of the damage."

I consider his argument carefully. "You're right, as much as I don't like it."

"What did Leo say? I saw you talking to him."

"He's worried; he thinks Kaylin should come back."

"I told her not to go. We're already up shit creek without a paddle, and the current is only dragging us deeper."

His words prove themselves prophetic.

****

The lorry makes it to the gates, thanks to some hard work from both our teams. There's no way it'll make it into the compound—for two straight-forward reasons. Firstly, the driver is just a very clever dummy; and Shadow, who had been the real driver, disappeared and hightailed it out of there.

Secondly, the lorry is filled with explosives. Not just any explosives, mind you: there's an anti-field generator on board, a very sophisticated piece of equipment donated by the Spanish. It creates a field that neu-tralises the force field protecting the compound—the explosives just finish the job.

The anti-field ripples out like a bright, electric wave. The bomb goes off a split-second later. The carnage simply cannot be described: there is rubble everywhere, fire, and many dead bodies. The people living on the nearby street no chance—but eggs and omelettes and all that.

Now that they have the initiative, the Communists attack en masse. With a bit of reconnaissance from us, they found a secluded spot in the woods where they hid thousands of men alongside many androids. They roll in on armoured electric cars—modified in secret with additional weapons—and storm the city. The element of surprise is crucial: the Party men outnumber them, but they flounder in confusion, and that puts them at a huge tactical disadvantage.

Blitzkrieg, they named this strategy. A German technique devel-oped in some long-ago war.

Still, this is the Party we're talking about: they're going to have something up their sleeve.

"Warning!" the alarm sounds in my headphones. "Incoming fighter craft!"

I'm sitting in a Q-car overlooking the battle; we're on top of a small hill. Elizabeth, the pilot, is next to me.

"So the Party managed to scramble some Q fighters, eh?" I ask.

"Yes. Our early warning system picked it up. Do you want us to en-gage?"

"Nah. Much as I trust your skills, Liz, we are still outnumbered here. No, let me try something."

"Are you going to call up a storm?"

I smile bleakly. "Something like that."

I've been practising my magic for two months now. I don't think I can summon a full-blown hurricane, but I don't think I need a god-damn hurricane to destroy these Party bastards. I close my eyes; I withdraw deep into myself, probing the air with my consciousness. I try to understand the nature of the wind, the clouds, the distant ocean.

Slowly, I push my power outwards, drawing from the environment. The wind picks up, buffeting the Q-car, but this is just a prelude.

The Q fighters are in sight now, moving fast. Down below, several Communist androids take note of the threat, angling their lasers upwards. As fearsome as those robots are—they've torn down everything that stood in their path—they are a poor solution against airstrikes. Those Q fighters are rapid, well-protected, and the androids are sitting ducks.

I strain, using my power to its fullest. As the clouds grow darker, sweat drips down my forehead. Power floods into me, charging me like a juiced-up capacitor. I've managed to merge the wind and rain into a vortex, and it makes me feel invincible.

I raise my arm, and lightning erupts from the sky, arcing towards the Q fighters. It instantly incinerates the first fighters. The second Q fighter explodes. The third target manages to charge up its shield, but it is scant protection against my magic. It, too, falls from the sky in a burning heap.

"Three Q fighters in under a minute—I'm impressed," Liz comments. "But two more are right behind them."

"I see them."

With one final push, I collect the lightning into a ball. Everyone in Derry—man, woman, and child—cranes their neck to stare. I send the giant ball of lightning towards the Q-fighters; they try and separate, but slowly, far too slowly. In an instant, the lightning ball detonates. Nought remains of the Q fighters but ash and debris.

Dark spots dance in my vision, and I feel myself sagging before I lose consciousness.

****

"Diana? Are you OK?" I recognise the voice as Grumman's. I open my eyes and find Liz, Grumman, and Shadow by my side. Leo is here too.

"How long was I out?"

"A few hours. We've taken Derry; the operation was a success."

"Wonderful."

"Are you feeling alright?"

"I'm feeling much better," I say, standing up. "Casualties?"

"Few, thanks to you," Leo says. "What you did with the lightning... it made me feel like an amateur."

I smile shakily. "You'll get better with practice."

"Don't celebrate yet," Grumman warns me. "We took very few casualties, but there were numerous people caught in the crossfire. Also, the taoiseach knows about our supernatural assets. If he didn't believe the footage of Michael, he's going to believe this."

"Difficult times ahead," I agree. "Now, I better get some more sleep. I need to recuperate my power."

"Did you need to make it so dramatic?" Leo asks.

"No, I didn't. But I wanted the Party to be afraid. We're not playing the nice guy anymore."

Little did I know how right I was.

Chapter Twenty-Two: The Fall

Mark

"Ready?" I ask Steijn, Javalook, and the other imps.

"The question is, are you ready?" Javalook replies. "Have you practised your glamour, de-warding, and destruction spells? Do these bombs work?"

"I tested three of the bombs at random in Shahar's ward chamber. I've been doing the spells against various targets for two days now."

"Good enough," Javalook agrees.

"I trust you," Steijn adds.

"You're a strong demon—one of the strongest I've seen," Pip says.

"Thanks, guys. Let's get this show on the road, eh? Go over the plan with me one more time."

"We will place the bombs in specially chosen locations throughout the Cauldron," Javalook begins. "It will create a pattern that will draw attention away from the Citadel, where the Arsenal lies."

"And you'll contact me telepathically when everything is in place?"

"Precisely. You detonate the bombs, go in, and destroy the Cup."

"Steijn, last chance—"

"I'm going with them."

I nod. "Okay, then move out."

The imps take off, and Steijn strides through the corridor, feigning nonchalance. I walk in the opposite direction, deeper into the Citadel. As a Fallen, my old life helps here: I'm entirely calm, even smiling at some of the demons I know. My insides feel like a tangled knot of worms, and the feeling intensifies when I pass Archdemon Tim (who waggles his eyebrows at me). Yet on the outside, my deception is picture-perfect.

Several tense minutes pass before I try to contact the imps.

Javalook? How's it going?

We've planted a couple of bombs, only a few left to go. Steijn helped us with some of the more difficult parts.

Tell me when you're ready.

I keep smiling and keep walking. Shahar informed me of the Arsenal's exact location inside the Citadel, but obviously, I can't just beeline for it. I need to take a circuitous route; this has to look like a sightseeing trip that just co-incidentally puts me near the Arsenal, located in the underground part of the tower. There are fewer demons here, which is good—it means fewer eyes to watch me—but it also makes me stand out more.

Okay. Done. Moving out.

Thanks, Javalook.

I reach out, expanding my consciousness like a balloon. I feel each bomb like a bright point in my awareness. The activation spell is like a flick of the wrist, though I don't move a muscle.

The bombs' effect is immediately apparent: several lamps flicker, and some go out, even though I'm a reasonable distance from the nearest bombs. The impact on Hell proper must be similar to an electric blackout.

I move quickly, searching my mental map for the exact spot. I find myself in a corridor: the floor is smooth marble, and there are no windows, only dim lamps. The darkness doesn't bother a creature like me. A small, detached part of my mind observes that there are tapestries depicting battle scenes on the walls.

I would surely have paused to examine them in different circumstances—they depict Lucifer fighting an army and then a dragon. Big and red pretty much sums it up, I think wryly.

I almost miss it, even though I'm looking for it. The tell is so subtle—a faint shimmer, a barely audible hum, a vibration under my feet. I'm not sure how many of these effects are *physical* and how many are created by my brain processing magic.

I stop. I reach out, feeling for the edges, but the glamour is sly, confusing, like a tangled web. It takes me a minute to get a feel for it, but I tear it off like a cheap curtain once I do.

A door opens before me. Not, not a door; such a word is too trivial, too quaint, too *proletarian* to describe this. Two massive wings stand guard to a vast aperture. The doors are granite, yet their surface is smooth and dark, like marble. A poem of demonic runes adorns the exterior, and they glow with a strange inner light.

The glamour did more than just conceal the appearance of the Arsenal. It also suppressed the *power* that lies behind it. However crudely, I can only compare it to things in my world—a dam holding back a great river, a massive battery, or a nuclear bomb. There is a tremendous amount of magic here... enough to flatten everything on Earth into nothing but smoking rubble.

The doors open as I walk past them. I enter a grand hall with a tall roof held up by great arches. There is no apparent light source, but a dim red glow seems to thicken shadows. There is even an underground stream flowing alongside the path; it reminds me of the river Styx.

The corridor opens out into a chamber, or a cave, for it is staggeringly big. Doors emblazoned with runes guard off various rooms. The cavern's centre hosts a fountain (that must be where the stream feeds into), formed into the shape of a winged demon.

The demon looks like it's holding something, but there's nothing there. It takes me a moment to spot the figure lying underneath the stone demon. At first, I only see hair, long and dark and feminine, and next to her, the Cup: a large chalice, dark as the ocean at midnight, with a ruby glinting faintly in the light. As I get closer, the details start to solidify. Words appear on the Cup, visible to my sensitive eyesight, and I recognise the Latin: *Qui audet adipiscitur.* He who dares wins. (And is that Greek on the reverse side?)

It takes me longer to recognise the girl, not because I don't know her, but because I don't know what the hell she's doing here. It makes no sense; it's like my brain refuses to consider it until everything clicks into place.

"Suzanne? Are you OK? Did you drink from the Cup?"

"Y-yes," she stammers, smiling. Her lips are bloody.

"Did you drink blood?"

"Water. Poison."

"Lucifer poisoned you?"

"No, you idiot. I wasn't good enough to be a demon; the Cup rejected me."

My head is still spinning. "So—your Act—"

"I told Lucifer all about your little love scene with Steijn. I've been following you carefully, you see."

The universe seems to stop spinning, then, with a shudder, restarts. Only everything is wonky.

"You betrayed me? You put Steijn in danger?"

"You're so blind. But hey, what does it matter now? I'm dying—" she retches. Only it's not vomit, but blood. "Massive internal haemorrhaging, he told me. That's how we die—the failures. We bleed from the inside."

I try to pity her, but there is only ice in my heart. "I could kill you and put you out of your misery. But Steijn is in danger; he needs my help. You'll suffer, which you deserve to anyway."

"Fuck you."

"I don't swing that way, dear."

A spasm overtakes her; her spine arches upwards, and she vomits more blood. The pain is so intense that I can see her eyes rolling in their sockets. She won't be making any sarcastic retorts—now or ever.

I pry the Cup from her fingers. I won't have time to destroy it now; I need to save Steijn if it's not already too late. I don't pause to consider that scenario—it's simply not allowed to happen. I swore to protect him; I promised not to lead him to his death.

****

I teleport to the Throne Room, but he's not here, so I Fade to the central city, on top of the roof where I once stood admiring the greenhouse. I spot them, and with a burst of speed, take flight.

"Steijn, my dear. I expected you to be a faithful servant to Mark, to take care of his every need." He chuckles darkly. "Including the sexual. I'm sure Mark enjoys pretty blond boys just like I do."

"Sir Lucifer, I—"

"*How je mond*, stupid boy. But you see," Lucifer continues, resuming his speech, "I did not intend for you to *fall in love* with Mark. Nor did I expect you to betray me. You revealed valuable secrets, sabotaged Hell's infrastructure... These are grave crimes. Punishable with death."

"Leave him alone," I say, putting myself between them.

The Great Demon has his wings spread wide, and he is breathtakingly beautiful. And terrifying.

"I won't let you hurt him. It's me you want."

"I expected you to try something like this," he says with a shrug. "I would have been surprised if you didn't. I wasn't expecting my loyal subjects to aid and abet you, however. Suzanne told me Stein helped you, but surely he couldn't have known all this..."

"Does it matter? Suzanne is bleeding to death as we speak. I expect she's already expired by now."

"Pity. I told that woman it was too soon, but, well..."

"Screw her. Now let Steijn go; punish me instead."

"I will never punish you."

"Then I guess I'll just have to make you." I don't know what I'm saying. Lucifer is like nothing I have ever faced; he is a god, a giant among pygmies. But I have to protect Steijn—I made a promise.

I explode into action, wings half-folded, and dive towards him. I expected fire, pain, fury. But his counter-spell is more like smooth water or a perfidious kiss. I simply flow past him, and the spell binds me, solidifying into rock.

I see it all. And though I strain against the magic with what seems like all my power, I am powerless to stop it.

Lucifer turns into mist—a dark, bloody fog. Steijn is looking into my eyes, and I expected fear, anger, betrayal. But no: when Steijn looks at me, knowing death is coming for him, he sees only love.

His thoughts somehow flood into my mind. *I wished I had more time. But I do not regret helping you; I do not regret loving you. I still love you, Mark.*

The red mist tears through him, and in an instant, Stein's body is torn to bits.

The mist solidifies into Lucifer, who stands, wings outstretched. The very picture of the Angel of Death. I expected him to boast, to rage, to feel *something*. But really, he doesn't feel much at all.

For Lucifer, human life is meaningless. He does not kill humans for pleasure, so he is not a sadist. But a god who sees humans as pawns in a grand game of chess is worse than a god who is sadistic. At this moment, I understand what Shahar tried to teach me by reading the Old Testament. Humans understand kindness or cruelty, but not cosmic indifference.

"You killed him."

The sensation starts slowly at first: a stirring deep in my gut, a pressure in my temples, bright fire in my eyes. But it grows like a tsunami. It is a rage without end.

I brush his binding spell off me, and then I *grab*. There is a violent shudder, a great tremble. There is screeching and grinding. Lucifer turns around slowly, and for the first time, his jaw drops.

I tore the Citadel Bridge in two. A piece of the bridge—a massive chunk of stone weighing several tonnes—is hurtling towards him, ready to destroy everything in its path. I want it to end him.

The Great Demon turns into a pillar of blue flame. He incinerates the bridge. Then, like a tornado, his power reaches out and tosses me into the abyss.

What happens next is just a blur. I am flying, and debris is everywhere. Hell is receding into the distance, and a vast lake of lava approaches me at warp speed. It shouldn't be possible for me to lose consciousness, but all the same, I succumb to darkness.

PART TWO: A BROKEN EARTH

Chapter One: A New Enemy

Kaylin

"Pay attention now," Roshika tells me. "I've sedated the tiger using magic, but you must still be careful. He could go into shock."

I nod. "I know. But I still need to remove the teeth of the snare from the bone and repair the bone, connective tissue, and muscle."

The tiger is wounded badly from a snare that was meant for catching deer.

"Do we use magic for infection prophylaxis?"

"Yes. Antibiotics are a fine invention, but no organism has ever developed resistance to magic."

The sleeping animal is beautiful. He has thick, orange fur, a graceful feline shape, and a soft white underbelly.

"How come I haven't seen any mutant animals here? You'd think a remote jungle would be crawling with them."

"Nope, not so. The demonic magic needed to transform animals into mutants is primarily concentrated near where humanity dwells in great numbers."

"And no zoologist has noticed this?"

"Oh, it's a pretty well-established fact—but no one has been able to explain it. Anyway, pay attention."

It takes several minutes, but I succeed. Bit by bit, I remove the snare, repair muscle, bone, and skin. Roshika also teaches me a spell for killing bacteria (and other pathogens as well).

"Can't this spell be used to help people who are suffering from chronic infections?"

"Yes, but it requires some modification, particularly for viruses that replicate inside human cells."

We are momentarily interrupted by the arrival of a cat. I've never seen this particular feline before, so it takes me a moment to realise it's Daimon, Roshika's mysterious, reclusive feline.

"Hey, kitty," I say.

He ignores me, padding up towards the tiger. He begins licking the tiger's ears and face—and even unconscious, the tiger responds. His heartbeat slows; he is instantly more relaxed.

"Daimon doesn't like humans," Roshika explains. "But he does like other animals, especially members of the feline family."

"Well, my job done is here. I'll finish up and—"

Daimon turns his attention towards me, taking me by complete surprise. He paws at me, and I lift him into my arms, seating myself on a chair. The cat has piercing green eyes and a dark coat (though his face is snow white).

"That's strange; he never does that—"

I don't hear whatever it is that Roshika says next. The vision hits me like a freight train; the lights go out in an instant.

I see death and destruction. From the rubble of a torn building, a young man is brought out. He has long, platinum hair, and he is beautiful. The grief is like a poison burning its way through my veins. But these are not my veins; they belong to someone else.

I see her now. Her hair is like molten silver, and she shines bright as Apollo himself. Yet it is not beauty she represents, but rage. She has eyes like thunder, and there is murder in her heart. I see a name: Araya.

I wake up with Daimon licking my face. My heart is beating at one hundred miles an hour, and sweat glazes my forehead. I stroke the kitty's head, and gradually, I return to normal.

"Feeling better?" Roshika asks.

"Yes."

"What did you see?"

"A woman. A young man died—I think it was her brother. And she's furious. I need to go to Ireland now."

"I haven't finished—"

"I don't care. This vision is important; it threatens our efforts to take Ireland. My men could be in danger."

She sighs. "Very well, then I shall come with you and help you. But first, we must see to one important remaining matter."

"Which is?"

"A memory, a vision of some sort. I can only show it to you here, in the crystal cave. It belonged to Lucifer."

"Then show me."

****

Roshika takes care of the tiger first, releasing him into the wild. Daimon comes with us to watch, then, when neither of us is looking, he disappears. As we return to the crystal cave, I ask Roshika about her cat.

"So how come Daimon wanted a pet right before I had my vision?"

"Oh, he can sense when we're about to have a vision. Why do you think I named him Spirit?"

"And he's never affectionate with people outside of that?"

"Oh, he is, but I can barely remember the last time he loved a human."

"How old is he?"

"About fifty. He responds very well to healing magic, which is why he lives so long."

Nothing surprises me anymore. Roshika could have told me she brought a Woolly Mammoth fossil back from the dead, and I would have believed her without batting an eyelid.

Once again, I enter the crystal cave. Once again, it takes my breath away. The crystals shine in bright colours—iridescent blue, emerald green, ruby red—but the black crystal dominates. Roshika moves toward the dark crystal.

This close to it, I feel the magic is like a magnetic field; it sets my teeth on edge and makes my ears ring.

"You must sit down with your knees crossed and your palms across your lap. I will draw the necessary spells around you. Close your eyes."

"Is this vision different from the ones I normally get?"

"Yes, but it's hard to describe. You'll understand once you experience it. Believe me; it's an experience."

She begins drawing the runes, and I follow her advice, closing my eyes and meditating. I hear her chanting in a strange language—Sanskrit maybe? —but soon I hear no more. The vision feels like no other. Usually, I'm simply unaware of my surroundings while Seeing, but this... this is like I'm in a different *time*, on another planet.

My body is wounded, tired, and sore. Only it's not my body, but Lucifer's. Sounds reach me first: a flowing stream, a faint twinkling, like wind chimes. Then sight; bright sunshine against limestone. Gradually, smell and taste arrive too. There is blood in my mouth, and it tastes bitter.

I crawl inside the cave, but it is Lucifer who is crawling. Two of his ribs are broken, and parts of my face—his face? —feels like it is on fire. I realise that this Lucifer is a man; he is mortal. When was this?

He keeps crawling forward, never stopping, despite the pain. I must surely feel only a fraction of it, yet I want to scream. Few things hurt in quite the same way broken ribs do. His determination is a force in itself: it's like he's unstoppable.

His thoughts are my thoughts. *I loved him, but they killed him. He's gone. Now they're pursuing me. I killed many—but I'm severely outnumbered. I must become stronger, or they will kill me too.*

He feels rage and pain and grief. And when Lucifer feels something, he feels it like an earthquake. No man is his equal.

He draws closer to the crystals, and even in the vision, they seem to possess powerful magic. At times Lucifer manages to rise into a stumbling walk; at other times, he is forced to crawl. But he never stops. *They wounded me with magic, but they weren't good enough to kill me. Soon they never will.*

He reaches the black crystal and places his hand on its surface. I feel it to be smooth, cool on the surface, and yet warm, as if animated by some internal fire. I expect Lucifer to start drawing spells or to chant the way witches normally do spells. Yet, he does not do this.

There is no name for what Lucifer does. It isn't Great Magic, and it isn't a spell like any I know. He... *wills* the power into him. He is like a force of nature, a thirsty desert swallowing an ocean. Raw power floods into my body, and we both scream, but still, he does not stop. His jaw extends, then snaps, and the pain is horrific.

But still, he does not stop.

His wrists break; his ribs liquefy into molten agony. His femur shatters, and his legs collapse. It feels like I'm going to die. The darkness is merciful.

****

For a time—it could be moments, or it could be aeons—I wander alone in the darkness. I wonder if the vision is over, and Roshika needs to fish me out. Or perhaps I have died, and I am doomed to wander this place.

Awareness hits me like ice-cold water. I am back in Lucifer's body, but it feels different. I feel wings extending out of my body, and they are as natural as my limbs, my heart, my muscles. He flexes his wings experimentally, and the motion evokes strength and freedom. *I could fly forever; I could see Earth in all its glory. No one would stand against me.*

He walks forward, ripping off his torn and bloodied clothes. Our body feels alive, a rich organism bathed in power. He experimentally tightens his biceps and abs, and the sensation is strange to me but wonderful.

He walks towards the edge of the cave, surveying the vast landscape before him. Our wings twitch; the urge is strong. With a whoop, we take off.

Nothing on Earth can compare to this. It is like being god. We dive, building immense speed; the ground hurtles towards us. Then, at the last minute, he turns, moving parallel with the environment. The G-forces would have torn an average person in two—but then, Lucifer is anything except average.

For a time, we simply savour the joy of flying. Then Lucifer spots a glacial lake. He descends gradually, approaching the edge of it. The water is ice-cold; it doesn't affect our body physically, but it annoys Lucifer. His magic is like a bomb, ripping out with explosive ease. The air turns frigid as an Arctic night, and now the lake is steaming hot.

He relaxes into the water, gliding with his wings. He makes himself comfortable on a rock. (The sensation of having male genitalia is disconcerting, but once again, oddly pleasurable.) Yet his thoughts are anything except relaxed.

So much power. This is what it means to be divine. Lucifer's mouth curls up into a cruel smile. *They called me a monster, an unclean being. They said God would punish me. Yet I know the Sadducees and Pharisees are nothing more than pathetic wizards who dream of godhood. They wear robes of fine silk and claim to know the word of Heaven, but these are lies to control the ignorant and superstitious.*

Soon, all will know that there is no God—only me. And I am not merciful.

****

The spell reaches out and tears me from the vision; I gasp awake. I am sitting cross-legged next to the crystal, exactly where I started the vision.

"I made you sit cross-legged to prevent you from hurting yourself. The vision is very..."

"Physical."

"Yes. It's quite easy to injure yourself thrashing about."

"That was... something else. I've never had a vision like it. I believe I understand Lucifer better now, but I fear that we are still missing many parts of the puzzle."

"There is still a great deal that we do not know about Lucifer; this vision is the most complete that we have."

"Do you know what he did to become a demon?"

"In short: no. Many have tried to replicate what he did. We have all either failed or, in one unfortunate case, died trying."

"It's not a spell?"

"Not like any I've ever seen."

"So, how do we fight him?"

"For your sake, I hope you don't have to fight him yet. You need more training, more preparation."

"He is more powerful than anything I have ever seen."

"Yes."

"But if I have to fight him, I will. Let's get a move on; I'll call my pilot. Can you also help me heal John when we get back?

"There are no guarantees with someone in a coma. But I promise I will do my best to aid you."

"Understood."

"Give me a minute to prepare. I chiselled small pieces of crystal from the big ones and connected them using magic. They will allow us to channel a portion of their power from afar. They will help our healing efforts—and your military efforts too."

"You did mention the crystals, but I never got around to using them. So you're saying that in this cave is where we are strongest?"

"Yes, but since a demon could attack us anywhere, I made contingency plans."

I nod with approval. Smart woman.

****

Diana

Thanks to our successful conquest of Derry, the Communists have moved on to bigger fish. Even they don't dare attack Belfast or Dublin head-on, but they are planning a major offensive to take West Ireland. The reasoning is simple: the Western part of Ireland is less populated, less militarised, and makes for an excellent symbolic conquest.

Of course, it's one thing to take a small town and quite another to conquer half a country. The logistics are more challenging, the risks higher, and not everyone is on board.

"Have you thought everything through?" Leo asks Andrew, the Secretary-General of the Communist Party. (That's a fancy way of saying Andrew is their boss. I laughed when I heard it.)

"Yes, we've checked and double-checked our plans."

We are once again at their base in Letterkenny, in the central control room.

"Even the best-laid plans don't usually survive the first contact with the enemy," I point out. It's what Kaylin taught me—she studied military history.

"I agree with you, Diana. I am inclined to pause, to think twice."

"But, the more zealous figures in your ranks won't let you?"

"They want results; they think now is the time to get it. There is some merit to that position since the Party is aware of us and is certainly mounting a counter-attack."

"So, if you take the initiative, you have a better chance of success?"

"Exactly."

"But I'm nervous about your plans for the South," Leo says warily. "You're sending most of our forces to Omagh and Enniskillen. I get it; they're the toughest targets. You're sending another division to Longford, who will then take Roscommon. Fine. But I don't think the forces you're sending against Limerick and Cork are sufficient."

"Are you just anxious because I made you commander of that division? I realise it's your first time leading a mission."

"I'm anxious because the numbers aren't there and because you're expecting the people to aid us against the government."

"The Party is very unpopular in the country; their support is concentrated in Belfast and Dublin," I point out.

"In Donegal or Roscommon, I would agree, sure. But Cork?"

"Do you refuse to command the mission?" Andrew asks. "I can put someone—"

"No, I'll do it. Diana? Will you follow me?"

"Sorry, Leo. The main offensive hinges on my powers. Shadow, though, he might want to join you."

"Really? The invisible guy?"

"You'll like him, I promise."

We go over the plans one more time, then begin to arm ourselves. I follow the men outside, towards the city centre. They've assembled the army there. If you'd told me a few months ago that Irish Communists had an *army*, I would have laughed in your face.

I can see many soldiers getting into formation and many more androids moving into place. They hold their lasers, plasma cannons, or rifles at the ready. Our group has supplemented their forces with Q-cars and other armoured vehicles. Speed will be the key; this army has to move fast to encircle and cut off the enemy. If we fight the Party head-on, we lose.

Chapter Two: Dragon's Lair

Mark

I return to consciousness in fits and starts. I dream, but my dreams are insanity: I know only heat, darkness, and death. It's like I can't breathe.

When I finally wake up, I realise I'm lying next to a lake of lava. Well, that explains the heat. It's a miracle I'm still alive. My trousers—a nice pair of jeans that Steijn got for me—have been burnt to a crisp, so I tear them off. I toss aside my sweat-soaked shirt with my jeans.

As soon as I remember Steijn, tears start to fall from my eyes. I haven't cried in years—not from being beaten up by drug dealers, not from being falsely imprisoned, not even when the Gardá dragged me away from my uncle's home. But now I cry rivers of tears, which hiss and steam as they fall.

He died because of me. I swore to protect him, and I failed.

I look around and spot the Infernal Cup a few feet away from me. I grab it, feeling its smooth metal surface on my fingertips. Even in this cauldron, it remains cool to the touch. I spot another inscription on the reverse side. I touch the Greek letters, reading them aloud: *O tolmón niká.* Who dares wins. For a moment, I wonder if I should destroy it. The word *Abad* almost forms on my lips, but for some reason, I stop. Instead, I carry it with me.

I begin walking, not thinking where I'm going. Maybe I'm trying to escape the heat, which is everywhere. Or perhaps I'm trying to run from what happened.

I should have kept him out of it; I should have known Suzanne was an evil bitch.

Like a blind man pushing a boulder, I walk and shuffle, shoulders hunched. I remember the story Shahar had taught me: Sisyphus, an evil man who had wronged the gods, was condemned to eternal torment in Tartarus—an abyss deep in Hades. The irony is too thick to appreciate.

Somehow, through the heat and the smoky darkness, I find the entrance to a cave. Relieved, I make my way towards it. Here, the heat is not so oppressive, and I lie down, exhausted. A demon should not feel any of what I'm feeling, but this is Hell. There is magic from another world here; it knows I do not belong in this place, and it fights my being.

The creature is giant, yet it moves silently, like a snake. In my wearied state, I don't see him until his claws curl around my chest. I open my eyes and find myself face-to-face with a dragon.

****

Hello, Mark.

I jump out of my skin, but his claws keep me pinned to the wall. A part of my mind coolly observes the beautiful red scales, the elegant shape of the dragon's neck, and his irises, which are bright orange mixed with green. Another more primitive part of my brain is screaming at me to run away.

"Who are you?"

I am Rex.

"Are you going to kill me?"

Not at all. I've been waiting for you.

"You're... the dragon?" I realise how stupid my question is.

I am a dragon, yes. I am the rightful ruler of this place: Lucifer, the scoundrel, tricked me and imprisoned me in this cave.

"Why are you holding me like this then?"

People have a tendency to be frightened when they meet me. I did not want you to do anything rash.

"Can't I Fade?"

No.

I realise that I can't Fade at all—the dragon is holding me with magic, not just physically.

"Okay. Nice to meet you, I guess. How come you know my name?"

I have been watching you ever since you came into my domain. The magic binds me to this cave, but it does not stop me from knowing everything that goes on in Hell. I am its master.

"You knew I wanted to talk to you?"

I did, but there was nothing I could do to initiate contact. It was frustrating.

"And your name—Rex. That means king, right?"

Precisely. My actual name is unpronounceable to you, but I've learned many human languages in my long imprisonment.

"So that's how you speak English. And Latin."

The dragon releases me, puffing with amusement. I notice his underbelly has differently pigmented scales—a bronzed orange rather than an intense crimson. He withdraws into a cavern, opening his wings while he does so. They are enormous and reptilian, like a pterodactyl. He takes my breath away.

"Wow."

Thank you for the compliment. It is rare for me to see a human or a demon up close, so the experience is novel for me too.

"The lava lake kinda roughed me up a bit; I usually look better than this."

You are beautiful.

"Are you sure you're not going to eat me?" I joke.

He snorts. *No.*

"How come the firelings didn't attack me?" I ask.

I ordered them not to. However, I could not suppress the magic of Hell itself, which rejects your presence.

"I never felt like this in the inhabited part of Hell—"

Lucifer's magic is responsible for that.

"Gotcha. So, we're together in this cave. You can't get out, I can't Fade back to Earth, and I doubt Lucifer would be happy to see me. That means we're stuck together."

You could take the Road back to Earth—

"That doesn't solve anything. It also means breaking my promise to Lucifer, which gives him free rein to attack Conall and anyone else I care about."

You can free me. We both want Lucifer dead.

"But how?"

It won't be easy. You'll have to deceive Lucifer, and you'll need to Ascend.

"You're right; that won't be easy. But tell me more. How did you end up cursed here? What do I need to do to free you, exactly?"

The dragon sighs. *It's a long story. Follow me, and I'll show you.*

I follow the dragon to a point deep within the cavern, where darkness shrouds the walls, and the ceiling stretches high above, almost beyond my demonic sight. The dragon makes his large frame comfortable on the floor of the cave, then extends his neck, touching my forehead with the tip of his snout.

I will share a memory with you. Try to be open to the experience, even though it will seem alien to you.

Though I don't move, the magic hits me like a bullet train.

****

I am mighty and noble. My power is without equal. I fly high above the Cauldron, raining fire and death on the creatures below. The demons. The dark invaders that besiege my land—that claim I am the monster.

"Go back," I call out telepathically. "You cannot win against me. Go back, or I will wipe you off the face of Hell."

The demons still resist me. Their leader, Lucifer, stands in the middle; the other demons stand in a circle around him, feeding him their power. Lucifer has cast a great dome, which resists my dragon fire. But not for much longer. Three phoenixes fly by my side, and down below, my firelings attack the dome at its base.

For three days and three nights, I've fought them. They are exhausted, and though I am wearied, I know I am stronger than they are. This stalemate cannot hold much longer.

"Almighty dragon! I call for a contest of wits to decide the outcome of this war," he calls out.

"You are a strong, vile demon, but you know you cannot defeat me in open combat. So you propose trickery." I laugh. "Go on; I want to hear it."

"See that yonder cave?"

"I see it."

"Whoever loses shall be imprisoned in that cave until the end of time."

"My firelings and phoenixes will still attack you. But I sense the reciprocity: without you, your followers are doomed. So be it. How do I win?"

"The winner must destroy an object that is precious to the other."

I laugh, and my laughter shakes the very foundations of Hell.

"I do not value any baubles, for I do not know greed. I am a noble creature, unlike you, demon. You are doomed if you do this. Turn back now."

"Yet I cannot, so the proposal stands."

I snort. "Fine. I accept."

"We must say the words of the spell: A contest shall determine the fate of Lucifer, the Great Demon, and Rex, the dragon. He who wins shall destroy an object valued by the other. He who loses shall be bound to yonder cave for all of time."

"He who wins destroys an object. He who loses stays in the cave." I say the words with boredom, not expecting much from the spells of this strange creature. Yet I feel the magic binding us as surely as stone.

"May the best man win."

With a great battle roar, I dive down. I smash right through their pathetic dome. I know what I'm looking for: a cup that Lucifer uses to create other vile beings like him. They thought they could hide it, but in Hell, no one can hide anything from me.

His Archdemons attack me all at once, but they cannot stop me. I smash them with my tail, catching one of them with my jaws; he perishes in an instant. Then Lucifer himself opposes me. He is fast as an angry bee—too fast even for me. His magic wounds me, but it is nowhere near enough to stop me.

I breathe fire all around me, forcing him to retreat. With a dexterous flick of my claw, I uncover the rock under which he hid his precious cup. I pause; something is not right. Though it looks like the Cup, I do not feel its power. I swivel my head, searching for the *real* Cup, which must surely be nearby.

"Did you think you could fool me that easily, demon?" I roar.

"No, I did not think the Glamour would fool you, Rex. The Cup is right here in my hands."

The strange creature smiles wickedly.

"But while you were distracted, I did manage to steal one of your scales." In his other hand, I see a beautiful, gleaming jewel—one of my scales.

"NO!" I let loose a savage roar and lunge towards him. But it's too late. The demon marshals all of his power towards destroying the scale; it blackens and withers.

An agreement made between two gods is sacrosanct; it cannot be defied. Not even by me. Powerful magic rips me away from the demons and smashes me through the opening of a cave. I fall into deep unconsciousness.

****

I gasp awake. The vision was so complete; it overwhelmed all my senses. I *was* the dragon: I understood his thoughts and his power. But now I am Mark again—the lost boy.

"So what happened to your scale?"

I regrew the scale, eventually. Nevertheless, Lucifer did indeed destroy something precious to me; the magic understood this.

"Yeah, don't ever try to outsmart Lucifer."

I did not know that at the time; today, I might agree with you. Yet outsmart him, we will. You will have to deceive him.

"What do I do?"

You grab that Cup and go back to Lucifer. He'll accept you with open arms, I promise you—he's still obsessed with you. The Cup can act as a peace offering.

"Right. But how do I undo the magic that bound you here?"

You have to do to him what he did to me. But you cannot simply destroy the Cup: you must pervert its purpose.

"By Ascending?"

Yes, but by ascending against the power of the Cup. Think of it as becoming an angel rather than a demon. The Infernal Cup will shatter, and that will free me.

"But I need a Great Act to Ascend—"

You will tear down the Barrier.

"What the fuck? Can I even do that?"

Of course, you can. You're a demonic child born of love—the ultimate prize. Lucifer misleads you with all that stuff about faith and humanity. You're a being of both worlds; that's what's needed to destroy the Barrier.

"Both worlds as in Earth and Hell?"

Earth and Lucifer's demonic Hell, more precisely.

"This is crazy. If I tear down the Barrier, Lucifer will have free reign on Earth. He'll make himself king of the world and kill anyone who stands in his way."

Lucifer will manage the feat eventually. Another person like you will come up.

"But I want to give Kaylin and Diana more time—"

Neither of the witches or their Familiars will ever defeat Lucifer. They don't stand a chance. I do. And if I fail—you might succeed. You will be powerful beyond belief; they did not lie to you about that.

"This is huge. I need... a moment to think about it."

By all means, take the time you need. The deception will need to be so-phisticated; you can't just walk up to Lucifer and say you'll give him every-thing he wants.

"Okay. Thank you for this, by the way. I'm going to owe you a lot, Rex."

We haven't won yet.

"No, but you've given me a real fighting chance. I had no idea how to defeat Lucifer. I thought I would have to stay with him, away from Co-nall, forever."

Plus, the Great Demon is a slut.

I laugh. "That too. Do you have a lady friend, by the way? Are there little dragon babies somewhere?"

I'm a god, not a species, Mark.

"That makes a lot of sense, actually. Okay. Can you leave me alone while I think?"

Go to one of the tunnels. I'll stay in the cavern since my bones need a good rest.

A dragon has to rest his bones, I guess. Despite my sadness, Rex manages to elicit a chuckle. Who could have thought a dragon would have a sense of humour?

Chapter Three: Regret

Lucifer

What have I done?

I have killed countless humans. Many, with my bare hands. I have felled armies with my magic; the world trembled at the mere mention of my name. Yet, one boy put my plans in jeopardy. Steijn—a servant, a nobody. Mark represents freedom, power, desire. He is everything I dream about, and I would do anything for him. Except I couldn't spare one harmless boy for him.

Do I feel guilt? No. I have long since forgotten the emotion. Regret, on the other hand? Oh yes. Punishment is a tool that the strong use to control the weak. But when a ruler punishes indiscriminately, without mercy, then he shows himself to be a powerless ruler.

"My lord?" Dacia says, interrupting my train of thought. "We've killed the last of the firelings and rebuilt the wards. The way you reconstructed the Citadel Bridge was marvellous."

"I don't care about the damn bridge. Where is Mark?"

"We have no idea. I'm sorry."

"If the firelings or the dragon get their claws on him, he could be finished. And it would all be my fault. Everything, ruined."

"He opposed your righteous rule; he wanted to shield a criminal from justice."

"A criminal? Steijn was just a dumb boy in the wrong place at the wrong time. Trouble is, I have no idea who helped him and why. Suzanne, that silly bitch, only overheard Mark talking with Steijn."

"Whoever helped Mark knew how to cover their tracks."

"You're right. But there's no use pondering that now. We have more immediate problems to deal with."

A group of imps comes bounding into the Throne Room. Javalook and Ezekiel lead them, two of my favourite imps. They gaggle around me; they clearly flummox Dacia.

"Master, master!"

"Out with it."

"We've been spying on the humans," Ezekiel continues. "The silly Communists are planning a major offensive to take West Ireland. They've already taken Derry."

"Why wasn't I made aware of this sooner?"

Ezekiel, who has unusually curly horns, shrugs. "We didn't think it was important. It's a small state and a bit player."

"True, but you did find Mark there, did you not?"

"We did."

"So Ireland is important in more ways than one. You must continue spying on everything that goes on there, including that ugly Party, those silly Communists, and that annoying witch."

"And Conall, master?"

"The boy is safe in Spain, is he not?"

"Beelzebub is off to spy on him, but yes, he should be safe."

"Good. I want him safe; I have damaged Mark's faith in me too much as it is. His boyfriend must be protected at all costs."

"Have you abandoned your amorous intentions towards Mark, sire?" Dacia asks. I turn and give her a calm smile.

"As much as I desire Mark—no, as much as I *love* him—I am not a fool. He clearly does not reciprocate those... feelings."

"I think you are right and that Conall's safety is imperative," concurs Ezekiel.

I scratch him behind his horns. "I knew you would agree."

"Lord Lucifer? What should we do?" Dacia asks.

"Nothing, for now. Javalook? I want you to find Mark. Do whatever it takes."

"We can't fight the dragon!"

"If Mark encountered the dragon, he would already be dead. I want you to help him fight off the firelings and guide him back to safety."

"Understood. I'll get the bravest imps to go with me on this mission."

"I trust you.

Chapter Four: A Troubled Being

Conall

I did my best, didn't I? I convinced the Spanish government to aid Ireland's Communist movement, to supply them with androids and weapons. Now Mother tells me the Communists have taken Derry, with a major assault planned.

Yet, much as I despise the Party and wish to see them toppled, my main concern lies with Mark and Lucifer. I feel that the Party's demise will be hard-fought, but that it is ultimately inevitable. But what if Lucifer succeeds? Then it will all be for nothing. An immortal dynasty of demons will rule the world forever.

Despite our Spanish villa's pleasant surroundings, I pace around the complex, feeling anxious, disturbed. Something big has happened down in Hell, and Mark could be in danger. I have no idea how I know this; it is merely a feeling that won't go away.

The sun is setting, and the hour is late; the sky is alive with hues of gold, fuchsia, and blue. Wispy clouds cover the horizon, and the light hides many shadows. The villa is usually a hub of activity as men and women, quite of few them young adults, work to keep it clean, maintain the crops (among them grapes, olives, and herbs) and run the household. I've been practising my Spanish with the staff, and I'm improving steadily.

I almost don't notice the shadow that detaches itself from one of the buildings, for it is barely perceptible. But I know what it is. I turn and call out: "Who are you? Show yourself."

If it's a demon, I want to be ready.

The shadow turns out to be Michael. He is elegantly dressed, as always.

"Ah, it's you."

"Hello, Conall. I wanted to meet with you again."

"Aren't you supposed to be busy in Ireland?"

"I've spoken with Diana, and she's told me to keep out of sight for now. The Party knows of my existence, but they don't know everything I can do. She hopes to keep it that way."

"Why don't you just go and kill the new taoiseach? It would speed things up."

"We need Kaylin's help to find him."

"And she's busy trekking up the Himalayas."

"Exactly. Besides, assassinating the leader would cause more chaos, which is not our intent. We want to defeat them in detail. A complete victory would ensure a stable new government—a government toppled through assassination would make ruling the country extremely fraught."

"Smart. OK then, spit it out. Why do you want to talk with me? I hope it's not to lecture me on my relationship with Mark."

"I realise that it would be hopeless. And in any case, I am the last person who should give lectures. Follow me; I want to tell you a story to try and explain who I am."

"You should do that with Mark, not me."

"Mark is in Hell. Going there would be suicide—at the very least, Lucifer would imprison me."

I sigh. "Of all people, I can understand that. Fine, I'll follow you. Where do you want to go?"

"To a little wood just outside. I don't want to frighten the locals."

We chuckle at that. Mark's father leads me to a secluded grove, where we sit on two fallen trees.

"Go on."

"My name is Michael, though Lucifer sometimes called me Moloch to annoy me, I suspect. I met him in the year 29BCE, not long after he became a demon. He turned me into what I am today a year after that."

"How did you become a demon?"

"I don't want to talk about it, but you deserve the truth. I murdered the woman I loved, my first wife."

"Ouch. Wife-beater is bad enough, but wife-killer?"

"I did everything for Lucifer because I wanted power. And you're right. I had no conscience for a long time, and I killed with impunity—men, women, even children. I ripped babes from their mothers and raped women in front of their families."

"And did it make you stronger?"

"Not one bit. I was a ruthless demon—one of the cruellest, worse than Lucifer himself—but I was pretty low on the pecking order. I became stronger once I met Bridget."

"Mark's mother?"

"Yes."

"He knows so little about her."

"She was beautiful," Michael says. "By this, I mean to say she had a beautiful heart. I had my fair share of pretty girls, so that didn't interest me as it had once. Bridget, though, was kind, smart, and brave. The bravest woman I ever met."

"How *did* you meet?"

"I was conducting a mission for Lucifer—some mischief or other, I think it was to kill a Party figure."

"Why did Lucifer want that?"

"He neither loved nor hated the Party; it was merely that killing the man would lead to chaos."

"Right. And Bridget stopped you?"

"No, she told me to go ahead because he deserved it. But she always said that murder leaves a mark on the soul and that I needed to balance out the dirty work with doing more good. She put me in touch with a refugee charity who smuggled people out of Europe and into South America."

"There's civilisation there?"

"There is, though European governments keep it hushed up. Spain was also the destination sometimes."

I file away that piece of information. "So, you're telling me that you just met her and started doing all this?"

"She was very persuasive. You're right to be sceptical, though. The old me would have murdered her for sport, especially since I hated do-gooders. But after two millennia, I slowly grew disillusioned with Lucifer and with myself. I started to regret my actions."

"Did you fall in love with her straight-away, or was it a gradual thing?"

"Gradually. I was too old for love at first sight and far too cynical."

"You were still technically Lucifer's minion during that time?"

"Initially, yes. But when you love a woman like Bridget, and your boss is the Devil... well. Lucifer knew how brutal I was, and one day he asked me to commit another atrocity. I couldn't do it. It was at during moment that I decided to fight. I vowed to become stronger, and I gained the power to resist."

"And Mark? When did he enter your life?"

"It took us time to realise Bridget was pregnant. I thought it was impossible, so I asked her if she had any other lovers, honestly and without prejudice. She didn't. So we had to do a DNA test, and her brother, Eoin, did it in secret."

"Why in secret?"

"We worried that Mark had some DNA which would identify him as different. And he did, though without knowing his parentage, you might think it was just a naturally occurring anomaly."

"What anomalies are we talking about?"

"You surely noticed how beautiful he is, even before becoming a demon."

"And he healed so quickly, even with regenerator solution; he was fine in two days. Heck, he ran faster than me while he was injured." I never realised how odd that was at the time.

"I bet he never suffered from a single cold," Michael points out. "Or a toothache."

"And he was ripped, even though I never saw him at a gym."

"Alas," Michael says, sighing deeply, "his supernatural make-up came with a cost. Bridget could not survive the birth. Her pregnancy went smoothly until after she delivered; that's when everything went to Hell fast. Eoin and his finest team of doctors could not save her."

"So, the million-euro question: why did you leave him?"

"I gave him to Eoin and left a little souvenir to contact me, should the need arise. I instructed Eoin never to let Mark know about me unless the situation became dire."

"Let me guess: you hoped Lucifer wouldn't find out about him."

"I also hoped the Party wouldn't find out about him because of his genetics. I never counted on the new law, which came into force less than a month later."

"Not your fault, that. I'll be sure to tell Mark."

"Thank you."

"So, how did Lucifer find out?"

"He has imps spying for him."

"Imps?"

The demon smiles then whispers a spell: *Capio*. I feel his magic rippling out like a net. Something *yelps* like a startled cat. Michael walks to a tree and grabs something from a branch. The squirming figure in his hand has horns and doesn't sound happy at all.

"Fuck you! Fuck you! I'm just doing my job."

"I know you, Beelzebub. You're reporting to Lucifer. But I also know you don't tell Lucifer everything."

"That's an imp?" I ask.

The little creature blows a raspberry at me.

Michael smiles. "Yes, he is a creature wrought by Lucifer's magic. But they have free will, and they're playing Lucifer like a fiddle."

"True, true," the little imp agrees.

"They can cross the Barrier?"

"It's a loophole in the Barrier spell," Michael explains. "It bound demons, but not other things created with demonic magic. An oversight."

"So why hasn't Lucifer conquered Earth already?"

"We're not demons, silly," Beezelbub explains. "We aren't immortal. You can't take over the world with imps."

"But you can use them to spy on people. So tell Lucifer we had a perfectly inane conversation. Make up some random shit; I don't care."

"I'm very creative," purrs Beezelbub.

"You are that," Michael agrees.

"Do you two know each other?"

"A bit," Michael says. "He was tasked to spy on me during my missions to Earth. I guess Lucifer suspected something already, even then. He misled Lucifer with just enough omissions and half-truths to let me escape his clutches."

"It was a tough tightrope to walk on," Beezelbub explains. "You should be more grateful."

"Oh, I am grateful to you and your friends. But you're still an annoying git."

The imp giggles.

"Do you know anything about Mark?" I ask. "Is he OK?"

"Mark and Lucifer had a little spat about a boy, and Lucifer cast him out of Hell. But Master is desperate to mend things over."

"But, where is Mark?"

"Somewhere in the lava lakes or a cave. We're working on it."

"If the dragon gets him—" Michael starts.

"What dragon? Is he in danger?"

"Grave danger," Michael says.

"Don't get your knickers in a twist!" the little imp cries out. "If the dragon wanted Mark dead, he would be sending an army of firelings to kill him. We would notice it. So either the dragon doesn't know where Mark is..."

"Or the dragon wants him alive," Michael fills in. "Which is plausible. The dragon hates Lucifer."

"I'm confused."

"It's a long story," Michael begins. "I'll explain later. For now, you need to know that the dragon is incredibly powerful, dangerous, and sympathetic to Lucifer's demise. He might be a valuable ally. Beelzebub, we're relying on your imps."

"Understood. Free me, and I'll go do what I can."

"Libero," Michael says.

The imp waves at me, then he disappears into thin air.

"Okay, explain," I order.

Michael is frowning.

"Michael?" I ask.

"I just got an emergency signal from Kaylin's medallion. I need to go."

And with that, he disappears too.

Chapter Five: Burns

Mark

I won't forgive Lucifer for what he did. Steijn was just a boy, and I cared for him like a brother; yet he was taken away from me in an instant, without a hint of remorse. I know that when I go back, I will have to deceive Lucifer. I will have to pretend to believe in his apologies and regrets.

But I will kill him, I vow. For Conall. For Steijn, who died too soon. For all of humanity, even if humanity is cruel and undeserving of salvation.

I try closing my eyes, but the tears keep on coming. The cave is dark and quiet, save for a distant underground stream and the faint *splash* of water. I am alone with my grief. But then, a man is always alone with his grief. He can try to distract himself with the company of friends or to lose himself in sorrow. But until vengeance is served—with blood hot from the source—he can never rest in peace.

Eventually, the tears dry, not because the sadness fades, but because even my demonic body simply can't keep crying any longer. That's when I emerge.

"Rex?" I ask the dragon.

Are you ready? Have you decided?

"I'll do whatever it takes to beat Lucifer."

The deception will need to be perfect. No being is more difficult to fool than the Devil.

"I know that."

Do you? Wait, don't answer that. There's someone here.

I spin around. "Who?"

The enormous reptile moves fast, faster than I can believe. The dragon's claws reach out, scratching a deep groove through the rock. But I catch the flash of movement that evaded the strike—something small, something with little horns.

"Stop!" I cry.

Imps. Spies. I will kill them before they report to their master.

The dragon snarls, opening his jaw to blast the area with fire. I leap, placing myself between him and the imps.

"No."

Rex pauses, then closes his mouth, teeth grinding in frustration.

You're crazy. I could have killed you.

"I know, but the imps are my friends. They're on my side, which means our side. Guys, you can come out now."

I recognise Javalook and Pipa as they cautiously make their way out of a tunnel. The dragon watches them with cold anger in his eyes.

Lucifer created these monstrosities from the firelings he trapped.

"Hey, I'm not a monstrosity!" Javalook says, affronted. He puffs up his chest and returns the dragon's stare.

"They have their own free will," I say. "Give them a chance."

The dragon snorts. *Very well. Explain yourselves.*

"Lucifer tasked us to find you," Javalook begins.

"He's anxious about you and wants you to come back," Pipa fills in for him.

"Oh, I'm coming back. But Lucifer is going down."

"What's your plan?" Javalook asks.

"I'll tell you on a need-to-know basis," I reply. "You will help me with the deception?"

"We will," they both agree.

Hang on; it's not that simple.

"What is it, Rex?"

The dragon sighs. *Lucifer, and his demons, need to believe you fought my firelings. If they see you unharmed, it will raise suspicion.*

The realisation slowly dawns on me. "So... I need to be hurt?"

Unfortunately, yes.

"How?" I ask. I've faced pain before when I became a demon. Very little could compare to that kind of agony.

My firelings... they will burn you, superficially. Nothing that won't heal on a demon. But...

"It's going to hurt."

Yes.

"Javalook? Pipa? What do you think?"

"Sorry, Mark. The big lizard is right," Javalook says.

Big lizard? Rex asks, slightly offended.

"Well, you've got teeth and scales and a big tail. So yeah," Pipa points out.

I am a dragon, not a lizard.

"Don't be a pedant," Pipa chides.

It doesn't take long for the imp's childish humour to wear away the dragon's hostility. The two banter while I think.

"Rex? Are your firelings sentient? Do they want to hurt me?"

Sentient? Sort of, but not really. They are destructive by nature but bear you no ill will. They will simply obey my orders.

"Good. Bring them in," I say, steeling myself for what is to come.

I've never seen the creatures up close before—even when they attacked the demons I was fighting, they were always far away—and I have to admit they're fascinating. Imagine a big campfire. Now imagine that the fire is *alive*, a living, breathing creature of air and magic. This is the fireling.

Whoopee!

I realise the firelings are communicating with each other telepathically.

Fire! Fire! Fire!

We want to burn!

Calm down, Rex orders. *You must do what I tell you and do it carefully. Mark here is to be burned, but only skin deep. You are not allowed to hurt him, only... singe him a bit.* I can tell the dragon is downplaying his words for my sake.

Yes, master! We is burning!

I open my arms wide, keeping my eyes open. I'm ready for the pain, and I want to know when it comes. I think of Conall, the boy I love, who waits for me on Earth, desperate for my return. I think of brave Kaylin and how she will fight. Most of all, I think of Steijn with his blond hair and his cute Dutch accent.

I remember when Lucifer killed him; he was so fearless, so beyond his seventeen years.

This is for you, Steijn.

Few words can describe the agony. I know what a burn is like, from when I was human: a boiling pot of water scalded me once, and I touched a flame out of curiosity. But this is a fire like no other. It melts my skin, chars my bones, and burns into my soul.

Stop!

The pain is over. I grin, then collapse. Once again, the darkness claims me.

****

I awake sometime later, returning to consciousness in an instant. I touch my skin experimentally, then bite back a hiss of pain. It doesn't hurt too much—assuming I don't touch the burned skin. I get up, trying to walk, then fall back down. *God damn, that hurts.*

"Are you OK? We were worried about you," Javalook asks.

"I'm fine."

He is wounded, but he will get better, Rex says.

"I sure hope so."

"You look like a cooked sausage," Pipa says.

"Thanks, Pipa."

That was the intent; Rex points out. It has to be convincing.

"It's convincing, alright," Javalook agrees. "Mark? Can we go now? We'll lead you back."

"Give me a minute," I say, gritting my teeth. Slowly, I lift myself off the ground. "Can't we just Fade?"

"The wards will prevent you unless Lucifer takes them down," Javalook tells me. "You can fly with us."

"You imps can fly?"

He shakes his head. "Of course we can fly, silly. How do you think we get from place to place so quickly?"

I extend my wings, realising, with pleasure, that they are unharmed. "Okay. Let's go give Lucifer hell."

Good luck.

We take off, two imps and a demon. The dragon watches us from his cave.

Chapter Six: Dangerous Secrets

Leo

Why did I agree to command this mission? It's a question I've been asking myself a lot. I think it's risky, ambitious, and clouded by too much optimism. Andrew would have let me opt-out and have someone else do it if I pressed the issue.

Was I afraid of losing face? No. The more I think about it, the more I come to understand the real reason: it's a dangerous mission, and I don't feel anyone else could do it except me.

This is how I find myself in an armoured car, a binocular in my hands, examining the military installation at Cork city. We'd taken Limerick just hours earlier, at the crack of dawn, and had met no organised resistance. However, I feel this is going to be different. The military installation here is big, well-armed, and seems to have double the amount of soldiers than previously reported. They must have called up reserves.

The October sun is still high in the sky, and the day is warm; I wipe the sweat off my eyebrow. Next to me is Shadow, one of Kaylin's men.

"I'm guessing you don't much like our chances," he says.

"No. The base is big, well-defended, and well-supplied."

"And no offence to your troops or anythin', but this isn't an army."

"True. We've less than a thousand men, and they're not battle-hardened."

"So, what's your plan?"

"We can't attack them head-on. We could try a diversion?"

"Not sure it would work," Shadow says. "They won't send the entire brigade out of the city; they are expecting a diversion."

"You're right. So... how about we sneak in behind enemy lines? We sabotage them, blow some shit up, and cause chaos in the ranks? Then signal the men to move in?"

He looks at me like I've just grown horns. "That's the craziest thing I've ever heard. You're supposed to be a general—"

"Lieutenant Colonel."

"Whatever. The point is, you can't just leave your men here while you go off on your own; you're supposed to lead them."

"There are other men and women I'm confident can handle things until I come back."

"But why you?"

"Because I'm strong: I have magic, and they do not."

"True," he concedes. "And looking at that bleedin' fortress, it might be our only hope. But I still think your leader made a poor choice in asking you to command this mission."

"I agree," I say quietly. "But I don't think anyone else can accomplish this. Are you with me?"

His blue eyes fix on me. Shadow has red hair, and freckles dot his face. They move when he smiles.

"It's crazy, but I love it. I'm with you."

****

After explaining my plan to the men and entrusting a competent man to lead them in my absence, we say goodbye. Shadow and I locate a civilian vehicle—we hotwire it quickly—and he starts driving it. A regular car will attract a lot less attention.

"So, how does your power work?" I ask him.

"I can make myself invisible and unheard."

"Do you control light and sound?"

"I have no idea."

"Okay. But can anyone smell you? Dogs, maybe? Do androids pick you up with their vibration sensors?"

"Nope. Dogs ignore me, and humans actually get out of my way while I'm invisible."

"Really? Kaylin told me her invisibility spells—"

"Yeah, but I'm better than Kaylin."

"And you can make others invisible too?"

"So long as I'm touching them, yeah. So stay close to me and don't wander off."

"I promise I'll hold your hand," I joke. "Do you want a ring?"

"A wedding ring? Oh, for feck's man, stop joking. Kaylin might think you're gay."

He stops, noticing my expression. "Wait, are you bi or something?"

"A little," I admit.

"Cool. I had no idea. I have a daughter and a divorced wife—did I mention that?"

"No, I imagine you didn't. We keep that sort of thing quiet so we don't put our family in danger if one of us gets captured. You're taking a pretty big risk telling me anything."

"I want you to know who I am because whatever happens, we have to trust each other."

He takes a deep breath: "I discovered my power when I was a teenager, but I kept it a secret, thinking it might make me an outcast. I tried to live a normal life with my wife Jeanne; I was so happy when Deirdre was born."

"Let me guess: it didn't last."

"No. Jeanne divorced me, and I agreed not to see them because the Party might come after me."

"If we win," I say, "do you think you could come back?"

"Jeanne and I don't love each other anymore. But I want to be a father for Deirdre."

"I can understand that."

"So what about you? Who are you?" Shadow asks me.

"I used to work as a military engineer before I joined the Red Army."

"What did you do? Design Q fighters and androids?"

"While I was on active duty, I was an expert in detonating mine-fields safely. After that, I worked on designing field artillery and armoured vehicles."

"Grand. So you're a Technical?"

"Yes, though I don't identify myself as one. I'm an Irish citizen who wants freedom and prosperity."

"Damn, those commies got you good. So what do you know about Kaylin and us?"

"Not that much, if I'm honest. Kaylin told me she's fighting an even bigger enemy than the Party, but she refused to say who or what."

"Aye, that's true." He's smiling, but it's a grim sort of smile; it's not pleasant at all.

"I guess you're not going to tell me?"

"I respect Kaylin's judgement, and I'm not sure you'd believe me, anyway."

I want to press him, but we're getting close to the base; there's a checkpoint right up ahead. We get out of the car.

"You ready?" I ask.

"Ready as I'll ever be, my man," he says, offering me his hand.

I grasp his forearm, and a moment later, we turn invisible.

****

The experience of being invisible is... strange. Men and even androids move out of our way to prevent a collision, which is bizarre. We pass undetected through an array of cameras and sensors (although Shadow made me store the com phone back in the car). Soon we're inside the base.

I get to work. I use telekinesis to cause all sorts of chaos: I rip wires, trip lights, and break computers. Confusion erupts all around us. To add to the chaos, I set random objects on fire. Shadow, meanwhile, manages to locate some explosives in a basement, which we rig to explode in ten minutes. (It takes some gymnastics to keep a hold of each other while synchronising our tasks.)

A soldier comes walking down the basement stairs, and he sees the explosives. He doesn't have time to call out or touch his com phone—I snap his neck telekinetically, and he crumples to the floor without uttering a cry.

"That was mean," Shadow says.

"I had no choice."

We make our way out of the base. Within minutes, a fireball explodes from the building.

"Get in the car," I say. "We need to get out of here ASAP. But do it calmly, without making it look like a getaway."

He turns the car and starts driving, remaining totally cool.

"That was great," he begins, "what you did with the telekinesis. Now order your men to—"

He hits the brakes, and we lurch forward. A woman is blocking the road. She's just standing in the middle of a road, wearing nothing but a dress. The woman has platinum hair, a molten sheen that cascades down her shoulders.

"Hey, lady," Shadow says, getting out of the car. "What are you doing on the road? Do you need a ride or something?"

"The question is, what are you doing sabotaging a military base?"

Shadow freezes, speechless. A moment later, the woman raises her arm, and Shadows goes flying like a football.

"Who are you?" I ask. "Are you sure you wanna fight? I'm dangerous."

"Oh, you're not half as dangerous as I am."

Her attack is like a telekinetic punch, but it's not so much a punch as the hand of God. I brace my power against it, but even so, I stagger backwards, falling down.

"You lot killed my brother," she says venomously. "Now I'm going to kill you."

The woman shines bright as an angel. She raises her hands to smite me, and I try to attack her. My telekinetic strike bounces off her like a ping pong ball hitting a concrete wall. I guess this is it—I'm going to die.

There's a cry of rage from behind her, and she spins around faster than I can believe. She sends Shadow sprawling away from her; a rock falls from his limp hand. Was Shadow going to bash her head with a rock?

The woman seems intent on him, fury rising out of her like a tornado. This isn't the time to be brave, I realise. This madwoman is way too powerful for me to defeat. So I do something cowardly but rational. I jump inside the car, floor the accelerator, and a burst of electric torque sends me careening away, wheels spinning.

****

"Mayday, mayday!" I cry on my com phone. "Shadow and I were attacked by an enemy, Familiar. We need Kaylin and Diana here—"

"Roger that. What about Shadow?" the man on the phone asks. Was Harry his name?

"He's been captured. I've no idea where he might be taken, or even if he's still alive. I'm sending you my co-ordinates now; I need firepower pronto."

A Q jet suddenly flies overhead. A moment later, the car bucks, then twists sideways. I hit the brakes.

"Shit! I just got hit by an Anchor." An Anchor is a specialised bomb used to disable vehicles. I spare a look out the back of the car. "And a bunch of Gardá cars are coming at me."

"Pretend you're innocent," Harry suggests. "It will buy you time. The Gardá will want you alive to interrogate you, anyway."

"I'm throwing the com phone away," I say before crushing it with my foot.

The Gardá men soon catch up with me, weapons pointing at the driver's seat. I open the door and raise my hands in surrender. To my surprise, two men tackle me, while a third stands pointing a laser at me. Guess I'm too risky for non-lethal force.

"You are under arrest," he says. The man has his knee against my neck, pushing me down towards the asphalt. Dark spots begin to dance across my vision.

"We need him alive," I distantly hear the other guy saying.

"Yeah, but he's dangerous, and no one will complain if we rough him up a bit."

"Can't—breathe—"

"Shut up."

Rage builds up inside of me; this is wrong. They think I am helpless and want to take advantage of me. I lift both men off me using my power, keeping a tight hold on their necks while I do it. The laser wielder is caught off-guard, and he's slow, much too slow. In the blink of an eye, I snap his neck. I dust myself off, keeping the two men in the air.

"That was bad form," I say. "You could have killed me. But I'm not a murderer, so I won't do the same to you."

"You killed—James—" the guy who was pinning me rasps out.

"He was going to shoot me with a laser; I killed him in self-defence. Whereas I surrendered to you, and you abused your power."

He tries to speak, but I wrap my magic tighter around his throat, cutting off whatever it is he was about to say. I calmly handcuff the men to each other using their own handcuffs. I rifle through their supplies and inject them with their own drugs. Job done. Now I need to get back to the car.

"Where do you think you're going?" My blood runs cold; I recognise her voice immediately. But how did she get here so fast?

I turn and find the woman smiling at me. But her smile is more like a feral grin.

"I want to talk—"

My words are cut short by an explosive fireball. I wait for the pain and the oblivion of death, but it does not come. Opening my eyes, I see a man standing in front of me.

But this is no *man*. He has wings, dark as the night, which coil around him like a serpent. And he has so much *power*—I feel it like a massive charged battery. I am before a god, and to be in his presence is to feel awe.

"That was rude," the winged being remarks. "One does not usually murder strangers, particularly strangers with whom you've not exchanged so much as a word."

"So it's you," the lady remarks. "The guy I saw in the video feed. Let's see how tough you are, then."

The woman flings a fireball at the elegant winged man, and he tosses it aside like a volleyball. Enraged, the woman lifts her hands, and lightning arcs out from the sky. The bolt does not find its target; instead, it blows a crater in the spot where the winged man had stood.

"Nice try," he says from behind her. The man throws a fireball at the woman, and she staggers back, trying to deflect it. I can see that the fire has burned her.

She seems to realise she's met her match. With a curse, she takes off, *flying* up into the air. The man unfurls his wings and makes to follow.

"Stop!" I cry. "Whoever you are! I need your help."

He stops. "Yes? Who are you?"

"My name is Leo."

"Ah. Kaylin might have mentioned you."

"You know, Kaylin?"

"She asked me to help you once she got your message."

"Who *are* you?"

"My name is Michael. I'm afraid we've not got time for more introductions. You said somebody had captured Shadow?"

"I think so. Can you... fly me? I'll show you where."

"Yes, and glamour us too."

He offers me his hand, and once again, on the same day, I find myself touching another man—another *gorgeous* man. I really need to get a grip and tell Kaylin. The beautiful man smiles as if sensing my thoughts.

Flying is like nothing I have ever experienced. Sure, I've flown in planes and Q-cars and stuff—I'm an engineer, and I used to work for the military when I was younger. I flew to wars in the Middle East, Africa, and once to Australia. The European League of Nations fought the Chinese in every theatre. (Usually, we won, except in Australia.)

But this... this is something else. This feeling is pure and free, and joyous. The wind ruffles my hair, and the world stretches out below me, the man's strong hands holding me firm.

"There!" I cry, hoping the wind doesn't blow away my words.

You may speak to me telepathically if you wish.

I'm too shocked to be surprised. A man who can fly, who wields magic like it's child's play, would indeed have mastered telepathy. Before I know it, the strange man has landed, turning me upright at the last moment. I take a few unsteady steps, still reeling from that incredible flight.

"Wow. Okay. Let's see if we can find Shadow."

We search the area. After a moment, I locate skid marks where my car was launched, and we follow the marks until we find a figure. He is slumped over by the side of the road, one arm outstretched. I initially don't recognise him. Shadow had such a lovely shock of red hair, but now...

"She burned him," I whisper.

The strange man—Michael—bends over and takes his pulse.

"He's still alive."

I breathe a sigh of relief, feeling tears form in my eyes. I wipe them away; I need to concentrate and keep a hold of my emotions. "We need to get Shadow to a hospital."

"Kaylin can help him."

I nod. "Can you get us both out of here?"

"Yes." He gingerly lifts Shadow's unconscious form in his lap, looking for all the world like a hero.

"Grab my arm," Michael says.

Then he does... something. The world seems to twist and blur around us; it's like space and time are being manipulated. A moment later, we're inside a building. I recognise some of Kaylin's men, even though my head is spinning with dizziness. I put a hand on the wall to steady myself.

"Shadow!" a woman cries, running up to Michael.

"He needs medical help," Michael says. "He's been burned by another familiar."

"Who?" the woman asks.

"I don't know, Elizabeth."

"But I do."

We all turn as Kaylin stomps into the room. "Her name is Araya."

Chapter Seven: The Return to Grace

Mark

We fly unmolested towards a vast metropolis. With a start, I realise it is the Cauldron—the place I'd lived in for over a month, and which, slowly and inadvertently, I'd started to call home. From this angle, it's almost unrecognisable: a vast, amorphous mass that blots out the landscape.

As we approach, I notice the faint blue sheen that surrounds Lucifer's domain. The wards.

"How will we get in?" I ask the imps. "Will I be recognised?"

"Of course you'll be recognised, you silly thing," Pipa says. "Lucifer has posted sentries to await your return. Also, we warned him of your arrival, telepathically."

Nothing surprises me when it comes to the imps. Not any more.

A whistle breaks the silence. "Ahoy there! Mark!"

I recognise the voice: it belongs to Archdemon Tim. He's waving at me, looking delighted to see me. I wave back.

"I was just about to call Luci—oh shit. Behind you."

I turn and see a *swarm* of firelings following behind me. Of course. Rex didn't make me suffer all that without following through on the plan—to make the demons think that he is my enemy. I turn back and see the wards go out.

"Follow us! Dive!" Javalook cries out.

We dive down towards the protection of Hell. At the same time, Tim unfurls his wings, then leaps into the air. He's fearless, I realise, with a bit of awe. He's going to meet the massive pestilence of firelings head-on.

The fight is epic, like something out of the *Iliad*. Tim is everywhere, fast as a mosquito, teleporting at the most unexpected times. The fire lings vainly try to hit him, but he is too quick, too agile. Tim throws fireballs, one after the other in quick succession until the swarm is noticeably thinned. To my astonishment, the firelings retreat.

"You god-damn little bastards," he cries out. "Running away when I was just beginning to have fun!"

I realise that if I ever have to fight Tim, it will be one of the most challenging fights in my life.

"I think you've had quite enough fun," a voice drawls. I start; it's Lucifer. He's appeared next to us on the roof of a building. We turn and face each other.

Seeing him is a shock. He is stunningly beautiful as always, but I notice subtle imperfections in his ordinarily inscrutable face: fine lines, shadows under his eyes, a tight pull to his mouth. The last few days have not been pleasant for Lucifer. I almost want to pity him, but then I remember Steijn's death, and hatred steels my heart.

Lucifer's reaction, on the other hand, is pure shock. Followed by instant affection.

"Oh, Mark... what did they do to you?"

"I had a little run-in with the firelings," I said raggedly.

"When I get my hands on that dragon..." he snarls. "Come, I'll take you to the infirmary. I've already set up the wards again."

I turn and see that, indeed, there is a faint blue shield glowing above us. In a moment, Lucifer is by my side, one hand touching my cheek. I force myself not to shy away; he misinterprets the gesture.

"It hurts?"

"A bit."

"Sorry. Can you hold my hand instead?"

The moment I touch his hand, we Fade. I turn and see the infirmary, the same place where Max had been taken after helping me fight Acheron.

"Sit on the bed and relax," he tells me.

"Are you going to bring Shahar?"

"What? No. Shahar is a competent healer, but he's still only human. He can't possibly compare to me."

"You're going to heal me?"

"Of course. Why the surprise? I am an extremely able healer."

"Well, the healing arts aren't associated with the Devil."

He smiles with amusement. "Mark, those are just silly stories I came up with to scare the humans. I am capable of a vast array of magic, including the medicinal sort. Let me show you."

He touches my hand and begins muttering words in Latin and Greek. His other hand traces runes on my chest. Almost immediately, a warm glow seems to saturate me. The pain fades away until it's not even noticeable.

"Open your eyes," he says, and I see a mirror held in his hand. The face reflected in the glass is barely recognisable as being mine: my skin is charred, blackened, and peeling. Only my eyes retain their bright blue colour.

"Now watch," he breathes. I feel his magic like a cool river on a hot summer's day, coursing through my veins, making my skin tingle. As I watch, the burns slowly heal, revealing smooth, peachy skin underneath. Within minutes, I am back to my old self again—the cherubic boy everyone wants a piece of.

"Wow," I say.

"Does anything still hurt?"

I put a hand to my cheek. "No, nothing."

"Wonderful."

"I have to ask," I start, "because I want to know. If you can heal me like this, can you also heal humans?"

"Naturally. Why ever not?"

"Can you bring back the dead?"

For a moment, he does not say anything. He looks troubled.

"Mark... To bring back the dead is cruel, crueller, indeed, than anything I have ever done. My most heinous acts would not compare to the vileness of necromancy."

"Why?"

"Because what is dead must stay dead. They can not be as they were in life; it is impossible. One can only reconstruct their body through their remains, but the end result is a walking corpse, a parody of life."

"You can't find another body and put their soul—"

"Mark, there's no such *thing* as a soul. That notion is pure nonsense that humans are wont to believe because it makes them feel good, and because the Abrahamic religions use it to manipulate them."

"But there's magic—"

"Magic is part of nature. Mortality is a fact of life, except for those of us who succeed in becoming immortals.

"Let me explain necromancy to you in simple, mechanical terms: there is no soul, only life that creates consciousness. Necromancy recreates the original body through a process called Resonance, which amplifies the memories from a body's remains. Those memories are weak or strong, depending on the condition of the remains. A complete, preserved body makes the best candidate for necromancy, whereas scattered remains produce only an animated, jerking skeleton."

"So you destroyed Steijn's body so that he could not be brought back—"

"Absolutely not. A full corpse creates a better facsimile of life, but ultimately, it is crueller still. Believe me; I tried it once."

One look at his expression tells me all I need to know: the pain and sorrow are real. Even a cruel immortal like Lucifer still feels the loss of a friend or a loved one.

"So, he's gone for good."

"Yes, and I'm sorry. I know I did the wrong thing."

Yeah, but you knew it was wrong. And you didn't care. The only reason you're apologising is that you can't bear to lose me.

I don't say the words; he needs to believe that I accept his apology, even though I really want to just rip his vile heart out of his body.

"Guess that's as good as I'm going to get. Thanks for healing me. Now leave me alone."

He nods solemnly before Fading away.

****

As I leave the infirmary, I am stopped short by Archdemon Tim, who is lounging in the corridor.

"You look much better," he says. "The hamburger look didn't suit you."

"Yeah, but it's not like I chose to look like that; firelings burned me."

"I meant no offence! I meant it as a compliment; you look fantastic."

"Well, thanks, but I'm not interested in campy guys if that's what you're thinking."

He smiles wanly. "Don't worry; you have nothing to fear from me. Actually, I meant this conversation to be a serious one."

"Go on."

"Lucifer explained the whole situation with Steijn to me. On the one hand, I'm sorry for you—I knew Steijn in passing. Nice guy. On the other hand, I'm concerned by the attachment you show to mortals."

"Concerned? Or do you just not like it?"

"Oh no, I love mortals too; I've had many mortal lovers over the centuries. Yet I do not allow myself to think that such a relationship will last forever, for mortals are but a flickering flame in the vast darkness of eternity."

"Well, you'd make a good poet. But I'm not sure I follow: I accept that my mortal friends will die while I will keep on living. That doesn't mean they should be murdered; that's cruel."

"But that's precisely the point: life is cruel. You can't save mortals, as mortals are beyond salvation."

"How cynical."

"Not cynical, just pragmatic. Experience has taught me to be realistic. The truth is, we love mortals for their frailty and beauty and hopeless innocence, the way we might love a lamb. But the truth is, we are wolves, and eventually, we will slaughter the lambs—they make a fine meal after all."

"So that's what humans are to you? Lambs before the slaughter?"

"I was only using a metaphor. But if you insist, let me try another metaphor. We are lions, and mortals are hyena cubs. Cute when they're young, but vile once they grow up, and unnecessary competition on top of that."

"Humans aren't vile."

"Aren't they? We demons might cause some mischief and have some fun at their expense, but humans kill themselves by the millions. Either through nuclear war and nationalism—the way my country perished—or through sheer indifference and contempt. They treated you like garbage when you were a Fallen; they treated me like garbage too. Do you know how many called me a poof and a fairy?"

"You got bullied as a kid—I get it. So what? Lots of people get over being bullied and become strong adults."

"Bullied, harassed, and attacked physically. Once they broke my arm."

"Once a guy tried to kill me with a knife; it didn't make me lose faith in all humanity."

He only smiles as if pitying me. "I envy your optimism. But I suspect it will wither like vines in a drought. Don't say I didn't warn you."

He walks away.

****

I didn't come back here to parley with demons about philosophy. My ultimate goal is deceiving Lucifer, but that will take some time, and until then, I might as well talk to people I actually like. After questioning the servants and demons, I find Max talking with Adrianne in a corridor.

They stop talking when they see me.

"Well, well," I say. "Gossiping about me behind my back?"

"Yes, if you must know," Adrianne replies. "The whole situation is weird. We have never known Lucifer to show so much contrition, to be so... desperate. Nor do we believe your story about coming back and being pals with Lucifer again."

"Well, I don't care one way or another. Believe what you like; it doesn't change a thing."

"You're playing at something," she says, eyes narrowed. "I just don't know what."

Max and I watch as she moves away from us.

"She's such a bitch," I tell him. "Why do you even keep talking to her?"

"I'll explain. Follow me first."

I follow him down the corridor to a balcony, where he spreads his wings and takes to the air. With a shiver of delight, I follow. We whoop and laugh—flying makes me ecstatic every time. I don't think I'll ever get bored of it.

I follow Max to the Boiling Lake, where we once fought in the arena. I can see that the lake has thawed and regained its namesake. Nobody is about now, which probably explains why Max brought me here.

"Spill," I say.

"I was talking to Adrianne because I wanted to get a feel for what the demons think about your return."

"And?"

"Opinions vary. Most demons seem to accept your story: you had a falling out with Lucifer, threw a tantrum, destroyed the Citadel Bridge, and Lucifer cast you out. You got burned by firelings. Now you're back, and you're Lucifer's favourite again."

"Good to know."

"Some demons, like Adrianne, are suspicious. But they have no idea what your plan is; they can't put their finger on what makes them uneasy."

"And what do you think?"

Max only smiles. He raises his hands, muttering a spell: *Silens*. I feel his magic like a bubble around us.

"That's a spell to protect us from prying ears. What I think, Mark, is that you hate Lucifer. He killed Steijn, whom you loved like a brother, and who was dear to me as well, by the way. So you made a deal with the dragon. You free the dragon, and he kills Lucifer."

"Wow. You almost figured it out—it's a bit more complicated than that, but the gist is correct."

"How do you plan on freeing the dragon? That's what I don't understand."

"By tearing down the Barrier and Ascending. I warp the power of the Infernal Cup, which breaks the spell that binds the dragon."

"Yes, I do remember how Lucifer managed to trap the dragon. Your plan is daring, I have to say."

I smile like broken glass. "So now that you've figured it out, what are you going to do? Join me? Or am I going to have to kill you?"

"Do you want to kill me?"

"No. I rather like you, Max, though I don't know why. I feel you're different from the other demons."

"The truth is, my Accession was very different. I killed a man in open combat, a powerful Roman general whom Lucifer despised."

"You really aren't like them," I say with surprise. "So why did you follow Lucifer? Why did you want to become a demon?"

"I wanted to be a powerful warrior, but I also loved Lucifer; he was my comrade-in-arms before he became a demon. In time, that emotion has softened. I feel a fondness for Lucifer, but I cannot ignore his actions, and I know that his rule would be a disaster for Earth."

"You're either with me or against me, Max. We cannot afford to sit this out by playing both sides."

"I'm with you, Mark. The more I've gotten to know you, the more I admire you for your love, bravery, and soul. What's more, I'm willing to prove it."

"How?" I ask, shocked.

"I am willing to put my life in your hands. I saw your duelling Lucifer with that sword of yours—a mighty fine weapon. So here's the deal: you stab me with that sword in the shoulder. It won't kill me instantly, but it will kill me eventually, sure as sure."

"Are you crazy?"

"Not at all. After you stab me, you will heal me."

"But I have no idea how to heal someone—"

"You'll figure it out; Shahar will help you if you ask."

"You'd do this to prove your loyalty to me? Why? Why not choose to do something less likely to kill you?"

"What else would you have me do? Besides, *audentes fortuna iuvat.*"

"Fortune favours the bold."

"Exactly."

I breathe in deeply, then exhale. "Okay, we might as well not waste time then. Are you ready?"

"Yes."

I lift my arm and cry the word that created the sword: *Pyr.* Fire races up my elbow and merges into a ball in my hand, which lengthens and darkens into a sword. A golden, shining blade.

With my hand holding the sword, I walk towards Max, who lies with his knees on the stone floor, unmoving. His eyes are clear blue.

"Are you sure? There are other ways to do this. You could steal something for me or kill another demon."

He smiles wanly. "Killing and stealing is what demons do to prove their loyalty to Lucifer; it's not what a warrior should do for his liege lord."

"Guess you're right. I hope I don't kill you."

"I know you won't kill me."

I raise the sword. In a flash, I stab it through his shoulder. He cries out in agony; the wound is burning.

"Max?"

"That weapon of yours—" he says, gasping, "is tremendously powerful. You must take me to Shahar immediately."

I nod. I extinguish the sword with a thought, and it vanishes into dust and flame. I lift Max, then Fade us to Shahar's study.

****

Shahar might be surprised to see us in his room, but he definitely doesn't show it. He takes one look at the wound on Max's shoulder—which is smoking and smouldering—and rises to his feet.

"Let me guess: Max asked you to stab him with your sword."

"How did you know?"

"It's just the thing Max would do. Come on; I'll teach you a healing spell. Max doesn't have long to live otherwise."

Shahar tears open Max's shirt (the old man is stronger than he looks) and then writes runes on his chest. I can see a dark line, like ashes, where the wound is spreading to Max's heart.

"Hold my hand," Shahar orders, "and say the word *agapó*. I will handle the rest of the spell."

I nod. "Agapo means love, right? Like, familial love?"

"Yes. The word will power the spell."

Shahar's hand is rough with wrinkles and calluses. I whisper the word *agapó*, saying it faster and faster, almost like a chant. Shahar is casting the spell. Like a bright golden band of energy, I feel my power snap out towards Shahar, then to Max. It touches the wound, which is like poison. It burns through the diseased tissue and calms the fire in the way water might extinguish hot ashes.

Max gasps, then his eyes open.

"Feeling better?" I ask.

"Much better, thank you. I take it my shoulder is no longer on fire?"

"No," Shahar says, "and fortunately for you, it will heal quickly. Mark's magic is a clean one. A weapon forged by Lucifer would probably have left you writhing in agony for days."

"I was counting on that."

"You were very foolish," Shahar admonishes. "But then, you always were brave."

"So, you're my knight Max?"

"I am your *Ypaspistès*. Your shield-bearer."

I grasp his hand, feeling the strength underneath. Max has forearms like steel vices.

"Glad to have you. I'll not forget this."

Chapter Eight: Healing

Kaylin

I stop moving, frozen to the ground. Roshika bumps into me from behind, but I barely notice her. My eyes are on the figure in Michael's arms. His burned hair makes him almost unrecognisable, but I can tell it is Shadow.

"What happened?" I ask. "Did she do this?"

"The crazy bitch with supernatural powers? The one you called Araya? Yeah, she did it," Leo informs me. I hadn't even noticed he was here.

"I had a vision of Araya, and I came back as soon as I could. But clearly, I was too late."

"I'm not sure if I blame you," Leo says. "I disagreed with your decision to leave for Everest, but no one could have foreseen we'd be attacked by another Familiar."

"She attacked you as well?"

"Attacked me? She nearly killed me. If it weren't for Michael here, I'd be dead. Speaking of which, who the hell is Michael?"

"He is... an ally."

"Kaylin, you have to tell him about us," Michael's gravelly voice intones. "You can no longer protect him by keeping him in the dark. Believe me, I would know."

"Kaylin?" Leo asks.

I sigh. "Leo... Michael is a demon. A former disciple of Lucifer."

"The Devil, you mean? He's real?"

"Very much so," Michael says with a hint of irony.

"Lucifer was trapped in an alternate dimension known as Hell, through a great spell called the Barrier. However, the barrier is weakening, and more demons can cross into Earth, at least temporarily. Michael here is one of the few demons who can stay here indefinitely."

"How come?" he asks.

"It's quite complicated," Michael says. "What you need to know is that other demons can cross over too, for a short while. They are extremely dangerous."

"If they're anything like you, I can imagine," Leo says. "So let me get this straight: Lucifer, the Devil, is trapped in Hell, but his minions can cross over from time to time. But what I don't understand is why does Lucifer care about any of us?"

"He wants to rule the world," Michael explains. "And he will should he get out."

"Starting with Ireland?"

"Someone very precious to him lived in Ireland. Someone we tried to protect but failed," I say, with a slight edge of bitterness.

"Oh, come on, Kaylin. Someone precious? You need to tell me more than that. You've already kept so much from me; you can't expect to bullshit me with something that vague."

I sigh deeply. Leo is right, of course.

"His name is Mark. He's a boy of about nineteen."

"Why does Lucifer want him so bad?"

"Because he is my son," Michael interrupts. I shoot him a grateful look. "He is half-demon and can cross the Barrier at will."

Leo whistles. "That makes sense."

"Gentlemen, as important as this conversation is," Roshika says, and we all turn towards her, "We have a wounded man to take care of."

All of them are staring at her, entranced by her strange garb and her incredible age. Roshika is hundreds of years old, and she looks the part.

"This is... your witch friend?" Leo asks.

"She is most certainly a witch," Michael confirms. "I can feel it."

Roshika fixes him with a level look. "Indeed. I have been training Kaylin here at my base in Everest, but there was only so much I could do in so little time, despite Kaylin's talent and eagerness to learn. She will have to learn more on the job. Find a bed for that wounded man, and let's get going."

****

I examine Shadow carefully, though it's painful to look at him. A sizeable portion of his body is burned through the dermis and into the fat, muscle, and bone. It's a miracle he's still alive.

"His vital signs are OK," I say quietly. "But the injuries he has sustained... they are horrible, beyond description. Why would she do this? Why not just kill him?"

"I think you know the answer to that," Roshika says.

"This... this was punishment. For killing her brother."

"You are probably right. But, there is a silver lining: your friend is alive, and I am one of the best living healers on Earth."

"Do you think... that he will look normal again? The way he did before? He had such bright red hair, and he was pretty young, only thirty-two."

"I cannot say for certain, not at this moment in time. But I am confident of the odds."

"Modern medicine would not be able to return him to his old self. He would live, the doctors would apply regenerator solution and stem therapy, but the burns..."

"Wouldn't quite fade. Yes, I have been keeping track of advances in medical science. Fortunately, Shadow has both modern medicine and magic to help him. We'll begin by healing the bone, which is the most important damaged tissue."

Roshika withdraws the White Book from her sari and looks for a spell. The runes and words on the page make me dizzy; it looks staggeringly complex.

"I'll guide you through it," she says. "Place your hand on Shadow's chest. Say the words after me, exactly as you hear them. You must push your mind out to encompass his body; I will tell you where to look."

I repeat a complex sentence of Latin and Greek words, feeling the magic grow with every syllable. My power rises inside me, but so does Roshika's, until the whole room seems to pulsate with healing magic. Roshika is sweating; I feel like I'm running a marathon. *Now,* she says telepathically.

I reach out with my mind, feeling the damaged muscle and liquefied fat. The skin has burnt off almost completely. But it's the bone that interests me: the bone marrow is where B-lymphocyte cells are produced. I feel Roshika's mind like a gentle presence, guiding my magic as it repairs cells and structures. The task is slow, even trying, but after several long minutes, we finish.

"Good," she says with approval. "It will take multiple sessions to repair the damage he has sustained, but we have completed an important step. Tell your doctors to apply the TGF-β solution in combination with hyper-oxygenated water. Most importantly, they must watch out for signs of infection. I prefer to treat infections with magic and use antibiotics only if necessary."

I nod. "And what will you do? I need to leave and convene with my men. We're expecting a counterattack—"

"I will take care of your friend here. But now, I must rest; that spell tired me more than you realise."

"I understand. Thank you for your help, Roshika."

****

I leave the infirmary and find myself face-to-face with Leo. He looks... exhausted. There are dark rings under his eyes, and he seems a little haggard. I realise that he must have cared for Shadow and that facing Araya was a traumatic experience.

"Kaylin," he whispers. "Will Shadow be OK?"

"Roshika seems confident."

"What do *you* think?"

"Me? I'm not sure. He'll live, that's for certain."

He nods. "It was my idea to attack the base incognito. I realise it was a mistake—"

"It wasn't. Your men took the city."

"But at what cost?"

"You could not have predicted the turn of events. I had a day's warning, barely, and I came here as soon as I could, but I still could not save one of my men from Araya. It is understandable to blame yourself, but I don't think we could have done anything better."

"How much did Roshika teach you? Was it worth it?"

"She's taught me a great deal."

"I realise this is very important for you; it's who you are. A witch."

"You're still wondering what exactly you and the other Familiars are?"

"Yes."

"Your power is demonic in origin."

"What? Like Michael's?" He sounds taken aback.

"Yes, though weaker. I was shocked, too, when Roshika told me, but it all makes perfect sense."

"I see. It's too much for me to process right now," Leo says.

"You suffered a trauma, seeing a friend get burned. I understand you barely escaped with your own life."

"I ran away," he admits. "When Araya attacked us, I abandoned Shadow."

"You would probably have died if you'd stayed. Araya is very formidable."

"But I feel like a coward!"

I place my arms around his shoulders, leaning into him. I kiss him lightly on the lips; he touches my hair.

"I have wanted to blame myself many times over the years, whenever I failed to protect my men, or a mission went awry. It's hard to shrug off the sense of responsibility, even when you are blameless. Believe me, I know."

He mulls my words in silence, holding me tight.

****

I summon my men to the main antechamber of the Dublin base. Michael, Leo, and Diana are also here.

"We stand at a pivotal point in the history of this country," I begin. "With the help of our allies, we have taken half of Ireland, from Derry to Cork, and the west coast to Roscommon. But we have not won yet. Belfast is an impenetrable fortress, and Dublin, the capital, is still beyond our reach."

"We might not be safe here," Grumman says. "The Party knows who they're facing. We can't keep operating in the capital. I suggest moving to Letterkenny, next to our allies; it's the most secure location."

"I agree—Letterkenny is a good choice. Currently, Shadow's medical condition is such that I would prefer not to move him. But we will begin moving our operations away from here; once Shadow is sufficiently recovered, we will mothball this place."

"How long will it take for Shadow to recover?" Diana asks with concern.

"Roshika thinks we can move him after a few weeks."

"Kaylin, Shadow could be the least of our worries," Grumman says gently. "The Party is mounting a huge counter-attack as we speak, as reported by our spies. Even the media is talking about how half the country has been overrun. This woman, Araya, is the Party's weapon against us. We need to be ready."

"We can handle Araya," I say confidently.

"But do you think our allies can hold out against the Party while you hunt her? They may need our support, including your magic."

I sigh. "Then we will need to split up, won't we? I will go to the North, Diana, to Roscommon, and Michael will go to Cork."

"I've no doubt the demon can handle Araya," Grumman says, not calling Michael directly by name, "but can you? Alone?"

"I'm ready for the bitch," Diana says with venom.

"Michael can teleport," I say. "Roshika can help us remotely."

I show them my obsidian medallion, the one I gave to Conall, who told me to wear it. "I can use this medallion to signal for help. I'll make another one for you too, Diana."

"I don't know much about magic," Grumman says, "so I can only take you at your word. I hope you know what you're doing, Kaylin."

****

I am inside an armoured car stationed in Enniskillen. Andrew, our allied leader, is beside me. We're watching our men as they barricade the city, set up mines, and DIY air defence systems.

"We're most vulnerable from an air attack," he says. "But I agree with your decision not to deploy the Q-cars you own; they are too valuable to waste on a fight we can't win. We'll have to beat them on land."

"It's my job to use magic to destroy the enemy's air forces," I say.

"Diana and Michael can do that, but I'm not so sure you can. Even Diana was rendered unconscious by the fight."

"Fair enough," I say. "Guess we'll have to find out."

We won't have to wait much. Our spies tell us that a sizeable armoured convoy is fast approaching from the East, and with them are several aircraft. They'll attack any minute now.

"What have your visions told you?" he asks.

"Nothing we don't already know from—"

A loud alarm goes off, interrupting what I was about to say. Defensive missiles are fired off from somewhere inside the city. A moment later, I see their target: a squadron of Q fighters. One of the fighter craft goes down in a fireball, but most of the missiles miss. The ground shudders as bombs detonate all around us—one is closer than the others. My ears are ringing.

"Kaylin?"

"I'm preparing a spell."

I close my eyes, searching my memory for a good spell. As my lips start to move, we hear a scream, and the street in front of us lights up like a Christmas tree. Only this is no festive show: this is real fire. The kind of fire that Michael or Diana can conjure.

"She's here," I say.

"Kaylin, don't confront her! We'll send androids and men—"

"No. I want to know why she joined the Party's side; I want to recruit her."

"Are you crazy? A bomb killed her brother!"

"And that means we should kill her? I can handle her, Andrew. I'll disable her, and then we can talk."

He protests, but I'm already out of the armoured car and walking down the street. I place a shield on my skin; the spell comes naturally, the way swinging a bat is familiar to a cricket player.

I find her walking down the middle of the street and notice the fire and destruction surrounding her. Smoking husks, formerly androids, decorate the apocalyptic scene like obelisks. There are also corpses mixed in with the robots.

"So you're Araya," I say, taking in her thin blue dress, her long blonde hair. "I would be pleased to meet you in other circumstances. I'm Kaylin."

"Intelligence gathered that the leader of the rebels is in the north. That's why I came here; I figured that if I cut the snake's head, the body will die with it. Are you the leader?"

"As far as you are concerned, yes."

"Good enough for me. Guess if I kill you, I won't have to deal with that *thing*."

"You mean Michael?"

"Whatever his name is. I'm smart enough to know that if an enemy is too strong, you should go for the weaker foe first."

"And do you believe I am weak?"

"Let's see, huh?"

I parry her fireball with the shield spell. But it's harder than I thought—the magic makes my nerves tingle.

"We don't have to fight," I say. "I know how your brother died. For what it's worth, I'm sorry."

"Yeah, apologies won't help now."

"Nor will harming others bring him back. My friend, Shadow—"

"The redhead? That idiot?"

"You didn't have to burn him, and he's not an idiot."

She just laughs; it's an almost hysterical sound. "You're the one leading a fucking *revolution*. You don't get to choose who lives and who dies. There's no such thing as being neutral in a civil war—you choose one side or the other. And I think you're worse than the Party."

"I hope to convince you otherwise."

"Tough luck, 'cos you're not going to convince me. I'm going to turn you into a candle like I did with your pretty little friend."

That makes me angry. The spell comes instantly to my mind, even though I've never used a Shatter spell like this one before. I cast the magic in my mind's eye, then grab hold of it, like it's a physical thing, and *fling* it towards Araya. It whips out from my hand, striking fast and true.

Araya raises a telekinetic shield. The Shatter spell explodes her protection like broken glass; the blast sends her flying.

"That was for Shadow," I say, gritting my teeth. Had she not protected herself, the spell would have killed her instantly by tearing her into shreds.

She dusts herself off. "Not bad. Now let me try."

Chapter Nine: A Meeting with Lucifer

Mark

"Lucifer has important news for you," Archdemon Tim says, lounging on my bed. I sigh.

"And did you have to come into my room to tell me that?"

"What was I supposed to do?"

"Knock?"

"Knocking is too proletarian for me."

"Whatever. Where will I find him?"

"It's a special room you haven't seen before. I'll take you there."

"Is that why he sent you?"

"Oh no, I volunteered. I wanted to make things up with you. For, you know, the conversation we had."

"Ah, you're afraid you've fallen afoul of Lucifer's protégée."

"Something like that. Shall we?" Tim asks, opening my window with a flick of his wrist. I jump after him, unfurling my wings mid-air. The euphoria is timeless.

"Fancy a race?" he asks.

"Sure."

I immediately regret my words: Tim darts forward like a cannon-ball. I push myself hard, narrowing my wings; I too gain speed, but more gradually. We fly around the Citadel in an arc, staying inside the wards. (Rex's firelings won't hurt me, but Tim doesn't know that.)

Soon, I'm gaining on him, but it's too late. He stops in front of a balcony and enters. I spread my wings wide, slowing down, but the granite still gives way beneath my legs.

"A hard landing," he comments.

"You win."

He only smiles. "Gotta go."

****

I enter the room and find myself alone with Lucifer. The Great Demon examines an enormous device that looks like a cross between a giant mirror, a gyroscope, and a laser. "What the bleedin' heck is that?"

"That is the Protequistator."

"What does it do?"

"It can do many things; you should think of it as a tool that allows a demon to project his presence."

"Like a Projection?"

"Yes, but better. You can influence minds and control mutants. How did you think I was able to influence Finn? Or command the mutants to attack?"

"Right, so that's how you did it. Did you bring me here just to show me this... protequistator?"

He turns around and smiles. "I thought you would be more interested in knowing what's going on down on Earth."

"You've never told me before," I say, but my breath hitches in my throat.

"Conall is doing well in Spain."

"You stay away from Conall now. We had a deal, Lucifer."

"We still do, and I respect it. I was only checking in on his welfare."

"What about my father? My uncle?"

"Your uncle is also in Spain. As for Michael, he is busy helping the witch fight the Party. Actually, they're in the middle of a huge battle, which I quite enjoy following. That Leo fellow is smart; he would make a good demon."

"Are they winning?"

"Well, Michael is killing everyone in his path. But they're losing, on the whole. The witch is having a hard time dealing with another Familiar—who, by the way, would make an excellent demoness."

"You're wrong about Kaylin; she will come out on top."

The Great Demon only chuckles. "If you say so, my dear. Now, there's one more thing I wanted to show you."

"Go on."

"You must follow me to a room I call the Arsenal."

"This should be interesting," I remark as we make our way down from the Tower and towards the basement of the Citadel. We encounter many demons on the way who bow to Lucifer and fix me with curious glances.

"Still the Chosen One, then," I mutter.

"Of course. You have the power to free us, Mark. And you are unique."

We descend several flights of stairs until, at last, we reach the area of the Arsenal. This is where I stole the Dark Cup and found Suzanne dying. Lucifer must be aware that I know *something* about this place— but he must never know how I found out. The imps would be in grave danger should their secret ever be revealed.

Lucifer pauses at the door, easily stripping away the glamour concealing the entrance. I whistle.

"It is very impressive, is it not?" he asks.

"I'm impressed, all right."

"I still haven't figured it out—how *did* you know where to look for the Infernal Cup?"

I can see this question is a test.

"Well, I'm not just going to tell you, am I? You're the Devil; you can figure it out on your own."

"You want to play the game then. Very well," he says, chuckling. "I suspect you pestered Shahar into giving up his secrets. I expected that from you; you are too clever, and Shahar is too sentimental. But I suppose no harm was done, so I shall forgive my old friend this transgression."

"You said you wanted to show me the Arsenal?" I ask, changing the subject.

"Indeed. This is where I store a great many powerful spells. Some are used to power the wards here in Hell or to keep the lights on—literally and not figuratively."

"So do you have to... recharge them?"

"Not quite. It would be more accurate to say I maintain them; the warding spells draw their power from nature."

"What about the other spells? I'm guessing you don't call it the Arsenal if it doesn't have some kick-ass spells."

He laughs. "Yes, the Song of Fire is one such example."

"What does it do? Rain fireballs from the heavens?"

"It does exactly that."

"And... how do you store all this power, exactly?"

"Good question. Follow me." I walk alongside the Great Demon as he leads me through the corridor and into a great cavern. At its centre lies a fountain, shaped in the form of a winged demon. This is where I stole the Infernal Cup. I notice that the Cup has been returned to its original resting place: the winged statue is holding it.

"Where do these doors lead?" I ask, motioning at the great barrier doors, which are warded with glowing blue runes. Some appear to be made from stone; others hardwood, perhaps oak or ash, but most of the doors are forged in black metal. It is like no metal known to man, for its surface glimmers, like the edge of fine obsidian.

"Let me show you." The Great Demon stalks forward, stopping near one of the black metal doors. He raises his hands, muttering an arcane sequence—a password of some sort. The magic protecting the door fades to an almost imperceptible glow. Lucifer pushes the door open.

Beyond the door lies a crystal—a very big crystal, easily as tall as two men. It is red, like blood, and seems to emit a sanguine glow.

"Did you bring these crystals here?" I ask.

"No, they were already formed when I arrived in Hell. I merely took advantage of them, adapting them to my own purposes. I strongly suspect they are tied to the crystals on Earth."

"Why do you think so?"

He smiles. "I know a great deal about these crystals, Mark. How do you think I became a demon?"

I freeze. "I have no idea. I tried to ask you before, but you always evaded my questions with poetry."

The Great Demon laughs mirthfully. "I did not think you were ready then. Now I am willing to tell you."

"I'm all ears, Lucifer. Where did you get the power for the transformation?"

"From a cluster of crystals on Earth, located deep within the Himalayas."

"So, what? You just walked up to a bunch of crystals and POOF! Demon."

"Well, actually, I crawled towards them while grievously injured. I took the magic—the force that underpins nature—and claimed it as my own. There is power out there, Mark. The Universe is full of magic. Yet the vast majority of humans frolic in the mud, incapable of grasping what the stars can offer us."

"Some must have tried, surely?"

"They did, but they never had what it takes."

"Which is?"

"Will. Desire. Vengeance."

"Could I become like you?"

He smiles widely. "Yes. You are the only one I have known, after all these millennia, to truly be capable."

His eyes are wild, intense, electric. I have to turn away.

"You've told me the how," I whisper, "but you haven't told me the why."

"The humans like to believe I fell from Heaven," the Devil says, amused. "But once again, these are stories that appeal to mankind's incorrigible love of morality tales."

"There is no Heaven, is there? No soul? No God?"

"If there is a Heaven and a God, I have never seen it. No, Mark. In my long existence, I have come to realise that there is only Nature, and we can either choose to be pawns in Nature's game—or we can choose to master it."

"But *somebody* must have had an interest in inventing these stories," I point out. "Until a few centuries ago, religion was one of the dominant forces in human society."

"I am impressed by your sagacity—you learn fast. Indeed, the stories were propagated by a bunch of witches. You might know them as the Sadducees or the Pharisees, but they went by many names."

"Who were they?"

"In short? A cabal of power-hungry wizards. They were the *real* conspiracy, you know. To the Jewish tribes, they were prophets and demigods, like Moses. They also ran the Roman Empire, but very few knew of their involvement."

"So it wasn't really about a heroic figure rising up against the Roman oppressors?"

"Oh, that heroic figure was partly me."

"Wait, what?"

I examine Lucifer more carefully, trying to determine if he's pranking me. Could he really be the Jesus from the tales? The defender of the downtrodden, the enemy of the rich and powerful? This prince of gluttony?

He laughs. "Don't look so surprised. I was very different back then—I was much more naïve, to start with."

"But you're a Roman citizen."

"I never really gave a shit about the goat-herders, that's true. But we fought a common enemy. And I was friends with many of the sheep lovers."

"So you threatened their power? And the Sadducees wanted you dead?"

"The Romans wanted me dead too, in the end. I might have been a general in their army and a powerful sorcerer, but I was becoming too much of a liability. The Roman high command didn't appreciate loose cannons."

This is a lot to absorb; it makes my head spin.

"Then why do you want to rule the world?" I ask him. "You saw what monsters the Sadducees were."

"Because I am a true god. I don't need to hide in the shadows, to claim a divine right and build messianic cults. The world is ruled by the powerful, Mark; the meek will not inherit the Earth. You can choose the wolf who swallows the occasional lamb, or you can choose the pack of rabid dogs who will rip apart the whole flock."

He certainly looks like a wolf, this Prince of Darkness: he lounges in mid-air, relaxed, but I know that Lucifer is always a split-second away from tearing somebody apart. It's what makes him so alluring. Wolves don't need to wear sheepskins because the lambs come to them willingly.

"Thank you for telling me this, Lucifer."

"You are welcome, Mark. I am glad you understand."

"Tell me: is it wrong for the wolf to love a lamb? Can his nature be changed?"

"The wolf will always remain a predator. But he can choose not to kill; he can choose to show mercy. I know what it means to love a mortal—I am not without compassion."

Maybe you did understand the meaning of compassion, for you were a hero once, I think. But not anymore.

Chapter Ten: The Battle for Ireland

Leo

We watch the incoming Party division with trepidation. I have returned to command my men in the defence of Cork, but once again, I fear the odds aren't good. The Party is throwing everything they have at us.

"Why Cork?" I ask to no one in particular. Harry, one of my subordinates, answers me anyway.

"They probably think that Roscommon isn't worth as much effort, and they believe they'll take Enniskillen anyway. Too close to Belfast."

"We have the fight of our lives ahead of us."

No sooner do I say the words than a squadron of Party Q-fighters swoop down and rain hellfire on our position. The plasma cannons are one thing, but the bombs hit even harder. We've barricaded the city, with us in it, but I know our position is precarious; our air defence systems are inadequate.

"Michael!" I cry.

Harry starts when he sees the demon, who emerges from the daylight like a shadow. Even with his wings furled, Michael is beautiful, radiant, and unnatural.

"Is he the Familiar you said was going to help us?" Harry asks.

I smile a twisted smile. "You could call him a Familiar, but that does not do him justice."

"How can I help?" Michael asks.

"See those Q fighters? Go and destroy them. We'll manage the land forces on our own."

"Is he going to blow them up like Diana—"

"No, Harry. Watch."

Michael unfurls his wings, which are long and velvety dark. Harry is staring at him with open-mouthed wonder. The demon takes off like a rocket. Despite the oncoming enemy, I simply can't help but watch; this is a truly spectacular fight. Twelve Q-fighters engage Michael, shooting plasma, launching missiles, and lasering him. Michael casually evades the missiles and simply ignores the rest, which does him no harm at all.

"What—how isn't he dead?"

"Harry, be quiet."

Michael teleports, cutting a Q-fighter in half; it falls to the ground in smouldering pieces. He fires not one but multiple fireballs, hitting two Q-fighters and downing them. The remaining Q-fighters assess the situation and decide to turn tail and run. But Michael has one more trick up his sleeve: raising his hands and hovering, he begins to *glow*. Sparks fly off him like lightning.

The sky opens, and a bolt of lightning arcs out from the demon, instantly destroying another two Q-fighters.

"Holy shit," Harry says.

But he says no more, for soon the land forces are engaging us. The Party has androids, fast armoured vehicles, and, most of all, *tanks*. Until now, we had not fought any tanks; they are all kept in Dublin and Belfast. They're the finest land-based weapon the Party fields in a conventional war, and boy are they mean.

My men had rigged the main streets with mines, but the tanks are keeping their distance. Instead, they're bombarding us with long-range laser fire, missiles, and plasma cannons. Several of our androids fall. My men return fire with plasma cannon, but it takes multiple hits to take down a tank. Their ordinance eclipses our own.

"If only they came inside the city, the mines would have given us a huge advantage," I curse.

"They're not that stupid," Harry points out. "They suspected something like that. They want to weaken us first, then finish us off."

Michael, I cry out telepathically. *Where are you?*

Trying to finish off the Q-fighters. I have only a few more.

Well, come here, right now. Leave the fighters for later.

The demon once again appears next to us; Harry almost jumps out of his seat.

"Yes?"

"We need to take those tanks down."

"Certainly—" He pauses.

I feel it, too: a *pulse*, a magical vibration. "Is that...?"

"It's Kaylin's medallion. She needs my help."

"Wait!" I shout.

He looks at me, perplexed.

"Kaylin has Diana and the other witch to help her. But if you leave us now, it will be the end of us. We've already lost half our androids and multiple men. We have no way of gaining the upper hand on the tanks."

"But—"

"No buts. I know Kaylin; she can take care of herself. Trust me."

He meets my eyes, nodding. "I trust you."

****

Kaylin

I deflect a series of Araya's fireballs using spells, trying to preserve my energy. I quickly realised that blocking her attacks in full would be my death sentence: Araya is powerful, the most powerful Familiar I have met. Her raw power easily exceeds mine.

I've tried catching her with non-lethal binding spells, but she either evades them or brushes them aside with telekinesis. She is also the best telekinetic user I have ever seen; I still can't believe she is able to counter my spells so easily!

"Just die already," she screams, throwing another fireball. I shudder as I catch it on my Shield spell, having failed to parry it properly. I feel the magic exhausting me. My insides are like jelly.

Realising the situation is dire, I activate my medallion. She must have felt the magical pulse because she halts her attack for just an instant and narrows her eyes at me.

"What are you doing?"

"I know when I'm outmatched; I'm calling for help."

"A little late for that, isn't it?" she asks, smirking.

"I still have one more trick up my sleeve."

I whisper the word of the death spell, knowing it's my best shot: *Nekros*. Death rises around me, rotten like the grave, and I target it—

Before I can unleash my spell, her telepathic attack hits me like a hot knife through my mind; it takes everything I have just to block it. I know that if I fail, I will lose my sanity. She raises her arms, a fireball coalescing around her hands—

Then the sky goes black. Her telepathic assault stops, and we both crane our necks upwards. A swarm of mutants has appeared out of no-where: there are flying pterodactyls, giant wasps, and leathery, wyvern-like creatures in the group. A moment later, they swoop down on us.

Araya cries out, raising a telekinetic shield. I place a Glamour on myself. The mutants throw themselves at Araya with zeal, and Araya burns them all to kingdom come.

Or at least, it *looks* like the mutants are being burned to death. Araya certainly thinks so. But I am more perceptive than she is: I can feel that there is magic at work here. Those creatures aren't real—they're illusions!

Araya shrieks with rage, frustrated by the endless stream of mutants. She does not spot what is behind her. A light. Something like... a portal? An old, hunched woman walks from the light. I recognise her immediately: Roshika.

"*Capio*," Roshika intones, her arms stretched out. A band of blue light snakes out and twists itself around Araya. Roshika says another word, *nullum*, and this time a string of red light detaches from her hand and binds Araya. The red spell and the blue spell entwine and trap the enraged Familiar. She's helpless.

I stare at Roshika, not quite able to believe what I'm seeing. "Roshika? Is that you?"

"Did you think demons were the only ones who could teleport?"

"But I never found a spell—"

"You just never had the right tools. Now, tell me, what are we going to do with this bitch?"

Chapter Eleven: Prisoner

Kaylin

"I say we kill her," Leo declares.

"I want her alive," I argue. "Besides, killing her would be a war crime. She's a prisoner of war."

"This isn't a normal god-damn war we're fighting," Grumman points out. "We're rebels, and rebels in a civil war have zero rights, even if we suspended disbelief and took the European Declaration of Human Rights at face value."

"She's a liability," Diana says, looking at the figure inside the cell. In the days following our victory, we'd moved operations from our Dublin base to a new headquarters in Letterkenny, just a few miles from our allies. Shadow's condition had improved such that we could transport him safely.

"She's a murderer without a conscience," Leo adds. "We can't trust her."

I turn to Roshika, pleading with my eyes. She assesses the situation carefully.

"There are advantages and disadvantages to both positions. To kill Araya would send a bad message; it would make us like the Party. On the other hand, Araya cannot be trusted."

"So, we keep her bound with magic until the war ends?" I ask.

"It is the most sensible course of action if you wish to avoid bloodshed."

"What did Andrew say?" I ask Grumman.

"He agreed with me; he thinks we should kill Araya and be done with it."

"No."

My men only sigh—they know that tone. It means the argument is over.

"What about the strategic situation?" Grumman asks, changing the subject. "We've beaten the Party's forces and have secured the western half of Ireland. That was good going, Leo."

"Michael did most of the work," he points out modestly.

"But you made the right decision in keeping him with you," I say. "We would have lost Cork otherwise, and many men would have perished."

"I thought you would be cross. Since, you know, he didn't come to help you out."

"I decided to confront Araya one-on-one," I reply. "I am responsible for my actions."

"Speaking of which," Roshika begins, "Kaylin, you need to be more careful. If it weren't for me, you'd be dead."

"I had the death spell—"

"You were too slow and left yourself undefended. Araya was able to interrupt your spell with a telepathic attack."

"Ladies," Grumman injects, "I have a question. Roshika, how did you manage to teleport and help Kaylin? Could you teleport some of our own men? What about tanks, or maybe... weapons."

I can see what Grumman is leading at. "You think Roshika might be able to bring a cache of weapons across the blockade in the Irish Sea, using magic?"

Ever since we won the Battle of Cork, the Party had declared a state of emergency. No air traffic and no maritime shipping are allowed. Nothing can get in or out of Ireland right now.

"I'm not convinced it's possible," Roshika says. "With you, Kaylin, I had the medallion to guide my magic. I can use the green crystal—which, by the way, is named the Crystal of Navigation—to teleport pretty much anything. But I still need a beacon."

"OK. Kaylin, we need to think about how we're going to take Dublin."

"We don't have enough weapons to take Dublin. Without heavy artillery, there is no way to defeat Party tanks or fortifications. You know that, Grumman."

"Can't the Spanish send us more weapons?"

"I've talked to them, and the answer is no. If they are caught trying to smuggle something into Ireland, it will be seen as an act of aggression. They don't want to declare war on another Member State."

"Can you get something on the international black market?"

"Not without fighting the Party's air-force and navy to break the blockade."

Grumman nods at my words. "That may be our next plan."

****

After the meeting, I returned to Shadow's room, where I helped Roshika with the healing spells. He's asleep on the bed, no longer unconscious. Roshika informed me that Shadow regained consciousness yesterday. He even stirs a little in his sleep.

"When is he going to wake up?"

I start. I hadn't heard Leo enter the room. "Soon. Maybe a week."

"He's already looking better. There's even some hair growing on his scalp. Did Roshika do that?"

"She did."

"That woman is remarkable."

"Careful now. I did a lot of healing, too, remember?"

"Of course. Don't assume I think any less of you, Kaylin."

He places his hand on mine.

"So you really cared about Shadow, didn't you?" I ask.

"I only just met him, but I liked him straight away. And when Araya burned him..."

"It's like he was snatched away from you right in front of your eyes."

"Exactly. I couldn't have put it better myself."

"It's strange how we can end up caring for the people we least expect."

"Tell me about it."

****

Days have passed, and my men have been cooperating with the Communists to smuggle a shipment of weapons from a dealer in China. The Chinese government wants to encourage rebellions within the European League of Nations, hoping it might weaken their enemy.

Grumman is formulating a strategy for sneaking the ship through, but it's much harder to get a boat to pass unnoticed than to get a Q-car. Plan B is to have Michael and our Q-cars attack enemy submarines while the ship makes a getaway.

"How close are we to launching the mission?" I ask him.

"Not long now, maybe in two, three days. There are a lot of contingencies to plan for; the biggest headache is the subs."

"It's hard to hit a sub if you can't see it. But just because you can't see them doesn't mean they can't see you."

"Exactly."

"What about sneaking the weapons through using submarines?"

"Do you have any submarines?" he asks.

"No, but—"

"Even if we could get some on short notice—and your wealth is great, Kaylin, I do not doubt that—the problem is that we can't fit tanks and artillery inside a sub. It has to be a ship."

"Good point."

"Have you had any more visions?"

"Not yet, but I will try. What does Diana think? Andrew?"

"Ask them; they're here in the room with us."

Our new base in Letterkenny was bigger by far than Dublin, and we had a vast control room all to ourselves. It takes me a moment to spot Diana among my men. She is speaking to a holographic projection of Andrew.

"Okay, so we rely on the cover of darkness and the jamming devices to sneak through, and if not—"

"Diana, how are things going?"

"I was just talking to Andrew here. He thinks—"

She stops mid-sentence, mouth agape. I follow her eyes and see the cause of her surprise. On the table, a small red creature is standing, arms crossed, looking very superior.

"What is that...?" Diana breathes.

"*That* is being called an imp. My name is Pip."

"You're an imp?" I ask. "Are you allied to Lucifer?"

"Lucifer is our master, but that doesn't mean I'm on his side. Actually, I'm helping your friend, Mark. You need to listen to me."

I project my voice telepathically. *Everyone! Silence!*

My men instantly stop what they're doing and turn around; they, too, stare at the creature on the table. She gives a little wave.

"Hello, humans, imp here! Stop staring like idiots and listen. I have important news about Mark."

"What about him? Is he safe?"

"Safe? Oh, he's perfectly safe for now. He's going to tear down the Barrier."

At first, I simply can't process what she's telling me. It's like a wrecking ball has hit me.

"Hello? Is anyone there?" the imp mocks.

"But... why? Why would he do that? He knows it would condemn us all."

"He has a plan, don't you worry. He's made friends with the dragon."

"The dragon?"

"Big scary reptile. Apparently, by tearing down the Barrier, he frees the dragon."

"But why didn't he ask me!" I explode.

"Uhm, it's kind of difficult to get out of Hell. Impossible, actually. I'm only here because Lucifer sent me to spy on you."

"You've been spying on us? For how long?"

"Oh, a month, give or take. You didn't even spot me, silly witch."

"What have you told Lucifer?"

"Nothing *important*. Anyway, what matters is that I'm telling you this now. Forget about your stupid plan; you need to prepare for a fight with Lucifer."

I run my hands through my hair, feeling frustrated, angry, and confused. Somehow, Lucifer is always one step ahead of me.

"Get Roshika," I bark to Diana. "What is Mark *thinking*?"

"Oh, he's right. I don't think you stand a chance, whereas Mark and the dragon might win against my master. But, hey, don't say I didn't warn you. Now, I need to be off."

"Wait! Do you know when Mark is going to do it?"

"Tomorrow."

With that, the imp bounds away, disappearing in a puff of smoke. Roshika and Diana arrive moments later, looking around the room in confusion.

"What happened?" Roshika asks.

"We need to prepare to wage war against Lucifer. All Hell is going to break loose." In a whisper so quiet only I can hear it, I add: "Mark, I hope you're not sending us to our doom."

PART THREE: FINALE

Chapter One: Let it Burn

Mark

In the beginning, I did not believe in power. I was a nobody, a lucky Fallen boy who fell in love with a soft-hearted Upperclassman. I told myself that love would save me, but that was a lie I did not believe: my story was doomed to tragedy. Teenage love would blossom, and then, as surely as night would follow the day, it would wilt and die. Conall would marry some female and get his boys on the side. As for me, a mutant or a drug dealer would finish me off.

But in time, I grew to understand my power and what it could do. I fought against the Party and won battles; I even killed Big Brother. I could not protect Conall from Lucifer's demons, but that was only because I was too weak.

Power is neither good nor bad; it just is. But for good to prevail, the righteous must be strong.

So I find myself face-to-face with Lucifer in his room, having requested to meet with him.

****

"Hello, Mark. I confess I'm surprised to see you here."

"I thought I could call on you for a change."

"I like that."

I clear my throat, feeling slightly nervous. The Infernal Cup is in my hands; I offer it to Lucifer. He raises an eyebrow in surprise.

"The Infernal Cup. Are you telling me that..."

"Yes. I want to Ascend. To become like you."

He pauses, looking me in the eye. It's not easy to lie to someone to their face, especially when they are the Devil himself. His countenance is beautiful, his eyes dark and probing.

I used to think that Lucifer knew everything and that no one could keep a secret from him; that he could uncover any lie. Maybe that's true for most, but not for me. Despite what he's done, Lucifer still loves me in his own twisted way.

Too bad I hate his guts.

"I've been thinking," I start, "about what you said to me when we first met in Hell."

"About power?"

"Yes. In time, I have come to realise the truth of your words. I still love Conall, but I no longer think of you as my enemy. In fact, I want to be your ally. And I want to be stronger."

"What changed?"

What changed is that you murdered someone I cared about in front of my eyes.

"I am tired of being too weak to get what I want. What's more, I've started to admire you, Lucifer. You can be cruel, but you can also be brave and kind and fair. Human leaders are all corrupted by power; they chase that which they can never truly possess. You are an immortal god. You can rule without fear, and thus you can rule justly."

"I am glad you finally see the truth. Humans do indeed chase the power they can never have—I couldn't have put it better myself. But Mark," he says, holding my hand, "this is about you. Why do you want to do this?"

"Because I want to rule by your side. It's time I turned the tables."

He smiles brilliantly. "Well said, Mark, well said. Give me a few days to prepare everything for your Ascension."

"Turns out this cup is useful after all," I joke.

"Oh, it's beneficial. You are going to be stronger than you can ever imagine."

****

I turn and examine myself in the mirror. Usually, I don't particularly care about clothes—I would happily go about my business naked, and I told Lucifer as much. But he insisted I wear something nice. "You should wear trousers, at least," he joked.

I am in my room; Max and Shahar are with me. A couple of days have passed since I spoke with Lucifer.

"The jeans suit you," Max says of the black, boot-cut denim.

"The boots too," Shahar adds. "You chose them perfectly. The dark brown complements your attire well."

"Thanks," I say, with a hint of irony. "Too bad I'm not wearing a shirt, eh?"

"The ceremony is unique to you," Max says. "It's about you gaining power and agency. That means you shouldn't wear what other people tell you to. Social convention is just another form of coercion."

"Did you get my scabbard?" I ask.

"Yes, here. Shahar and I did our best to ward it, but I would keep the burning effect to a minimum," Max says, winking.

I take the scabbard I asked for—a beautifully-crafted artisan's piece, made in the Scottish style—and sling it across my back. My sword appears in my right hand at my command, though it's not on fire this time. I place the silvery blade in its scabbard; only the tip is sheathed in order to allow me to draw it. Turns out you can't actually draw a blade on your back if the length of the sheath exceeds past your elbow—it took me a couple of attempts to figure it out. Max had died laughing.

"You don't look bad yourselves," I comment, taking note of Shahar's robe—a decadent, embroidered affair, dyed navy blue. "Is that traditional Jewish garb?"

"No," Shahar says. "I was ostracised from my community a long time ago. I no longer wear the garb."

"I had no idea, sorry. No toga, Max?"

"It's out of fashion; we Romans prefer suits these days. But I'm carrying the enchanted spear and shield I used when I fought for Lucifer."

He hefts a rounded shield on his left arm, which is black as a starless night. In his right arm, he holds a spear whose point glimmers like ice.

"Before we do this," Shahar says, "you have considered the full ramifications?"

"There's no way for anyone to anticipate the full ramifications," I point out. "I'm just following my gut."

"It's the best we can hope for," Max points out. "You know what the ceremony involves, right?"

"First, I tear down the Barrier. Then, I drink water from the Infernal Cup. I either survive, or I die."

"You will survive," Shahar says. "The question is, will you break the Cup's power?"

"Only one way to find out."

I Fade to the Throne Room, Max fading Shahar with him.

****

The Throne Room is full to bursting: every demon has come here to watch the ceremony. I spot Tim among the Archdemons, wearing his usual pink tank top, and Diego is among the ranks too. I expected to see fear, anger, or hate, but he looks at me like I'm a god. I turn away quickly.

"We come here to watch Mark Ascend," Lucifer begins, "but also to bear witness to our freedom. For millennia, we have been trapped here in this place. You have followed me through victory and defeat, through Hell and high water." A few demons laugh at his remark.

Lucifer continues, smiling. "You have shown great faith in me, my dear beloved demons, even when the Barrier seemed impregnable. Many of you joined our ranks after we were imprisoned here, confident that one day we would prevail and Earth would be ours.

"But perhaps the greatest faith has come from Mark. I kidnapped him from his beloved and killed a boy he was fond of, yet he chose to accept me as his ally. He chose to free us. Mark, we are all in your debt now. Know that I will respect your wishes regarding Conall, for my desire is nothing compared to your actions."

Such pretty words, I think. If I didn't know better, I might actually believe him! But I know Lucifer for what he is: the most extraordinary liar ever to walk Hell or Earth. The danger is not that he might kill me; the danger is that I would corrupt myself willingly for him.

Out loud, I say, "Tell me how to break this damn Barrier."

In an instant, Lucifer is in front of me. "You must reach out and feel it. I perceive it as being like a shield. Beyond that, I can offer no help. This power is unique to you, and you alone."

I nod, take a deep breath, and close my eyes.

I feel it like a... veil. It's the only way I can describe it. Yet this veil is not diaphanous but solid and robust. I reach out, grasping the shroud with my mind's eye. Then I tear it off.

The effort is *mammoth*. I feel like Atlas holding the entire world on his shoulders. My muscles strain, despite making no physical effort; I fall to my knees. Even as I do this, I feel only distantly aware of my body. The veil has the strength of steel, but I must be stronger.

With a final, loud cry, I succeed. The Barrier comes crashing down like the shards of a broken stained-glass window. The noise is incredible. I hear it like the rushing of a great river, mixed in with grinding noises as if the river were tearing down a decaying stone wall.

My vision swims, and I sway; Max is at my side in an instant. Then the moment passes.

I blink, looking around the room. The demons are still and silent. For a second, I wonder if I failed. But no: everything feels different. It's as if a pane of glass has been removed from a window.

Slowly, Lucifer starts to clap. The demons begin clapping, too, until the whole chamber echoes with thunderous applause.

Several long minutes pass and the room is abuzz with conversation and cheers. Lucifer has seated me on a chair to recover, though I am already feeling much better. Eventually, he calls for silence.

"While we are all anxious to finally see Earth again, do not forget Mark's Ascension. You must bear him witness, for he will soon be the greatest among you. Dacia, the Cup?"

"Here, Master," the Archdemon says, bringing him the Cup half-filled with water.

"Mark, you must drink."

"Will it hurt?"

"It always hurts. But after what you did, I know your power is true. Normally the transformation takes a few days, but in your case, it could be hours. I will place you in the infirmary just in case."

I nod. "Let's do this shit."

He chuckles. "I forget how young you are sometimes."

"Even younger than Tim when he Ascended."

"And stronger still."

He places the Cup to my lips.

"Are you going to chant a spell?"

"Hardly," he says. "I worked many moons on the spells used to create the Infernal Cup. But using it is child's play."

I take the Cup from him, toss it back, and gulp the liquid down.

It may have been water in the Cup, but it tastes like acid. The pain starts immediately as a burning sensation in my throat and stomach; it spreads to my entire body within moments.

I have survived worse than this already, I know. Before becoming a demon, I suffered from agonising spasms and random paralysis. This pain is similar, only more bearable. Shahar explained the reason: I am already a half-demon, so Ascending is easy.

The real problem? I need to be stronger than the Cup. It needs to break.

I grit my teeth, hold the Cup tightly, and *slam* my power against it. Against the Infernal Cup, against Lucifer's magic, against the venom in my stomach. I rebel against evil. I embrace strength, but not as Lucifer did, not through darkness and rage, but with light.

I remember Conall's hand wrapped around mine. I remember when I said *I love you* and meant it. I remember Steijn, too, with his cute boyish looks that hid so much bravery. I even see Uncle, who cared for me like a son, even though I caused his sister's death.

Agony splinters through my spine. I black out instantly.

Chapter Two: Born Anew

Mark

I see a golden light. For a moment, I wonder if I've died, and this is Heaven. Even in my dream state, this seems preposterous.

Gradually, I regain the sensation of my body. I feel my chest rising and falling and feel the power in my muscles. I am stronger than I have ever been before; I feel divine. I open my eyes, and instantly the world resolves into brilliant clarity. It's as if a filter has been removed from my sight: I can see the finest detail, from tiny motes of dust to the individual fibres of my blanket. Colours seem impossibly bright and intense.

I lift myself off the bed, discovering that I am still in my jeans, though sans boots and scabbard. I pad down the infirmary and open the door.

Max is leaning against a wall outside the room. He startles when he sees me.

"Mark? You're awake already?"

"Why? How long has it been?"

"About two hours."

"Two hours?"

"Normally, this takes days. How do you feel?"

"Different. Stronger. It's as if I see the world anew."

"It was the same for me when I Ascended, but you are unique."

"What happened to the Cup? Did I succeed?"

"The Cup lies broken. Lucifer wondered what happened, but the pull of Earth was too strong for him, and he forgot all about it. He's there now, along with nearly all of the demons. Only a few stragglers are left."

"Good."

Mark? Can you hear me?

Rex!

I am free, Mark. I am ready to attack on your command.

I breathe a sigh of relief; Max looks at me perplexed.

"Rex—the dragon, I mean—just contacted me. He's free."

Max relaxes infinitesimally. "Our plan is working."

"What plan?"

We turn around and see Adrianne walking towards us. "What are you two plotting?"

"Are you not even going to ask how I'm feeling?"

"It was a foregone conclusion."

"So why are you still here?" Max asks her.

"I don't trust you; I thought the whole ceremony was a charade, but to what purpose, I don't know."

"So, you're going to babysit us and see if we do something naughty?" I ask sweetly.

"No one returns to Lucifer's graces so swiftly. You deceived him."

I exchange a look with Max; he nods ever so slightly. Adrianne, not being stupid, immediately picks up on it.

"What?" she asks.

The sword is in my hand instantly. I move phenomenally fast—Adrianne does not even have time to look surprised. I drive the blade through her heart; the flames consume her in a flash. Not even ashes remain.

"Well done," Max says approvingly. "She was getting suspicious, fast."

"Let's get out of Hell," I say. "I want to see Earth again."

"I have longed to see Earth for millennia," Max says wistfully.

We head towards a window, where we will fly out from above the Citadel. At that moment, Dacia arrives. We freeze.

"Mark! It is good to see you well. Lucifer asks for you to join him—on Earth." Then, with surprise, she asks: "Where is Adrianne? I saw her a moment ago."

"Adrianne?" I ask, feigning surprise.

She narrows her eyes. "Didn't you see her? She said she wanted to talk to you. Said something about..." She pauses, and I see the pieces of the puzzle click inside her head. I have to give credit where credit is due: Dacia is very clever. She sees right through our web of deception.

"Something about?" I ask innocently.

"Betrayal."

"Do you think we betrayed Lucifer?" I ask, walking closer to her. She shrinks back, instinctively. I've never seen an Archdemon truly *afraid* of me. The feeling is exciting, almost addictive. I relish this power.

"I'm going to find out," she says, then charges. Her wings are outstretched, points aimed at my heart.

I simply kick her, and she goes flying backward. She retaliates with fireballs, which I simply ignore; I don't even feel any pain.

Her eyes widen in terror. "I must warn him—"

Instinctively, I draw my power towards my hands, splaying my fingers. Chains of light arc out through the air and wrap themselves around her. I close my hand, and the chains tighten, dragging her down on the floor. She writhes there, helpless.

"How is this possible—" she gasps.

"Doesn't matter," I say, and the sword appears in my right hand. I pull back, preparing to stab her through the chest. But I hesitate.

"Please don't kill me," she whispers.

It's one thing to kill someone attacking you, but to kill someone who is helpless against you? Even if they are a demon?

Strong arms grasp my own. The blade surges forward, piercing Dacia's heart. Fire engulfs the Archdemon, and she perishes with a strangled scream.

"Max! What did you make me do?"

"What was necessary. Do not think that Dacia was a helpless little girl whom you cruelly executed, for she murdered more souls than I could count and never offered mercy to anyone. Those who do not show mercy should expect none in return."

"But I'm better than her—"

"You are, but even heroes must kill their enemies."

I sheath the sword and turn around.

"Max—"

He hugs me then, and the words die on my lips. It's a powerful, manly hug, the kind warriors give.

"Trust my judgement as I trust in yours, Mark. Now let's get out of here."

"Wait!"

We turn and see Shahar running towards us.

****

The old scholar leads us to his tower. It's so strange to see the Citadel empty; it's as if I've landed in some alternate reality.

"Is this important, Shahar? Lucifer is free to wreak carnage on Earth and my boyfriend—"

"Lucifer shan't harm a hair on your boyfriend's head, and you must come with me. What I'm going to tell you might tip the scales in your favour."

The old scholar leads us to his room and sits on a chair; Naem, his cat, is instantly by his side. Shahar strokes her fondly.

"First off, you should know that if you kill Lucifer, I am going to die."

I blink in shock. "I wondered if that might be the case, but I didn't know. Shahar, I'm sorry—"

"No, don't be sorry. I've lived far longer than most humans get to live, and I've recorded all my knowledge in books. I am happy to meet my end. There's more." Shahar takes a deep breath. "Killing Lucifer will kill all the demons except you."

"You mean—Max? And my dad? Did you know?" I ask Max.

"Yes," he says simply. "Like Shahar, I am ready to meet my end. I am simply glad that I get to see Earth before I go."

"I... don't know what to say. Thank you."

"You must not only defeat Lucifer," Shahar continues, "but you must also fight his demons. They will kill many on Earth."

"Kaylin will help me defeat Lucifer," I say. "The dragon will take care of the rabble."

Max smiles at my comment.

"I leave the strategy to you. You must know that defeating Lucifer will not be easy. He understands Great Magic better than anyone alive, so don't assume you can repeat another Mary Magdalene—he will see it coming."

"Do you think I can beat him single combat?"

"I have no idea. Whatever you decide, I can only bid you good luck. *Shalom Aleikhem*, Mark."

"*Aleikhem Shalom.*"

Shahar only smiles at my attempt at Hebrew and kisses his cat on the forehead, who meows in protest. I realise this is the last time I'm going to see him.

****

"So, how do we get out of here?" I ask Max as we stand on the balcony. Above us, I see stars—the world of Earth. Freedom, in other words.

"We fly up through the Citadel."

"What country will we arrive in?"

"What country do you think?"

"Israel? Palestine?"

"Hah, no. You'll find out soon."

He continues to accelerate, and darkness envelops us. Below, the Cauldron stretches out, a world of fire and sulphur. Above us, there is only the stars' cold blue light, set in a canvas of infinite black. I realise that there is no breath in my lungs.

Max? Are we in space?

Yes. We cannot communicate verbally because there is no air and no sound.

But where is—oh.

The blue planet is visible now. A vast rock, most of it covered by ocean, only the thinnest layer of atmosphere ensuring life's survival. It is beautiful, green, and fragile. It is my home, and I'm going back—to protect it and everyone who lives there.

Max, here's what I want you to do. You will head over to Lucifer and pretend everything is normal. We can't let him know something's up—at least, not yet—so lie and tell them I'm still sleeping. Can you do that?

Yes, but first you must give me a memory of the place you want to meet in.

I had almost forgotten that he couldn't Fade to a place without having a firm idea of it.

Touch my hand, and I'll share a memory with you.

I show him the green fields of Ireland, Dublin's harsh, concrete landscape, and through it all my feelings—of rage and bitterness, loss and longing.

I will find you. Good luck.

Chapter Three: Vengeance is Best Served Cold

Lucifer

Oh, how I've longed for this moment! Humans have hated me for millennia, and none more than the witches. The Sadducees and Pharisees curse their hides, thought to destroy me. The Roman witches came to agree. I was too powerful, too dangerous, and too rebellious.

For so many centuries, Mary Magdalene kept me locked up in Hell. But now, at last, I am free. Thanks to Mark, I can once again taste the cool, clean air of the ocean; I can savour the salty tang of sea spray as it blows off the Mediterranean; I can gaze upon the sun as it rises from the East. I have been in that dark pit so long, I have forgotten what it's *really* like to experience the sun—its caressing warmth, its rosy fuchsia tones, and its incredible brilliance.

Nearly nine hundred demons congregate around me, ebullient and restless. I had taken them with me almost as soon as the Barrier went down—I left only a few to keep my human subjects in Hell under control.

Thinking of him makes me shiver. I almost didn't believe he could do it, but he beat all my expectations. The way he drank from the Infernal Cup... it was as if he wanted to prove not only that he was *worthy* of being a demon but that he was *better* than any other demon. The Cup had shattered, and at the time, I was simply too distracted to pay it any attention. But now that I think about it... how strange. I do not know what ramifications it could entail.

Archdemon Tim is at my side, his face radiant with joy.

"I forgot how much I missed Earth!" he cries.

"You're telling me."

"When are we going to begin the attack?"

"Are you done with the honeymoon so soon?"

"I want to have some fun," he says, smiling darkly. "I'm just itching for a fight."

"You'll get your wish," I say. *Faithful demons! I want you to arrange yourselves based on what Continent you're from.*

They obey my commands immediately, even Tim, who flies off with a wave. I take them in: a horde of dark-winged beings, ready to bring death and destruction at my beck and call. Ready to make me Emperor — and to crush all who stand in my way.

I will search your memories, I warn them. *Be ready.*

I fly towards each demon, touching them on the forehead, taking in their memories. I learn of Brazil, Argentina, Australia, China, Japan, North Africa, and South Africa—and every other far-flung corner of the globe.

The spell I am about to use is named the Mass Fade. It is one of my Grand Spells—the most powerful spells I know other than Great Magic—and the demons have never seen it in action. I draw a pentagram inside a circle, then whisper the words of the spell.

Power builds inside my body, like a great storm on the cusp of a wide sea. It explodes outwards, guided by the symbols. My demons fade, each teleported to exactly where I wish them to go.

The ocean is silent once more. But soon, its waters shall run red with blood.

Chapter Four: Coming Home

Conall

The imp appears in front of me as if from nowhere, and I jump back, startled. I had been reading a book in my room—a treatise on European politics.

"You shouldn't do that," I rebuke the little creature.

"What, did I scare you? Wee Javalook scared a big boy like you?"

"Well, you came out of nowhere. Did you teleport or something?"

"No, I can't Fade in the way demons do. What I did was take an interdimensional shortcut; we imps are very good at doing that."

"OK. Why have you come to me, then?"

"I wanted to warn you. Didn't you feel it?"

"Now that you mention it, I did feel *something* happening about two hours ago. What was it?"

"The Barrier came crashing down."

"*What?*"

"Mark has freed Lucifer and Ascended."

"Why would he do that?" I demand.

"To free the dragon known as Rex, who is extremely powerful and could defeat my master."

I breathe out slowly, trying to keep calm. "Okay. So this is it? Lucifer is going to attack?"

"The offensive against Earthly governments has begun; Lucifer is sending out demons as we speak."

"Am I safe?"

"You are. Why do you think Lucifer sent me here? To chat? Much as I like your boyfriend, I don't normally discuss Lucifer's plans with random mortals."

"You're here to protect me?"

"To keep an eye out for your safety and to call for help if needed. I'll watch you, discreetly. Now, if you don't mind—"

The little imp suddenly leaps away; a moment later, President Meow lands on the bed, yowling with frustration. The feline pulls back his ears and stalks towards the intruder, ready to pounce.

"Get your cat to stop attacking me," Javalook complains shrilly.

But I can only laugh. "You don't expect me to control that feline? He couldn't care less about what I tell him to do." As if to prove my point, the President leaps again, and the imp rolls over to evade his claws.

"You're enjoying this, aren't you?"

"Maybe. If you want my advice, hide somewhere where the cat can't see you."

"Point taken," the imp says, jumping away and perching himself on the light fixture.

"I'm going to take a shower," I say. "Try to get along with President Meow—I don't want to babysit you two."

"How am I supposed to get along with him? That cat is trying to kill me!"

"The President likes treats. Go and pilfer something from the kitchen."

I make my way out of the bedroom towards my en-suite (Mother always takes care to provide me with luxury) and strip off my T-shirt—I went for white to compliment my jeans, which are light blue and fit snugly on my hips. A moment later, I throw off my jeans, underwear, and socks. The water greets me like a warm kiss.

****

What is Mark *thinking*? Freeing Lucifer is literally Armageddon. The Devil has been plotting world domination ever since he was imprisoned.

He is prepared to do *anything* to get it: he will slaughter countless millions, raze cities to the ground, and destabilise governments world-wide.

But at the same time, I know Mark is not stupid. Freeing this dragon gives us a chance against Lucifer. Besides, what's the alternative? Mark cannot stay in Hell forever, for Lucifer would either corrupt him or kill him. He took matters into his own hands.

My rationalisations still can't stop my body from tremoring uncontrollably. I have never been this afraid in my life. I thought maybe a shower would help, but no amount of warm water can wash away the chill inside my bones.

I almost don't notice the *presence*. So subtle is he, so quiet, that only my subconscious sixth sense tells me he's there. Glamoured as he is, he still radiates power—something divine in nature, something that cannot be mistaken.

His strong hands wrap around my abs, and his teeth nuzzle my neck.

"Did the imp not notice you come in?" I ask breathlessly.

"He was too busy stealing food from the kitchen—I assume to feed the cat, who *did* notice me but didn't give a damn."

I laugh brokenly. "Maybe you're not real, then. A figment of my desperate imagination."

His fingers casually reach down to my bum, and I give a soft gasp when he touches me.

"God fucking *dammit*—"

"Have I convinced you now?"

"Oh, yes. I've missed you so much, Mark. You wouldn't believe how much."

He clasps my jaw in his hands, turning me around to face him. He's so beautiful that for a moment, I still think I'm dreaming. Surely no one can be this handsome? His eyes are impossibly blue, like a finely cut diamond, and his hair shines precious as gold.

"I've missed you too, Conall. Sometimes I missed you so bad it hurt."

I wrap my arms around his neck, kissing him with all I have. He tastes of the ocean, sweet and salty, with more than a hint of something wild. He lifts me onto his chest, holding me as if I weigh nothing at all.

"How strong are you now?" I ask once I've taken a pause from kissing him. (Hey, a guy needs to get his breath back.)

"More powerful than you can imagine. Even I haven't wrapped my head around it yet."

"All part of the plan?"

"Yup. Freeing Lucifer made me stronger and ultimately planted the seeds of his destruction."

"How fitting," I say before kissing him again.

I kiss him deeply and thread my hands through his hair, which is soft and pleasantly damp. I release the kiss, then begin planting smaller kisses along his jawline.

"I always loved your hair," I comment.

"You have pretty nice hair yourself."

"You flatter me. Now put me down; I want to suck you off."

"Oooh, how very direct. You really must have missed this."

"You bet I did."

He places me back down, and in an instant, I'm on my knees, taking him in my mouth. I grab his ass at the same time—I like keeping him in control when I'm doing my business. What can I say? I'm a pro.

He goes along with it, letting me do all the work. He closes his eyes and moans when I pleasure him. He tastes delicious.

"Oh, wow, Conall. You didn't do this before. I feel like a virgin again."

"Learn from the master," I say with a wicked smile.

"But I want to make you feel good, too," he whines.

I roll my eyes and turn off the shower. "Fine. In that case, I want to ride on your back to the bedroom."

"I can do that."

He leans forward, and I hoist myself up, holding his shoulder blades between my thighs. I confess—it feels wonderfully possessive.

"You're enjoying this," he comments with amusement.

"The view is nicer up top."

He walks towards the bed, where I push hard with my legs, toppling him over. I stand up next to the bed.

"Get your knees," I order.

"With pleasure."

I smile as I take him in: he is like a Greek sculpture, with muscles hewn from marble. I trace the lines of his body, entranced by his abs and shoulders. I thrust myself into his mouth, and he takes me willingly.

"Keep your eyes open," I whisper, "and look up at me."

I could get lost in those eyes, for they are dark as the deepest ocean, and they hide nothing. Mark always tells me everything, from the brightest joy to the darkest despair. It amazes me the way he can be so strong and yet still carry a hint of vulnerability. Even now, he's not sure how best to please me.

"I like it deep, too," he says.

I lift his head, thrusting upwards with my core muscles.

"That's it," I say approvingly. I withdraw, lean down, and kiss him. I hold his jaw with one hand and play with his ass in the other as we continue.

I pull back, my breathing ragged. It takes everything in me not to just explode. Mark senses this and pulls me back towards the bed. I lie with my head on his chest, and he strokes my hair gently.

"You're too much," I complain. "No mortal can hope to match you."

"I am no mortal."

"Well said." I smile. "How do you want to do this?"

"Can you top?"

"Absolutely."

"I want to lie face-down on the bed, stomach flat, and with my wings stretched."

"I like the sound of that."

He arranges himself into position, unfurling his wings. They are dark as the night, velvety to the touch, and take up a good chunk of the room. I brush them gently at first, starting from the edges before moving my hands towards his shoulder blades, where the wings are thickest. I crush his wings in my fists, and he moans in ecstasy.

I turn my attention to his bum, kissing him there. I give him everything I have, and he growls. Feeling when he's ready, I lean forward, grab his wings again, and thrust myself inside him.

He's panting hard, eyes wild. I lower myself to kiss him, and he twists his head to meet me. So I kiss him while simultaneously threading my hands through his wings. I don't know what he feels—he's beyond words now—but I can describe my pleasure.

Everything starts and ends where Mark begins. His feathers send tingles through my fingers. His lips are soft and warm, his tongue firm. And his ass is too tight around me; it makes stars dance across my vision.

Harder and harder I go until I cease to know anything but wild ecstasy.

****

"Did you enjoy that?" I ask.

"I like it when you touch my wings. And I love having you inside me—you're just so dominant, and you know exactly what you're supposed to do."

"Is it uncomfortable? I know if a guy does it wrong, it can really hurt—"

"No. It just feels great."

"Did you like it? Because I'm pretty spent."

He chuckles. "Yeah, you probably are. I did very much enjoy it, though."

"Was it a little... too much?"

"You are pretty gross. But..."

"But...?"

"That was the best sex of my life."

I chuckle darkly and lean against him. "I'm glad to hear it. Because we might not survive to feel something like that ever again."

"I will protect you to my dying breath, Conall—"

"That's what I'm worried about. You'll fight the Devil, not me."

He kisses my forehead. "Have faith in me. It's still daylight outside, right?"

"Late afternoon. Why? You don't plan on going out now?"

"I have to talk to Kaylin and—"

"It will wait for another hour. Mark, I want you to be mine, at least until darkness falls. Don't leave my side."

"Okay, Conall."

So we lie in each other's arms, not speaking, merely content to savour the last moments before the battle. The sun casts a rose-gold light as it sets, illuminating his golden hair, his perfect, peachy skin—so smooth I could bite into it—and the fine hairs on his chest. In that strange, fleeting moment, I realise I'm the luckiest man on Earth.

Chapter Five: Preparations

Kaylin

"Roshika, I—"

"You need my help," she interrupts. "Yes, I too felt the Barrier coming down. It was hard not to."

"It was like a dam broke," I whisper. "And then this huge body of water just came crashing down."

"Are your friends here?" she asks. We are in our new Letterkenny base, but in a side-room off the main control room. Grim concrete walls surround us, and bright LEDs shine a clinical blue light. This place had been an abandoned warehouse which we had fortified and upgraded—but there had been no time to fix the décor.

"Yes, Diana and Leo are in the main room with everybody else."

"Good. I have the Books with me, and there's a spell I would like to show you in the Red Book." She withdraws the Red Book from her voluminous sari and walks over to a nearby table. I follow hastily.

She thumbs through the Book to a spell. "These are the Marks of Power. You draw the runes on the target's skin, and their powers become greatly enhanced for a short while."

"How long are we talking about?"

"Everything from a couple of minutes to a few hours. Anything longer than that is too risky."

"I'm guessing there's a cost?"

"There is a big one. Lifeforce fuels the magic; the stronger the spell, the greater the cost."

"You're telling me the person loses some of their life? How much? Months, years, a decade?"

"It's not quite so simple as losing a few years off your life—it also impacts your health—but I estimate two to five years."

"I will do it—"

"No, you won't. I'll need you for the Great Magic spell we'll end up using against Lucifer. This magic tends to make the target go a little mad, especially if you're casting the Marks on yourself. Ask one of your friends."

"Okay. I shall do that. Are you going to research a Great Magic spell?"

"I've been doing that since the Barrier came crashing down. I have a few candidates in mind, but I'll need a bit more time to prepare."

"We're all counting on you, Roshika."

"Believe me, I know."

****

I take the Red Book with me, feeling its unfamiliar texture and weight in my hand. I find Diana and Leo where I left them. I take them aside, making excuses.

"Diana, Leo, I know a spell that can greatly enhance your powers for a short period."

"That's great! What do you need?" Diana asks excitedly.

Leo is not so naive. "I'm guessing there's a price to pay?"

"The spell will drain part of your lifeforce; Roshika tells me it's something like two to five years. Are you willing to pay that price?"

"Yes," Diana says straightaway. "If it means we stand a chance against those immortal bastards, I'll do it."

I never really expected anything else from Diana. Say what you like about her, but she is brave. "Leo?"

"If this were any other war, I would say no. But we're talking about the fate of the world here. If this makes me stronger—if this means I have a real chance of fighting off a demon—then I will do it. I do not want to be a liability for you to worry about constantly."

"Leo, that was never—"

"I almost died fighting Araya, who is at best equal to a middling demon."

I sigh deeply. "You are right, Leo. Very well. I will need to draw the Marks on your arms, legs, and back."

I start with Diana. The Marks I inscribe on her skin are made using a simple spell and the tip of my index finger, yet simultaneously, I have to keep a chant going. It had not taken me long to memorise the Latin words—it's a simple phrase—but it takes all of my concentration to do both simultaneously.

Once I have drawn all the Marks, I whisper the closing spell, *Signati*. The Marks glow a strange blue, then return to their standard reddish-black colour. They resemble a series of strange tattoos in geometric forms, not unlike those of hieroglyphs.

"How do you feel?" I ask Diana as she changes back into her dress.

"Like there's a huge lake of power inside me, and all I have to do is drink."

"You need to wait—you don't want to run out prematurely. Leo?"

The spell is even more demanding for me this time around because I have never been this intimate with Leo, and he is distracting me. My eyes want to follow the curve of his biceps, the planes, and the angles of his back... Diana pinches me. I shriek.

"Keep your mind on the spell," she orders.

I start the chant, making sure to draw the runes correctly. After what seems like an age, though it is probably mere minutes, I finish. I flop down on a chair, exhausted.

"I feel like a battery zapped with a big charge. Is that normal?" Leo asks.

"I have no idea; this is the first time I have used them."

"Thanks for this, Kaylin. I'm sorry you didn't get to see me half-naked before."

Diana rolls her eyes while I go red. "That was completely unprofessional of me—"

"No, it was completely normal. If we live through this, Kaylin—"

"You two love birds can carry on with this conversation at a later date," Diana interrupts. "Need I remind you that we still haven't decided what to do with Araya?"

****

"I doubt she's willing to help us," Leo says as we walk towards Araya's cell. "If you don't kill her, at least keep her locked up, so she doesn't mess up our plans."

"I want to give her a chance," I say. "She doesn't know what we're up against—"

I freeze mid-step, nearly falling over; only Diana's quick thinking saves me from landing face-first on the floor. Then I forget the physical world entirely.

The world is on fire. I see Beijing's smouldering remains and countless other world cities: Paris, Berlin, and even Dublin. Armies lie broken on fields, felled by giant fireballs and deadly magic. In Rome, Lucifer has raised a palace, which floats in the air like a great leviathan.

The view changes, and now I am in his Throne Room. Sunlight streams in through vast gilded windows. Lucifer lounges on a Throne made of black stone, glittering with veins of gold. He is sipping from a champagne glass while a naked man and woman dance in front of him.

He has conquered the world, so why shouldn't he have his fun?

I return to consciousness like a swimmer coming up for air. I gasp, looking around in confusion. I am lying on a bed; Diana and Leo must have moved me. I focus on their expressions. Leo looks slightly worried, while Diana is merely curious.

"What did you see?" she asks.

"A vision of what would happen if Lucifer won the war."

"And? Was it sunshine and roses, drinking wine by the seaside?"

"Something like that, but with a lot more death and destruction thrown in."

"Who could have guessed?"

Leo doesn't seem amused by our cheery black humour. "I guess you could show this to Araya," he says practically. "It's the best chance you have of getting her onboard."

I nod. "Let's go."

We find Araya exactly where I had ordered her to be kept: in a large, comfortable cell, complete with a nice bed and en-suite. Of course, Roshika's spell still binds her powers—it is visible as bands of light encircling her forearms. Araya is pacing angrily.

"Hello, Araya."

She turns and sneers. "Have you come to gloat? Why don't you just kill me and be done with it?"

"Because you can still be useful to me."

"I'm not going to help you fight the government."

"But will you help me fight a demon?"

"What?" She stops pacing.

"You heard me right. The Party isn't our only enemy—indeed, it's no longer our main concern. A powerful being named Lucifer is preparing an army of demons to conquer Earth."

She laughs. "The Devil is going to attack us? Are you kidding? Have you gone bloody mad?"

"No. Come here, and I'll show you a vision."

Bemused, she walks over and touches my hand through the cell bars. A quick whispered spell does the job of transferring the vision. She reels back, dropping to her knees (at least she's not as clumsy as me).

We watch her for several long moments. When she opens her eyes again, I can see they are changed.

"If this is a trick—"

"I can't fake a vision."

"But this means... god, this is bad. I don't know what to say—you're clearly not the bad guy if you're willing to fight this."

"I'm glad you think so. Will you help?"

"Can I help?"

"Of course you can. But we need to trust you."

"I can't possibly earn your trust in so little time—but I will fight these creatures."

"Good enough. Roshika can bind you in an instant if you fall out of line. Just warning you."

"Duly noted."

As we walk away from her cell, Leo comments: "I really didn't think that would work, Kaylin."

"I am happy to prove you wrong."

"I agree," Diana says. "We need all the help we can get."

****

Mark

I found Kaylin's new base easily enough—Pip told me after I asked Java-look—but I decided not to go in straight away. Well, Conall convinced me. He told me I should go in with style.

So Conall and I stand alone in a field, waiting, the air heavy with expectation. The late October sky is grey, the sun peeking through only occasionally. The air is cool and humid against my skin.

It starts as no more than a scent, carried in the folds of the wind. The smell of fire, lava, and sulphur. Then we feel it like a sound, a tremendous beating of wings. Then the ground shakes; I hold Conall to keep him upright.

Like a phoenix arisen from the ashes, the dragon falls from the sky and lands on the Earth. He cranes his neck, taking in the surroundings. The dragon grins when he sees us, showing long teeth.

Conall stares, open-mouthed, for a long moment. I worry Rex has scared him. But he soon proves me wrong by running up to meet the dragon.

"Hello, Sir Reptile," he begins. "Mark tells me your name is Rex."

Indeed it is, little human.

"*Salve.*"

The dragon grins even wider. *You speak Latin, little one. I, too, learned Latin, but that was a long time ago, and I did not think you still understood the language.*

"Well, only a little bit," Conall says modestly. "I admire the Romans."

I am pleased to meet you. Your name is Conall, yes?

"Yes."

"Rex," I interrupt, "I want you to meet a witch named Kaylin, who will help us against Lucifer. Their base is not far from here. Shall we go?"

Lead the way.

We walk—if it could be said that a dragon walks, for the Earth trembles whenever he makes a step—towards the base. Once we approach the main doorway, two men and two androids immediately train their weapons on us. With a flick of my wrist, I send the androids into a wall, crushing them.

"Don't shoot," I order. "It's Mark."

"Wh-what is that?" one of the men asks.

"His name is Rex, and he is a dragon. Did Kaylin not mention it?"

The men exchange a glance, then put down their weapons. "Right ahead, sir, if the dragon will fit."

I believe I will, Rex comments wryly. The men leap backward in shock. We make our way past them into the main room.

****

Everyone stops what they are doing and stares. Kaylin, Diana, and Leo stride purposefully towards us.

"You could have told us you were coming," she says. "Might have saved us two androids."

"The androids won't help you against Lucifer. And besides, aren't you happy to see me?" I smile wickedly.

"I am, but I wish the circumstances were better. This is... the dragon?"

My name is Rex.

"I apologise then. You must think we were quite rude."

The dragon chuckles, and it is like a rumble of stones on a mountainside.

I think that Mark played a practical joke on you. Who are your companions?

"Diana, meet Rex," Kaylin says. "This is Leo, my friend."

I raise an eyebrow at the mention of "friend."

Pleased to meet you all. Shall we begin planning?

"Roshika is still preparing the spell, and I haven't called Michael over yet. Can you give us half an hour?"

I narrow my eyes at the mention of my dad. But it's clear we have other priorities now.

"I'll go and talk with my uncle in Spain," I say. "See if he wants to come back to Ireland. I'll be back soon. Rex, you can kill some time with Conall—I'm sure he'll be happy to talk to you."

"Certainly," Conall agrees.

Then it is settled.

****

I Fade back to Spain, then fly to Madrid through the cover of Glamour. I land on a deserted street, retract my wings, and strip off the Glamour. I walk to the nearby hospital, asking for my uncle's name. It takes a while, as most of the nurses don't speak English, but eventually, they pull up uncle's address from the database. Another Glamour and a short flight later, I find Uncle's new home.

The sun is setting, and it casts long shadows across the street. The trees are shedding their leaves, and they form a carpet of gold, tinged here and there with fuchsia tones.

His house has a wrought iron gate opening out into a front garden. The building itself is made from stone and strikes me as very pretty. It looks protected against mutant attacks—there are subtle re-enforcements if you know where to look—but otherwise, it could belong to a different century.

I smile wanly. I used to fear the mutants, but not any longer. They are not difficult to control. Once I defeat Lucifer, the mutants will die along with the demons. Eventually, the Familiars will lose their powers, and Earth will be free from demonic influence.

I knock on the door and wait calmly. Uncle curses as he fiddles with the lock. When he sees me, he freezes.

"Hi, Uncle. I'm back."

"But this means—what did you do, Mark?"

"I tore down the Barrier, and yes, Armageddon is coming. But I have a plan."

"I sure hope so. Come in, please."

I sweep past him, taking in the laminated hardwood floor and the stone walls. I whistle. "Not bad, Uncle."

"I'm just renting this house; it's not mine."

"Still, you're well paid, even in Communist Spain."

"Communism is a bit more subtle than paying everyone the same wage; it's about overthrowing the chains of capital accumulation."

"Really? I had no idea you knew anything about Communism."

"I didn't until I came here. The Party suppressed a lot of history."

I walk past the corridor to the living room, where I make myself comfortable on a sofa.

"Tea?" he asks. "It's hard to find black tea here, but I manage."

"Yes, please."

Once again, I sip the warm liquid, enjoying the buzz of caffeine. I don't need sleep, and I suspect this night is going to be special.

"So Lucifer is going to attack Earth?" he asks. "Should I expect to see a lot of casualties in my department?"

Trust Uncle to think about the patients. "It depends on what the Spanish government will do. Conall told his mother to advise peace talks, as that will buy time and prevent many casualties."

"The Spanish are not stupid. The Party in Ireland, I fear, will not give up without a fight."

"No."

"So it's clear I'm needed back there and not here."

"Yes, I think so. You... don't want to go back?"

"I will go wherever sick and wounded people need me. But you're right—I never liked Ireland. Mark, if we live through this, can you promise me you'll settle down in Spain?"

"And do what? Marry Conall and live happily ever after?"

"You can do that here. And... I would want that for you. Will you consider it?"

"I'm not sure—but I guess I'll consider it. For now, I have to defeat Lucifer. This might be the last time we ever see each other, Uncle."

"I realise that. I don't know how you'll defeat Lucifer, but if anyone can do it, it's you. You've gone to Hell and back already. Good luck, Nephew."

"Thanks, Uncle."

He ruffles my hair, just like old times. I smile nostalgically.

"Time to go," I say and offer him my hand.

He clasps my hand in his, and a moment later, we Fade away.

Chapter Six: Dragon's Gift

Conall

"So you're immortal?" I ask.

Yes. I have lived for thousands of years, but I spent a long time trapped in a cave, all because of Lucifer.

"Then you've got plenty of reason to want him dead."

Exactly. Besides, I have studied humans for thousands of years—I have learned of your dreams, your fears, and your desires. You are not perfect, nor are you always honourable, but you are worth saving.

"Thanks."

Rex grins wryly.

"Can I tell you something? I've always wanted to ride a dragon," I say wistfully. "But I can't imagine you'd agree."

Why not? No human has ever ridden on my back. It would be a novel experience.

"But won't people notice a huge reptile flying in the sky? I mean, people in this part of Ireland are quite provincial and superstitious, but still—"

I can Glamour myself. That won't be a problem.

"So... you'd really let me ride you?" I ask hopefully.

Yes. Just try not to fall.

"I'll do my best. How... how should I saddle you?"

The dragon leans forward, putting one foot in front of him.

Climb my leg and take a seat on my back, just behind my neck. Hold on tight.

I clamber awkwardly up his leg, holding on to bony protrusions, and try to make myself comfortable between two spikes on his back. I feel his powerful muscles contract; it's the only warning I get. A moment later, Rex leaps into the air.

I had flown with Mark before, but even that fantastic experience doesn't quite prepare me for this. The dragon takes off like a rocket, not even bothering to flap his wings. As we gain speed, the wind buffets me left and right. Soon, Ireland is but a patchwork of green fields and lone forests beneath my feet. Rex continues ascending until we are past the clouds, and brilliant sunshine illuminates the world once more. His scales sparkle like rubies in the light.

"Wow!" I call out. "This is fantastic! Have you ever seen the sun?"

I have, but only in human memories. It doesn't quite do it justice.

"No, it doesn't."

For a while, we only fly, and all my fears take a backseat. I revel in the sensations: the wind races across my face and Rex's wings beat out a strong rhythm.

A calmness descends over me; thoughts evade my conscious mind. I see the world through Rex—he can see not only the visible rays of the sun but also the purple shades of ultraviolet and the deep orangey-reds of infrared. I feel the flap of his powerful wings, the swish of his tail as it balances his flight.

When we land, it comes as a shock. I blink, feeling as I've just awoken from a dream.

"What... Rex, that was incredible."

You saw through my eyes and felt through my body.

"How is this possible?"

I felt it the moment I met you, but I was not sure until now. Conall, you are a witch.

"Wait, what? But I can't do spells—"

No, you probably cannot. You are a weak witch; there is only a spark of magic inside you. Even so, you see many things that mundane humans do not.

"Wow. I had no idea."

You have only a spark, but even a spark can become a great fire with the right kindling.

"What are you saying, Rex?"

I can grant you a gift—a blessing.

I jump off Rex's back, landing with my knees bent and my hands outstretched.

"What will your blessing do?"

I will place a portion of my fire inside you; it will make you stronger.

"Will I be able to defend myself against demons? Will I be able to fight them?"

Yes, you will easily defeat weaker demons. But avoid the strong ones, as I cannot make you indestructible.

"That's still more than I could ever have imagined. I was so afraid that I would put Mark in danger simply because I am mortal and cannot defend myself. This gift means more to me than you realise, Rex."

I am glad to hear that.

"Is there a cost to this magic? Kaylin says that every spell has a cost."

The power comes from me, so it makes me slightly weaker. I can only grant a small portion of my fire to you, as too much would kill you. You are still a mortal. Also: it will not last forever.

"There's always some sort of catch, I guess. How long does it last?"

You'll be at full power for a couple of days. I estimate the fire will fade completely after approximately two weeks.

"Sounds good to me. I accept your gift, Rex; it would be an honour."

The honour is mine, little one.

Thus, the dragon extends his head towards me, touching my forehead carefully with the tip of his snout. He says no words, but power floods into me like a raging inferno. I cry out, burning with pain, and collapse.

****

Are you okay?

I wake up, rubbing my eyes. The feeling of weakness soon dissipates, replaced with incredible strength. I jump to my feet, flexing my muscles experimentally. I can see a faint light burning underneath my skin.

"I feel much better now. How long was I out?"

A few minutes. It's understandable.

"I can't wait to show Mark my new tricks."

The dragon chuckles with glee. *Indeed. Shall we go?*

Needing no further encouragement, I break into a run.

Chapter Seven: Armageddon

Lucifer

I could have gone anywhere to claim my right. I will be a world ruler soon, so why not start with a romantic city like Paris, Jerusalem, or Rome? The Romans cast me out, so what better irony than to conquer their great city?

But somehow, I find myself looking upon a different city entirely. Dublin may not be beautiful (the Black City is a more fitting epithet than the City of Angels), but this is where I found Mark, who gave me my freedom. I feel the need to repay him. And what better way to do that than by slaying his old nemesis?

I fly above the city one more time, Glamoured by magic and the starlit night, taking in the sights. Soon it shall all burn.

I land in front of a huge, spiralling tower. Big Brother's abode, apparently. I reveal myself to the humans and androids guarding the door.

"State your business," the captain says.

"I'm here to kill you, your precious Big Brother, and pretty much everybody else."

The androids are programmed to respond to my hostility, and they turn their weapons on me. I cast the Spell of Undoing on the android farthest away from me; the robot breaks apart into little pieces, each perfect and undamaged. I shall let Shahar study the contraption. The android nearest to me aims a punch at my face.

I catch the robotic fist in my hand. Robot and demon battle together in a contest of strength—a contest which I win, naturally. I tear the robot's hand right off its body. I level a kick and send the rest flying into a nearby wall, where it crumples.

The men stare at me, open-mouthed.

"Run away, my darlings." Would I let them live? Maybe, maybe not. I haven't decided yet.

The captain charges his laser and fires. I laugh. In an instant, I Fade next to him, grab his head, and decapitate him. The other guy is smarter and decides to run away. I spear him through the back with a bolt of energy. What can I say? I'm not feeling charitable tonight.

A simple spell blows the alloy door off its hinges. From there, it's carnage—complete, mindless destruction. Human and android falls until nought remains but splattered blood and torn metal.

"Come out, come out, wherever you are," I say, though I know exactly where Big Brother is. I can sense his mind.

I race up the stairs with superhuman speed. In less than two seconds, I cover twenty stories. I open the door to his penthouse apartment.

I admit: I expected Big Brother to look more intimidating. True, those dark eyes of his eyes hide ambition and cunning—but also fear. He is of moderate height, with black hair. He wears an elegant black and white suit with a red tie.

"Who are you?" he asks. He tries very hard not to make his voice tremble but fails. Pity. I expected more of him.

"They call me Lucifer, the Devil, Satan—all sorts of things. You may think of me as your doom."

"I can give you anything within my means," he says. "Money, power, connections—"

I snort. "You can give me nothing."

"If you want to kill me, just get it over with."

"Oh, but wouldn't that spoil all the fun?"

Before he can say anything, I tackle him, shatter the window behind him, and fly him out of the tower. I land just outside the city, binding him with a spell.

"THE IRISH GOVERNMENT!" I call out, projecting my voice using magic. "I HAVE YOUR LEADER. COME AND GET ME."

The effect is nearly instantaneous. The police and military instantly gather forces, and several Q fighters scramble to attack. All within minutes.

"You must have been expecting a kidnapping," I say.

"Yes, but who are you?"

"I am a friend of the boy your government repeatedly tried to imprison and kill."

"Are you part of the rebellion?"

"No, silly. I'm going to rule the world."

Several Q-fighters dive towards me, firing lasers and plasma cannons. I retaliate with fireballs, bringing each of them down in a flaming heap.

"Aren't they worried they'll kill you in the crossfire?" I ask.

"I told them my life would be forfeit if kidnapped and to kill the rebels at any cost."

"Good. All the more fun for me."

A procession of tanks is rolling down the bridge over the River Liffey. An idea pops into my head. "Mark isn't the only one who likes bridges," I say to myself.

I need no formal spell for this, only Will and power. I raise my hands, feeling the edges of the bridge with my mind. I grin wickedly. The bridge groans loudly, then, with a loud tearing sound, it separates from the supporting structures. With a wave of my hand, I fling the bridge—tanks and all—into the surrounding buildings. The carnage is just glorious.

"Please, I will do anything you ask; just spare the city."

"Since when do Party leaders care about their people? You are motivated by nothing except power and self-advancement."

"I am not a monster if that's what you're saying. A monster is someone who annihilates a city just because he can."

"True, I am a monster. I find life more interesting that way."

"I will recognise you as Sovereign and rule in your stead as Prime Minister, a simple administrator—"

"Even now, helpless before my power, you try to bargain and weasel your way out of the situation. Mark was right to hate you. You are worthless."

I remove the binding spell from him. "Get out of my sight," I order. "I don't ever want to see you again."

Seeing unexpected freedom, he runs. I smile cruelly. This man is ruthless, power-hungry, and surprisingly naive. Big Brother forgot all about bargaining and saving people when freedom presented itself.

I strike true and fast as the serpent. My hand coils around his heart, and I tear it from his chest as easily as plucking a bird. Now everyone will see how heartless he really is.

****

With my business in Dublin complete, at least for now, I Fade to Beijing. I have sent the largest contingent of my forces here, and I wish to see how my valiant demonic subjects are faring.

My intelligence services told me about this city. They said it was a place of extremes, a country so divided by class, tradition, and economics that Ireland seems like an egalitarian paradise in comparison. The slums of Beijing are like no other—they are the champions of human misery and suffering. The Forbidden City, on the other hand, was said to be graceful and beautiful.

No one can say the Forbidden City is beautiful now, though. Only blackened wreckage survives. My demons are battling Q fighters in the air and the land army outside the city. Fires pour black smoke into the air. I smell ashes and death. Flashes of laser fire, plasma bolts, and demonic fireballs light up the area. The noise is deafening—the Chinese are firing their heavy artillery.

"Lucifer!" I turn and see Archdemon Tim flying towards me.

"How goes it, Tim?"

"We're finishing off the airborne defence. We offered the Chinese government a chance to surrender as you ordered, but they refused. Naturally."

"They are certainly stubborn. Why is the city on fire? I told you to attack the Forbidden City and *only* the Forbidden City."

"Hey, don't blame us! They started shelling the Forbidden City once we slaughtered the government. That's why the city is on fire."

"I see. Summon the other Archdemons; I wish to prepare a Grand Spell."

"The Song of Fire?"

"Precisely."

The Archdemons are soon by my side. Oh, how long I've prepared them for this. The Song of Fire requires raw power, unlike anything seen on Earth. I took a small piece of the crystal with me from Hell, allowing me to use the power I have stored for aeons, but even that is not nearly enough. I need their strength as well.

They raise their arms and circle me; I feel their power bolstering mine. I do not chant the spell's words but *sing* them: it is a song of burning rage, death, and decimation. The song gains tempo, taking their power and shaping it to my will.

Though it is night, the sky begins to glow. It is not the pleasant, life-giving light of the sun but something infinitely more destructive. It's time to enjoy the fireworks.

Enormous fireballs rain down from the sky, arcing towards my intended target. Indeed, no witch has ever cast a spell like this one. There's no need for the subtlety or complexity of Great Magic; there is only a need for annihilation. Each fireball lands like a flaming asteroid: the ground shakes with every explosion. The fire is blinding, and the noise is unholy.

Then there is silence.

Once, there had been an army. Millions of men and thousands upon thousands of tanks, androids, and artillery pieces. Now there is only the desolate earth, littered here and there with the corpses of fallen soldiers. A breeze stirs the ashes, and it feels oddly gentle.

Chapter Eight: It's Time to Die

Mark

As soon as I teleported Uncle back to Ireland, Kaylin put him in the medical ward and asked me to join her in the main room. Conall and the dragon are there, along with another witch named Roshika. I spot Diana and Michael there as well. I lock eyes with my father, then look away. We'll talk later. For now, we need to plan.

"I have called you all here," Kaylin begins, "to discuss our strategy. Lucifer is the greatest threat we have ever faced, and he endangers not just us, not just Ireland, but the world. We need all the help we can get— even yours, Araya."

I spot a platinum-haired woman in the back who looks sullen but determined. It takes me a moment to place her: didn't Lucifer mention a Familiar who was giving Kaylin a tough time?

"Didn't she—"

"Attack me?" Kaylin asks. "Yes, but she has agreed to move past that to help us combat the demons. Leo, my friend, and Roshika, my mentor, are here as well. I brought Michael too. Is there anyone else you think should be here?"

"Yes. Give me a moment."

I reach out, searching for the now-familiar mental presence. *Max? Can you come now?*

Yes.

Mere moments later, Max appears in the main room. He looks around, observing everyone in the room, but especially the dragon. Rex snorts but otherwise chooses to ignore him.

"This is Max, my friend. Max, meet Kaylin, our leader; Conall, my boyfriend; Roshika, Diana, and—"

"Michael."

The two men clap one another behind the shoulders, smiling. I don't think I've ever seen my dad smile before, not like this.

"It's been a long time, Max."

"Only a few decades, but yes, I missed you too, old friend. Your son is a remarkable man."

"That he is. How was Hell? Is Lucifer just as I remember him?"

"You mean, a violent tyrant with grandiose ambitions and a soft spot for beautiful men? Yup. Same as always."

They laugh. Kaylin clears her throat, and I smile with amusement.

"Gentlemen, your attention, please. We need to prepare a plan of action. Rex, we are glad for your assistance in this fight."

Don't mention it. I hate that wretched demon even more than you do.

"We want to know... can you defeat Lucifer on your own?"

Defeat? You'll have to be more precise. I possess greater power than him, but Lucifer is cunning and immortal.

"You can't kill him? The Dragonfire—"

Oh, I can give him a very bad day. But even Dragonfire would not kill him, not permanently. I believe only another demon can truly kill Lucifer.

There is a moment of silence. "Roshika?" Kaylin asks, worried.

"I agree with the dragon. The Books have not been forthcoming with any spells that might vanquish Lucifer. We can trap him, yes, but not kill him."

"Then, we must find a way to entomb him. Does anyone know a good place?"

Might I suggest the cave where he imprisoned me for millennia? I confess the irony would be rich.

"I quite agree. Out of interest, Roshika, why did Mary Magdalene not imprison Lucifer to a more secure prison, back in the day?" Kaylin asks.

"You forget that she had to imprison not just Lucifer, but all of his demons. We have the dragon to mop up the stragglers."

"Then it's settled?" Kaylin enquires.

I speak up. "I could kill Lucifer. It's better than trapping him somewhere only to worry that, at some point in the distant future, he could rise again and wreak vengeance on the world."

"We can't risk it, Mark. We don't know if you can defeat Lucifer. He beat us before when he was only a Projection—"

"But I am much stronger now."

"Mark," Roshika butts in, and we all turn towards her. "Let us attempt Great Magic first. Sending you to fight Lucifer would be a measure of last resort."

"Okay. How are you going to do this Great Magic then? You need Foresight, Activation, and—"

"Sacrifice," she says, and at that moment, she looks incredibly old.

"Roshika has agreed to give up her life for the spell," Kaylin says quietly.

"She's a brave woman," Max comments. There are murmurs of agreement from the others.

"But still," I continue, "what's your plan?"

"Kaylin will cast a shield tuned to my life-energy. We will attack Lucifer."

"So, you give up your life to power a shield while Kaylin does some other juju?"

"No, our attacks will just be a diversion. Lucifer will destroy our shield, killing me. That will Activate the Great Magic."

"That's clever. But how are you going to get him alone? If the other demons break down your shield spell before Lucifer—"

That's where I come in, Rex interrupts. *I gather, Roshika, that you wish me to fight the demons and keep the bulk of them occupied?*

"Yes. Mark, Michael, and Kaylin's friends will deal with the remaining stragglers."

"What about Conall?" I ask. "Lucifer might think to attack him. I want to protect him—"

"I don't need protecting."

We all turn towards him, incredulous. "But you're just human," I say. "You've brave—"

"And now, I am strong. It was a gift from Rex. I can demonstrate if you wish?"

I meet his eyes, so confident and yet so different from the boy I know. Conall's eyes are brown, like chocolate, but now they glow red as if lit by the remnants of some great inferno.

"Max," I order. "See if Conall is as tough as he says."

We all walk outside to watch the fight. Max's joints pop as he stretches, the muscles underneath his shirt rippling like water. Conall has his hands in his jeans, looking nonplussed by the intimidating demon.

Max charges at him, fast as a bolt of lightning. To my surprise, Conall does not try to evade him. He simply slugs the demon across the jaw; Max goes flying. We watch him open-mouthed.

"Next," he says.

"Michael?" I ask, meeting his eyes. He nods.

My father raises his hands, and fireballs materialise out of the air. He sends them towards Conall, who does something I never believed possible. Conall manipulates fire, making it coalesce around him in a spherical shield. The fire is deep red, like embers. The blue demon fire meets his own and is snuffed out.

With a raised eyebrow, Michael fires a bolt of lightning towards the shield. Conall's protection doesn't so much as flicker. With a wicked grin, Conall sends a fireball of his own towards my dad. He Fades, narrowly avoiding death by immolation.

Conall moves, quick as a viper. He wraps his hands around Michael's throat and throws him down towards the ground.

"I surrender," Michael says.

I stare at the boy I love, mouth agape. It takes me a moment to fully process what has happened.

Conall turns and faces me, a feral grin plastered on his face; I recognise a challenge when I see one. I stride forward, and Conall raises his shield again. I form a band of light in my hand and lash out, whipping it towards him. The shining magic cuts his shield in two. Before he can react, I charge, tackling him to the ground.

"You're sexier with all your newfound superpowers," I whisper against his ear.

He wraps his hands around my neck, cradling my head as he kisses me.

"I can still surprise you," he says. I yelp back as something unbelievably hot scorches the back of my neck. He shows me his hands, which glow like coals.

"For that," I say, "you're going to bottom next time."

He only chuckles. "The pleasure will be mine."

"If you two love birds are quite done," Kaylin says, a little bored, "then we may continue our deliberations?"

"By all means," Conall agrees.

"I'm still not leaving you unprotected," I say. "Kaylin, I want you to modify Conall's medallion so that I can sense it."

"I can do that."

If I might make a suggestion?

We turn towards Rex. "What's your plan, Rex?"

I think Conall should ride on my back during the assault.

"What? Are you crazy? You're going to lead the attack: there will be demons everywhere—"

Yes, but no place is safer than on a dragon's back. The demons will be far too busy trying not to get burnt to a toast. If you try and hide Conall somewhere, Lucifer might find him and send an Arch Demon to finish him off.

"You have to agree with the logic," Conall argues.

"Fine. I just never expected to see my boyfriend riding a dragon and fighting demons."

"There's a first time for everything."

****

We return to the main room: there's more to discuss. I notice that Michael looks a bit... agitated?

"Kaylin," he begins. "While your plan is solid, you always need to have a contingency when dealing with Lucifer. He will find ways to surprise you."

"What do you suggest?"

"Why not use a similar spell on me?"

"You would give up your own immortal life?"

"Yes."

"It's not that simple. We still need Foresight and Activation—"

"I thought about that. Let's say that if something goes wrong, I attack Lucifer. We know he will kill me, and when he does, it will Activate the Great Magic."

"That's not a bad idea," Roshika says grudgingly. "It's worth considering, Kaylin."

"Very well. Thanks for this, Michael. We appreciate it."

"So let's recap the plan," I say. "If everything goes right, Roshika's death will trap Lucifer in a cave system within Hell. Rex, you, and Conall will attack the demons in China to keep the main force occupied. What about you, Diana?"

"I will come with Kaylin and her team to Dublin. Roshika, Araya, and Kaylin will attack Lucifer while we keep the demons off her back."

"You can do that?"

"Kaylin has put a spell on us that enhances our powers at the cost of our lifespan."

"A hard price to pay."

"It is necessary," she says firmly.

"What will I do?" I ask.

"Don't attack Lucifer," Kaylin warns me. "You'll help Diana and Leo fight off the demons. Try and stay out of trouble."

"And if it all goes wrong?"

"Run, and prepare to fight another day. You and Rex will be Earth's only remaining hope."

I nod, acquiescing to her logic.

I catch my father looking at me. I move across the room, pulling him away to a side corridor.

****

"So, you've decided to play the hero?" I ask him.

"Yes. But then, you're a hero too, aren't you? A far better one than I ever was."

"You weren't a good man, were you?"

"No. I like to think I became better when I met your mother, Bridget. Your existence is proof of that much."

"Did no other demons have sex with a human? Why is it that I'm the only half-demon in existence?"

"Demon women are sterile, and in pregnancies where the father is a male demon, the result is always a miscarriage. At least, that's what we knew—but perhaps that was simply because we demons were simply too twisted to ever really love someone."

"I exist because you loved my mother?"

"Yes."

"Who told you this?"

"Shahar did the last time I went to Hell. He also told me that your existence is what makes it possible for me to circumvent the Barrier."

"It's too bad you were never around."

"I realise now that abandoning you was a mistake—but I can't be the father you always wanted. It's too late."

"Yeah, that's true. You know, this could be the last time we ever see each other; you might not survive this battle."

"Believe me, I know. If I die, I am content—I have lived a long life, longer than any mortal could have lived. I was rarely a good man for those two thousand odd years, but I always lived life to the fullest."

"*Carpe diem*, right?"

He smiles without amusement. "Luck be with you, my son. May you live better than I did."

Chapter Nine: The Final Battle

Lucifer

"Sir, the Israelis have offered to discuss the terms of their surrender," Archdemon Julius informs me.

I smile. "Of course. They have always been a pragmatic nation; it's something I admire about modern Israel. They joined the European League of Nations because it was the Great Power, and now that I'm here, they want to play nice with me."

"Well, we did decimate a good portion of the IDF air force and land army."

"That would have given them the right incentive. But I sense from your tone, Julius, that there is more."

"The Saudi Arabian government is petitioning us for negotiations as well, but there are several insurgency leaders within Saudi and the greater Middle East who have refused to accept our rule."

"Refused?"

"They say they will never bow down before the Devil. Allah will smite you—"

"Ah yes, the imaginary man in the sky."

"They will fight to the bitter end, my lord. It wouldn't look good for you as ruler."

"True, and I know many humans will call me leader because I can ensure peace where there was only chaos. But tell me, Julius, these insurgents—they don't survive without popular support, do they?"

"They need people to hide them, yes," the Archdemon agrees. "And to smuggle weapons, provide intelligence, and give them inside help. The Europeans have been fighting them for decades, I hear. A lot of airports have been blown up."

"I propose a solution," I say cunningly.

"What solution is that, my lord?"

"Without popular support, the insurgents will crumble. People won't support them if they fear me more than they fear the insurgents."

"You plan on... making an example?"

"*Pour encourager les autres*, of course."

"What are you thinking of?"

"Oh, you'll see.

I grab Julius' hand, Fading us to Mecca. I hear poets call it the Golden City, and it's easy to see why: there are countless domes, minarets, and turrets, all resplendent with golden roofs.

"Do you plan on speaking to them?" Julius asks. "We need an Arabic speaker—"

"I can speak the language well enough; I have learned from Shahar and my subjects. I can handle it." I use magic to project my voice, speaking in Arabic: "Faithful believers! Your leaders claim to negotiate with me, but I know that many of you support militant groups. These militant groups refuse my generous terms of surrender."

I feel the weight of a million gazes upon me.

"But like your Allah, I too am a wrathful god. And unlike him, I have the power to punish you. Which I will relish doing."

The reaction is instantaneous. Many humans flee, while others fall to their knees and pray. A few even manage to launch some SAAMs our way.

"Run while you can! Or die praying on your knees—I don't care either way."

I raise my arms, preparing the greatest of the Grand Spells. I toiled on this magic for millennia in Hell; I nurtured it with my hate, with furious malice. The rage instantly consumes me, burning through my veins. This power is like no other.

I feel my body spasming and arching. Julius watches me with concern. "My lord? May I help you with the spell?"

"No. This spell shall be the work of my hands and my hands alone."

The power builds within me, centuries upon centuries of despair and loss, reaching its ultimate apotheosis. It is like a great river bursting a dam. I reach out, feeling the nearby Red Sea, the same sea that Moses was said to have parted so many millennia ago. Humans idolised Moses and thought him a god, but really he was a witch. He didn't do it alone, though—he needed help.

I am greater than Moses.

The weight of it all is immense. I cry out, in pain or ecstasy, I don't know. A great mountain of water flows across the desert, moving at two hundred miles an hour. It charts a path of destruction across the country.

The humans start to panic. Families herd children out of the way, carrying their possessions with whatever they can. The smarter fanatics try to flee with the general population, but most stand and pray.

Prayer will not stop my magic. The buildings collapse under the great mass of water; there is a terrible grinding and tearing as steel bends and snaps against the torrent. Anything that didn't escape the city is surely dead.

I have achieved my goal: that is what matters. If a few unlucky souls didn't escape, they have none but themselves to blame. I gave them ample warning.

****

Diana

Kaylin always warned me about my passion for destruction. But now, I can finally put it to good use. The Devil and his cronies are going down.

The City of Dublin is as black as I remember it and even more chaotic. With Big Brother dead, killed by Lucifer's hand (Pip told us), the Party is in total disarray. I don't expect them to be more than a nuisance. Lucifer has, however, left a contingent of demons here. Killing *them* will ensure the Bad Boy comes to us.

I close my eyes, raise my arms, and reach out with my power. The day is overcast and cold, the final day before November. I summon the clouds to me, feeling their energy, drawing from it. I feel Kaylin's runes burn on my skin, matching the power. The clouds blacken and begin to spin. A wind picks up, at first a strong breeze, but soon it becomes a raging hurricane. The world grows dark and pregnant with battle.

Lightning forks down from the sky, and I laugh hysterically, the mad witch that I am. Leo, who is by my side, only rolls his eyes.

"The battle isn't starting yet, honey. Don't play all your best cards."

"Don't you worry, Leo, I know what I'm doing. And look—there! A demon!"

A figure with black wings swoops down from the sky, two more following on its wingtips. I summon my power, and it responds to my call with glee. I obliterate the first demon with a bolt of lightning.

Leo's hands explode with flame, and the second demon falls with a scream. But the third demon is smarter. I parry his fireballs with my magic, but then he teleports. Where has the bastard gone?

I turn around and see him coming. He's too quick; there's no time—

There is a bright flash of light, and the demon falls to the ground, screaming—he dies an instant later. I turn towards my saviour.

"Kaylin did tell you to wait for me," Mark says, still holding a colossal burning sword in his hand.

"I wanted a piece of the action. You spoil all the fun."

"That demon could have killed you."

"Leo had my back."

"Sure."

A figure suddenly bounds from a rooftop, startling me. It takes me a moment to recognise it as Pip, the imp. Mark is watching her with amusement.

"Lucifer has noticed what you're doing," she says. "Be prepared for a big demon attack soon."

"What about Rex? Conall?"

"They left for Shanghai; they should be there soon."

"OK, good. In that case—" Mark doesn't get to complete his sentence. Pip's head explodes in a shower of blood, and a loud CRACK follows a split second later. Pip has just been shot!

Mark's reaction is instant and terrifying. He unfurls his wings and takes off with unbelievable speed. Moments later, he returns, a struggling figure locked in his arms. I expect him to land, but instead, he keeps on flying. Mark drops the man a moment later; he drops to the ground with a sickening *crunch*.

Mark Fades back to us. He's breathing hard, eyes wild with rage.

"I'm sorry," I say. "I liked the little imp, too, you know."

"She was helping us fight Lucifer. She had nothing to do with the Party!"

"The sniper just picked an easy target—it could have been one of us instead."

"Mark," Leo says quietly, catching his gaze. "We will mourn later, once the battle is over. We need to stay alert."

The boy nods silently. We turn and face the oncoming demons.

I count ten demons; this is going to be a tough fight. Their leader howls a war cry and dives straight after us. I reach out, feeling the storm around us, understanding its power, moulding it to my will. I slam all of the demons at once, buffeting them with air and lightning. They crash to the ground.

Leo seizes the opportunity. He sends a wall of flame towards the demons. A couple manage to Fade away, but several are not so quick-witted and die burning. Four demons spring at us. Leo and I burn the two nearest to us. From the corner of my eye, I see the other two slam into Mark, who seems to shrug off their attacks. He drives the sword into one demon and binds the other demon with a chord of light.

"You traitor," the demon screams.

"Now, now, Diego, there's no need to state the perfectly obvious."

"We should have killed you when we had the chance—"

"But you were too weak then, and now you are nothing."

"*Hijo de puta*—"

Mark decapitates the demon, ending whatever he was about to say. He turns towards us; I raise an eyebrow.

"You knew him?"

"Me and Diego had a history together. Anyway—" He pauses. "He's here."

"Who is?"

"Lucifer."

****

Conall

"So, how are we going to get to Shanghai?" I ask Rex.

You shall ride on my back, and I shall turn to fire. This will allow me to travel at incredible speeds.

"Are you sure I won't die?"

I'm certain. The fire will not hurt you.

Just as I'm about to climb the dragon, Max appears. I look at the demon curiously. Mark trusts him, and earning his trust is not easy. This guy has to be good.

"What are you doing here, Max? Aren't you supposed to be off with the others?"

"Mark ordered me to accompany you."

"Really? Why?"

"He wants to keep you safe."

"Fine. But keep up, will you? The dragon flies fast."

"No need; I will Fade to Shanghai. Lucifer teleported me there, so I have a good idea of the place."

"Smart thinking, then. We'll meet you there?"

"Yes."

I settle atop Rex, and he unfurls his wings, propelling us high into the air. There's the now-familiar rush of air, the sensation of my face liquefying from the incredible acceleration. Rex levels out, flying above the clouds. Then he does something else. He becomes immaterial, yet at the same time, still solid. I feel myself changing too—I feel lighter, more insubstantial. I glance at my hands with amazement. I am made of *fire*, a glowing incandescent substance with a curious solidity, like frozen lightning.

Rex propels us forward at unbelievable speed. I know that travelling faster than sound—travelling *much* faster than sound—should produce a sonic boom that would kill an ordinary human. Yet I feel hardly anything at all.

I watch as we cross seas, mountains, and whole continents. I recognise Siberia's icy wilderness below, though we are high in the upper reaches of the sky. I am not sure exactly how long the flight takes—an hour, perhaps slightly more. It feels completely surreal.

Eventually, a city materialises on the horizon. As we get closer, I see that the city is burning, and countless dark-winged beings circle the air above. From this distance, we can hear the din of Q fighters and artillery—even a few old-fashioned jets.

"They really threw everything they had at Lucifer's demons."

To no avail, little one. Without magic, there is no hope of fighting either me or the demons. Now let's go and give them Hell.

Rex slows down, then materialises again. The shock of having flesh once more is indescribable. I whoop, then shout a war cry. The dragon roars, and it is a roar so deep and so savage that the Earth trembles.

****

The dragon rears back and breathes fire at a group of nearby demons. Some manage to Fade, but many perish in the inferno. Through the corner of my eye, I see one of the demons heading for me. But I need not worry: Rex flicks his tail, swatting the demon like a fly. He falls to the ground, burning, before disappearing into the void. I spot another demon coming in from above. I raise my hand and send a fireball her way. Taken by surprise, the demoness dies instantly.

"How many was that?" I cry.

A *dozen*, his mental voice rumbles in my head. *But there are hundreds here. The fight is only just beginning.*

Rex dives down towards a river—the Huangpu? —and concentrates on one of the bridges, a steel pylon affair that's many metres long. I only get an idea of his intent from our telepathic bond before seeing his plan materialise in full glory. He separates each metal pylon from the bridge and sends them flying into the air. But it doesn't stop there: he breathes a quick gush of flame and sets each pylon on fire. He telekinetically throws the pylons towards the demons.

Taken by surprise, countless demons fall in the hail of burning metal.

"That was so cool!" I cry. "I didn't even know you could do that."

I can do many things.

Something flashes in the corner of my eye. Rex twists away, but he is milliseconds too late. The demon slams into me, and we fall towards the ground. He wraps his hands around my throat, purple eyes gleaming with malice. White fangs grin from his open mouth.

Moments before we hit the ground, another figure tackles my captor. I slam into concrete; the breath is knocked right out of my lungs. But I know a normal human would not have survived this fall.

I summon the power within me and haul myself to my feet. *Rex? Where are you?*

Fighting—Archdemons—they ambushed us—

I have faith the dragon will fight himself out of it. Instead, I turn to the two struggling figures: I recognise Max and another demon with long green hair. The strange-looking demon has Max pinned using telekinesis.

"Max, darling, you shouldn't have betrayed us."

"What do you know about loyalty, Tim? You don't care for anyone except yourself."

"I am loyal to Lucifer."

This is not just any demon; this is *Archdemon* Tim. Mark had warned me about him. The Archdemon raises his hand, where a bolt of blue energy has materialised. Max is about to die. So I do the only thing I can: I throw a fireball, hoping to distract the creature.

He moves incredibly fast, almost dodging the surprise attack. The fireball still catches him on the edges of his shoulder blades, and he shrinks back. Max instantly explodes into action, firing a shadow bolt towards the demon's chest. He Fades away.

I feel hands gripping my throat, strong as iron. "Move, and the boy dies," Tim warns Max. "And I don't think you'll want to be responsible for the death of Mark's little human lover. Who, I must admit, is quite sumptuous."

You underestimate me, demon; I communicate telepathically.

"Oh? How so?"

I bring fire into my throat and *push* it through his hands and into the core of his being. The demon reels back, crying out in agony. It is the last thing he ever does. I watch as his body explodes into flame, and his wings—webbed and silvery, like a dragonfly—catch fire and melt.

Then he dies.

"Who was that guy?" I ask Max.

"A so-called friend of Mark. He was strong even by Archdemon standards—you did well, Conall. Really well."

We hear a great roar and look up. Rex has scattered the Archdemons and is heading towards us.

"Go," Max tells me. "Before the others think to attack you."

But how do I climb a dragon's back mid-flight? There's only one solution: I must fly. Instinctively, I summon the power within me, push against the ground, and *lift* into the air. I accelerate, gunning for Rex. He turns around, allowing me to land on his back easily; I slam into him, barely hanging on.

You are still clumsy in flight, little one, he says with amusement.

"You did mention I could fly, but I had no idea how."

War is the mother of invention. The dragon turns his attention to the enemy. *Well done with the Archdemon. Now let's finish them off, shall we?*

With a roar, he charges at the demons. And with fire in my hands, I bellow an equally savage cry.

Chapter Ten: A Plan Gone Wrong

Kaylin

This is it—the moment I've always lived for. We are about to face one of the most powerful beings ever seen on Earth, a tyrant greater than any that came before. I have placed the binding spells on Roshika and Michael, which should trigger the Great Magic under the right conditions.

We are three: Roshika, Araya, and I. We walk under a blue, spectral dome. Michael is to our side, ready to intervene. Our plan is working so far: Diana and Mark have taken out many of the demons present here, and Rex is keeping the bulk of the demon horde occupied in Shanghai.

We pass only scattered resistance from a handful of demons, which our combined magic defeats easily.

He is waiting for us by the River Liffey, next to the ruin of a bridge. I expected many things from the Devil, the Great Demon, the most feared individual in our collective human imagination—but I never expected to see him filing his nails. He seems very absorbed in the activity, almost completely ignoring us.

"The very least you could do," I begin sternly, "is acknowledge our presence."

"What is there to acknowledge? Two annoying witches, a girl who picked the wrong side, and my old darling Michael." He smiles wickedly. "It's so nice to see you after two decades, Moloch."

"My name is Michael."

Lucifer waves away his protest. "Semantics. The point is, you were my lieutenant, and you betrayed me. Ordinarily, I would punish such insubordination harshly—but given that you *are* Mark's father, I give you the chance to surrender; my punishment will be lenient if you do."

"I will never surrender to you."

"Ah, well, it was worth a try. In which case, you will perish with these foolish mortals. Now, tell me: where is Mark?"

"You will never have my son," Michael says hotly.

"What you wish is of no consequence. You have filled that boy's head with nonsense, making him turn against me. He even freed the dragon! Do you know what a menace that damn reptile is?"

"Mark acted of his own free will," I interrupt. "He freed the dragon without our help or advice."

"Then, I shall have to ask him. Once I kill you all."

"You can try," I say. "I've always wanted to fight the devil." My words are pure bravado, of course. We cannot compete with his raw power or his skill as a witch; he is unrivalled. We can only outplay his arrogance.

Lucifer sends a wave of fireballs against us. Michael Fades away while I, Roshika, and Araya hold hands to combine our power. The shield wavers but holds. I wipe sweat from my forehead; Lucifer was just testing us, and already, he shows his superiority against our combined might. Frankly, we are nothing against this being.

"Not bad," he says, laughing cruelly. "The bit with the Great Magic is especially clever."

"What Great Magic?"

"Oh, don't pretend you have no idea!" A bolt of lightning scissors from his hand, narrowly avoiding Michael and weakening our shield even more. I just have to keep him attacking us; once the protection breaks, Roshika will die, thus sealing Lucifer away forever. (I can already feel Roshika shaking against me.) Lucifer must not figure out the ruse!

The Great Demon just sighs. "I am the oldest witch ever to have lived, the strongest, the most daring, the most cunning. Did you really think I would not see how you bound the witch's life to that shield? Or figure out you'll try and use Great Magic against me? Fooled me once; shame on you. Fooled me twice; shame on me."

"So what are you going to do about it? Put us to sleep? The shield protects us against all magic—"

"Oh, I can unbind your little spell, but it would take too much effort to do it that way. So I set a trap of my own." He waves his hands, clearing away the dust and rubble with telekinesis. A pentagram is inscribed on the asphalt below us, surrounded by a circle drawn with runes.

We try to move, but it's too late. The runes activate, glowing blue. I feel our magic cut like a string.

It all depends on Michael now. He must attack; Lucifer must slay him. The old demon bellows a war cry and charges at the Great Demon. Lucifer catches him, holding him in a macabre parody of an embrace. They lock eyes.

Michael is frozen solid.

All is lost—we're going to die. I summon the rest of my magical reserves; I intend to die with dignity. Araya shrieks out a cry of rage and attacks Lucifer with everything she has. Fire, thunder, even telepathic attacks, which I feel like a volley of knives. Lucifer does not so much as flinch. He parries all of her magic attacks and ignores her telepathic assault, the same way one might overlook a toddler punching on one's leg.

I think of the forest clearing, the peaceful place Roshika had taught me to find when being attacked by death magic. Lucifer's death spell falls flat. Rolling his eyes, the Great Demon slams Araya, sending her flying into a wall, where she crumples soundlessly.

He turns towards us. "Any last words?"

"Go to hell," I breathe.

I wait for the end. But then something... happens. I feel it like a great tearing in the world, a feat of magic so monumental it warps the universe's fabric. Lucifer is thrown back as if by an invisible hand, and I feel myself being transported someplace far, far away.

There is light and then darkness. Infinite darkness.

Chapter Eleven: Duel with the Devil

Mark

I feel the Magic like a soundless explosion, filling my ears with silent noise. I blink and wait for my senses to come back. That was Great Magic, without a doubt. Yet, I know that Lucifer is still alive on this Earth. I can't describe precisely how I know this—it's like a connection, an invisible tie to Lucifer.

Whatever Great Magic Kaylin or Roshika cast, it was a desperate one.

I turn towards Diana and Leo. "Hold the line, don't let any other demons interfere. I'm going to fight Lucifer."

"What? But surely Lucifer is bound—I felt the magic—" Diana complains.

"It was indeed Great Magic, but Lucifer is neither dead nor bound. Trust me."

Diana sets her mouth grimly. "Then you are our only hope. Good luck, Mark."

"Fate be with you," Leo adds.

I unfurl my wings and launch myself into the sky. As I fly, the world begins to darken. The clouds are like angry giants, lords of the sky, and lightning flashes in their depths. The wind, too, buffets me left and right—it takes all my new-found flight experience to keep a steady course. I can feel Diana working her magic, moulding the storm to her will. I spot the occasional demonic figure falling from the sky and smile to myself. Diana is brilliant.

I find him in the city centre, next to the River Liffey. A body is crumpled somewhere against a wall—Araya?—and it takes me a moment to recognise the ice statue next to Lucifer: Michael, my father. There is no sign of Roshika or Kaylin. The Great Demon himself looks annoyed.

"Your witch has been teleported away somewhere," he says, "so she can't trouble me again."

"Kaylin, you mean?"

"Whatever her name was. The old one sacrificed herself to power the spell. Annoying little martyrs, witches."

"What have you done to my father?"

"Oh, Michael? The witches put Great Magic on him, assuming I would just kill him straight away. But of course, I froze him, which ruined their pathetic plan. It also allows me to deal with him at my leisure."

"You'll have to go through me first."

"Oh, Mark," he says, sighing. "We don't have to fight. I could give you a place beside me at the palace. I will build it in Rome; we can rule together. You can keep your Conall—I don't mind."

"You really think it's that easy? You sent me to prison, hoping I would turn into a demon. Then you threatened my boyfriend and kidnapped me to Hell. If that wasn't enough, you killed Steijn, who was barely more than a teenager—and a friend to me. Now you offer me power, assuming I will ignore the millions you have just slaughtered across the world."

"I did get carried away with Mecca, but the situation in Beijing wasn't my fault—"

"It doesn't matter. Millions more will have to die for you to call yourself emperor."

"Is that so special? Millions have already died in pointless wars, and millions more will continue to do so as the millennia pass. With me, there is peace."

"You lie. Humans will never follow a sorcerer-king. They pray to gods, yet while you have the power of a god, you cannot command human loyalty. You offer punishments and favours, but human faith cannot be brokered with mere favours. Yours would be a rule of constant subjugation and brutality."

"Oh, come on, Mark. It's not like you ever cared about politics. What does your heart want?"

"My heart wants you dead, Lucifer. For what you did to me, Conall and Steijn, I will relish seeing you fall." With that, I unfurl my wings, which are no longer black, the wings of a demon. My wings shine white, like a fresh blanket of snow. They burn with radiance. It's purely superficial, but it reflects something deeper inside of me; a fundamental change in my nature, my very core being.

All of Lucifer's demons are alike—except me.

"You will regret this, angel-boy." The Great Demon unfurls his wings, long and slender, and dark as the void.

He is still blindingly quick; he is still the Devil I know. Yet, the dynamics of this fight are different. Before, I was weak, and Lucifer only toyed with me. This time, it's for real.

A series of lightning-fast punches send me reeling, but not for long. I place my body so that his next punch goes wide, and I retaliate by slamming into him with my shoulder. He goes flying into a building.

"Not bad," he says, dusting himself off. "You managed to survive the first skirmish. But you still fight only a fraction of my true power."

The Great Demon turns into mist, a black, tenebrous substance. I saw him do this before when he killed Steijn. But now it will be different. I summon my power, raise my hand, and slam my fist into the ground. A wave of radiant energy emanates from my hand. The shockwave forces Lucifer to materialise, and sends him reeling.

"You didn't really think that would work?" I ask him. "That trick is old."

Lucifer smiles a slow, chilling smile. A sword and a dagger appear in his hands, and they glimmer black, like sharp obsidian. "Let's see how good you are with that burning sword of yours, shall we?"

I raise my arms and grasp my golden sword with both hands on the hilt. I mould the weapon to my will, making it longer and more massive. Liquid fire melts from the blade, melting through the asphalt below like plastic.

We meet in a clash of blades. Our movements resemble those of dancers, for they are fluid and graceful. Yet this dance is savage and macabre. Lucifer Fades several times, thrusting with the long blade, trying to find an opening in my defences. I keep him at bay with powerful, sweeping arcs, never breaking my stance. I wield the massive sword effortlessly, but I know it is only a matter of time before he wins. Lucifer has had aeons to practice his swordsmanship; I had to make do with scant weeks.

So I manipulate the fire from within the blade, sending slags of burning magic in every direction. A hiss tells me one found its mark.

"You little shit," he growls.

"Not everyone is a pushover, Lucifer. You have grown arrogant in that castle of yours."

He growls, and suddenly, black tendrils suppurate from his hands, binding me like prey in a spider's web. I feel the magic like a cold emptiness eating through my skin. I set my jaw and fill myself with power. I shine bright as a star. The tendrils evaporate, mere shadows in the face of the light.

We exchange a barrage of fireballs, which I counter with ease by creating a wall of fire. Around us, the storm howls, occasionally shattering a window. We remain unaffected in the eye.

Lucifer zaps me with lightning, which I block with my sword. Finally, he erupts into a column of flame and sends a swirling vortex of demonic magic crashing into me. I wrap my wings around me, imbuing them with power, and shield myself.

I smile. Lucifer has thrown everything against me, and I have not so much as flinched from the onslaught. He might yet win—for he is still the being from legend. He is the serpent that seduces you with beautiful words; he is the wily fox, the dreaded wolf. But clearly, his raw power no longer eclipses mine.

I can fight him as an equal.

"Have some of your own medicine," I say before I erupt into a golden flame. I send a torrent of my magic towards him, and he counters it with his own malevolent power. For the span of moments, we lie locked together in a contest of strength. Slowly, my magic advances, getting closer to scorching him. He Fades away.

"You have power now," he says bitterly, "but you are still callow. You lack subtlety and finesse."

"Show me some of your finesse then."

The Devil raises his arms, and from one, he is many.

I blink, trying to figure out if this is some mirage, some trick. But the horror is real: there are now six versions of Lucifer surrounding me—all of them identical. Lucifer laughs at me, a sound as cruel as it is sweet. I look around me, trying to decide how I might fight them. Surely one must be the real Lucifer, and the others are only inferior copies? But how can I tell what is real from what is a lie?

I transfer the sword to my right hand and cast a spell. Perhaps I speak some words, or maybe I do not, relying purely on the force of my concentrated will. I fashion my magic into a shield of iridescent light.

"You think a shield will save you?" he enquires sarcastically.

"Shut up, Lucifer. I'm sick of your gloating. Why don't you come and get me?"

Six copies of Lucifer spring at me, a pack of wolves ready to devour their prey. I catch three of them on the left side with my shield, tossing them aside and adding some burns, too. I swing my sword in an arc, and two of the copies fall under my blade.

A sharp pain explodes up into my shoulder. I turn enraged. One of the copies attacks me from behind.

"You're losing, Mark. Face it."

"You're a sick little bastard, Lucifer."

"Oh, but is it really me you're talking to?"

I close my eyes for a fraction of a second, fighting past the numbing pain in my arm. I feel the magic Lucifer has woven like a living thing, a chameleon of many shades. I dig deeper, piercing the spell. I know what I'm looking for: a dark heart, rotten on the inside.

Once again, the copies spring at me. But I ignore the duplicate I was talking to, Fading ever so slightly—*blinking*—so that it misses me. I parry the others' blades with my shield, but I leave myself deliberately exposed on the sword-side.

The viper moves in for the kill. But I know Lucifer's purpose, his true twisted nature. At the last moment, I strike.

I shatter his spell like so many broken mirrors; my sword blow separates truth from lies, villainy from virtue. No evil can resist its sharp point, its fine edges, or its annihilating fire.

I drive the point of the sword right through his heart.

At first, he is simply shocked. He stares at the weapon, not quite believing it. He has lived for millennia; I am just a boy. A mouse has slain the lion. Slowly, realisation dawns on him. He falls to the ground, trying vainly to pry the blade from his chest. He succeeds only in singeing his fingers.

Then his expression dissolves into fear. Authentic, genuine fear.

"I'm... going to die."

"Yes, you are," I say the words simply, without any inflection. Lucifer is not bleeding, but that is because there is nothing inside him to bleed. There is only empty darkness, which seeps through the wound like poison.

"*Half sunk a shattered visage lies, whose frown, and wrinkled lip, and sneer of cold command...*"

"Is that Ozymandias?" I ask.

"Ozymandias mocked tyrants. But the tyrants always have the last laugh—you should know that by now, Mark. Even as I lie dying, I am summoning what remains of my magic towards a spell. I'm going to blow this ugly city to kingdom come."

"The people of Dublin have done you no harm," I say, alarmed. I have no idea how many are still left in the city, but it could easily be a million souls. I have no idea how I might contain such a burst of magic.

"Do you think I care? They don't call me the Devil for nothing. If I cannot rule the world, then I will destroy it out of spite so that none may rule in my place."

I scramble for a solution to the problem. I can think of only one desperate option. Slowly, I drop to my knees, at eye level with Lucifer.

"You did love me, didn't you?" I ask simply. "I could never have done this otherwise—you would have seen through the deception. Love blinded you."

"Yes, it did. Though I am two thousand years old, I am doomed to repeat past mistakes—just like those stupid mortals. You are no better than Judas was."

"No. Judas only used you for sex. I never reciprocated your feelings, Lucifer, but I never scorned your love."

"You didn't?"

"Even after all you did to me, even when you pressured me for sex, I could not bring myself to hate you. Though you are beyond salvation, you do have your redeeming qualities."

"Such as?"

"Your wicked sense of humour. Your sense of justice—you recognise evil in others, even though are you are blind to that same evil within you. But I admired your affection most of all: you loved with a wide-open heart. Though you are crafty and smart and could have played all sorts of games with me, you chose to be honest."

"I... I don't know what to say. No one has ever left me speechless before."

I kiss him on the forehead. "You need not say anything; your actions will speak louder than any words. You don't have to kill all these people— you're too good to murder without reason. You're ruthless, yes, but not spiteful."

The Devil closes his eyes, smiling. "You are naive to believe in my redemption, but you are right about this much: I do not kill without reason. I have lost; you have won. I should accept my fate with dignity."

"Thank you."

"Even as I fade away into the abyss, I will remember that moment, Mark, when you hugged me, without desire, without asking for anything in return."

I hug him one last time. "For old time's sake," I whisper.

"*Ave atque vale*, Mark."

The Devil closes his eyes one last time before melting away into the void. I grab my sword from where it lies discarded and raise it high above my head. A burst of power shoots up from within me, rises high into the sky, and explodes into a brilliant flare.

Victory is ours.

Chapter Twelve: Queen of Spies

Kaylin

The Crystal Cave is beautiful, like I remember it, but empty without Roshika. I say goodbye to Marten, the raven, who caws mournfully, easily understanding my telepathic message: *Roshika is gone.* I free Roshika's ball python, Cassandra, from her cage, hoping she can make her own way in the wild. Catching Daimon, the cat, is the most difficult challenge. I am eventually forced to use a spell.

While the feline certainly thinks of himself as independent, I know Roshika feeds him and takes care of his injuries. Life for a domestic cat, even a half-wild one, would be challenging in the mountains.

With a limp cat in my arms, I call my men at home, asking for a Q-car to Mount Everest. I felt Lucifer's death like darkness lifting from the world. Therefore, I don't bother asking how Mark defeated Lucifer—I know he will tell me personally.

We failed where one boy succeeded. Mark truly deserves to be called a hero.

The flight home is long but mostly uneventful: I am not in the mood for conversation, and the pilot lets me be. Even in the short while that I knew Roshika, I came to admire her bravery, stoicism, and warm demeanour. She taught me a great deal about magic, but she had precious little time. Learning magic without her will be hard—but it is my destiny. I will carry on her legacy.

Gradually, the Q-car begins to descend, and green fields become visible on the horizon. We are home.

****

Grumman meets me at the door to our base.

"It's good to see you again," he says gruffly. "We worried you didn't make it."

"Roshika sacrificed herself to power a spell that teleported me back to the cave on Mount Everest."

"But you don't need Great Magic for a teleport spell. Right?" He scratches his stubble, looking confused.

"I suspect she did more than simply teleport me. She threaded spells of protection and concealment and used her life force to make them more powerful. Lucifer could have searched the ends of the Earth for me."

"Right. Smart woman, that Roshika. Still, we're lucky to have Mark, aren't we?"

"Luckier than we could imagine."

"Did someone mention me?" The boy in question swaggers towards us, relaxed and confident.

"Don't brag about saving the world," I warn him. "Or we'll never hear the end of it."

"Aww, and here I thought I was going to be the golden hero, ready to parade across the world. Women would swoon and fall at my feet."

"You don't even like women, Mark."

"I know. But a guy can dream, can't he?"

I roll my eyes. "Thank you. Is that good enough?"

The humour leaves his eyes. "Diana is in the hospital wing, you know. You should go see her."

"I will."

I know Diana is unconscious, but I have no idea how bad it might be. It could be that she will wake up on her own in a few days, right as rain. Or else the blood magic drained all her life. She did, after all, wield a power that no mortal could ever hope to match.

I find her on a bed, attended to by a nurse. I ask her about Diana's condition.

"She's stable, ma'am. Her heart is doing fine."

"But is there brain activity?"

"We haven't put her in the MRI yet—we didn't have time."

"No matter, I will know soon enough. You are dismissed, Wynne."

"Yes, Mistress."

As the nurse leaves the room, I reach out with my mind, searching for Diana's consciousness.

I am in a land of ice and fire, a world of dreams. I walk on a flat expanse of ice stretching as far as the eye can see; the sky is black with smoke, and on the far horizon, a volcano spews lava.

I must find Diana—but where is she? Her mind has created this place, and her consciousness is lost within. I fear that I, too, may become lost, for this place is featureless and vast.

But magic is strong here; I feel that. I must rely on spells. I draw a Seeking rune and cast a Tracking spell. A wisp of light travels across the wasteland, parting away the smoke and snow. There, in the distance, is a flash of brown hair. Diana.

I call to her, but she does not hear me. So I pull her, using my magic like a rope.

"Kay... Kaylin?" she asks.

"Diana, you must come with me."

"But I have to do something—have to fight—"

"Lucifer is defeated. You are dreaming."

"How do I know I can trust you?"

"Cogito ergo sum."

She smiles, a trace of the Diana I know and love. "Of course. You know better than anyone."

We turn around, the dream world fading to oblivion.

I return to the waking world like a diver coming up for air. I forcibly calm my breathing, as hyperventilating would do me no good. Diana recovers more swiftly than I.

"Are you OK, Kaylin?"

"Am I OK? The question is, are you?"

"I feel fine."

"You were trapped in some sort of dream-world."

"Yeah, I just... lost consciousness. I don't remember much about my dream. Was it because of the blood spell?"

"Frankly, I'm not sure. If Roshika were here..."

"She is no longer with us?"

"She sacrificed herself to protect me."

"A brave woman. Do you know how I got here?"

"I understand Mark carried you slung across his shoulder. Don't mention it, though—the boy is cocky enough as it is."

"He did save the world, you know. He deserves some credit."

"Who are you talking about?" I turn and see Leo in the doorway.

"Leo!" I exclaim before I run towards him and catch him in a hug.

"Well, hello to you too, Kaylin. How are you doing, Diana?"

"I'm fine, really. Just embarrassed that I fell unconscious, and you didn't."

"You commanded a huge storm—I accomplished only a fraction of your feats. It's no wonder you paid a higher price than me."

"I'm just glad you're both safe and sound," I say. "Is anyone else hurt?"

"Non-Familiars stayed out of the fight," Leo informs me. "John is still in a coma, though."

I almost forgot—John was a brave pilot who sustained an injury while fighting the Party Q fighters.

"I know that look," Diana says. "Do you think you can help him like you helped me?"

"Roshika taught me a good deal, but still... I don't know. I can only try."

****

I find the stricken pilot alone in his room, electrodes connected to his head; the monitors are beeping regularly, showing heart and brain activity. His friend and various family members had been allowed to visit, but pretty much everyone has given up hope. Well, everyone except me. But then, I am one of the last remaining humans who still has access to magic.

I move the bed to the middle of the room and draw a circle on the floor. I inscribe numerous runes on his forehead. The spell is ready; it's time to enter his mind

I start to feel drawn into a dark pit. The sensation is like falling, except the air feels sticky, almost tar-like. I search for thoughts, for emotions, and find them, but they are scattered. John's memories are like pinpricks of light in a vast, empty darkness.

Now I understand what I have to do. John's mind is broken, and my job is to put it back together again. What's more, I have to do it fast—or neither one of us will survive. But how do you fix a shattered mind? All the king's men and all the king's horses couldn't put him back together again.

Then I have an idea. Diana escaped into a dream when she fell unconscious. Could it be that dreams act as a defence mechanism for the mind? If only Roshika were here to answer that question.

What I need is a grand, unifying narrative. A place where all the memories can come together. I think of the meadow, the place I retreated to when I needed to defend myself from a death spell. I project that sense of well-being, of peace, onto the world around me, moulding it to my will.

The air is alive with the scent of freshly cut grass. Birds chirp a melody in a tree, and the wind whispers gently. I am sitting on a bench, and besides me is John. He looks disorientated.

"What happened?" he asks. "I was flying—we were attacked—"

"You were attacked by Party Q fighters. You sustained a head injury that left you in a coma."

"I'm in a coma now? Is this a hallucination?"

"Not quite. I am a real person; my name is Kaylin."

His eyes focus more clearly on me. "Kaylin? The witch?"

"Precisely. I am here to get you out of this coma, John. You need to follow me."

"Follow you where?"

"To waking life. This is a dream I have created for you."

I offer him my hand, and he takes it. We walk away from the meadow, and it fades away into nothing. Once again, I feel a swimmer coming out from a deep dive. Pinpoints of light appear above me, then materialise into the real world.

I am back in the infirmary room. John is awake and removing the electrodes from his head. He tries to get up and almost falls over. I move to help him.

"Stay on the bed," I order. "You have been in a coma for several weeks. You need to recover."

"My family? My friends?"

"They will come as soon as they can. Rest."

"Why did you do this for me? I'm not even one of your men."

I smile. "I helped save the world. Healing a comatose man is just another day in the office for me."

****

I find Diana and Leo waiting for me outside the door. They seem pleased.

"Nice going," Leo says.

"Thank you. How is Shadow, by the way?"

"The doc expects him to wake up soon."

"I should—"

"No, you shouldn't."

I turn towards Diana, surprised. "What is it, Diana?"

"Shadow will be fine on his own. You need to meet Andrew, the Communist leader, who has invited you to Dublin. He's unofficially the Taoiseach now."

"That makes sense." I had almost forgotten about our allies. It stands to reason that they would take control of Ireland with the Party gone and the demons defeated.

"Andrew wants to negotiate a power-sharing agreement with you," Diana continues. "Be careful, Kaylin. They've been allies up to now, but with so much power in reach, they might not be so friendly."

"We can always use Mark to threaten them," I point out.

She smiles slightly. "I was thinking of a more diplomatic approach. Mark is a teenager, not a weapon. If we abuse his trust—"

"He could become worse than Lucifer."

"Exactly," Diana agrees. "The future of our country is on your shoulders, Kaylin."

****

I am escorted towards a secure building and pass through multiple X-rays, metal detectors, and searches. Since Lucifer had trashed the tower, Andrew had decided to move the country's headquarters to a more secure building. Of course, these measures are pointless against me: there are various spells I could use to bust myself out of here and kill anyone who gets in my way.

Diplomacy, Kaylin.

Finally, I am brought face-to-face with Andrew. He is the same as I remember: a well-built man in his late forties, sporting a salt-and-pepper beard. The suit is new, though, and the beret with the red star is clearly just theatrics.

"Hello, Kaylin. It's nice to see you again."

"Cut to the chase, Andrew. I nearly died fighting the Devil, and I've been busy healing injured men today."

"Very well." He sighs. "I have thought about making a supernatural crack squad with you as the commander. I figured that, since everyone has seen what demons are capable of, no one will dare go up against a witch. Your power cannot be contended with; no one will dare threaten us."

"You know better than that, Andrew. People do not respect leaders who consort with dark powers. They fear the supernatural, yes, but fear breeds resentment, and resentment leads to rebellion."

He looks away, then sighs."You are right."

I allow myself to relax slightly. I was worried the man wouldn't see sense—I should have more faith in him.

"Let me propose something else in that case. I want you to be a covert force," he starts. "You will be my eyes and ears; you will also help with difficult missions that require unique talents. Officially, you'll be Permanent Secretary of the Interior."

"Unique talents," I say, smiling. "What a lovely euphemism."

"So, are you in?"

"You want me to be your Queen of Spies."

"Simply put, yes."

"What's in it for me?"

"All the money and resources you could need. But I know you're not motivated by money."

"No. If you want me to help you, then I want democracy."

"Kaylin, it's not that simple. Ireland hasn't had a real election in centuries. The people have just been through a civil war and a worldwide invasion by *demons*. This country is not stable enough to hold an election—we don't even have a constitution or political parties."

I want to argue, but I know he's right. "Okay, then promise me we'll have a referendum on a new constitution within two years—and an election the year after that."

"Of course you would ask for this. To be honest, my first offer wasn't very serious—I knew you would turn it down."

"You're trying to negotiate with me by bluffing?"

"I was thinking more along the lines of *give and take*. Two years is too soon, Kaylin—we need a *decade* of rebuilding."

"Fine. Five years then."

"You win. In five years, I promise a referendum."

"Good. I'll hold you to your word."

I turn heel and leave the room. There is nothing more I need to say.

Chapter Thirteen: Proposal

Conall

It took some doing, but I managed to find a rock that is the correct size. If this sounds a little strange, bear with me. It had to be the right kind of rock: granite, a durable stone, grey and weathered by the elements. It can't be too small or too big, as stone is tough to work with. It helps that we have the Manzanares mountains here next to the villa.

I examine the rounded piece of granite which lies in my hand. I concentrate hard, bringing the fire inside me to the surface. My hands glow like an electric forge, and the flames swirl around the rock. Soon it is red hot.

I work the stone with willpower alone, moulding it with magic. I let all the unneeded stone slag off, then place my work on some gravel to cool. I'll come back once it's ready.

I walk back to the villa, seeking out my bedroom. I expected to find President Meow on the bed, but I never expected to see Javalook next to him. The little imp is curled up next to the cat; the President embraces the imp with his paws.

I raise an eyebrow. "Now, that's something I never thought I would see."

"Hey! For all you know, I could be held hostage by this evil feline," the imp complains.

I snort. "I doubt it."

"Okay, it's true! We made friends. It turns out this kitty likes me a lot more when I feed him treats."

"That sounds like him."

"Anyway," Javalook continues. "Rex sent me here to talk to you."

"How is my fine dragon doing?"

"He is now the ruler of Hell. He had to step in to stop the riots."

"Riots?"

"The humans had been ruled by the demons for millennia. With them gone, chaos was bound to follow."

"So you're the dragon's spies now, I see."

"How did you guess?"

"Rex needs good spies as much as Lucifer did."

"True."

"I'm sorry about Pip, by the way. Mark called to tell me the news."

"You didn't know her."

"I didn't, but I sympathise with your loss."

"Thanks, human. You know, the funeral will be tomorrow. We rarely lose an imp, so everyone will be there. Maybe you and Mark...?"

"We'll think about it."

For a moment, there is silence, broken only by the contented snoring of the cat.

"So, they're all gone?" I ask. "The demons? I can't quite believe it."

"Neither can I. Our master was a constant in all our lives. He created us, and he continued long after our natural lifespan ended."

"How long do you imps live?"

"About three centuries, give or take."

"We'll be safe now, then?"

"Who knows?" the demon asks sorrowfully. "The world is a strange place. But you have nothing to fear from us."

"Thanks for telling me this. Tell Rex I'll come to visit him sometime. I'm off to speak with my parents."

"See you."

****

I find Mother speaking with father in his office—a small wooden affair, lit by only a single window. Mother's operations room, I know, is considerably grander than this. They turn towards me as I open the door.

"So we're safe?" asks Niall, my father.

"Mark managed to kill Lucifer once and for all. The imps and the dragon are friends. So it would appear that we are, indeed, safe."

"I'm not leaving this country," Father says. "The Party could still have supporters back in Ireland—people who are staying under the radar but who wouldn't hesitate to put a bullet between my eyes."

"Mother?" I ask.

"For once, I agree with your father."

"There's something else you're not telling me."

She laughs, a sweet, tinkling sound. It is at odds with what my mother really is: a scheming politician and canny businesswoman.

"Oh, darling, you are so wise. Yes, there is something, good news, in fact."

"What?"

"After I told the Spanish government of your heroic efforts fighting demons—on the back of a dragon, no less!—they decided to make you a national hero. You will receive a salary, and as your family, we are entitled to protection from the state."

"Wow. They believed you?"

"Hundreds of thousands of people saw the dragon, and a few brave souls even managed to capture some footage. It was possible to see you on the dragon's neck."

"Great. If anyone still harbours doubts," I say, smiling wickedly, "I can always provide a demonstration." I flick my fingers, and a fireball glows above my hand.

My mother is delighted, clapping like a small child. Father looks slightly worried.

"Son, are you sure you're not going to burn down the house?"

"Positive. Anyway, I'm going to meet Mark."

"Do you have any big surprises in store for him?" Sianna asks cunningly.

"It's not like I would tell you, Mother."

She tuts. "No, you would not."

Father only sighs with frustration.

****

I call Mark with my com phone, telling him to pick me up at the villa. I make sure to grab my work before he arrives. It doesn't take long—he teleports in an instant. The moment I see him, I launch myself, catching him in a hug. To our surprise, I actually manage to knock him down.

"Whoah there, Conall!"

"Look who's talking! Here I thought you were unstoppable."

"Not against you, Dragon Boy."

"Shut up, Angel Boy. I want you to fly me to Barcelona."

"OK. Do you want to see the beach?"

"Yes."

He lifts me up and turns me around so that he can glide his hands from my back down to my abs. He unfurls his entrancingly beautiful wings: they are not quite white but silvered and majestic. My guardian angel.

Then we're off. The take-off is smooth; Mark is an accomplished flyer now. He ascends at a shallow angle and flies at low altitude, at a gentle speed of perhaps seventy miles an hour. He threads his legs through mine.

"Faster, Mark. There are six hundred kilometres between Madrid and Barcelona."

"Sure." He accelerates in a sudden burst, rocketing up past a hundred miles an hour, then two hundred. I guess it's two hundred based on the way the air buffets my face.

"That's more like it!"

The journey to Barcelona is pleasant and beautiful. The late-morning sunshine is glorious, and the landscape below is pleasing in a rural sort of way. We pass the hours talking (telepathically, since the wind makes it hard to hear anything). We don't discuss anything important, and even though I'm travelling at two hundred miles an hour on the wings of an angel, I feel like a normal teenage boy talking about banal teenage stuff.

The sea appears on the horizon like a blue diamond, perfectly flat and smooth. Mark dives, then pulls back, slowing us down. We land gently, both feet forward.

I turn around and kiss him; his tongue is salty like the sea. The wind blows his hair and caresses my bare skin.

"So do you want to swim?" he asks.

"Swim, and fly, of course."

"You can still fly?"

"I have some of that dragon's juju remaining in my veins."

"So, why did I have to fly you here?"

"Because I wanted you to hold me in your arms."

"That's a load of rubbish, and you know it."

I chuckle. "What can I say? I'm a hopeless romantic."

"More like a hopeless idiot."

I laugh, then shoot into the air, flying above the sea. "Catch me if you can."

He unfurls his wings, moving through the air like a raptor. I whoop and jeer, flying in circles and loops, but eventually, he catches me, slamming me into the sand. I take a moment to breathe.

"That was fun," I say. "Can we swim now?"

"Sure." He unceremoniously takes off his shirt, then jeans, and in two seconds, he's naked.

"You know," I say, "you might as well not bother with a shirt. Or underwear, for that matter, seeing how keen you are to get rid of it."

He only smiles. "You only have to ask, Dragon Boy, and I promise never to wear a shirt again. Now take off those designer jeans before you get them wet."

I carefully unbutton my shirt. He rolls his eyes and practically rips off my jeans. He gives my ass a good squeeze once I'm naked.

"Swim," he orders.

I dive into the water and propel myself through it, quick as an otter. He uses his wings to swim. We lark about in the water for a while. I swim a few kilometres (I *am* superhuman), leading him away from the main beach, and towards a smaller beach with more rocks. There's even a cave.

"A death trap," he points out. "Soon as high tide comes in, you better breathe water."

"But I can always fly," I say. "Anyway, enough talk." I lift him, holding him with my thighs, and fly him over to a large rock.

He raises an eyebrow, clearly surprised. "It's still hard for me to understand your strength. That dragon is quite something."

"He sure is." I shut him up by kissing him hard on the mouth. He doesn't notice me placing the ring on the sand next to us, nor did he see the ring beforehand when I removed it from my finger. The way I carefully unbuttoned my shirt? A magician's trick—and all part of the plan.

I give him a quick blowjob to get him up, play a little with his ass, and lift him off the rock. I twist around and pull him on top of me.

"Oh," he says, pleasantly surprised. "I'm topping again, I see."

"I'm not fragile. At least, not as long as the fire is in me, and it will take a couple more days for it to leave my system."

"Ah, so you want it rough."

"Exactly."

He places his fists next to my head, cracking the rock as he does so. He kisses me, nuzzles my neck, and moves down, biting my nipple. I grin widely. Then he puts one hand on my neck, the other touching my hips. I lie back, savouring every moment. Soon he's inside, working his way into me. I gasp.

I lose myself in the experience. The sun is bright; the wind is gentle; he is forceful, but I am never uncomfortable. We both finish in ecstasy.

Satisfied, we lie on the beach, butt-naked, the sun in our eyes.

"Perfection," I say wistfully. "I never dreamed we would have this."

"Me neither."

I trace his chest with a finger, letting small wisps of flame curl around his skin. He hums appreciatively. I take a deep breath, and with my other hand, I take the ring.

"I want this moment to last forever," I say.

"I don't know about forever, Conall. Who knows what lies in our future? I live in the present."

Live in the present. Yes, I agree.

"Mark, I want to ask you something."

He sits up, noticing my tone. "What is it?"

I uncurl my fingers from the ring, letting him see it. The grey stone is perfectly formed, smooth on the inside, rough on the outside. Two words are emblazoned on its surface.

He gently puts his finger on the Greek letters, reading them aloud. *"Se agapó."*

"Do you know what it means?"

"It means you love me."

"Yes. Mark, will you marry me?"

He smiles, touching the ring reverentially. "You know I'll live forever, right? At least, if someone doesn't kill me, and there aren't many people who can kill me."

"And I am but a mortal, a blossoming flower, so sweet in life, so sad in death. Any blade can slay me; I can fall to any disease or slip in a moment of carelessness. I wake up knowing this day might be my last and go to sleep knowing the darkness could claim me forever."

"You say that like it's a good thing, almost."

"It is what it is and always will be."

"I have to think about it, Conall."

"Is something bothering you? Something you're afraid of."

"I have to show you. Lie back, and close your eyes."

He touches my forehead, and then I am gone.

****

I see it all from the beginning. It is easy to understand what Mark sees in him, and I do not envy him for it one bit: Steijn is lovely, slender, and lithe, with a mop of blond hair and sparkling blue eyes.

But I know so much more than sight, scent, or even the touch of the boy's skin. I feel everything Mark feels. At first, it is no more than a flicker of attraction. Then it is a fire of brotherly protectiveness, duty, and love.

I see the plan unfold and know Steijn to be a brave boy who would have made a fine man. When Lucifer kills him, it is like an icy dagger plunging into my heart. All the life drains out of me. There is only darkness, a depression that welcomes me with open jaws.

****

I breathe sharply, returning to the present world. Seagulls fly above, cawing raucously. Mark watches me with concern, his blue eyes wide.

"Mark... I didn't know. I'm so sorry about him."

"It's not your fault; it is mine. At least I avenged him."

"You feel guilty for what happened to Steijn—and that guilt makes you wonder if you can ever have a life with a mortal boy. Or if he will be taken from you, plucked like a mouse by the talons of a hungry owl."

"Yeah." He wipes away a tear, but he's obviously crying. I touch him gently on the cheek.

"I'll give you as much time as you need."

"We should get back home," he says. "And we need to find our clothes."

"I quite agree. Clothes would be nice to have."

He can't help but smile, just a little. Seems I haven't lost my charm yet.

We return to the beach and eventually locate our clothes (luckily, this part of the coast is almost uninhabited). We do not say anything, for words are not needed: Mark needs to come to grips with this trauma, and it is my duty to aid him as a good lover and friend. Mark wraps his arms around me, teleporting us back home.

Chapter Fourteen: Old Friends

Mark

Conall's mother let me have my own room in the villa, and as the sun set, I received a visitor. Javalook, my old friend.

"Hello, Mark," he says, looking downcast.

"Hey there, Javalook. I'm sorry about Pip."

"About that... we're holding a funeral. Not just for Pip—Shahar too. We would like you to join us."

"I've never been to imp's funeral. Will there be other imps? Humans?"

"It's not a very common occurrence, true. There will be lots of imps, and many humans, since Shahar was liked by all. Rex has also accepted our invitation."

"The dragon will be there?" I raise an eyebrow. "He didn't seem to like imps."

"He's changed his mind about us. Besides, he's the new master of Hell. Everyone who stays there has to accept him as a sovereign."

"Yeah, you don't just replace two thousand years of tyranny with a functioning democracy overnight."

"Precisely. Your witch friend Kaylin agrees; the spies have discovered plans about a new constitution to be put forward to the Irish people in five years."

"Spies? You're back to your old ways, I see."

The little imp beams. "Guilty as charged."

"Okay, so how do I get back to Hell? Can you take me there?"

"Only imps can take the interdimensional shortcuts. You will need to make a portal using magic."

"Can't I fly into space?"

"And enter through the sky above the Citadel? No—that's one way only, I'm afraid."

"Okay, then teach me the magic. Damn, I'm really going to miss Shahar, aren't I?"

"As soon as Lucifer died, the magic within Shahar faded away. He collapsed from a heart attack immediately."

"Pity."

"It could have been worse," Javalook points out. "We could have lost many more people to Lucifer's mad quest for world domination. Anyway, the portal spell starts like this..."

The little imp gesticulates wildly and explains the working of the spell in a rapid sequence. I have to ask him to repeat himself—twice—before drawing the correct runes on the floor and name them. The first time I attempt the spell, it does nothing.

"You drew the *taxidi* rune incorrectly," he points out.

"You're not half as good a teacher as Shahar," I mutter. But I try the spell again, and this time a portal appears—a swirling vortex leading into a vast unknown.

"See you later," the Imp says and winks. A moment later, he disappears.

I roll my eyes and step through the portal. It engulfs me like a blanket of warm darkness.

****

In many ways, Hell is just the same as I remember: dark, hot, and oppressive, with only magic lights to illuminate the cavernous halls. Yet, it is also different in some fundamental ways. As I walk the streets, I notice signs of vandalism—and several buildings have been incinerated. Some were set alight through banal means. Others, I sense, were destroyed by magic.

It looks like the dragon had to resort to some drastic measures to maintain order. I never realised how difficult the situation in Hell would become without Lucifer and his demons. I scoff. I was a hero saving the world; I hardly imagined that there might be negative consequences if I succeeded in killing Lucifer.

But the consequences would have been much worse if Lucifer had lived to rule the world.

A group of men accosts me in one of the smaller alleys. They're mostly carrying knives and swords, although the leader is toting a gun. I raise an eyebrow. Guns are not easy to get a hold of when you live in another dimension.

"The tax is five denarii," he begins. "Or twenty sestertii, if you're too thick to know how much five denarii is."

"Uhm, excuse me? I don't know about any tax." I know these guys are trying to hold me to ransom, but I'm just playing them to see where this leads.

"Have you been living under a rock? The Devil is dead. Hell is a free country now, and I'm making the best of it."

"By robbing people? Won't the dragon slaughter you once he finds out?"

"Shut up. This part of the city is mine. You pay the tax, or—"

"Or what?"

"You leave and try your luck with the guys next door. But they're not as friendly as me." He smiles a gap-toothed smile.

I just laugh. "Is that a threat?"

"This boy sure is cocky," one of his accomplices mutters. He probably thinks his voice is too low for me to hear him.

I move faster than the eye can follow, pulling the guy away from the group before they can so much as flinch. I lift him by the throat, one-handed.

"Guess who killed Lucifer?" I ask, smiling brightly as if this were just a walk in the park.

The colour drains from their faces. "We didn't mean no trouble—"

"The Hell you didn't." I let go of their comrade, and he drops to the ground like wet tissue paper. "You will give up your weapons to the authorities. If I catch you robbing people again, you won't need to worry about the dragon—I'll kill you myself."

I stride past them, and they shrink away from me. I have a funeral to attend.

****

The funeral is held next to the boiling lake, which I suppose is as good a place as any. I immediately notice Rex, who stands at the head of a procession, his body still, his head held low. Then I notice the imps—many imps, perhaps hundreds. I realise I've never seen so many imps at one time, but then, why is that a surprise? The little guys are incredibly secretive.

I make my way towards the dragon.

Hello, Mark.

Hey Rex. I noticed you were having a hard time keeping order in the city?
Did you run into trouble?

Some guys tried to mug me; I had to give them a piece of my mind.

The situation has been challenging, the dragon admits. *I have no experience ruling over humans, imps, or anything except firelings.*

Oh yeah. Where are the firelings anyway?

I ordered them to stay away while I work to bring the situation under control—they are too troublesome to deal with right now.

Good idea. So, Pip, Shahar... did you know them?

Pip, I never got the chance. I did know Shahar, for he lived long indeed.

"Really? In what way did you know him?"

I listened to him speak. He was a wise man, who knew a great deal, but he spoke only rarely and with purpose.

His comment is incredibly astute, and for a moment, I don't know what to say.

I am saved from answering by Javalook, who jumps on top of the dragon and eyes me haughtily.

"He lets you ride him?" I ask, amused.

I rather like the imps, Rex confirms. Javalook sticks his tongue out.

Then the humour drains from his face. "I miss her already," he confesses.

"We all miss people. I miss Shahar and Max—even my dad. They all perished along with Lucifer."

"True," he agrees. "I rather liked Shahar myself. But now we are free of Lucifer, and we can build something better in his place."

"Let's hope so."

A group of imps enters our congregation, carrying Pip's body on a stretcher between them. She seems whole and perfect, as if merely asleep.

"But how did you fix her head injury?" I ask.

"We created an illusion based on our memories of her. We wanted to remember her as she was, not as a headless corpse."

We all bow our heads as the imps carry Pip's body across towards the lake. A wooden raft is waiting for her; the imps gently lay the body on the raft, then set it moving with a touch of magic.

A group of humans marches in, carrying a sarcophagus on their shoulders. The figure within is wrapped in ornate mourning robes, and it takes me a moment to recognise that it is, in fact, Shahar. The old scholar really *does* look the same way he did when he was alive. I exchange a glance with Rex; he nods slightly.

The men place Shahar's coffin on a second, larger raft, and I walk towards it, ignoring the steam from the lake. I lightly touch Shahar's hand, which is warm but still unmistakeably dead.

"Goodbye, Shahar. *El Maleh Rahamim.*" I say the phrase as a courtesy, knowing full well that Shahar did not believe in God. He knew that divine power is not something to be worshipped; it is something to be feared.

Rex rears his head and blows a jet of fire towards the rafts. They instantly go up in flames.

****

After the funeral, I say goodbye to the imps, leaving them to their mourning. There is another person who is mourning, and it is my duty to comfort her. I unfurl my wings and take off, ignoring the previous no-go areas. That's one of the perks of being friends with a dragon: his minions no longer attack you.

I descend towards a Victorian house, a work of grey stone standing morosely atop an outcropping of granite. I unfurl my wings and calmly knock on the door.

Femke, Steijn's mother, opens the door. Her eyes widen as she takes me in.

"It's Mark," I say. "I want to talk about Steijn. Can I... may I come in?"

She nods mutely, wiping away tears. I follow towards the living room—the same place where I spoke to her and Steijn, in what seems like another lifetime. She beckons me towards a seat and gets busy making tea. I suspect it's a ritual, something she does to calm herself down. Dutch people don't usually drink this much tea.

We watch each other from across the coffee table. She starts talking first.

"I don't hold you responsible for what Lucifer did. Steijn wanted to help you—truth be told, he wanted to be a hero. You didn't encourage him; he told me as much."

"That's... unexpected. I thought you might be angry at me."

"No, I'm not. You simply... brought back some memories. Tell me, was my boy in love with you?"

"I thought of him as a brother. But I think Steijn was very much in love with me, yes."

"He gave hints, though he never said it outright. I... *ach*, this is so hard."

"I know," I say simply. "You don't have to say anything. I just thought... I don't know—maybe you wanted closure. Perhaps I could help you in some way, however small."

"Can you bring him back?"

I immediately know what she means. "No. There's nobody, and even if there were, that would be a fate crueller than death—for Steijn, for everyone."

"I shouldn't even have asked. If bringing back someone from the dead were that easy, you would have done it already."

"Yes."

"I guess there might be one thing you could help me with. There's been trouble lately."

"I know what you mean."

"Is there anything you could do to protect me? A spell?"

"Several. I'll start by warding your house, then your person."

"Why not just ward me directly?"

"It's easier to ward a structure," I explain. "Plus, since this is your home, warding the building first makes it easier to then apply the magic on to you."

"I understand."

I begin by drawing a series of runes on the house's perimeter, then draw a central rune in the very middle of the house. I chant a Latin sentence, finishing with *Aere Perrenius*—which means "more lasting than bronze." I feel the magic leave my body, imbuing itself in these four walls. The windows seem to glow with a faint sheen.

"Now for your personal wards," I say. "These are connected to the house wards and would, theoretically, fail if the house wards were ever breached."

"But, I'm guessing that's not going to happen?"

"There are only two people known to me who could break these wards, perhaps three."

"Go on."

I draw a rune on her forehead and another on her throat. I whisper a few words, and the runes glow blue, then fade away to invisibility.

"That's it?"

"You will be safe from anyone who tries to attack you, either with magic, bullet, or blade. But I can't guarantee safety from poisons, and certainly not a natural death."

"What about accidents?"

"The spell should protect you from most accidents."

"Thank you, Mark. You've done me a great favour—me and the world. That bastard had to die."

"It was the least I could do, Femke."

****

I find myself on a rooftop, staring at the greenhouses, as I did before. It might be the very same rooftop—or it might not. Does it matter? The feelings are the same, but they are also different. Before, I was filled with longing, with hope, and with dread. Now I feel melancholy, uncertain, and lost. I thought victory would taste sweet, but I never expected the bitter residue.

I examine the ring Conall had given me. It is hewn from solid rock, and the outside is rough-edged, but the inside is smooth as molten stone. It is pleasantly warm in my hands and feels very solid. I put it on my ring finger, experimentally flexing my hand.

I unfurl my wings and hurl myself towards the open sky.

Epilogue

Kaylin

I never expected to succeed in my ultimate aim—to defeat the Devil, overthrow the Party, and usher in a new government. Nor did I expect the price that victory would entail or how it would change me. To take a trivial example: meetings. I have been in countless meetings with Andrew, his staff, the Spanish, and old-guard Party members. (Fun fact: if you want to lead a country out of a civil war, you need to play nice with figures from the old regime.)

I was born to lead rebellions, covert forces, and even armies. But throw me in a meeting, and I want to hex everyone in the room.

As I walk from a makeshift government building (repurposed following the battle with Lucifer) towards the newly re-opened Dublin base, I think of Shadow. He has been steadily improving but has not awoken yet.

I unlock the secret door to the glamoured house. Even though I am now technically part of the government, I do not allow myself to get too comfortable. We still have enemies—many mundane, and perhaps even a few supernatural, lurking unseen in the shadows.

I enter the room and stop dead.

****

He greets me with a smile, walking gingerly towards me. I hug Shadow, taking care not to hurt him.

"Hey, Lazarus."

"Technically," he points out, "I wasn't dead. Just very badly burnt."

"You spent time in a *coma*. You should take it easy."

"I feel alright, all things considered. Was this your doing? Or Roshika's?"

"Mostly Roshika, but I helped a great deal, especially towards the end."

"Where's Roshika? I want to thank her."

He immediately notices my crestfallen expression. "She didn't make it?"

"She died saving me from Lucifer. Mark ultimately killed him."

"And Diana? Your boyfriend?"

"Both are fine. Though Leo is not officially—"

"He is *so* your boyfriend. You really should spend more time with him."

"I've been knee-deep in meetings. Running a country is hard work, you know."

"Meetings, *schmeetings*. You just saved the world! Take a honeymoon or something."

"A... honeymoon?"

"Is the concept foreign to you? Do I have to spell it out for ya?"

"No, it's just that I never considered it."

"Well, you should. Now, where's the kitchen? I'm hungry."

I watch, bemused, as he pads away, still in his hospital gown, looking for food to wolf down. All in all, Shadow has survived his ordeal remarkably well. I have no doubt he will leave us soon to spend time with his daughter and live a normal life free from homicidal arsonists.

In time, he will even become normal. But I will always remain a witch.

****

I leave our base, saying goodbye to Diana and Shadow. The train ride to Cork is short and mostly uninterrupted, allowing me to relax and think. The other passengers are few, and they seem mostly shell-shocked. They have learned to fear witches and demons, though none know that I am a witch. Andrew had taken special care to conceal my true powers; I have even assumed a different name, complete with an official passport. (A fake passport is one thing, but an *official* passport with a phony name? Now that's something.)

I walk on a country path and pass inside the property's Glamour. To a passerby, it would seem like I vanished in a field. Before, they would have ascribed such phenomena to an over-active imagination or a simple illusion. But these days, people are more paranoid. I really need to buy a house somewhere in the woods.

I open the door and find Leo lounging on my sofa. He smiles when he sees me, and I smile back a little shyly. I may have faced the Devil in battle, but relationships are still pretty scary to me.

"So we've won," he says.

"It seems so."

"I'm thankful to be alive, and I'm glad I get to experience life next to you."

"That's... very romantic. I don't know what to say."

"Take a break from government business. Follow me somewhere else."

"You know, Shadow suggested the very same thing. There's no way you two could have planned this, as he had only just woken up from a coma."

"You've obviously been through a lot, Kaylin. Andrew can handle things on his own. Why not take a break?"

"I guess I can do that."

"I'm glad to hear it," he says, pulling me into a hug and kissing me gently on the cheek.

"Is this a honeymoon?" I ask quizzically.

"It might be."

"Do you have any skeletons in your closet? Because I have several," I say.

"Do your skeletons dance?"

"They sure do."

"Well, I might be bisexual," he blurts out. "Does that count as a skeleton?"

"No. A skeleton is when you assassinated someone by making them tear their eyes out with a hex."

He gulps audibly. "Right. You sure have a flair for the romantic, Kaylin."

"Sorry. It's fine that you're bisexual, Leo. A lot of my friends are queer."

"Queer?"

"Ah, I keep forgetting. The Party scrubbed our history from the books; there was once a thriving queer scene in Ireland. We had gay marriage like in Spain."

"I had no idea. I just thought... well, I thought that part of me would always have to remain hidden. It wasn't something you talked about."

"You've met Mark and Conall. You know it doesn't have to be like that."

"You're right." He breathes in deeply. "Thank you for understanding."

"You're welcome, Leo. Now, take me on this honeymoon of yours."

"Yes, my princess."

I roll my eyes. "I'm the evil witch, not the princess."

****

Conall

"So, do you think 'perfect boy' is going to marry you?" Jake enquires sardonically.

"I'm counting on it."

"Why can't you just fly off into the sunset and be content with that? Marriage is for making babies and shit. I wouldn't marry a girl if you paid me, never mind a guy."

"Who knows? We might adopt."

"You're still kids."

"Like you're any older."

"Yes, but I'm not romantic enough—or stupid enough—to get married."

"Fine, Jake. Have it your way."

"What's this about?" We both jump when Mark enters the conversation out of thin air.

"You shouldn't do that," Jake pouts. "It's... unnerving."

"Yeah, yeah."

"How was the funeral?" I ask him quietly.

"It was alright. I met with Steijn's mother, helped put some protection spells on her."

"There is unrest in Hell?"

"Oh, you bet. Some guys tried to mug me."

"I bet that didn't turn out well for them."

"Nope."

Jake seems a bit put out—he is rarely kept out of a conversation. "It's rude to ignore people, you know."

Mark just rolls his eyes. "Really, Conall? This guy?"

"In my defense, he can be very charming," I reply.

"And he is hot," Mark agrees. "But still. What a dickhead."

"Hello! I'm right here."

"I suggest you make it up with Mark," I tell him. "He has good reason not to like you."

"But he's immune to all of my charms!" Jake protests. "Besides, how can a man compete with an angel?"

"I am not, technically speaking, an angel," Mark points out.

"Semantics. I really didn't think you were as punctilious as Conall."

"I have received a fine education, you know," Mark begins, smiling.

"From which institution?"

"From the Devil's finest scholar."

"Well, I guess I can't argue with that. I'm not the one who challenged the Devil to single combat—and won."

Mark simply laughs. "You're such an idiot, Jake. I think I might actually like you."

"You? Like me? I'll believe it when I see it, angel boy."

"Will a hug suffice as proof?"

Jake eyes Mark sceptically. "A hug from you might be the end of me."

"I promise not to crush you into a pulp. Pinky promise."

"You're like a primary school child with an inflated vocabulary."

"Guess there's a compliment in there somewhere."

I watch, amused, as Jake and Mark hug. Jake even gets a pat on the back.

"So... does this make you BFFs now?" I ask.

"Not a bleedin' chance," Mark says.

"I concur."

"Whatever. You two had to get it out of your systems. Now, Mark, will you come with me? I had a picnic planned on a nearby mountain."

The weather is sunny and warm; a breeze flits through the trees. It's a perfect day for a picnic.

"Works for me," says the golden-haired boy.

"Enjoy your picnic, lovebirds," Jake mocks.

"I'll go and grab the basket." I return a moment later, handing it to Mark.

"Now catch me if you can," I say and take off. Mark follows a split second later. Jake is just left standing with his mouth slightly open.

****

We whoop and cheer as we gain altitude, although the flight is brief. Soon we're on top of the mountain. I chose it because it offers a great view of Peñalara—the highest peak—while being pleasant and wooded. I spread the blanket on the ground and lay out the menu of this afternoon's vittles: various local cheeses (*quesos*), tomatoes, bread, *chorizo*, and a nice bottle of *rioja*. We munch in contented silence.

"I still don't believe it," he says.

"What don't you believe?"

"Any of it. The blue sky, the bright sun, your hair as it catches the light."

"You won, Mark. We all won."

"But now that I have it all," he says, "I find myself in doubt. How is it that I was so sure of myself when the odds seemed impossible, and now, I find that I am plagued with uncertainty?"

"The Greeks have a saying. Χαλεπα τα καλα."

"Khalepa ta cala? What does it mean?"

"It means that what is beautiful, wondrous, and just is not easy to come to by—it must be fought for, endured, and truly earned."

"You're saying that when something is too easy, it's not valuable."

"That is what I am saying."

"Well then, I guess..." He takes in a deep breath, unable to complete the sentence.

My heart is beating double-time. I hold my breath, incapable of saying anything.

He does not resort to words, for Mark has never been a wordsmith. He is a man of action. Gently, he takes my hand in his, concentrating tightly. Warm, white light pools from his fingers and slowly coalesces into a shape.

A golden band of light shines bright on my finger. The words are engraved with silvery light, and they match the words I wrote on his ring: Σε αγαπω. *I love you.*

I blink the tears from my eyes, but they keep on coming.

"Does this mean...?"

"Yes, Conall. I want to marry you."

I laugh brokenly. "Father will have a fit. And Mother will want to organise the wedding herself, complete with the decorations."

"I don't see what's wrong with that."

"Have you *seen* Mother's decorating?"

"Too... stark?"

"She likes concrete. A lot of concrete."

"I think we'll manage." He takes me in his arms, kissing me on the forehead.

"And so we come full circle," I say.

"So we do," he agrees. "From the day we met in that dark alley, our life has been one struggle after another."

"Now we stand on the edge of destiny," I continue. "Ready to make our own choices."

"I've made my choice, Conall. *Te Quiero.*"

"Wow, you have a flair for languages. I've been studying Greek for years and Spanish for months, and you're already catching up."

"I guess I have a talent for it."

"*Te quiero más,*" I whisper. He smiles. He knows exactly what it means.

The sun drops below the horizon, painting the sky with brilliant shades of crimson. Gradually, the more intense shades fade into fuchsia and then a dark, cerulean blue. Finally, the night claims its rightful tribute; the world is swallowed by the canvas of darkness and painted with starlight.

"I used to think the stars were cold and merciless," he adds quietly. "But now I want to be among them. Nothing is stopping me."

"But I cannot follow you there."

"No, and that is why I will never leave Earth."

"Maybe you will, one day," I whisper quietly. "You are a god, Mark; you are no longer truly of this Earth. At least, not entirely."

"But until that time comes," he says, "I will be at your side."

He holds me tight, his warm body smooth and powerful next to mine. We say no more, for no more need be said.

Fin

About the Author

Alex Stargazer is an author of epic fantasy tales that snare you in with imaginative worldbuilding—and keep you reading with beautiful love stories and intricate plots. He currently resides in the lush campus of a Dutch university, where he gazes forlornly upon the wet landscape, and dreams of living in another world. Alex, when not otherwise occupied with programming stuff, likes to read, play RPGs, and go to the gym.

Alex can be found on Twitter @AlexStargazerWE or on Facebook at Alex Stargazer Writes Books. Don't forget to follow him on Goodreads, where you can also do other useful stuff like shelve his books and leave him reviews.

Read More Books by Alex Stargazer

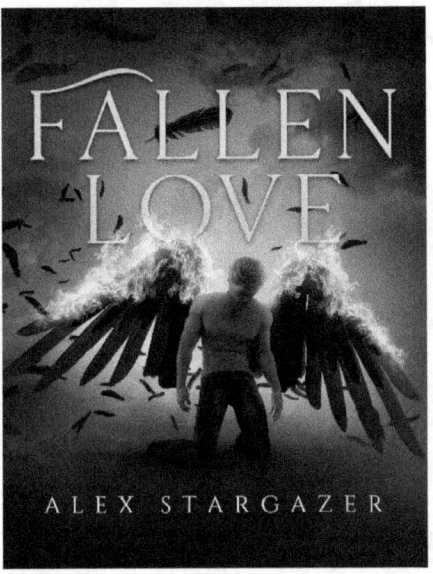

Upperclassman Conall is rich, impeccably dressed, and set for a prestigious career in the Party hierarchy. He doesn't lack for anything—except, maybe, love.

When he finds Mark, alone, abandoned and hurt, he doesn't expect one act of kindness to alter the course of his life forever. There is more to Mark than Conall can even dream of. The beautiful, vulnerable boy Conall knows is not human. A dark power lies within Mark. It can make him immortal... but love might be the price.

Reviews for *Fallen Love*

"The writing is polished, even compelling in spots. If you're looking for an entertaining read with ambitus world-building, give it a try." — KD Edwards, author of *the Last Sun (Pyr)*

"This book was nothing short of amazing. I loved the characters, the action, it's safe to say I loved everything about this book. I hope to see more in this series because I'm hooked." — Ashley Tomlinson, author of *Becoming Grim*

Reviews for *The Vampire Eirik*

"I enjoyed the sexual tension between the characters, it was exquisite." — Margaux, Goodreads Reviewer

"I was riveted to the drama; it is my hope that their story has just begun." — Teressa, Goodreads Reviewer

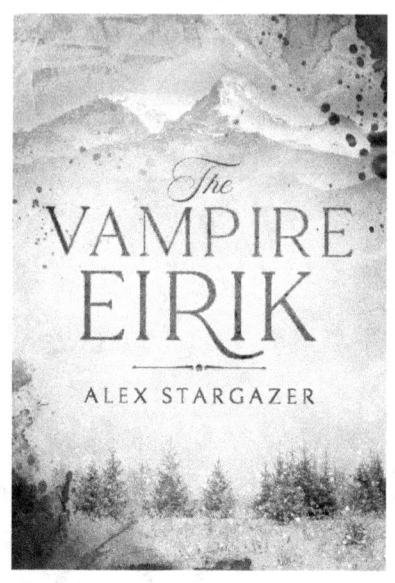

For Peter, a young, carefree engineering student, Norway means a chance for a better financial future - and the opportunity to see a beautiful landscape of fjords, primeval forests, and windswept peaks. A friendly vampire on the other hand - that's just an unexpected perk.

Yet the landscape conceals a darkness, a hidden ferocity: nature is older than man and it does not always welcome him. To survive, Peter will have to rely on Eirik. But Eirik is still a vampire, and nature always wins in the end... A tale of friendship, intimacy and magic, the Vampire Eirik is a short story that's perfect for bedtime reading.

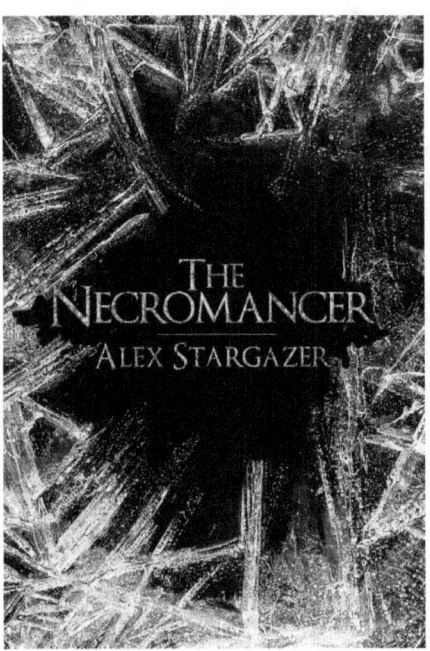

The wind of the North whispers a name, and all who hear it are frozen in fear. It is the name of the Necromancer. And it means death...

In the South, Linaera dreams of becoming a healer. A novice at the Academy of Magic, she skips most of her battle magic classes (because who needs battle magic anyway?) When her mentor, Terrin, decides to send her on a quest to the icy North, Linaera will have to learn far more than a simple fire spell to survive the ravenous undead.

Even so, greater dangers lie in wait. There is a dark secret hiding in the depths of the North; a secret that will make her stronger—or destroy her.

THE SCEPTRE OF FIRE

ALEX STARGAZER

The Sceptre of Fire is an old school fantasy romp: it's got elves, dwarves, orcs, necromancers, and a campy mage. But there's a twist—a pretty big one. The orcs? They're not really the bad guys. The necromancer? Yeah, he's got history. And the knights in shining armour aren't always noble...

The necromancer was once a pretty decent guy: he killed pirates on the high seas and did his duty as an Empire subject. But he loved another man, and for that, he had to be punished. Now driven by an insatiable thirst for revenge, he has turned to dark magic—and enlisted the help of orcs. The orcs have their own, very good reasons to hate the Empire. Driven out from the Empire lands and into a freezing, inhospitable territory, the orcs know that hunger is a stronger motivator than most.